THE WATER
TRAVELERS

THE WATER TRAVELERS

Heir of the Unknown

By Daniel Waltz

For

Dan,

Bree,

Brad,

and Harry

Table of Contents:

Chapter 1

"Madi," Jake, a high school block whose IQ wouldn't be accepted in most foreign high schools shouted, dragging Madi from her thoughts.

"Hello, Jake," she said, unenthused. "Somehow you've managed to find me today."

"I looked all over the school for you. Madi we're having a big party tonight, to kick off summer break and all, you know?"

"We?"

"Everyone."

"That's a lot of people."

"It's gonna be at Samson's place. You know, big pool, huge TV, lots of private space, and plenty of drinks—pretty much anything you want."

"It's funny, Jake," Madi turned, eyeing Jake down, "I don't have any interest in what you're saying. Quite frankly I don't think I ever have."

She turned away from him and walked down to her locker. Class was over, and using it as an excuse to get away from Jake, she acted like she was actually going to get something from it. Madi dialed her combination, screwing up the first time. She barely knew what the books inside were anymore. Picking them one by one she placed them on the floor for a janitor to take and return to the library.

"Madi, I'm sorry. I don't know where we went wrong," Jake said, returning to her sightline. "Can we just start fresh? I know that's a cheesy thing to ask and probably stupid, but I'd like to try."

Madi looked up at him. This came as a surprise to hear from Jake, so she listened.

"I mean, if we're being real with each other, I'm a great looking guy and you're a hot—"

Typical Jake.

Madi shut her locker, not really hearing what else he was saying. Jake followed her out the door, babbling behind her all the way to her Jeep that was parked in a dirt lot because she got to school late. She ripped the school parking ticket off the front of it and tossed it in after opening the door.

"Parked right next to you," Jake commented before clicking his car's remote unlock on his keys.

Of course you did. Madi swung her light brown backpack into the passenger seat and climbed in. Jake held her door when she tried to shut it.

"What gives?" he said, sounding a little more frustrated. "I've been trying to get with you for three years, and I've tried everything."

"Jake, let go of my door," she said, staring at him.

"All's I'm saying, is I want to be in that passenger seat with you."

"You want…" she pointed to him "to be in that passenger seat…" she sassed, looking to the seat, "with me? Like both of us at the same time."

"No, I mean…well, if you want to sure."

"You're a douche."

Madi kicked his chest, knocking him to the ground, and slammed her door shut. Before he could get back up she had already pushed the lock button.

"Someone's feisty. Madi."

She pretended his voice was almost completely muffled through the window.

"Your top's down, I know you can hear me."

She buckled herself and started the Jeep.

"Madi."

Music started playing and Jake seemed to

still be talking. She paid no attention to him. He knocked on her window but she only turned her music louder.

Putting the Jeep in first gear, she looked over to him. His hands were in the air and a fake, upset smile was across his face as if to say, "Cool."

Madi smirked back and drove off, flinging dirt behind her.

Taking a few deep breaths, she returned to her thoughts before Jake had interrupted them. *One more year…one more year in this horrible place.* She took another deep breath. *Then I'll be out of the house.*

Madi turned her steering wheel at a light and then shifted back to a higher gear. *Then I go to college. Awesome. More studying and more stress. Can't wait.*

Madi shifted to the Jeep's highest gear as she cruised down the road. The warm wind slipping through her hair felt refreshing. It was summer, the top on her Jeep was down, and she was on her way to spend the day with her closest friend, her grandma.

Over the past year and half Madi had grown extremely close to her. She was always there, understood what Madi had to say, and never judged. And she could trust her—something so simple yet hard to find.

Chapter 2

"You want us to go around the west side of the lake and you take the right?" asked the Captain of the Guard to Aaron.

"I'll cut him off at the river; just stay on his trail. Put pressure on him, Ugine. Don't allow him to plan out his next move," replied Aaron as he ran across the green land into the fading fog.

The dew glistened on the grass as the sun climbed over the hills; nature was just waking up as footsteps rushed through its home. A man, dressed in attire that blended with the forest, came up to a swampy pond and seemed to peer into it to see if it was one that could change his fate.

Obviously not knowing if it was and pressured by the footsteps heard in the distance, he ran deeper into the woods. The glow of torches through the fog clearly extinguished the hope from his eyes. Panic filled his mind and forced him to continue to flee. Never facing this situation before, the well-trained spy was outmatched.

"Whatever water he goes in, follow him;

don't let him escape on Earth," ordered the Captain of the Guard to his men.

The guards wore dark armor from shoulders to toes and appeared as the bringers of death to their enemy. With black-bladed swords in one hand and flaming torches in the other they pursued their escaped captive as he dashed desperately into a murky lake. Like a fish, the spy dove under the water, temporarily disappearing from the guards.

The spy resurfaced, choking on some of the now-clear water. Gasping for air, he made a last attempt for land, trying to leave his followers behind in the water. Not getting more than a few steps onto the dirt, he seemed to realize his hunters had already emerged out of the water themselves. Drenched, but not showing any signs of weakness, the guards continued their hunt.

"Don't let him get to the cliffs!" shouted the Captain as his head rose from the water. His now-wet, brown beard sagged down his face. Drops fell onto the dirt below his feet.

The criminal, using all the energy he had left, made it to the top of the cliffs and turned around. The spy choked out the words, "You know you're unable to dive this far and still hit water." Coughing to regain some of his breath, he spat out, "You tried, O great 'Captain of the Guard,' but fortunately for me, destiny has created a new path."

The Captain of the Guard, in his last attempt to catch the man, drew his black bow with a roped arrow attached. As his frail aged hands laced the arrow, the spy smiled and leaned back toward the edge of the cliff, releasing himself over it.

Brushing the feathers up against his wrinkled face and breathing out calmly, the Captain fired the arrow between the heads of two of his men in front. The arrow ripped through the air and crossed only a breath away from the spy's now-horizontal nose as he plummeted over the cliff.

The Captain and the guards rushed to the edge of the cliff and watched the spy's body spiral down the treacherous gorge, heading straight for the speck of water at the bottom.

"He won't hit that, sir; death is his fate," said a guard to the Captain.

"Oh, he'll hit it all right. That's what he was trained to do."

The spy's body did one last flip before

straightening out and slipping into the pool of water.

"Death is not his fate, but escaping isn't, either," said the Captain as he grinned.

***

The spy emerged from a river like a salmon hopping out of a stream, only to face the arms of Aaron. Aaron threw the man to the ground, proudly saying, "It was a good try, but you really thought a trick like that was going to work? I discovered this passage."

The spy, overcome with exhaustion, accepted defeat and looked as though he was trying to enjoy his last breath of freedom, as he lay drying on the grass. Aaron examined the armor of the seemingly dead carcass. It blended with the ground so well that it seemed if the man were to lay lifeless, nothing would ever notice him. Aaron examined it further in hopes of discovering an emblem, revealing who sent him.

"Take off your armor," he ordered.

Without even attempting to resist, the spy

snapped his hand quickly toward his shoulder, causing the armor to unlock and fall to the ground. The spy was left wearing only a black silk undergarment that covered all but his head. Aaron bound the spy with rope and left him lying on the grass. He examined the armor more thoroughly now that he had possession of it and could move it around as he pleased.

Unsuccessful in finding an emblem, Aaron rolled the chain mail-like armor up and stuffed it in his bag. Its linked construction made it easy to store and although Aaron couldn't explain how it blended so well, he knew it was forged with some kind of magic. He sat on the ground and ran his hands through his dusty brown hair. Aaron's dark navy vest and leggings now dry, he laid back on the grass and waited for his comrades.

Ugine and the guards emerged out of a bed of water in the river and approached Aaron and the prisoner. The guards lifted the captive and waited for their orders.

"Take him back to the castle," Aaron said.

"Good job, Aaron. I'm glad you were one step ahead of him; he was clever."

"Don't give me all the credit. It wouldn't have been possible without you there. If he had a moment to think, he would have realized several ways out."

"Are you referring to Earth as one?" asked Ugine.

Aaron laughed. "You think he could last one night on Earth?"

Ugine chuckled for a moment, but then recomposed himself. In all seriousness, he said, "Whoever we're up against, they know how to use the waterways, and they know how to use them well. They know the connections between here and Earth seemingly as well as we do."

"We need to figure out who they are," replied Aaron.

"We'll let the King question him. Maybe this one will give us answers."

They crossed through the brown stone arch suspended more than five hundred feet above the entrance to the kingdom. Handcrafted architecture of two lions on their heels lined the front wall of the castle all the way to the top of the arches. Between their front paws was a blue and white circle. There was a black lion with a green eye and a brown lion with a blue eye. The two lions symbolized Earth and Upitar; brown being Upitar and black being Earth. The blue and white circle resembled the orb that allowed the people of Upitar to travel back and forth between their world and Earth, through water.

Behind the lions, at four points around the castle, water flowed from the top and middle of the walls into rivers.

As the group proceeded through the archway, Aaron glanced up. In the blackness at the top stood ten precision archers on each side. They served as watch guards of the archway. Coming through the other end of the main gate, they entered the inner walls of the kingdom. Without wasting time, they headed directly for the throne room.

Having ascended up the steps to the castle throne room, Aaron took hold of one of two five-foot, golden, vertical bars on the door and pulled it open. Seizing the hair of the spy, the Captain of the Guard dragged him into the room and threw him on the floor. Aaron then stepped in, followed by the guards, who lined themselves up in the shadows at the back of the throne room out of respect to their

King.

"Well done," said the aged man with steely brown eyes and a tidy graying beard.

The King got up from his throne, slowly stepped down the three steps, and crouched next to his facedown, lifeless prisoner.

"I'm going to ask you this once," said the King calmly and slowly. "Who sent you?"

The prisoner tilted his head in the direction of the King and lifted his eyes toward him. His lips shaking, he spat, "I would rather die tha—"

"Enough!" ordered the King as he stood up.

"I have heard that one countless times! Lock him away, torture him—just do something to get anything out of him," said the King as he waved away the Captain of the Guard and his men.

"Yes, sir!" the guards said in obedient unison.

The King slouched in his chair with one hand covering his eyes as the door shut.

"That was a little quick, don't you think, Father?"

The King sighed. "I can't waste my time with pitiful attempts to try to get information. We are at war, Aaron, and our enemy is unknown."

"I know, but just listen to me," Aaron said stepping toward his father. "If we free a spy, I'll follow him back to where he came from. I can find out who's against us and I can kill the spy before he can tell anyone what he knows. And I'll still be able to escape."

"Aaron, it's a good theory, but someone has to replace me. I'm growing old, Son."

"I'll be fine, Father, no one can catch me and..."

Aaron's father interrupted him. "Aaron, I have another task for you."

"Father, we don't have time for me to do these pity quests," Aaron pleaded.

"This is not a pity quest, Son."

Aaron mumbled as he paced back and forth, complaining about previous jobs. "Swab the chicken pen, cook your dead grandpa dinner, go catch me a blue fish with magical yellow spots..."

"Aaron! This is serious. It could end this war, and..." The King looked up toward the ceiling and took a breath. "...It's the last task I have for you before I give you the kingdom."

Aaron stopped mumbling. Looking into the dark brown eyes of his father, he said with concern, "But you're still young, Father."

Avoiding confrontation, Aaron wittily said, "You're not going to poison yourself, are you?" Aaron looked over to one of the throne room guards. "Keep an eye on my father, he might…" While acting like he was drinking a poison vial, Aaron made a gulping sound then grabbed his throat. "…himself."

"Aaron! Enough games! You've been around those humans too much, you're starting to pick up their humor and the last thing I will have in this kingdom is an heir who thinks like a human!"

Aaron's father moved to the opposite side of the throne room, away from Aaron. He stared silently at the stone walls of his castle. The flaming candles that lit the room outlined their bodies on the white marble floor. Sunlight poured in through the windows in the roof.

"Sorry, Pops," commented Aaron.

His father responded with a tone of love and understanding combined with laughter. "What did you just call me?"

Aaron smiled. "Nothing, nothing, Father. Sorry, continue what you were saying."

The King sighed, ending the cheerful gags between father and son. Pausing he looked into the eyes of his child. "Aaron, I need you to travel to Earth and kidnap the daughter of a man named Michael Harper. After you kidnap her, I need you to bring her here...and kill her."

Aaron looked into the eyes of his father, perplexed and confused as to why a girl's death was part of his initiation to the monarchy. But, the stern, challenging eyes of his father showed no signs of changing the conditions. Aaron's father looked away and then broke the silence. "Aaron, a king must be able to do what is best for his people, regardless of the difficulty."

"But death, Father? Can you at least give an explanation as to why this is just?" Aaron's eyes shook back and forth while trying to make eye contact with his father.

As the King looked back into the eyes of his son, he said, "Aaron, she is the one we've been searching for. The one who is prophesied to destroy the waterways. She is the legend who is supposed to cut off our world from Earth, and everything we have come to know will cease. Upitar will not be stable without the waterways connecting it to Earth."

Aaron looked at his distorted reflection on the marble floor. Trying to take his mind away, he looked into his own eyes in the reflection. He ran loops in his mind around this idea of death. Forcing himself, Aaron looked up and muttered, "I'll do it."

Even though he said it, he could not bring himself to accept it or believe he would. The King grinned slightly, evidently not wanting his son to believe he was happy for bloodshed, but happy that his son was ready to be king.

"I'm proud of you, my son. You will have seven days, including today. Do not delay."

"Why does this have to be done so quickly?" Aaron turned toward his now-seated father, who stared at Aaron like he looked at a member of the kingdom requesting something; both hands out front on their armrests.

"Because soon she will begin to take steps toward this fate. She needs to be killed before she gets too far along in her studies of the waterways and becomes too powerful to overcome. We do not know what sort of sorcery she may possess, but if she is to destroy the waterways, she is not to be trifled with. The time is coming, Aaron. I fear we will be no match for her if we do not strike now."

"But why can't I bring her here and you kill her, or a guard kill her?" Aaron's voice contained frustration.

"Aaron, the people of Upitar need to see that their new king is capable of even the most difficult task for the sake of his people. By you defeating this — this legend, this wretched prophecy — it will cause the people to feel safe, and they will trust you. Your brother would have been able to do it." The King paused briefly. "But he's not here."

Aaron's mind went into deep thought. It only lasted a few seconds, but felt like hours. He remembered his older brother, Samuel, and how he had disappeared six years ago. Samuel was more well-built than Aaron, even at a young age. Despite his muscular features, the brothers looked similar, with the same dusty brown hair and defined jaw structure. A few small freckles rested on their cheeks under their blue eyes. As similar as they were, Aaron and his brother never got along. There had always been constant strife as to who was better. Who did Father really love more? Competition controlled their lives.

His brother, like Aaron, was a very gifted water traveler and knew the waterways well. Although Samuel was two years older than Aaron, he didn't know them any better, though. Nevertheless, Samuel taunted his brother with the fact that he was the rightful heir to the throne. This ate at Aaron. He knew he would eventually surpass Samuel in water traveling capabilities and would be wiser than him, but it meant nothing.

Aaron was enraged by the fact that something was just going to be given to his brother when he didn't even have the chance to earn it. Samuel hung it over Aaron's head as a tool for submission. Aaron never subjected himself to his brother, and this only increased their distaste for each other.

Naïve competition sparked one night about the qualities of a king and who had better attributes. The question rose among them: Who was braver?

"A king has to be brave. You know that,

right?" asked Samuel in a derogatory tone.

"What are you getting at?"

"Just making sure you understand how brave I am, and that's why I will be a better king," smirked Samuel.

Aaron knew Samuel took joy in his brother's aggravation. He fed on Aaron's frustration. Samuel enjoyed watching people get angry and try to fight back. Regardless, Aaron took the bait.

"What are you challenging me to?"

Samuel informed Aaron, "In the basement of the castle there's a sacred pool, from when the castle was first built. It hasn't been used in centuries, but I guess it goes to the home of the orb."

"So you want to go into the basement and see if it exists?"

"Not only that, I want to travel through the pool and see where it goes; see if it really takes us to the orb, if it even exists."

Aaron was afraid to respond. He didn't even want to look for the pool, let alone travel through it. But he couldn't let his brother know he was afraid, so he replied calmly, "It's not actually there. It's just a legend, Samuel. Father would know of it and he would have told us. Now I'm going to bed; it's late." Aaron turned his back on Samuel and began to walk away.

"I am braver, then."

Aaron stopped walking.

"If we get caught in the lower parts of the castle, at this time of night, without the Captain, do you know how mad Father will be?" he replied, trying to get his brother to implement a truce between them.

"You just have to say I'm braver. It is the truth, anyway. A king should be braver than his subjects."

Not seeing any way out of it and not wanting to let Samuel believe his own words, Aaron agreed to go. Samuel smiled and they snuck out of their room to the staircase. The people in the castle were asleep, aside from several guards patrolling the halls. Few torches lit the grey stone walls but darkness primarily settled everywhere. Aaron and Samuel slipped around the halls and approached the back entrance to the throne room.

A guard came around the corner holding a torch. Aaron and Samuel scurried into the darkness.

They knew if the guard caught them they would be reported to Father for being out past their curfew. They held their breaths. The guard walked directly in front of them. Not shining his torch in their direction, he stayed his course. Both let out their breaths.

They opened the back entrance to the throne room and closed the door without making a sound. Behind the giant throne was a wooden door with no locks. Everyone who knew it was there knew opening it could result in death. Aaron took a torch off the wall. "It's going to be dark down there."

As much as the brothers fought, they still looked out for each other and enjoyed each other's company. As much as they competed, they still shared the same family blood. And as much as they hated each other, they loved each other.

Aaron held the torch as Samuel took hold of the door handle. It didn't even creak as it gracefully opened. Blackness covered the stony steps descending into the basement. The brothers looked at each other. Both of them were undoubtedly afraid now, but overcome by curiosity.

"We've come this far," Samuel said, followed

by a smile.

The brothers descended. The stairs were unforgiving, not absorbing anything. When they reached the bottom, they came into an open room. Aaron scanned, noticing archways with tunnels lining the walls of the room. There were five archways on each side and one at the end of the room. Whether it was instinct or luck, they decided on the tunnel at the far end of the room.

The tunnel was seemingly endless and only led to more stairs, leading deeper into the chamber. The brothers tiptoed close to each other, spooked by the slightest twitch. The further they walked, the more darkness consumed them. Finally they approached an old wooden door. A black knob rested on it. Its black coarse hinges showed no age. Aaron put his hand on the door; it was a soft wood.

Samuel wrapped his hand around the knob and both boys breathed heavily. He twisted the knob and opened the door, allowing Aaron to shine the light in.

There was one room. Twelve foot by twelve foot, with a pool in the middle. The top of the water was crystal clear and the pool was circular. Aaron shined his light over it.

"Well, it exists," said Samuel.

"Yeah, but where's the bottom?"

The boys peered over the edge. The pool had an endless bottom — water as far as they could see. The deeper the water descended, the blacker the water seemed to become. They looked at each other. Both evidently thinking the same thing: Where would it take them?

"I don't think we should do it, Samuel."

"We have to now. If we walk away, you know it will haunt us for the rest of our lives."

As much as Aaron wanted to disagree and get out of there, he knew Samuel was right. Aaron set the torch on the ground, away from the water. The brothers looked at the pool and walked in. Submerging all but their heads, they looked at each other.

"On the count of three, we do it," said Aaron.

"One…two…three…"

The brothers stuck their heads under the water. Aaron water traveled. His gut pulled as he was taken to whatever water this pool was linked to. His feet touched a bottom and he lifted his head out of the water.

Stars lit the sky wherever he was. Getting out of the water, Aaron realized he was on some kind of a floating platform overlooking miles of land. Behind him was a rocky tunnel with a visible end and a floating path that connected the platform to the mountainside.

"Samuel?"

The land was beautiful. Trees were covered in starlight and mountains stained in moonlight. Aaron looked back down the tunnel and saw someone coming toward him.

"Samuel?"

He didn't get a response. Panicking, he shouted Samuel's name. The thing that looked to be the silhouette of another person was moving closer. Aaron stumbled back into the pool. He was so afraid he began to have trouble breathing. He dropped under the water as fast as he could and saw the silhouette standing above the pool. A hand reached toward him as he hid under the surface of the water. Aaron closed his eyes out of fear and water traveled.

Re-emerging in the pool in the cellar, he lunged out of the water. Samuel was laughing.

"Where were you?" shouted Aaron.

His brother continued to laugh at how horrified Aaron looked. Aaron was overcome by rage fueled from his fear and leaped at his brother, who was still in the pool. He began to throw punches at him. Samuel retaliated and fought back after the first punch.

Aaron knew not to water travel because something was on the other side, waiting. His brother didn't, though. Trying to pull a fast move on Aaron, Samuel sank under the surface and water traveled. Aaron froze. He waited, but Samuel didn't come back. Aaron frantically climbed out of the water and trembled with fear.

His stomach turned. His head shook. All his hair stood up. "Samuel?"

Scrambling to his feet, Aaron grabbed the torch and sprinted down the hallway, up the stairs and into the main chamber as fast as he could. Not looking back at all, he continued out into the throne room. He dashed out of the great throne room doors and did the only thing he could think of.

"Someone help!" Aaron cried.

Torches lit around the castle and within moments, guards and the Captain appeared.

"Aaron, what's wrong?" asked the alarmed Captain.

Aaron was at a loss; he stumbled out words. "Samuel, he's gone, taken!"

Aaron began to cry and shake.

"Aaron, where is he? I need you to tell me."

Aaron looked up at the Captain. "The catacombs in the basement, the sacred pool," he said, sobbing.

Letting go of Aaron, he ran toward the throne room. The King met him at the doors. Aaron scrambled to try and keep up with them.

"What happened?" the King barked in fear.

"It's Samuel. He traveled through the pool!"

The King said no words, only hurried down the stairs and into the basement, toward the pool. Only the Captain of the Guard and Aaron followed him, Aaron farther behind than the Captain, but not even the captain could keep up with the father running for his son. They dashed down the steps, skipping the bottom flight. The King darted through the main room and then down the stairs that led to the pool.

The door was already open. The King ran into the water and was gone before the light of the Captain's torch reached the room. The Captain dropped his torch as he dove into the water, wasting no time in setting it down.

Samuel was never found, and it was assumed he water traveled while part of his body was out of the water, something called miss-traveling. Aaron ran these thoughts through his head a thousand times. When someone miss-travels, the legends say, they go to a place called The Reverse. Because no one has ever come back, most believe they really die instantly while other theorists say it traps you forever in a mystical place on Earth.

If something were to have taken Samuel, it wouldn't have gotten far because there was no other known water on the mountain, and from the view available atop the mountain, it would have been seen running away. The King knew his son had miss-traveled, but sent out a search crew for him anyway. He didn't want to give up hope that his firstborn lived.

Aaron snapped back to the present and the matter of killing the girl for his people. Forcing himself to look up, he muttered, "Fine. I'll do it."

Aaron turned his back to his father and hung his head. "Father, the only reason I am doing this is because I love our people. No matter of gain could be worth taking an innocent life."

"She is not innocent, Aaron. She is of Earth, first of all, and second of all, she is the one who was prophesied about."

"But she's not guilty yet!"

"We won't have a chance to stop her when she becomes guilty! Her being of Earth should be crime enough!"

"Father, the humans are different than what you say they are."

"Enough, Aaron. One day you too will see the evil in them."

Knowing that the argument wasn't going to change anything, Aaron, discouraged and still puzzled, walked to the throne room door. His cold hands met one of the lifeless bars. He pushed it open and shuffled out into the bright sunlight, still not lifting his head.

Chapter 3

Aaron vigorously packed food and human clothes into his dark-colored navy bag. A tear fell from his eye and rolled down his red cheek. Even though he appeared tough and proud on the outside, he was broken. He had never taken an innocent life and had never planned on doing so, till now. It was not like it was someone they were at war with or he was killing a convicted criminal. With only walls surrounding him, he felt alone and cornered.

"Is this what it takes to be King?" he said to himself. *I don't really have a choice, do I? When have I had a choice?*

Aaron sat on his bed made of fine wood with soft animal hides for blankets. He stared aimlessly at his black wood cabinets. His thoughts were interrupted when a knock came. He opened the door, angered because someone broke his concentration while he was in deep thought. Ugine stood at the entrance and handed him a scroll.

"This is a new map. It contains the blood

coordinates of the girl. On the map is a red dot, and the closer you get to the girl, the smaller the red dot becomes. You'll have to do some investigating to find out who she is exactly. There can be no mistake."

"I know," mumbled Aaron.

"Are you okay, Aaron? You look a little worn."

Aaron wanted to express everything to Ugine, because he was the one person he had known all his life and felt a connection with. The Captain was his best friend. But not wanting to talk to anyone at the same time, Aaron replied, "I'm fine, just a little tired."

"Get some rest then; you have an early morning. We'll drop off some supplies at sunrise in case she tries to resist you."

"What is that supposed to mean?" Aaron asked, shooting a glance at the Captain.

"Well, nobody likes to be taken captive, so sometimes you have to do it by force."

Aaron was disgusted and appalled. Masking his anger, he muttered, "Okay," and broke eye contact.

Aaron yanked the scroll from the Captain, then slammed the door. Through the wood, he heard the Captain say, "Aaron, I know this is going to be hard for you, but for the safety of your people — for me, for your father, and for you — you have to. Nobody knows Earth better than you. You're the only one who can do this."

Aaron sucked up his sniffles and cleared his salty eyes.

"I know, I'll do it."

"Okay, see you in the morning," Ugine replied, seeming to feel Aaron's discouragement.

Aaron stayed in his room till nightfall, thinking and running the idea in his head. After thinking about it excessively for hours, he started to become desensitized to the thought of taking an innocent life, almost to the point where the idea didn't bother him anymore. It was the right thing to do; it was for his people. He still did not want to think about having to capture her while seeing the fear in her eyes, though.

I won't do that. I'll just trick her into coming here. I'm good with humans anyway; it's easy to gain their trust.

Aaron threw on his water traveling clothing and put his bag around his back. He decided to leave that night so he would not have to face the expectations of everyone in the morning. Quietly he sneaked outside his house. Because he was the son of the King, his house was made of stone when most of the residents' houses were made solely out of wood. He didn't take a torch. The light would have caused suspicion from the archers at the top of the archway and the patrolling guards.

Aaron snuck behind the houses and underneath the windows of homes. Excitement filled his veins as he slipped through the inner village. The darkness around him enthralled him. The thrill of running from everything created a fuel in him from the fear of being caught. Not wanting to go back to the life he lived, he contemplated leaving forever.

He felt free until he approached the archway. Torches lit the path to the outside. Never having snuck out before, he didn't even realize these torches were lit at night. There was no way he could stroll through the archway without the archers spotting him. Aaron had to plot out his next move. There was no water inside the castle walls deep enough for him to water travel through. It was a safety precaution in order to prevent intruders from invading quickly.

Without being able to completely submerge his body in water, water traveling couldn't take place. If a water traveler tried to travel while any part of their body was out of the water, they would miss-travel. Regardless if The Reverse existed or not, Aaron knew there would be consequences if he tried to travel without being completely under.

As the prince of the land, he knew another way out of the castle walls — an escape exit. Aaron snuck to the back of the castle; past the horse stalls and feeding sheds. In the far right corner of the kingdom were old storage sheds. The sheds were really only made for a hidden route, but in order to disguise them, they were filled with old useless artifacts. Below the floorboards was a hatch that led to an underground tunnel.

Aaron edged against the wall of the house next to the storage shed. As he moved his head around the corner, he caught a glimpse of three guard wolves protecting the shed. One of the wolves' ears picked up the brushing of Aaron's clothes as he peeked his head around. Snapping its head in his direction, it looked into the blackness of the night. Aaron moved his head back as soon as he saw the wolf's ear twitch. He let out a small breath of relief.

The only thing Aaron could think of was creating a distraction. He knew as soon as the wolves started barking, guards would appear. Aaron took a wrapped piece of bird meat from his bag. A sweet aroma filled the air when he removed the wrapping. Freshly seasoned spices encased the meat.

The sound of growling broke Aaron's moment of drooling. All three wolves had approached the adjacent corner of the house. Without hesitating, Aaron tossed the meat around the corner. It flopped on the ground.

Aaron heard the wolves growl and pounce. He peeked his head around and saw that all three dogs ran for the meat. Aaron sprinted toward the shed. The wolves fought over the meat until one caught a glimpse of him sneaking past. It viciously chased Aaron but he had a large lead on it as he approached the shed. Grabbing hold of the door handle, he discovered it was locked.

Panic filled Aaron's mind when he realized he couldn't run anywhere and the wolf was right behind him. Aaron lunged his body up and grabbed hold of the roof. The wolf leaped at his feet. Aaron didn't have the strength to pull himself up in time, so, in panic, he spread his legs and the wolf hit the door of the shed. Taking advantage of the moment, Aaron dropped onto the wolf. Straddling it, he noticed the key to the shed around its neck. The wolf squirmed when it felt Aaron's weight. In control of the fight, Aaron put his hands around the head and neck of the wolf and, with a swift twist, broke its neck.

Seeing that he had now not only drawn the attention of the other wolves but that torches were also approaching, he quickly unlocked it and slipped inside, tossing the key out just before he closed the door. He held it shut as he heard two wolves hit the hard wood. Hearing a click after the first wolf hit, he realized the door was now locked again. Without wasting time, he hurried to the back of the shed. He slid away the chest that rested over his escape and lifted up the hatch. Aaron jumped down into the blackness of the tunnel and the hatch slammed behind him. He sighed with relief as he took his bag off his back. Aaron removed a torch, some flint, and some steel and hurried down the tunnel without lighting it.

He heard guards searching the shed. "There's no one here, sir. They must have hid somewhere else in the castle," said one to the Captain.

"Lift the hatch on the escape tunnel and shine some light down there. Maybe that's how these spies keep getting in."

Aaron heard the latch click and dropped to the ground. Without moving, he tried to blend in with the dirt.

"What do you see down there?" asked the Captain.

"It looks empty! I don't see...wait, I see something! There's someone—"

Before the guard could finish, an arrow pierced his chest. Turning his head around to see more of what happened, Aaron saw a spy, dressed like the one he captured, turn and bolt down the tunnel toward Aaron.

"Stop him!" shouted the Captain.

Seeing his chance to get out, Aaron got up and scrambled farther into the darkness in front of the spy. Guards filled the tunnel and drew their bows. The sounds of strings snapping were followed by arrows whizzing past Aaron as he ran. He heard a gasp for breath behind him. Looking back, he caught sight of the spy falling to his knees, and then to the ground, with an arrow in his back.

He heard the voices of the guards shouting as they surrounded their new prisoner. Crashing into a wall, Aaron realized he reached a corner. Rounding it, he continued to flee without lighting his torch. As the voices and lights of the guards disappeared, he slowed down.

Wait, why am I running? I didn't do anything wrong. I'm just leaving early. Why am I fleeing from them?

Without further thought, Aaron decided to keep going and not worry about straightening things out. The note he left on his dresser, saying he wanted to get a head start in saving his people, would explain his absence. Touching another wall, Aaron looked back to see if he could spot any of the guards' lights. Not noticing anything, he figured it was safe to light his own torch.

Striking his flint against the steel, he created a spark and lit his torch. Dry dirt covered the walls of the tunnel. Rotting wood and hardened clay held the structure together.

He hiked down the tunnel with caution, always observing far ahead because he didn't know if other spies were hiding as well. Aaron's heartbeat slowed down as he walked.

"Why was I running?" he asked himself.

I mean, it felt right, too. It was exciting. What would I have said if I was caught, though? Aaron laughed at the thought of it. *That would have been hard to explain.*

Aaron spotted starlight at the end of the tunnel. The thrill of running left his body.

Things aren't as much fun by yourself, I guess.

The prince felt lonely as he pushed away a few branches and exited the tunnel, without anyone to laugh or joke about it with afterward. Forcing himself to think about something else, Aaron pulled out the map to the girl. The map currently showed Upitar. After scanning and observing the map, he realized where he was.

Aaron hiked through the night-filled woods with his torch and approached a small pool of water. He put his map and torch, after dousing it in water, in his bag. Walking into the little pond, he felt its coolness wrap around his hands and face as he completely submerged himself. The gentleness of the water was his last bit of peace. Aaron breathed out, creating a flow of bubbles as he sat under the surface to calm himself. He water traveled.

Lifting his head above the water, he found he was in the middle of a lake. The moon was still out, not like that of Upitar's, though. Earth's was always white where Upitar had a yellow, purple, and green moon that would rotate or sometimes multiple would be out on the same night. Aaron swam to the shore and took out his map again.

The map morphed and showed Earth's landscape on a first layer and the world of Upitar on a second layer. The map was magic. It knew where Aaron was and showed a red ring where the girl was based on blood. Aaron knew how this type of map worked. The closer he got to the girl, the smaller the ring would become.

The first layer of the map was almost see-through from the right angle. Aaron examined the red ring that appeared on the map, because he was now on Earth.

It's not even that far. I could do this in a day, if I had to.

Aaron trekked for the next body of water. As he approached, he scanned the area for witnesses. He checked the trees and looked as far across the lake as he could. On Earth, he had to be more careful of people seeing him. He knew some people of Earth had a fascination with the water travelers.

Some travelers claimed they saw flashes before they went under the water, which were later discovered to be flashes from cameras. Not knowing what the humans wanted from them — whether to prove that they existed or to capture one, or to try and learn how to water travel — water travelers had to take precautions before they traveled on Earth.

Seeing that it was safe, Aaron slowly slid into the water. Watching his reflection ripple across the surface, he questioned everything he was about to do. If he didn't kill this girl, he would be shunned and forgotten. If he did, he would be a murderer.

He was surrounded by people who didn't understand where he was coming from. People who had a grudge against the people of Earth. People like his father.

Aaron sat in the shallow water and it only covered up to his waist. He debated running away and never looking back. Fleeing from everything, friendships—not that he truly had many—responsibilities. And the things that were being forced upon him without any say on his behalf.

If I ran…I would never look back. As soon as I take that first step, I'm gone.

Conflicted by his integrity, his mind tore at itself. The thought of escaping from everything comforted him, but his love for his people forced him to do what was right.

Aaron said to himself, "Many times the most difficult thing and the best thing are the same," as if hearing himself speak those words would make it easier. As if they would cause his emotions to cease. He knew this was what he had to do for his people, and so he accepted it.

Aaron sunk completely into the water, traveling back to his world. Every waterway large enough to submerge a person in was linked with another waterway. For most, it was one pool on Upitar and one pool on Earth. Few would take you to another location on the same world. Aaron discovered dozens of same-world-waterways but was always looking for more because knowing of them gave him an advantage when it came to traveling quickly.

It was still night when Aaron climbed out of the pool on Upitar. *Hmm. Thought the sun would have just started to rise in this part.* Knowing the region well enough, he didn't even check his map. He didn't want to stall and to allow his mind to reconsider.

Aaron quickly traveled to his end destination: the pool of water that would place him close to the home of the girl. Aaron slipped into the final pool, feeling the purity of the water completely encase him as he water traveled back to Earth.

Chapter 4

Aaron slowly emerged out of the swampy Earth water. Only peeking his head out so he could scan the area around the lake before he exited the water completely. Weeds tangled around his feet as fish slipped past his legs. Having grown accustomed to all forms of water, this didn't disturb him at all.

The bright moon of Earth lit up the night sky. After checking a few times for humans, Aaron waded out of the murky swamp onto the mossy grass. Standing up in the moonlight, the water slid off his attire. His clothing only took seconds to dry because of the design and its material of tiny scales over a thin layer of blubber.

Mostly forest surrounded him. Deep through the trees, lights from local houses could be seen. Aaron leaned up against a tree. Moss surrounded the trunk, creating a cushion to sit on. He felt the ridged wood lines of the tree on his upper back and against the back of his head. Comfort wasn't something important to him right now, though.

Aaron pulled out the map from his waterproof bag. He was just where he planned to be. The house of the girl should be in the area directly through the forest, past the first subdivision.

Past the first subdivision. He memorized that fact. Aaron was putting his map back into his bag when he heard the crackling of sticks and speech from across the lake. He looked over and saw people coming down the hillside; it was guy and a girl. Not knowing who they were, Aaron became alarmed. He was still wearing his traveling clothing, and if they saw him, they could become fearful and call for help.

Aaron sat still, thinking that maybe without moving at all, they wouldn't see him in the dark. They started coming his way. He knew that they would see him because the scales on his traveling clothes contrasted against the pattern of the trees and grass, especially with the moonlight shining on him.

While they were still off about one hundred feet, Aaron remembered the spy's armor in his bag. He pulled it out and quickly unraveled it. Throwing it over himself like a tunic, he laid on the grass. The two people stopped right in front of him.

"I don't know what that means, Kyle. You're being so unclear. Are you afraid of having to take a risk for someone?" said the girl to the guy.

"Yes, no...I don't know. This is my future, Erica. I can't just make decisions like this, being so young. And neither can you," said the guy.

"I know, I know. It seems silly. But you did say you loved me, didn't you? You told me you would die for me. If you love me, then isn't it worth the risk? Or no? Was everything a lie?" The girl continued to walk along the trail around the pond.

The guy followed, remaining silent.

Aaron removed and rolled up the camouflaged armor and changed into Earth clothes so he would blend in more — slim black jeans with a blue hoodie. He updated his clothes frequently to keep up with the fast-changing styles on Earth.

Aaron slipped through the woods toward the girl's house he was supposed to find. He followed the trail, leaving plenty of room for the boy and girl ahead of him. Grass turned to pavement as he walked. The trail had become a small golf cart track.

He snuck up a steep incline and found himself approaching the backyard of a house with a few sparse trees.

Aaron backed down the incline of the trail to scope out the yard before he crossed it. He was professional. He wanted to make no mistakes. If anything went wrong, he was taught, it could endanger his people and, after all, they were the only reason he was here.

It's the second subdivision. This should be the first.

The headlights of a car shined into the woods. Aaron dropped to the ground. The lights shut off and he heard the sound of a car door closing. Aaron remained on the ground. He listened to the door of the house open and then saw some of the lights inside the house flick on and off.

A light in the second-story window of the house flashed on. Aaron remained lying down as he crawled onto the lawn. Staying at a safe distance from the glowing light, he looked up. There was a girl near the window. She was brushing her long black hair as she opened a window and sat along the edge of it. She had a brush in one hand and a phone held up to her ear in the other.

"What? Luke is not into me." She laughed and then smiled. "You really think so?" she said into the phone.

The girl smiled again. Even though Aaron only saw her from a distance, he instantly fell for her smile. He felt something for her. He felt things in his stomach for her. He didn't know what it was, but he liked her. The wind rustled through the trees and against his back. He felt a connection to her. His daydreaming was interrupted when, from behind him, he heard the voice of an old man say, "You lost, son?"

Just through the woods stood an old man with a short grey beard. He was hunched over as he peered through the woods at Aaron. Aaron looked at the girl to see if she heard the old man and would see Aaron standing there. She hadn't; she was still preoccupied with her phone. Aaron approached the man. He didn't want the girl to know he was there.

"No, I'm just... I'm just walking around," Aaron softly said to the man.

"What's your name, son?"

Aaron became slightly aggravated with the

man. What gave him the right to question him? Aaron wanted to tell the man off, but he didn't want to cause a scene, so he made up a name.

"John Smith."

There are millions of Smiths.

"And where are you from, John Smith?"

"Getting a little personal now, don't you think, Mister?" Aaron replied, with a hint of a smart-alec tone.

"Look, kid, I just don't like it when other people watch my girl in the window."

Aaron paused for a minute to process what the man just said. He spoke the only words that came to his mind. "You... You are very... What? What do you mean, 'when other people watch your girl'?"

Aaron became defensive, almost as if the girl was already his friend. "And you're, like, sixty; you're a pedophile. I might have to report you for what you've said; you...you are sick, sir."

Aaron was fluent in the way humans talked. He learned how people his age responded to other humans, for the most part.

The man slowly licked his lips and crept back

into his house. Aaron stood there.

I will never understand humans.

Aaron snuck back into the backyard. The girl was still in her window on the phone. Aaron took off his bag and set it in the woods.

"Well, I guess it could be possible. We'll see what happens this year," she said.

He heard another voice inside the room. The girl turned her head. Aaron snuck closer to the house to hear and see what was going on.

"I need to get up early and I can hear you through the walls. Get off the phone, Madalyne," said a man's voice.

He sounded older and stern, but still loving and caring.

"Okay." The girl sighed.

"Hey, Julia, my dad wants me to get off the phone because he's trying to sleep. I'll see you soon. Yeah. Yes. We will. Okay, okay. Bye." She laughed as she finished.

The girl hung up the phone and the dad's voice sincerely said, "Good night, Madalyne. I love you."

"Love you, too, Dad. Hey, how is your

research going?"

Sounding a little caught off guard, the dad responded, "It's…it's slow, but we're finding new things and making progress."

"Well, that's good, right?"

"Yes, yes, it is."

"Good night, Dad."

There was silence. Aaron moved closer to her window. Part of the roof ran along the bottom of Madalyne's window, about two feet below. Aaron noticed an old wooden swing connected to a tree by an aged rope on the side of the house, not far from her window. He snuck over to it.

Aaron looked around the tree for a branch to start his climb, but no branches were found until halfway up, where the rope to the swing was tied. He felt the rope. It was ridged and threads frizzed everywhere on it, but it was thick, and looked sturdy. Aaron lifted his right foot onto the swing and grabbed the rope. He put both hands around it and hung on to see if it would hold his weight. It seemed firm and capable of supporting him.

Aaron leaped up the rope and snapped his feet around the bottom of it. Slowly he inched himself up until he reached the branch it was connected to. He wrapped his arms around the branch and pulled himself up as smoothly as he could.

The sturdy branch held him as he regained his breath. Through the window, Aaron could see the girl sat on her bed as he sat in the tree. She began to write in a notebook, tucking her hair behind her ear when it brushed against the paper. It was a fair leap to the roof from where he was, about six feet. Feeling prepared, Aaron calmly moved his feet across the branch as it became narrower.

As he progressed down the limb, it wobbled the more it approached distant ground. A light turned on and lit up the darkness. It was a spotlight directly below the roof under Madalyne's room that had detected his movement in the trees. Aaron froze. He did his best to blend in with the dark green leaves.

Madalyne came to her window and looked out. She didn't seem to be very interested in what caused the light to go on, but she took a brief glance. She was beautiful, even more beautiful than at a distance. Her long silky black hair journeyed almost two feet down her back and appeared as though it had been brushed for hours. It looked refined and fine—nothing a brush could do, it had to be natural.

Madalyne left the window. Aaron stayed frozen in the tree. Still mesmerized by her, he unknowingly leaned over and fell off the branch. Hanging by his hands, he pulled himself up as quietly as he could, shaking many leaves free.

Now back on the branch, Aaron thought quickly. He knew the light would stay on if it detected movement. He needed to get onto her roof before the light went out. If it went out and turned on again, it might cause suspicion, and he could actually be caught.

Aaron moved faster down the branch. It became very skinny under his feet, and it bent drastically. The roof was about a foot away from him now. He couldn't hit it too hard or he would be heard. Cautiously he began to lower his foot toward the roof. Aaron knew since he was now above the spotlight, it wouldn't detect his motion.

He needed to get onto the roof and let go of the branch before the light went out. His foot had to be close. He stretched out his leg and all of his toes.

Shaking his foot, he desperately felt for the roof.

Aaron was running out of time and knew he had to let go. He had no idea what the distance was between the roof and his foot. He let go, and his foot touched the roof immediately. He had been only an inch away from it. The branch rose back up to its normal position. The only noise was a rustle in the leaves, and it sounded like anything the wind would do.

Aaron stealthily moved over to the edge of the house directly along Madalyne's window. He hid there and caught his breath. The spotlight went out. The light from Madalyne's room still illuminated the shingles underneath her window. Aaron waited.

Now what?

He hadn't really thought this through. Was he just going to knock on this girl's window and hope something good came out of it?

What am I even doing up here? I should just jump off this roof. I mean, I still have a mission to do.

As much as he thought about running, he couldn't bring himself to leave. He wanted to stay.

It's the perfect scenario. Every girl wants a

dreamy fantasy guy to become a reality and knock on their window. It happened in that movie once and I know I've read a story about it. But what if she doesn't consider me a dreamy guy? Who even cares? I've made it this far.

Aaron forced himself to remove the doubts from his mind. He slowly moved his hand to the window. As softly and friendly as he could, he bent his wrist so his knuckles touched the window. He knocked three times, and then, feeling compelled, he waved. After what felt like one second but was actually about three, he brought his head into the light, and then his full self, placing his hand on the window.

He made eye contact with Madalyne, and then did what felt right. He smiled.

She screamed.

Aaron's eyes grew big as he looked around frantically and scrambled to the edge of the roof. Lunging off, he rolled into the grass and bolted for the woods. The spotlight didn't even catch him.

***

Madi's dad busted into the room. Her door

swung open and slammed against the wall.

"What's wrong?" shouted her dad, alarmed.

Madi paused for a second. Rethinking what just happened.

Who was that?

She acted as frightened as she could.

"I...I... I saw this mouse, and it ran across my floor and..." She began to shake and almost cry. Acting horrified, she said, "...and it ran behind my computer desk."

"A mouse? You give me a heart attack because I thought somebody had broken into your room, and you only saw a fluffy little mouse?"

"Yes!" said Madi, still acting scared. "I'm a girl, Dad! Those things scare me!" She shouted at her dad, being as embarrassed as she could.

Her dad raised his eyebrows. "I'll get it tomorrow, okay? Do you think you can make it through the night?"

Madi brought her knees close to her chest and wrapped her hands around them. "Yeah," she responded innocently.

Her dad walked out the door, "Good night, Madalyne."

After she heard her dad's door close, Madi got up from her bed and closed her own door. She turned around, unsure of what to think. She ambled over to her window and stared at it. Madalyne placed her hand where she saw the boy's. She opened the window and gazed out into the blackness before her. Madi rested her elbows on the edge of the window as she leaned over it, not wanting to leave the spot.

Chapter 5

Aaron continued to flee. He dashed past the old man, now sitting in his rocking chair. When Aaron ran through his yard, the man shouted out a perverted question. Aaron didn't respond or even acknowledge the man's remark, but continued to hustle through that yard and into the next one.

Coming up on the pond, he turned around once he got out of the old man's view. He could still see Madalyne's window, barely. Although he knew he should, Aaron didn't want to water travel back just yet.

Aaron looked around to see if anyone was near him, but he was alone. He crouched on the ground, still feeling adrenaline pulsate through his veins. He perched on the lonely Earth and stared at her window. *Was that it?* He hadn't even had a conversation with her and he already felt like he knew her, and now any chances of being around her were gone. Aaron sat on the ground and took his mind elsewhere.

He thought about his mission — that was

what was important. He couldn't bring himself to leave yet, though. He still felt connected to her. Aaron did the best he could to take his mind off her but no matter what she bombarded his thoughts. As soon as Aaron tried to think of what he had to do, he noticed Madalyne walk up to her window. She leaned on the edge.

No way.

Madalyne seemed to gaze out.

Does she want me to come back? Why did she scream, then?

Thoughts ran through Aaron's mind. Positive thoughts—what if she was just scared and she actually really wanted to talk to him? Maybe something special was going to click between them. But just as the positive thoughts flooded his mind, so did the negatives—what if she was just making sure he wasn't still outside? What if she was looking for someone else, or what if she just wanted some air?

Falling in love and finding that perfect person had always frightened him, mostly because of the growing pressure his father put on him to find a bride. *What if there isn't a perfect person for me?*

What if I'm meant to be alone? Rule alone?

While these positives and negatives buzzed around Aaron's mind, so did these other thoughts. They seemed ever more relevant now. Then something happened. It was almost instinctive, as though Aaron had no input.

He began to walk. He came toward her window as though something was pulling him to her, as if something told him to. It felt right, like he was supposed to go back. He snuck back through the woods, avoiding the old creepy man. As he reached the bush right before the clearing in her yard, Madalyne stepped back inside and closed her window. Aaron paused.

What does that mean? Does it mean anything?

Aaron's heart sank, but only for a beat. It came back to life when he thought of doing the only thing that might work. He moved his hands around on the ground below him. Moving aside dried leaves and twigs, he picked up a few small pebbles with his cold hands.

Aaron stepped out of the woods and took one pebble. He held it in his palm and looked at it. It was funny how he felt this one pebble could change his entire life. This one, small, light-colored pebble. He took the pebble and, without hesitation, tossed it at her window. It hit the glass and made a small noise. He waited.

Nothing happened.

Should I throw another one?

Just before he was about to throw another pebble, Madalyne came to her window. She looked at him and a shocked look came over her face. Her eyes exploded in size and she put her hands over her mouth. She hesitated, then opened her window.

"Umm, hi," said Aaron, as friendly as he could.

Madalyne blushed. "Hello? Did you knock on my window earlier?" she asked, in almost a whisper.

Aaron let out a small chuckle. "Yeah, that was me..." He followed up with a smile.

Madalyne waved at him. "Come up here. I don't want to be to loud, otherwise my dad will wake up."

Aaron replied with an 'okay' and then walked over to the tree. Madalyne's eyes glistened and her pupils widened as she watched Aaron walk over to her tree. Without even examining the rope this time, he grabbed hold of it and began to climb.

"No, no, what are you doing?" Madalyne asked politely.

Aaron looked at her, confused. She chuckled and then pointed to some stairs at the side of her house.

"Take those, and then climb over that railing onto my roof."

I'm so dumb. He let go of the rope and walked up the steps, trying to avoid as many creaking noises as he could. He tiptoed across her patio and lifted himself over the wooden railing that separated the roof and the deck patio. He lowered himself onto her roof and scaled over to her.

Now being face to face with her and at a better angle, he restarted the conversation.

"Hi."

"Hello."

They both released a joking smile. With a flirty and puzzled chuckle, she asked, "So, you… climbed up to my window?"

"What I think is a better question is why you opened your window? Didn't your parents ever tell you not to talk to strangers, or open your windows to them late at night?"

They both laughed and then smiled.

"Well, when you started to throw rocks, I wasn't going to let this opportunity pass."

She tried to sound cautious. "But before this goes any further, who are you?"

Aaron thought for a brief moment. Madalyne didn't even seem to notice. He had to decide what he was going to say. His real name? His last name? Make something up? Nobody knew who he was, so his name didn't seem dangerous.

"My name's Aaron," he said. Before she could ask his last name, he asked, "What's yours?"

"My name's Madalyne, but most people call me Madi. It's easier."

"Well, Madi, would you be up for hanging out with a stranger for the night?"

"I…" She eyed him. "I would," Madalyne replied, revealing her excitement, but still keeping it contained with caution.

"Really? Awesome! So what fun things do you do on…ah, what do you do for fun?" Aaron caught himself. He had let his guard down because he was so focused on her and not saying something dumb, but as a consequence, he almost revealed he was not from Earth.

Madi giggled a little and said, "What I find fun is usually uncommon."

Aaron didn't know how to react to her. He didn't want to look weird but at the same time couldn't come up with anything to say. Without even thinking, his instincts took over, and he replied, almost challenging her statement, "Yeah, what does that mean?"

They both laughed quietly. "Well, what I do for fun is... different," Madi said, "and a little dangerous."

Aaron wanted to respond by saying, '*If only you knew,*' but he didn't. He thought that would just make him look weird. Instead, he responded, "Really?" With a mix of love and wisdom in his voice, he added, "Life isn't fun unless it's a little dangerous and unknowing."

Madi smiled sarcastically. "Look at you: Mr. Wise-Adventurer."

Aaron laughed and could not come up with a rebuttal.

"All right, Mr. Adventurer." Madi started to climb out her window.

She stopped halfway. "You're not going to rape me or something once I come outside, right?"

Aaron laughed, followed by a "no."

"Okay, good." Madi climbed out the rest of the window.

"You're going to trust me just because I said so?"

"Well, yeah. I mean, when is the next time some mysterious guy is going to come up to my window and want to hang out? This has been, like, my dream, and I'm not going to let it pass me by because I was scared." Madi closed her window, leaving it an inch open so she could later get back in.

Aaron soaked in that fact. At first he thought humans were just dumb, but then he realized he would probably do the same thing.

"Now, instead of running and jumping off my roof, let's take the stairs," she said.

Madalyne lifted herself over the railing and Aaron followed. They quietly snuck down the steps and into the grass. Aaron could tell she had snuck out many times before. She was quick and knew her way through the darkness, not even stepping into the spotlight's field.

"Now, I have this place I like to go to. It's a secret, though, so you can't tell anyone about it, okay?" said Madi.

"Yeah, I promise I won't tell."

"Okay. It's kind of a long walk, but it will be fun."

They slipped through the woods and around to the front of her house. They set foot onto the pavement and escaped from the light coming from her house. Even though they were far from her house, they were quiet, as though they still had to be cautious.

"So, where are we going?"

"It's a surprise," Madi said smugly.

Once they rounded the corner of her street, they saw a car coming down the road. At first they wanted to hide, but then they decided they didn't have anything to hide from. This car wasn't looking for them.

"Just act casual," said Madi.

They turned their backs to the car and kept

walking down the road. A black SUV slowly approached and pulled up alongside. A head leaned out the window and a male voice said, "Madi!"

Madi and Aaron looked at the SUV and saw two guys in it. Madi responded, almost acting disheartened. "Hello, Jake."

"Madi, you doing anything tonight? You wanna do something?" Jake laughed.

"No, Jake, I'm fine."

"Oow, come on, Madi," Jake urged. He talked to her like a puppy.

"I'll see you later, Jake," Madi said as she kept walking. "Come on, Aaron, let's go. He's obviously drunk."

"Oh no you don't, Madi. You're not going to hang out with that guy and not me." Jake got out of his SUV.

Another voice inside the car said, "Jake, come on. Let's get out of here. Don't hurt the guy."

Jake stumbled over to Madi and shoved Aaron out of the way. He put his hand on her shoulder and said, "Now come on, Madi. You know you want to come party with us. It will be fun, we're always fun!"

Aaron was confused. Madi said, almost crying now, "Leave me alone, Jake!"

"Come on, Madi, come with us. A pretty girl like you needs to have some real fun every once in a while."

Aaron didn't know exactly what was going on, but he could tell Madi was upset and this guy was causing it. He put his hand on Jake's shoulder. "That's enough, don't you think?"

The voice in the car laughed. "Show him what's up, Jake."

Jake took his hand off Madi and turned toward Aaron and swore at him while pushing him back. Jake then swung his fist at Aaron's face. Aaron raised his left hand and blocked the punch.

Aaron grabbed the boy by his collar and swung him around at the SUV. He pushed him up against the car as Jake tried to fight back. Aaron grabbed both of his arms and held them against the car. He squeezed Jake's arms so hard that Jake's hands started to turn purple from lack of blood.

Aaron simply said, "The answer to my question was, 'yes.' Don't let this happen again."

The prince let go of Jake's arms. Grabbing

hold of the back of his neck, Aaron then threw him into the SUV. The tires on the SUV squealed as it drove off and Jake stuck his middle finger out the window.

Aaron was stronger than most humans. Being a Upitarian, his strength was advanced on top of having to train and work harder than the average person. Being one of the best water travelers known, he was also one of the best fighters. He was constantly assigned tasks such as catching prisoners or hunting people down because he knew what he was doing, and he had never been beaten.

"That was... How did you do that? Jake's...Jake?" Madi was shocked.

"Jake needs to learn a few things." Aaron smiled as he dusted off his hands. "Now, where is this place we're going to?"

Chapter 6

Aaron and Madi walked through trees and around brush and swamps. Because of the darkness and not knowing where he was going, what seemed like hours to Aaron was really only a mile. Lights from houses were still visible, but at a distance. They came to a clearing where a tall, pillar-like structure stood.

"What is that?"

Madi seemed confused why he asked, but in a flirty tone she replied, "You don't know what that is? Just look at it."

Aaron really didn't know what it was. He had never seen one of them on his world, and because of the darkness, he didn't know if he had even seen one on Earth, either. He came up with the best excuse he could.

"I mean, it's dark. It looks like a...a...tower?"

"Yeah, silly, it's a water tower."

"Oh, yeah, now I see it!" Aaron acted like he knew what a water tower was. "So, why are we here?"

"We're going to climb it."

"That?" said Aaron as he pointed to the tower.

Madi laughed. "Yeah!"

"That's your secret place?"

Madi looked at Aaron and then at the water tower. "Well, the top of it is."

"You want to go to the top of that thing?" Aaron was very confused.

"Yeah, I do it all the time, sort of. It's really cool and you can see for miles! Come on, trust me; it'll be fun!"

Madi began walking and waved for Aaron to follow.

"Okay." Aaron hurried up next to her.

They went around the far side of the tower and there was a ladder.

"How are we going to get up to the top? The ladder only goes halfway."

Madi's voice rose happily as she spoke. "I have a friend who works for the water system in the city, and he kind of gave me a key."

"He just gave you a key?"

"You see, he sort of had a crush on me, and

he couldn't say no when I asked him for one." Madi smirked.

"Wow, using your attractiveness to get stuff you want? Pretty low," joked Aaron.

Madi joked back, "What? A good girl has to have fun every once in a while, and daring adventures is how I do that. He was just a piece in helping me."

Madi started to climb up the ladder and Aaron followed, giving her plenty of space so she did not think he was a pervert. He looked awkwardly at his shoes, in order to kill time.

Madi had reached the halfway point when Aaron set foot on the ladder. Madi sat on the edge of the opening where the ladder ended and watched Aaron as he climbed.

"I'm going to drop my shoe on you."

"You wouldn't."

Madi began to slip her foot out of her shoe.

"It's…it's…slipping off my foot."

"No, no, no, no, no! I can't see."

"Whoops," she said as her shoe slipped off.

It was a running shoe, something worn for jogging. It was grey and pink and had a pink bottom. The shoe fell and hit Aaron on the head.

"You suck."

The shoe continued to plummet and hit the ladder repeatedly as it hurtled downward, making a clanging noise that echoed in the night.

Madi giggled as Aaron reached her. He wasn't mad at all, he only smiled. "Have fun walking now, gimpy."

They stepped along the narrow metal walkway that came to a door leading inside the water tower. Madi reached in her back pocket and pulled out a small gold key and put it into the lock. The door unlocked and light escaped into the darkness as she opened it.

"That's bright," Aaron said as he leaned back.

The two entered the water tower and were consumed in its light.

Madi shut the door behind them. "Now all we have to do is climb this ladder up to the top."

The inside of the water tower was lit up well, but very enclosed. It was tube-like, small and confined. The light reflected off the white cylinder walls and made both of them squint, waiting for their eyes to adjust.

Madi was halfway up again before Aaron started climbing. The bars inside the tower were colder than those outside.

Aaron watched as Madi reached the top of the tower. She lifted a hatch that led to the night sky outside. He didn't like being alone in the tower and climbed faster to the top. Aaron began to think about all the water locked away in the walls of the tower. Where did it lead to in his world? What if he traveled and appeared in one of these "water towers?"

When he reached the end of the ladder, he put his hands through the hatch and placed them onto the roof. He lifted himself out and stood on the top.

The top was huge. It was very open and had a railing around the edge of it with a few panel like things along the backside. Aaron looked at the few antennas with red lights on the top that were placed near the hatch of the tower. They seemed familiar.

The wind was much stronger and it was even colder on the top. Aaron's eyes had to readjust to the darkness now. He looked over and saw Madi leaning along the railing of the tower, looking over the horizon. He drifted up next to her and leaned as well.

He wanted to be close to her, but didn't want to creep her out at the same time. Aaron saw that she noticed he was only an inch away from her and she didn't move away, so she mustn't have minded.

"Isn't it beautiful?" she said, looking far out across the moon-polished Earth.

"Yeah. It is."

"You can see everything — houses, trees, clouds — depending on how shiny the moon and stars are. And look, farther out there, it looks almost like mountains." He gazed at the trees and the clouds. The vast distance amazed him.

"Look at the stars," he said, looking up into the sky. They were bright and easy to see from where they were. They lit up the sky and only a few were covered by distant puffy clouds.

Together they watched the stars and then looked back across the horizon. Madi laid her head on Aaron's shoulder and drew closer to him. His heart raced and he wondered if hers did the same.

Aaron only moved his eyes to see her as she continued to look out. The wind blew aggressively and Madi snuggled her side into Aaron's shoulder and grasped his arm tightly.

As new as this was, he loved it. He felt connected to her. And she seemed to feel connected to him. It was a perfect moment and there was no risk in sharing it with each other, because they wanted to share it together. The perfect moment didn't last, though.

Down in the distance near the entrance to the subdivision closest to the water tower were the flashing lights of a police car. Madi paused, then lifted her head. She leaned over the edge, gripping the railing forcefully. She appeared to be alarmed. Aaron saw the panic on her face and was now alarmed as well.

"What's wrong?"

Aaron didn't fully know what police were or what they did. He just knew sometimes they were good and sometimes they were bad. In this case, he knew they must be bad.

Madi swore and said, "We have to go!"

She sounded scared and didn't seem to know

what to do. She scurried to the hatch where the ladder was and slid down. She only touched the bottom two steps before reaching the floor. Aaron climbed down, stepping on one bar at a time.

"Aaron, come on, we have to hurry!"

Aaron let go of the ladder and slid down. He clenched it toward the bottom, but still hit the ground hard.

"Are you okay?" asked Madi, concerned.

"Yeah, I'm fine. Let's go," said Aaron as he pushed Madi out the door.

Madi slid down the next ladder and landed on the ground. The police car began to round the turn as Aaron began to slide down the ladder. Madi grabbed her shoe and said to Aaron as he reached the bottom, "Someone must have heard my shoe hit the ladder and called the police!"

Madi slipped her shoe on and looked around with terror covering her face. Her eyes were wide and her head moved quickly as she tried to scan everything at once.

"I don't know what to do! This has never happened before!"

Aaron looked around, not knowing what to

do, either. He couldn't hide her under his camouflaged armor because he left his bag in the woods near Madi's house. He breathed out and thought quickly and calmly, just as he was trained to do if he were about to be taken captive.

All of a sudden, his brain revealed an idea. Somehow, he knew exactly where he was — why he remembered the antennas with red lights at the top. He grabbed Madi's hand and said, "Come on, this way!"

Madi held onto Aaron's hand as they ran. Behind them, the police car stopped and two men got out. Flashlights glowed on the grass as the men started chasing them.

"I've never run from the police before! My dad's going to kill me — my four point I worked so hard for will be ruined." Madi gasped for air. "Breaking and entering, that's what they will charge me with. This is a felony; I'm so dead."

Aaron was listening to her, but was more focused on where he was going. Turning his head from right to left, he said, "There's a pond-like thing around here somewhere."

Madi stopped. She pulled away from Aaron.

"What? That's your idea? Hide in a pond?"

In that moment, the imaginative dream that was created shattered as though all of it were a mistake.

"I should have never come out my window with you."

"Madi, you have to trust me," Aaron said quickly as he watched the police gaining on them. "I know there's a pond-like thing around here; it's our only chance. I promise you, they won't catch us if we find it."

The police officers had gained ground on them, being only three hundred feet or so away now. Madi looked into Aaron's blue eyes and he looked back into her green eyes. She grabbed his hand, not seeming to know whether it was out of total fear of being caught and it seemed like her only option, or because she trusted him.

They both ran again and Aaron scanned the area, searching for the pond. He knew there was a pond around here.

Madi pointed over to a hill and said, "Over there, on the other side of that hill there's a small pond. Is that it?"

Aaron ran in the direction of the hill and pulled Madi with him. Reaching the top, he saw the pond he remembered. He knew if they water traveled through that pond, they would appear in a cave in his world. While inside the cave, it appeared as though it was underground.

Aaron quickly made up a lie so Madi would not suspect anything when inside the cave. "Now listen, if we swim down, there's a pocket in the side of the bank that leads to an underwater cave. We can sit in there and hide until it's safe."

"What?" Madi was extremely confused and frustrated.

Aaron turned and saw the police were no more than fifteen feet behind them shouting, "Stop right where you are!"

Aaron grabbed Madi's hand. "Just…trust me; my brother and I used to play in it when we were little." This statement was not a lie.

Aaron leaped, pulling Madalyne with him. The two plunged into the murky pond water and sank under the surface.

Aaron knew that as long as he made contact with her and both of them were completely under the water, he could water travel, taking her with him. He saw the police jump in after them. Madi's eyes were shut as she clenched Aaron's arm, ready to swim where he went. Aaron water traveled.

The water remained dark, even though the cave they appeared in was slightly illuminated. Aaron's head emerged and Madi's followed.

Madi's feet touched the ground and she stood up in the pool. She rubbed her eyes clear of water and looked around the small cave, appearing to take it in.

Overwhelmed with joyous relief, she shouted, "It's real! I thought you were joking or that we would never actually find it!" Madi got out of the water and sat on a stone slab. "This is amazing."

The pool was about three foot by five foot, with mostly stone around it. In one area, it opened into a small tunnel of water that wrapped around to another part of the cave.

The room they were in was small, but big enough to move around and stand. Aaron lifted himself onto the slab and sat alongside Madi. "What, you didn't believe me?" he said, followed by a smile.

"I just…I don't know. I panicked. If I were caught, I could have done jail time or something for breaking and entering, so I thought that trusting you was literally my only option, even though I doubted it completely."

"Good to know you had such high faith in me." Aaron laughed, and then Madi laughed, too.

It was a laugh of relief, an overwhelming joyous laugh of relief. Madi stopped abruptly and stood. "Wait! What if they find us in here?"

"They won't," Aaron replied confidently.

Madalyne stood standing.

"Trust me, they won't."

Madalyne gave into trusting him this time and sat down.

"What leads down that tunnel?"

"It's…it's just a dead end. More water, and then a wall," Aaron said, adding to his lies.

Aaron knew what was really behind the wall. It led to the outside — the outside of Upitar. When Aaron and his brother were little, they found this place. They were out hunting and stumbled across the cave. Their young child minds had longed for exploration and the cave was like nourishment to their growing intellect; something they craved.

They found the cave and it was their place —
a secret fort for the brothers. It became the place
where they could go and not compete. The small
pool of water also excited the side of them that
longed for adventure. Discovering where it led was
not only an option, it was a must.

To their disappointment, it didn't lead to
some mysterious place on Earth. The only thing that
aroused their curiosity were the red lights at the top
of a mysterious structure. Aaron now knew what
that was — the water tower.

All these years later and not only did he
know what the red lights were, he had also been on
the top of the structure. As they grew older, they
had abandoned the place and Aaron never thought
he would enter it again.

Madi broke Aaron's flashback with a
question. "Where is the light coming from?"

Aaron didn't need to lie about this. "You see
those rocks on the ceiling? They're called — or at
least I call them — glow stones. They glow just like a
dim light, and it looks like light is peering through
the ceiling."

"Wow," Madi said as she examined the rocks. "I've never heard of them before. They're amazing."

Aaron reached and broke off a small piece of stone and handed it to her.

"Careful, it's fragile."

"It's so precious, like, it's magic or something."

"They're really rare, too. So don't show it to anyone." Aaron knew these stones only existed in his world, and Earth researchers would go crazy over them. "Keep it safe with you."

Madi smiled and went to put the stone in her pocket. "Will it break?"

"No, they're not that fragile — they're just not like normal rock. I have one, too." Aaron pulled out a necklace that hung around his neck. On it was a glow stone like Madi's.

"Is that from when you and your brother used to come down here?"

"Yeah." Aaron didn't want to finish the conversation and Madi seemed to notice.

They both sat on the stone ground and leaned up against the hard wall, gazing at the glowing rocks above them.

"It's so peaceful," Madi said as she dozed on Aaron's shoulder.

Although Aaron loved the moment, he couldn't avoid something. He brought an Earthling to Upitar—something he was told never to do and could result in death. But he didn't feel wrong about it, he felt like there was nothing more right. After pausing for a moment he wrapped his arm around her. "Yeah, it is."

Aaron started to feel a little tired. He knew he needed less sleep, being a water traveler, but he still didn't want to risk falling asleep in the cave and something happening while they were on Upitar. As soon as her breathing became steady, he knew she was sleeping. Aaron sat in the cave and watched the rocks, which almost looked like stars. He thought of his brother, Samuel. This was the one place—the only place—they didn't fight; the one place they could really be brothers.

Before he knew it, Aaron fell asleep as well. The two slept under the starry rocks while they waited for it to be safe to return to Earth. When Aaron woke up, he was startled. He hadn't wanted to fall asleep. He rubbed his eyes vigorously, trying to figure out how long he was out. It had to be safe by now.

He woke Madi up saying, "Come on, sleepyhead, we have to go."

Madi sounded exhausted.

"Already? Won't they still be out there looking for us?" she asked, still groggy.

Aaron walked her to the water. "No, silly, you fell asleep. We've been down here for a while."

Aaron figured it must have been only half an hour, because that's all a water traveler usually slept for, but he still assumed it was safe to leave. Madi slipped into the water and her body jolted awake from its coldness.

"Now, just hold my hand and follow me, okay?" Aaron grabbed her hand.

They swam under the water and Aaron water traveled. Reappearing in Earth water they swam to the surface and then to the grass. Madi squinted her eyes as she slowly looked around.

Aaron walked over to her. "Are you okay?"

"Yeah, my stomach just feels a little weird."

Aaron wondered if she sensed that they had

water traveled. Diffusing any curiosity Madi had, Aaron lied again. "It's just because of the pressure change. Because we were so far under the water, the pressure was different than up here. A stomachache is natural."

Madi rubbed her stomach. "Oh, okay." Her face showed she had no idea what really happened.

Looking up, Aaron saw that the moon was still in the sky. It wasn't in the right spot, though. It was farther along than Aaron expected. About an hour and a half farther.

Madi looked around, now completely awake, and asked, "What time is it?" She stretched. "Do you know how long were we down there?"

"Umm…I think almost two hours…"

"Two hours? I have to get back! If my dad doesn't find me in my room when he says goodbye, he'll know I snuck out. He has to leave at four for a flight!"

Madalyne dashed up the hill, followed by Aaron. They ran across the open grass, past the water tower, and through the brush, across the pavement, and then through the woods again. Whether it was because they were running or because Aaron remembered some of the way, the trip back seemed much faster.

Madi and Aaron ran up her steps as quietly and as in sync as they could, their clothes still soaked. Madi opened her window and climbed through it, and then turned to Aaron. She looked into his eyes and he looked back into hers.

"So, will I see you again?"

"How about tomorrow?"

"By that you mean after some sleep?" She beamed — her hair wet, dripping on the carpet and windowsill.

"Works for me," Aaron replied, returning the smile.

***

Madi closed her window and turned, startled from hearing her dad's door open. She jumped into her bed and flung the covers over her head so only her dry face showed. Madi's dad opened the door and stuck his head through. Madi had her eyes shut. She hoped Aaron was able to get well hidden alongside the house in time.

Madi's dad walked over to her bed and sat on it. Madi opened her eyes, pretending her dad woke her.

"Hey, Daddy," she said sleepily.

"Good morning, Madalyne. I have to go catch my flight. I'll see you later, okay?"

"Okay," said Madi as she pretended to doze off to sleep.

Madi's dad got up and seemed to notice the window was open and the motion light on. Madi rolled over in her bed, trying to make as much noise as possible to warn Aaron that her dad was coming to close the window. She heard Aaron's feet slide across the shingled roof as quickly and quietly as he could. Her dad didn't seem to notice the noise.

Madi knew he couldn't make a run for it because her dad would see him jump off the roof. She didn't hear any creaks from the roof, though. Aaron must have been standing as still as he could. Madi's dad rested his hand on the wooden window handle. Nothing happened. Her dad just stood there, looking out the window. Madi held her breath, waiting for her dad to peak his head out. The window shut. Her dad didn't see Aaron.

Madi's dad turned around and walked out of the room with a smile at his daughter. The door finally shut. Relief hit her body. Hearing one creak from the roof, she knew Aaron must have jumped off and ran.

Chapter 7

Aaron came up out of Upitar's water and walked onto the grass. Where he was in his world, the sun was also down. He was close to the kingdom grounds. Aaron rested underneath a tall bending tree in some high grass that covered his feet but didn't go past his shins. He hung his Earthling clothes on a thick branch of the tree in the warm night air. As soon as he laid down into the grass, it absorbed him as if it were a soft bed with freshly fluffed feathers. The wind blew a warm blanket over him that carried the fresh scent of honey. Aaron closed his eyes and submerged into a peaceful state.

The moon moved calmly while Aaron relaxed. A brisk wind rustled across the land and onto his face. Aaron was abruptly removed from his peace and reminded that he had work to do.

He rubbed his eyes. Before Aaron could return to Earth, he knew he had to report to his father. An update on his status was necessary. *Dad's probably wondering where I am — especially after taking off early.*

For only spending one night on Earth, Aaron thought he had made plenty of progress. He lifted up his pant leg, revealing a golden lapis dagger. Setting the dagger on the ground, he rummaged through his cluttered bag.

Aaron pulled out some of the food he had wrapped. After unwrapping it, Aaron realized he was starving. He smelled the fresh berries and cooked bird wings. Although the food was cold, he devoured it in seconds. He was full from either eating too fast or the food being enough for him.

Aaron picked the beautifully handcrafted dagger up off the ground. It had a lapis handle with gold twisting around it. The blade was gold, with a lapis line going down the middle on both sides. His father gave it to him as a gift, but it was more of a chain of responsibility. The dagger allowed him to send messages to his father through the water. The weapon had a magic element that supposedly came from one of the outer rim worlds. When he touched water with it, it connected to the closest pool of water that the other dagger was near — the dagger his Father had.

His father had a golden dagger with an emerald color gem wrapping around it. The blade was similar to Aaron's but had an emerald line going down the middle. When Aaron or his father touched water with their daggers, it opened up a connection system for communication and messages could be relayed.

Aaron walked back to the pool. He wrapped his hand around the hilt of his dagger. Aaron hesitated. He didn't want to touch the water. He didn't want to be reminded of what he had to do. But he knew he couldn't ignore it. If he did, his father would send guards to find him, and then his chances of seeing Madalyne again would be lost completely.

Reluctantly, Aaron touched the calm, flat surface with the tip of the dagger. A blue light appeared at the tip as Aaron held it in the water. He waited. After a few minutes, a green light appeared on the other side of the pool. His father now held his dagger in the water as well.

Aaron began to write in the water. He wrote out the word, "Father."

The green light of his father's dagger moved

around the water and formed a word.

"Safe"

Aaron swept his free hand across the water to clear what he had written. He then responded to his father's writing.

"Yes"

Aaron and his Father engaged in a conversation through their writing:

"Progress"

"General area"

"Time is limited"

"Plenty"

"Seeing signs"

"Signs"

"Changed variable"

"What"

"Unclear possibly her father"

"Confused"

"No explanation time short"

Aaron's frustration grew. He wrote quicker.

"How short"

"Less than half hurry"

"Father"

"War"

"More"

"I must go"

"Wait"

"Hurry stop prophecy"

"Yes Father"

Both Aaron and his father's lights disappeared from the water when he lifted his dagger from the surface. Aaron walked over to his bag and dropped to the ground. He was upset. Stressed. Angry.

Why is it that when one thing goes good in my life, it gets ruined because of something else?

Aaron continued to think and realized it wasn't that he would have less time to see Madi now — he knew he could continue to see her — it was the crash of him coming back into his world. He was able to escape everything for one night, and now he had to come back into it all.

Aaron pulled out his map, not even looking at it. *I could spend all day today with Madi, and have to spend all tomorrow finding the girl. Or I wait a few days to finish my mission and spend those few days hanging out with Madi. Then finish it.*

"It's a tough decision," Aaron joked to

himself.

The idea of spending the whole day with Madi made him forget about everything swirling around his conscience. He became cheerful again.

He looked at the moon and remembered she was still sleeping. The moon in the sky was yellow and even the outline of the green moon could be seen far in the sky, behind the clouds. As they glowed on the ground, he remembered something.

Aaron packed his things quickly and took off running across the field. At the end of the field was a giant tree, and then behind that were woods. In front of the giant tree was a small lake.

Aaron dove into the lake and water traveled. When he emerged, he was on the other side of Upitar. The sun was shining strongly above him. He was in a flowing river with the current pulling him downstream. He let the water guide him down the river for a little ways and then swam for land. He entered woods ahead of him, slowing down in order to not to lose his footing.

Hiking through the woods, he came to a swampy pool of water. Aaron dove in the muddy water, knowing it would all wash off later anyway.

The pool led to a clear lake with an island in the middle. The sun was gone and the two moons were visible again. Their green and yellow glow shined on the surface of the lake and island.

Aaron swam over to the island. Its land met him before he was even out of the water and Aaron walked easily up onto the small patch of land. In the middle of the island, which could fit no more than a few people, were flowers.

The flowers sprawled their petals out in the moonlight. *Perpatillians.*

The flowers had fourteen petals. They glowed yellow with speckles of red. Aaron picked a few of the flowers at their stems and held them together in his hand. They continued to glow like the others, even though they weren't connected any longer.

Aaron gazed at the flowers and smelled them. Their scent was calming. It wasn't too strong or overbearing, but peaceful. Aaron turned and sunk back in the water. He kept the flowers safe with him, holding them close as he water traveled. He worked his way back to where Madi was, arriving again in the same pool near her house.

The Earth's sun was already making progress in the sky.

Chapter 8

Aaron changed back into his Earthling clothes even though they were still damp. For a moment he wondered what she would think of that. Was it weird to wear the same clothes twice, especially if they were damp? He didn't think about it long because he figured it was a small, unimportant detail.

Aaron double-checked that his dagger was in its sheath along his right calf, just above his ankle, just in case he needed to defend himself. He could still run and move freely with it there; it was designed for quick and stealthy travel.

He ran through the woods, past the old man's house and up the hill that led to Madi's house with the perpatillian flowers in his hand. He didn't know if it was safe or not yet, so he snuck up her steps and over to her window. Poking his head around, he looked in her window, but didn't see Madi. He figured she was just in another part of the house, so he waited. And waited.

It felt like a really long time to Aaron. He

began to wonder if she was even home. He grew bored and decided to put his hand on the window. The handle was on the inside, but Aaron didn't see a lock. He tried to shift the window to the side to see if it would open.

Aaron applied more strength and the window slid along its tracks. Her room was now open for him to enter. He quietly slipped his right leg inside, being cautious in case her dad was still home.

After he got the first half of his body in, flowers still in hand, he scanned the room rapidly. Seeing no forms of life, he brought the rest of his body in and closed the window, using the handle this time. The handle was wooden, and looked handmade. There was something engraved in the wood.

Aaron leaned in and peered at it. He made out the letters "THEY'RE R..." when he heard something pounce and make a creaking noise on her bed. Startled, he let go of the handle and turned briskly with his hands down by his sides like a good boy. He looked at her bed and saw a small black cat with white stripes crouching on it. He sighed.

It's only a cat.

Aaron carefully tiptoed over to the cat. He pet it on the head and quietly set the flowers down on the bed. The cat rolled onto its back out of pleasure. Still cautious, Aaron crept to the wall on the left side of Madi's room opposite her bed. Her door was across from the window and was opened slightly.

Aaron slid over and looked through the small crack that separated the door from its frame. He looked around as much as he could, but all he really saw was a hallway. There were several pictures on the wall, probably of the family, and a few news articles.

Not seeing or hearing anyone, he shifted around to the opening and stuck his head out. He still didn't see or hear anyone, so he slid into the hallway. The walls were a light yellow color. To his right was a beautiful staircase that led downstairs, and to his left stood another door, closed.

Madalyne's door was brown, and so was the one at the end of the hallway. They were both made of an elegant wood and were rather smooth, nothing like he had ever seen.

Aaron moved toward the staircase and began to descend step by step. It spiraled down to an opening where the first floor of the house could be seen. He lowered his head to get a view of the entire downstairs.

He observed a room with couches and another hallway that he could not see around. There was light in a room at the far end of the hall. He stepped down one more step to get a better view and heard footsteps.

The noise of feet hitting the ground came out of nowhere. They stepped onto the bottom of the first step as Aaron backed up the steps. He tried to match his every step to the ones he heard. Once his feet touched the carpeting, he dashed back into Madi's room just before the person came around the top portion of the steps. The cat was now sitting outside of the door with its tail aimlessly waving. Aaron's heart was racing as he panicked, not knowing where to hide. He couldn't go back out the window, because the noise of it sliding open would draw attention.

He looked around and saw a dark area of her room — the closet. Aaron swiftly moved over to it. It was huge. Clothes surrounded him from wall to wall and he still had enough space to completely spread his arms out opened. He heard Madi's door open.

Aaron hid behind the clothes hanging in the closet and sat along the back wall, getting as far back into the wilderness of clothes as possible. He tried to make himself small and indistinguishable, but could still see through some of the gaps between the clothes.

Aaron saw someone's feet and closed his eyes, as if not seeing them would help him hide. The light on the closet turned on and a person began ruffling through clothes on the adjacent wall. He opened his eyes. It was Madi.

Aaron paused. It brought him relief to see Madi and not her father, but what should he do now? Pop out? He couldn't scare her, because he knew this was already beyond creepy.

Madi continued to look through her clothes and then selected a hoodie from the wall. She walked out of the closet and shut the light off behind her. She left Aaron's view and he became more composed.

Aaron still sat in the closet, thinking of the best way to let her know he was there. He watched what he could catch sight of in Madi's room, to see if she was still there. He saw a top piece of clothing fly by and hit her bed.

It was a shirt. Her shirt! Aaron panicked.

If she's changing and then finds out I'm in here, she'll really think I'm some kind of a creep!

Aaron wanted to shout and stop her just in case she crossed her room and came into his view. At the same time, he didn't want to scare her. While he was thinking, she passed by, wearing the hoodie she had pulled from her closet. Aaron was safe.

Madi walked over to her window and opened it. She had one of the flowers he brought her in her hand. Leaning on the edge she seemed to be looking for him. Aaron knew even if he were to come out now and scare her, she wouldn't even care. The side of her face he could see said she just wanted to see him again.

Aaron didn't know how he knew this, but he just felt it was the best time to let her know he was here. He quietly climbed out of the jungle of clothes and stood up in her dark closet. She didn't notice him. He slid to the edge of the closet and said, "Umm, hey?" with his hands behind his back.

Madalyne jumped and turned toward Aaron, who was now in the light. She put her hand over her mouth as she caught her breath.

"Oh my gosh, Aaron! You scared me!"

"I'm sorry." Maybe he was wrong about letting her know he was in there.

"It's okay!" She laughed, still catching her breath. "But why were you in my closet, might I ask?"

Reassured by her smile, he confessed, "I kind of snuck in your house to see if you were downstairs or something. I didn't want to use your front door because from what you said, your dad seemed kind of frightening. But when you started coming up the stairs, I freaked because I thought you might be your dad—"

Madalyne cut him off when she lifted the flower that was in her hand. She smiled wide.

"Did you bring me these?"

"I thought you might like them."

"They're beautiful, I love them! Thank you."

Aaron smiled and Madalyne looked at his

wet clothes. "Did... you...forget to change?"

"Sort of. I kind of tripped and fell in a puddle on my way over here. Do you have anything dry?" Aaron replied, glancing around her room.

"That's going to fit you? I might have a hoodie, but other than that, guys can't really wear my clothes," she said, laying the flower on her bed.

Madi looked through her closet and pulled out a red hoodie. A name crossed the front of it. Aaron attempted to slip the hoodie on while he asked excitedly, "So, do you have anything planned for today?"

"Actually, yes, I do."

Madi walked over to Aaron and pulled the hoodie over his head. For a moment, they beamed at each other. They still didn't know what each other was thinking, so they were unsure in their own minds of how each other felt.

"There's someone I want you to meet today," she said, releasing her grasp on the hoodie.

Aaron was confused. It was enough of a risk talking to Madi, let alone meeting someone else. Madi seemed to notice the worried look on Aaron's face and comforted him, saying, "Don't worry! I love and trust this person very deeply."

Aaron's mind took a brief turn. *What if it is another guy?*

Madalyne stopped his crash when she said, "It's my Grandma."

Aaron's worry left and he actually felt safe when this name came up. He had no idea why, but he actually wanted to meet her.

"Oh, okay," he said eagerly.

"She's super nice and she's the only one I trust with everything," assured Madi.

She walked over to her bed and petted the head of her cat who was laying against the flowers again.

She looked at Aaron and said, "Come on, you ready?"

Aaron continued to adjust to the small hoodie and followed Madi downstairs.

"Not having to climb out the window this time is kind of exciting."

Madi Laughed.

He tried to take in as much of the house as he could as they traveled through it. Things always baffled him in humans' homes, the lights, the furniture, the "television," the "computer," chargers, refrigerators — anything that was advanced compared to his world captured his interest. He had grown accustomed to things, but they still brought him wonder. It was hard for him to hide his facial expressions.

Madi obviously noticed his face light up as they walked through the house and giggled as she asked, "What? What are you looking at?"

Aaron provided a reason by saying, "Your house is just so…nice."

"Well, my dad's a researcher, so he does make some good money." Madi opened the front door that led to the driveway.

She approached a large black vehicle as Aaron followed. Aaron didn't know what to expect, or what to do.

"Hop in," Madi said.

"Is this yours?"

Madi giggled. "Yeah! My daddy got it for me for my birthday. It's my baby."

Madi opened a door as Aaron walked around the vehicle. He was puzzled as he looked at the other door, unsure as how to actually 'open' it.

He took his best guess and grabbed the handle on the side.

He pulled it and the door swung open. Holding the door calmly, he acted like he knew what he was doing. Following Madi's lead, Aaron climbed into the vehicle and sat in the seat. Madi started up the engine and Aaron became intrigued as music came out of nowhere. He tried to hide his curiosity by sitting back in the seat and acting nonchalant. Madi put her hand on a stick like thing and looked over at Aaron as he sat in the chair, thinking he was doing everything right.

"You going to buckle up?"

Aaron freaked. *Buckle up? What does this mean? What am I buckling up?*

He remained composed and responded in the calmest way he could. "Nope." He smiled and looked at Madi.

She looked back at him and jokingly said, "You are a daring one, aren't you?"

Madi backed the car down the driveway.

I can't believe that worked!

As the vehicle rolled down the road, Aaron was fascinated with how it moved, and how she controlled this — thing — with a small circle. He didn't know what the stick in the center was that she kept moving around, but he was still enthralled.

"My Grandma isn't too far away, just a few miles."

They left Madi's subdivision and began to pick up speed as they cruised the road. Aaron sank back into his seat and tried to become one with it. He had never gone this fast before and became alarmed as he fearfully tried to grip the side of his door without Madi noticing.

He looked over at her and watched as she calmly controlled the vehicle and mouthed words that matched the music. This made him calm for some reason. It was as if when she was calm, he felt safe.

Aaron noticed the belt going around her shoulder that connected to two points of the car. He looked over on his side and saw a similar belt hanging there. He took hold of it and dragged it across his body to match Madi's.

"Oh, Mr. Tough-Guy, putting on the seat belt. Don't trust my driving?" Madi joked.

Looking for something to connect the belt to,

he responded, "Maybe."

Aaron saw a small red piece with a black case around it and a small sliver of an open line across it.

This must be what it connects to. He plugged the two pieces together.

"Oh, really? Are you afraid of this?"

Madi looked at Aaron and began to force the vehicle back and forth across the road. Aaron was flung side to side between the console and the door. His heart raced.

"You know, it's very common for Jeeps to roll during turns at high speeds," Madi stated as she smiled at Aaron. "Do you trust me now?" she flirted as the car continued to move wildly across the road.

Aaron didn't know why, but it was actually exciting. He was scared but ironically having fun as adrenaline pumped through his body. He laughed as he tried to get out the words, "Yes, yes, I trust you."

Madi slowed the vehicle down. They both laughed at each other. After the laughter died, Aaron began to look out the window as the Jeep coasted down the road. He looked down and saw a lever attached to the side of his seat. Aaron pulled the lever and the back of his seat flung forward. Madi laughed when it hit him. Aaron held the lever and leaned the seat back. The Jeep had an open top where Aaron could watch the clouds. Together they peacefully coasted down the road, with warm wind blowing in their hair as they headed for her grandmothers.

Feeling Madalyne nudge him, Aaron opened his eyes.

"Hey, wake up. This is the house."

Aaron rubbed his eyes as he tried to see clearer.

"You fell asleep."

"How long did I sleep for?"

"Almost forty-five minutes, I think? I took the long way because I just felt like driving."

Aaron filled his lungs with air as he processed what he heard. "Forty-five minutes?"

"Yeah, about that."

"Wow." *Why am I sleeping so much?*

The surface went from smooth pavement to loose gravel and the vehicle began to bounce as it went down the driveway.

"Her house is way back here behind these

small woods."

Aaron watched as they passed tall pine trees on both sides. They came to an open meadow with short grass and a giant, beautifully decorated lawn. There was a large stone with moss growing on the bottom of it placed in front of a tree with red leaves, which was a little ways from the house.

On the right side of the driveway was a lamppost that seemed to greet people as they exited the forest area. On the left there was a large divot in the ground between the stone and tree, and then behind was the entrance to a wooden house that looked more like a large cabin than the other houses Aaron had seen.

The road veered to the left as Madi pulled up in front of the house. She turned the key and the engine shut off. Madi looked at Aaron and said, "Now, she's super nice, so don't be afraid of her."

Aaron smiled. "Okay."

They got out of the car — Aaron figured it out on his first try this time.

"Looks like it's going to storm," Madi said as they approached the door.

"Yeah, it does," Aaron replied as he watched

the dark clouds begin to roll over the trees.

"Here, stand over there. I'll say hi first and then I'll introduce you."

Aaron moved over to the left, behind Madi and out of the doorway. Madi clenched her hand into a fist and knocked against the door. They waited. Madi looked at Aaron and they both let out small giggle before their composure returned. The knob on the door turned and it opened.

"Why, hello there, Madalyne," said the voice of an elderly lady.

"Hello, Grandma!" Madi said excitedly as she hugged her grandmother.

"Hello, dear. To what do I owe this visit?" asked her grandma in a loving voice.

"Well, there's someone I want you to meet."

Madalyne waved at Aaron to come into the picture. Aaron walked into Grandma's view and gave a friendly wave and smile.

"Oh, he's a cute one, isn't he?" Grandma said with a chuckle.

"Grandma!" Madi said, embarrassed.

The old woman giggled and said, "Come in, you two. I'll throw on some cocoa."

Madi and Aaron walked in and both took off their shoes, Aaron following Madi's lead. The woman walked around the corner and into the kitchen.

"Just have a seat in the living room."

Aaron and Madi sat on an old couch that was surprisingly comfortable as it absorbed the two of them. A small fire crackled in one corner and a television flashed in the other.

The grandma entered, carrying three mugs of hot chocolate and set two on the small wooden coffee table in front of Aaron and Madi.

"Thank you," they both said.

Madi's grandma sat herself in an old brown chair that looked just as comfy as the couch. She looked at them as she sipped her own hot chocolate.

"So, Grandma, this is Aaron."

"Hello, Aaron," she responded kindly. "You can call me Granny, okay?"

Aaron was instantly filled with warmth when he heard her speak. "Okay, thank you, Granny."

"So, tell me a little about yourself, Aaron."

Aaron avoided the question because he

didn't know what to say to that without making up a complete lie.

Nervously, instead he rushed, "I actually knocked on Madalyne's window one night, and I know that sounds creepy, but I don't know, something felt special about it, please don't take that in the wrong way."

Granny laughed, almost as if it was directed at Aaron's nervousness.

"So, I take it this is a story that Grandma won't be telling your father, right?"

They all laughed. They conversed for a few hours about the night before and everything that had happened, and Granny laughed, entertained by the stories. After everything began to die down, a thought that was reoccurring finally dominated Aaron's mind.

Where's the grandfather? Was he dead? Aaron knew not to ask questions like that, so he continued to try and block them out. He looked around the room for things to amaze him but found none.

"May I use the bathroom?" Aaron asked politely.

"Oh sure, dear. Madalyne, show him where the restroom is."

"Yeah, sure!" said Madi as both she and Aaron tried to get up from the deep couch.

They laughed as they attempted to stand, only to fall back into it. Once they had gotten up, Madi walked Aaron out of the room and down the hall to the bathroom.

She flicked the light on and said, "Here you go," followed by a smile.

"Thanks." Aaron smiled back and shut the door behind him.

Aaron used the bathroom quickly. Afterward, he slipped out as quietly as he could. He wanted to look around the house and see if he could answer the pestering question in his head.

Aaron walked slowly down the hallway, glancing at as many pictures as he could. In the first one—no grandpa—only grandma and some kids. The second one—same thing. The third one—only the grandma. The fourth, fifth, and sixth were all solo pictures of the kids, who all looked relatively the same age.

Not one picture had a grandpa in it. *Why?*

Aaron walked back into the living room where Madi and Granny sat and was greeted by a friendly, "Hey," from Madi.

He sat back on the couch next to Madi, who was telling more of the story from last night.

"And then we went under water and came up in some underwater cave Aaron knew about! It only felt like ten minutes down there. Well, I did fall asleep, but I guess we were down there for almost two hours. Aaron woke me up and when we came back out, the sun was close to rising."

Granny laughed. "That's some story, isn't it? How did you know about that cave, Aaron?"

Granny looked at Aaron with her old curious blue eyes. Aaron responded with the same story he told Madi. "My brother and I actually found it when we were little kids. I remembered the spot at that moment and it just seemed like our only option."

Granny chuckled. She set her cup down slowly and then stared at Aaron for a moment. Just a moment. Her old, steely-blue eyes peered into his. It gave him a strange feeling, like she was staring deep into him, searching him. Aaron felt defenseless, as if he could hide nothing from her.

Light flashed around them, followed by a loud crack. Granny kept her eyes focused on Aaron and, as if in slow motion, then turned them to look where the light had come from.

Outside the window, a large tree tumbled over in the yard. It crashed against the ground and the whole house shook. Madalyne screamed and hugged Aaron for safety. Granny rose to her feet almost as quickly as the tree hit the ground. Her back facing the window, she spread her arms wide, ready to protect both of them with her body.

Chapter 9

After a brief moment of silence, Granny said, "Is everyone okay?"

Aaron and Madi looked at each other to see if they were and then said, "Yes."

"Oh my gosh," Madi said, still catching her breath.

Aaron stood up. "Why don't you sit down, Granny?" He held her arm and attempted to lower her back in her chair.

Granny shook her arm, causing Aaron to release it. "No, no, I want to see it! What happened?"

Granny moved over to the large glass window. Outside laid a great tree that appeared to be hundreds of years old.

"Oh my..." Granny put her right hand over her mouth.

"How long has that tree been around, Grandma?" asked Madalyne as she now stood next to her grandmother.

"For many, many years," muttered Granny.

The storm quickly dissipated and the skies began to brighten again.

"Let's go see it," said Granny.

They went out the back door to the house and onto a small stained wooden porch. They hustled down the three steps and walked cautiously over to the tree. As excited as Aaron and Madi were to see it, they didn't want to rush her grandma.

When they finally arrived at the tree, the burn marks along the side were obvious.

"The... the lightning split right through it," said Madi.

"That must have been one powerful bolt," said Granny as she examined the tree.

Aaron knelt down by the tree where it had split. There was still about two feet of the tree connected to its roots. A leaf already laid shriveled on the ground, dead.

He rubbed his hands along the ridged bark and could still feel the warmth of the lightning bolt. This was unusual. Aaron knew that lightning strikes like this didn't just happen.

As he examined the tree, Granny said, "Your grandfather would have been intrigued."

The statement was directed toward Madi, but it caught Aaron's attention and he listened closely. Aaron didn't hear Madi respond, but Granny continued to speak.

"He always told me that whenever something happens in our world, there is an equal and opposite reaction in their world."

Aaron shivered. He tuned in more carefully, and stood up to listen. Madi interrupted her as she looked to Aaron and explained. "My grandfather had a fascination with these creatures he called 'Water Travelers.' And… I guess you could say my father inherited the fascination."

Aaron did everything in his power to hide his worry and dangerous curiosity.

Granny turned to Madi and said, "You don't think they're real?"

"Well, I've never seen one," Madi rebutted.

Almost as soon as Madi finished her sentence, Aaron said, "But please, Granny, finish your story."

Granny gave a faint smile. "Madalyne's grandfather, my husband, believed that there is another world out there where a human-like race lived. He believed they use water to travel back and forth between our world and theirs. He would tell me, 'The world has to be so mysterious. There must be some form of magic that makes it all work. They use the waterways to travel quickly around their world.' He was obsessed with them."

"Why would he be so interested in the tree, though?" asked Madi.

Aaron knew the answer to this, but he held his tongue and listened to Granny's response.

"Because, Madalyne, according to him, whenever something happens in our world, something also happens in their world. Like an equal and opposite reaction. If a tree falls here, then a tree may fall over there. If a river is created, or destroyed, then a water source over there must be created or destroyed. The two worlds are linked."

Aaron knew she was correct, but still acted curious to hear more.

"But how did he even know they were real?" questioned Madi.

"He said that he saw them. That he watched people walk into pools of water multiple times and not come out for days. Was it true?" Granny's voice became hoarse and teary. "It's the only thing that makes sense."

Aaron could take it no longer. He had to know what happened to the grandfather. "If you don't mind me asking, Granny, what happened to Madalyne's grandfather?"

Madalyne's eyes widened and she stepped toward her grandmother, ready to support her, but to her surprise, Granny told him. "He disappeared. We don't know what happened to him, and no records or a body were found."

"What do you think happened?" Aaron asked.

Granny paused for a moment, and her voice grew more hoarse. "I think... I think they took him." She wiped a tear away from her eye. "I think he knew too much, and they took him to their world because he was too dangerous."

"Come on, Granny, let's go inside," interrupted Madalyne.

Granny didn't move, but she continued to speak. "And that's why Madalyne's father wants to find them so passionately. He found his father's entire collection of notes and sketches of the water people. He became just as curious about them as his dad was. But unlike his father, he wants to find them because he hates them — because they took his father away from him. He wants revenge. He wants to find them and destroy them."

"When did he disappear?" asked Aaron.

"After the birth of our third child. All of our children were born no more than a year apart, and four days after the birth of our third, he went missing."

Hiding his overwhelming curiosity, Aaron replied, "I'm so sorry that, whatever happened, happened."

Granny wiped a few more tears away and recovered. "Thank you, Aaron. Let's go inside and I'll contact someone to get this tree out of here."

As interested as Aaron was about Madi's grandfather, he was also concerned about what could have happened in his world to have caused such a powerful lightning strike. The bolt ripped right through the tree, even though it was almost five feet in diameter. Something drastic had to have happened in his world. He had never seen anything like this before. Was it the tree or the spot where the tree was planted the reason why it was destroyed? In the midst of his thoughts, Madi spoke as she held the door open.

"Aaron, you coming in?"

Aaron broke from away the tree and went back inside, forcing himself to block out everything that had happened because he wanted to focus on Madi. The two walked back into the house and sat back down on the couch while Granny was in the kitchen, pressing buttons on the phone.

"Sorry about my Grandma; she... she just misses him, and, and—"

"It's okay, I understand."

"Just a forewarning, though; if you ever meet my dad, he is kind of obsessed with them."

"What do you mean?" Aaron tried to hide his uneasiness.

"He's just really determined to find one." Madi laughed. "I don't know; he's just really persistent."

Aaron didn't want to personally ask her again if she believed in them. He didn't want to cause any questions, or suspicion, but even more than that, he didn't want her to have to make that decision.

"I'll keep it in mind." Aaron smiled.

Granny was in the other room, wrapping up her telephone call.

"Yes...yes. Tomorrow. Okay. Thank you very much. Okay... Have a good day... You too... Okay, bye."

Granny walked back into the room. "The fire department says they can make it out here tomorrow. I guess we got hit by a nasty storm; a tornado touched down not too far from here."

Madi's eyebrows rose and her eyes grew large at the sound of this.

"Lucky it didn't hit us, right?" Granny said.

Madi said a weak "Yeah."

She glanced at Aaron and seemed to notice the concern in his face. She put her hand on Aaron's leg. Aaron didn't even notice until she moved her hand a little, he was thinking about the repercussions of what could have happened on his world.

"We'd better get going, Grandma. We have some... stuff to get to."

"Are you sure? It could still be bad out

there."

"Yeah but the storms blowing past us, and I checked the sky — what's blowing in looks clear.

"I trust your judgment, Madalyne. It's always been good." Granny smiled. "It was lovely seeing the two of you. Drive safe, okay?"

"We will." Madi said.

Madi and Aaron got their shoes on, tapping their toes against the floor to make sure they were snug. While Madi was using her finger to fit her shoe on, she said, "Don't tell Dad about any of this."

"Oh, don't you worry, your secret's safe with me." Granny winked at Madi and then smiled at Aaron.

"Give Grandma a hug now, dear," Grandma said, opening her arms toward Madalyne.

Madi and her grandma hugged and Grandma whispered in her ear, "I like him; he's a good boy."

Madi giggled and pulled away. Aaron pretended not to hear or notice. Madalyne walked over to open the door and Aaron began to follow when Granny said, "Aren't you going to give Granny a hug, Aaron?"

Granny smiled, and Aaron did, too.

Grandmother opened her arms to Aaron and gave him a hug. While hugging, Granny also whispered in Aaron's ear, far more quietly than she did in Madi's ear.

"I know your secret."

Aaron froze. *Your secret.*

She knew. She knew everything. She knew that he was a water traveler. Pulling away from the hug, Aaron stared deep into her eyes. It was the same look she gave him right before the lighting struck. How did she know?

She knows.

Granny stared into his eyes, as if peering through every wall he set up to block people out. She grinned and then nodded her head gently. Aaron didn't know if her grin was supposed to make him feel safe knowing that he could trust her, or was a warning, telling him to run.

Granny winked. With her wink, he felt safe. He could trust her because she was hiding something of her own from everyone, too. There was more to her story, more that hadn't been told. More about what really happened to her husband,

and that only he could be trusted with.

"What did you say to him, Grandma?" Madi said, peering back at the two of them with the door open.

"Oh, nothing." Granny smiled, not breaking her gaze with Aaron.

"Grandma, you didn't embarrass him, did you? Come on, Aaron, we've got to go." Madi tried to get him away from her grandmother.

Aaron stumbled backward a little, mentally tangled in what just happened. He quickly glanced at Madi to see if she had heard anything. She was too far away.

"Bye, Grandma, I love you," Madi said.

"Love you, too, sweetie," said Granny as the two of them walked out the door.

Aaron had no trouble opening the car door this time. He was more focused on Granny.

"Hmm. No rain," Madi said, getting into the Jeep. "See, she is super nice," she continued, as though she was trying to get a sense of what Aaron was feeling.

Madi started the car and Aaron said, "Yeah, she is," still pondering everything that happened.

Madi moved the stick and drove around Granny's ringed driveway.

Aaron's heart still raced. As they reached the end of the driveway, Aaron looked back through the side mirror at Granny. She stood in the doorway, watching them as they drove away.

Chapter 10

"You looked like you kind of wanted to get out of there."

Aaron hadn't completely stopped thinking about all that just happened, but he tried to refocus on Madi.

"What? Oh, I didn't mind that much."

Madi giggled. "Sure. I could see the look on your face."

"No, she was nice. I enjoyed meeting her — she seems very trustworthy."

Madi smiled at Aaron. "Yeah, she is."

Aaron knew Madi was referring to their secret, but Aaron was thinking about his own secret.

"What would you like to do now?" Madi asked.

Aaron thought of things to do on Earth, but his ideas were scarce. He just looked at Madi, her one hand on the wheel and the other on the stick-thingy he could not remember the name of.

"I don't know. Got any other ideas?"

Madi saw him looking at her hands. "Do you

wanna drive?"

Drive? What does that mean? Is that what it means to control this thing?

"Come on, I can tell you want to!" Madi stopped the vehicle and got out.

She ran around to his side and opened the door. "Come on!" Madi joked as she reached over his stomach and unbuckled him. "Do I have to do everything for you?"

"I—I don't know how," Aaron said, looking away from Madi.

"Oh, you've never driven a stick? It's okay, I can teach you! It's actually super easy," Madi insisted.

Aaron had never driven, let alone driven a stick. He didn't even know what a stick was. He didn't want to elaborate to Madi on how he really had never driven, though. It looked like it was something everyone on Earth did and he didn't want to have to deal with the embarrassment of saying it. Plus, he was always up for something new.

"Okay," Aaron said hesitantly as he slid out of his seat.

Madi jumped into his seat and Aaron walked around to the other side. As nervous as he was, he was also excited. This seemed so cool, controlling this thing and telling it what to do. He hopped into the driver's seat with a little more joy in his step and then buckled up.

"There we go, now you're getting it," Madi said. Then she began her instructions. "Okay, so the gas is under your right foot, and the brake is near your left foot. On the far left is the clutch. In order to drive a stick shift, you have to push the clutch in and move the stick to first gear."

Madi took Aaron's hand and held it over the stick.

"Your hands are so cold," Madi said.

"Maybe yours are just warm," Aaron replied sarcastically.

"Oh. Clever. Is that really the first thing you could think of?" She smiled and said, "Push the clutch in first."

Aaron moved his left foot over to the clutch and pushed it in. *Wow! This is awesome!* The car hadn't even started yet.

"Okay, now use your right foot to hold down

the brake."

Aaron pressed on the brake, too.

"Okay, now, while keeping the clutch pushed in, turn the key."

After watching Madi do it several times now, he had a good idea what the key was, where it was, and how to turn it. He twisted it and heard something come from the front of the car. He let go just like Madi had done and then sat there as if this wasn't the coolest thing in his life. His heart beat fast and his breathing increased just slightly.

"Nervous?"

Aaron half smiled. "Not in the slightest."

Madi giggled. "Okay, now we're going to move to first gear. That's this position right here, like at the top left of an 'H,'" Madi said.

She moved his hand together with the stick and repositioned it into first gear. "Now, this is the hardest part. You're going to use your right foot to push slightly on the gas as you remove your left foot from the clutch. Does that make sense?"

"Not at all, but let's try it," said Aaron eagerly.

"Okay." Madi laughed.

Aaron removed his right foot from the brake and moved it to push slightly on the gas pedal while lifting his left foot off the clutch. The vehicle sputtered; Aaron froze. The Jeep jerked back and forth. Madi flew back and forth as did Aaron until he lifted both his feet off the pedals and it stalled, coming to a stop.

Aaron unfroze as Madi laughed. As Aaron began to thaw from her laughter, he too laughed as loud as Madi.

"Wanna try it again?"

"Of course."

Aaron put his left foot back on the clutch and his right foot back on the brake. He started the vehicle and moved the stick into first gear so he was ready to try again. As terrifying as this was, it was also fascinating. He wanted to do it—he wanted to get a feel for what being an Earth person was like.

Aaron moved his right foot over to the gas pedal just as Madi told him and applied some gas as he lifted his left foot off the clutch. The vehicle began to move. It didn't jerk, but it moved down the road.

"I'm doing it!" Aaron shouted.

"Yeah, you are. Now, apply a little more gas, and what you're going to do is take your foot of the gas, push in the clutch, and move the stick to second gear."

Only half of that made sense to him, but when Madi saw that he had started to do it, she directed him to second gear by placing her hand quickly on his and shifting the gears.

"There we go," said Madi.

"Wow! This, this is — this is amazing!"

"Isn't it fun?" Madi said. "Okay, we're going to go into third gear now."

Aaron duplicated his actions for second gear, and Madi directed his hand so that the stick went into third gear. She didn't take her hand off his this time but instead, hers rested there, right on top of his. The two continued to go down the road and through the gears with the wind gently kissing their faces.

Aaron came up to the first small turn in the road. Fear crept into his mind, but he let his instincts dominate his actions. He turned the wheel nonchalantly and the Jeep went exactly as he directed. Aaron could not contain his excitement.

"This is it. This has got to be the coolest thing I have ever done."

Madi laughed. "You're so weird."

Madi continued to show Aaron how to drive all the way back to her house. They decided to take as many back roads as possible, making the trip back double the amount of time it took them to get there because Aaron wanted to drive for as long as he could. When they got to the driveway, Madi decided to park. She didn't want him to hit her father's garage door.

"That was so remarkable," Aaron continued to say, unable to control his excitement.

"Come on, let's go inside." Madi laughed.

They walked in through the large main wooden door. The house was chilly and dark. Madi flicked on a light and walked over to a little box on the wall. She tapped it several times and the house began to make a noise.

"What's that?" asked Aaron, looking at the little box Madalyne poked several times.

"It's the thermostat. My dad programmed it to be cold while he's gone in order to save energy, but he forgot that I'm still here," Madi explained.

Aaron pieced together the information he just received about thermostats. "Things that change the weather inside the house," he said quietly to himself.

"You want some food?" asked Madi as she walked into the kitchen.

Aaron followed her and sat down on one of the dinner table chairs. "Umm, sure," he said, not knowing what kind of food they ate.

He had never had Earth food before, so he didn't know what to ask for. Madi pulled out some assorted fruit and, to Aaron's surprise, he knew what it was. After seeing the food, he realized how hungry he really was. As soon as Madi set the tray down on the table, he began to pick at it.

Madi sat down in the chair next to him and pulled her knees up to her chest so her feet were also on the chair. She munched on some food while looking at a newspaper.

Aaron looked at Madi and noticed how she was sitting, deciding to do the same. He pulled his knees up just like her and continued to eat.

"Are you mocking me?" Madi joked.

It took Aaron a moment to realize what she

said, but when he realized the flirtation in her voice, he quickly understood not everyone sat like this. He decided to play along with her anyway, though.

"What? What, I don't know what you're talking about."

"Oh, really? Really?" Madi nudged the side of Aaron's chair with her foot. The chair lifted on two legs for a split second.

"Oh someone's a little pushy," Aaron joked as he tapped Madi's chair with his foot.

"Pushy?" Madi lifted Aaron's chair again.

The chair fell backwards and Aaron landed on the floor. Madi jumped out of her chair to help him, sincerely saying, "I'm so sorry."

When Madi looked at him, he was laughing.

"Are you okay?" she asked, crouching down to his level to show her concern.

"I'm fine," Aaron said, as they got up from the floor.

They both stood there. Madi smiled. Aaron did the same. Not knowing what else to say he asked, "Hey, where's your bathroom at?"

"Have to go again, do you? It's the first door on your left down that hall," Madi pointed behind them.

"Thanks," Aaron said as he walked through the house. *I'm an idiot.*

The hall wasn't lit very well, and Aaron didn't know where the light switch was, let alone how to work it. As he walked down the hall, he saw some newspapers hanging in frames on the wall. He took a quick glance at one and it read:

WHO ARE THEY?

Below the words was a picture of a person sneaking into a lake. He skimmed the article and saw the words "Water Travelers" multiple times. He quickly turned around to see the other articles.

WATER TRAVELERS?

LEGEND OR REALITY?

DO THEY EXIST?

There were seven articles along the walls and all of them had to deal with water travelers, theories about them, and pictures of them. Aaron didn't recognize anyone from Upitar in the pictures and the dates on the articles was the 1950s, so they must have been Madi's grandfather's artifacts.

Aaron's need to use the bathroom reentered his thoughts. He stumbled into the bathroom as if it was a place of escape and hiding. He saw the small switch thing on the wall and it looked simple enough to work. He tapped it and light filled the room.

It never ceased to amaze him, that by tapping a little thing on a wall, light would immediately illuminate an entire room. Aaron refocused quickly, though, and locked the door behind him. He stood in front of it, as if he was trying to keep something out.

His heartbeat increased. *Where am I? Who are these people? What have I gotten myself into?* He breathed deeply and proceeded to use the bathroom. *I'm in deep.*

Aaron flushed the toilet and quickly washed his hands. *I can trust her. Right? Of course. She doesn't even think we're real. Even if she did, she will never find out, and, if she does, she won't do anything; she's not like that. She can't be. There's no way she could be like her father. If anything she's probably the opposite, and if the time comes for her to know, well then I know I'll be able to trust her. And if this continues, I just need to be careful around her dad. That's all. Simple. Sort of. Regardless, he isn't coming back for a little while, so I'm safe for the time being. And if I ever do meet him, he will never know. Right. Easy as that.*

Aaron took a deep exhale and looked at himself in the mirror.

I can't believe this. Of all the people, this girl happens to have the craziest family. My dad would kill me. But I have to stay. I can't run away from them now. If this father is hunting us, I need to know how close he his, for the sake of my people. That'll be good excuse if things go wrong.

Although perplexed, Aaron was satisfied with his conclusion. He shut the water off and wiped his hands on the towel hanging by the sink. All of a sudden, a loud noise screamed off in the distance.

It was high-pitched noise, with a clanging sound of metal on metal. It was blaring and sounded as if it was approaching quickly. Aaron threw open the door and rushed down the hallway back to Madi.

"What's that noise?" he shouted.

Madi looked at him and chuckled a little. "It's just a train, silly."

A train? What's a train? Because of the tone in Madi's voice, he figured that trains were something common on Earth.

"Oh, where's it at?" asked Aaron enthusiastically, because he really wanted to figure out what a train was.

"There are some railroad tracks by my house. You can see it if we walk back there a little."

"Let's go see it!"

He had never seen one before. It sounded amazing, and seeing it up close would be something he would never forget.

"Umm, uh, o-okay," Madi joined in on his enthusiasm. She got up from her chair and grabbed Aaron's arm. "Come on, we're going to have to run if we're going to catch it."

They rushed out the front door, slamming it behind them. The noise grew louder as they ran through a field. The tall dead grass rubbed along their legs and Aaron constantly stumbled from holes in the ground.

"How are you so good at running through this?" Aaron asked Madi.

"I used to run through this field as a kid, so I guess you could say I grew up with it."

"I've run through fields before, but this is—"

Before Aaron could finish his sentence, he tripped and landed in the grass. Madi and Aaron burst into laughter. Madi reached her hand out to Aaron. "Come on, it's right over this hill."

Aaron willingly grabbed Madi's outstretched hand. They grasped each other's hands and warmth spread between them.

They reached the top of the hill and below it, down in the valley, Aaron saw the train. It was enormous and long. Its wheels looked as though they were sliding across the tracks. The massive cars were all linked to each other by only a sliver of metal compared to their size. Some of the cars were wooden and some were rusted metal. It wasn't going as fast as he thought it was from the sound it.

The two stood there and watched it roll across the tracks.

"Let's get closer," Aaron said, now leading Madi toward the train.

The ground was not as hard to walk across here; it had leveled out compared to the patchy terrain behind them. Aaron noticed that many of the wooden cars had open doors.

"They look like little moving houses," he said.

"They kind of do." Madi smiled.

"Where's it going?"

"I think to the city. It's a little far from here, about twelve miles."

Aaron looked into the opposite direction from where the train was heading. He saw the end of it way off in the distance. He looked the other way and couldn't see the beginning of the train. The whistle screamed again from the front direction of the train. Never before had Aaron heard a whistle this loud. The train looked so mighty, so powerful. Aaron wanted to board it. It looked full of mystery.

"Let's hop on it. Come on."

"What? Aaron—"

"Come on, it will be fun!" shouted Aaron, pulling Madalyne toward the train.

"Aaron—"

Before she could finish, Aaron said, "Your

dad's out of town, and it will be easy to get back. Come on. When will you have another chance to do this?"

She didn't argue with that. Aaron approached the train and stood close to it, with Madi by his side. The train moved at a brisk walk. Aaron squeezed Madi's hand. Madi squeezed his hand back.

"You really do know how to have an adventure."

Aaron didn't look at her, but a grin came across his face. A run-down wooden car with an open door approached and Aaron grabbed the side. He ran along the train and quickly flung himself into the car.

Madi jogged along the side of the train. Aaron extended his hand for her to grab. She laughed as she tried to keep up. Once their hands locked, Aaron lifted her up into the car but lost his balance due to the swaying of the train.

They rolled onto the wooden floor of the car and remained on their backs as they laughed together. Madi sat up and said, "I can't believe we're doing this! We're actually doing it!"

Chapter 11

Madi and Aaron stood up. The car wasn't very big, only about eight feet by fifteen feet, with a ten-foot high ceiling. As they looked out the back of the car, they saw mountains in the distance and the sun was just setting between them.

Aaron watched Madi look out into the distance. She stood there, gazing at the mountains.

"Isn't it beautiful?"

"Yeah, incredibly."

The clouds mixed with the low sunlight and formed a brilliant pink, purple, and orange summer night sky. Trees ran along the mountain and created a dark blanket over it.

"Wow." Madi was in awe.

The train car shook slightly and Madi fell back into Aaron. He caught her, but fell over onto the hard floor himself.

"Ow," Aaron joked.

They laid there, Aaron holding her safe. Both looking at the ceiling.

"Maybe we should stay sitting," Madi said.

Both sat up in the back of the train car and leaned against the wall. They sat next to each other with their shoulders just barely touching.

"Have you ever been in this city?"

"Nope. I've never even been in any city, actually," admitted Aaron.

"Really? That's crazy. Never?"

"Nope. I guess you could say I live in a pretty old place. Not a whole lot of cities," said Aaron, even though the kingdom was almost the size of a city.

He continued. "It's right down the road from your house, actually. I guess, not right down the road — you would have to travel a little bit, but it's not far."

"Hmm, I think I might know a subdivision you're talking about," Madi said, completely wrong. "You're going to like the city. There's so much to do and so much going on. Imagine hundreds of little shops that have things like tea or clothes or old thrifty things."

"I love tea," Aaron said energetically as he leaned forward.

Madi laughed. "We'll have to get some tea,

then, won't we? My dad's office is also in the city, we can take a walk by on our way to the tea place."

Aaron paused for a moment and then said, "Uh, umm, okay."

Madi leaned her head back on the wall. "I like this."

"What do you mean?"

"This," she said, gesturing at everything around them. "This — it's like, perfect. An escape. It's away from everything and it just feels...good. You know, like, don't you ever think of the perfect getaway? This couldn't be any better."

"This is nice," Aaron agreed, leaning back against the wall.

"It just feels nice to get away, to leave the world for a little bit and not have to worry about anything. It's like we're in our own little world right now," Madi smiled, looking at Aaron. "Don't you ever get overwhelmed from responsibilities and school and things you have to do and becoming the best of the best?" Madi's voice became more emotional as she spoke. "To have to get good grades in school so you can go to a good college, and then what? So you can get a job that makes money and then do that job over and over again for the next forty years of your life? Doesn't that just sound awful? It sounds so boring and so repetitive. It just sounds lifeless and, actually, it really scares me."

Aaron didn't know what school was, but he still understood where she was coming from. His father constantly pushed the duties and responsibilities of kingship on him and it overwhelmed him. He didn't want that life. Just thinking about the mission that he had to complete made him downcast.

"I kind of know what you mean."

"Aaron, I've been meaning to tell you something. And maybe it's just because I haven't had a chance to see more sides of you, but I like how you're so carefree. Just enjoying the moments of life and taking in everything around you — being in amazement of the world. It's like all these things that bother me, that I stress over, you just don't even struggle with. You love life for what it is."

"I do have things I struggle with, though," Aaron said. "The responsibilities of life and how people tell me I have to do some things in order to become something — it stresses me out. Whoever said I have to do something I don't want to, in order to become something I want to? Why can't I just live life, maybe not do what everyone else does? I want to enjoy everything I do and sometimes — most of the time... I don't. But this — I like this, too." Aaron smiled. "I like this because...it's — it's just different. People don't do this because it's out of the standard way of thinking. Doing this is fun. It's a statement saying I'm not tied down to the average way of life — live, do what's customary, and die."

"Does your dad expect a lot out of you?" Madi said tilting her head and looking at Aaron.

"Yes! Yes, he does! He wants me to do so much, and, quite frankly, I don't want to do what he wants me to do at all."

"Me, too. I mean, I love my dad but he can just be so demanding. He wants me to excel so much in school and then go off to some college like Harvard or Yale. I'm sorry, personally I don't want to study half of my life away. And I don't want to get out of where I am now, only to be placed in an even more stressful life. It's all just stupid." Madi paused and took a breath. "Sorry."

"It's okay."

"What's your dad like?"

"He can be kind of uncaring. I mean, he's just not as loving as he used to be. As I've gotten older, he rarely ever has time to talk about anything besides duties. And I understand. It just scares me. I try to joke with him, but he rarely ever gets it and I'm afraid eventually nothing will ever get through to him. I know he loves me, but I feel as if some things are just more important than me sometimes."

"I know what you mean. My dad gets so caught up in his research about those water travelers that he becomes callous. He gets mad when people laugh at him or his work. And ever since my sister left for college, he has been even worse. It's like I have to compete with her, and if she could go to Princeton, than I should also be able to do as well as her." Madi paused. "Sorry, I know you probably don't care. It's just—I love my sister, but my dad expects me to be like her and I can't, let alone do I want to." Madi breathed out slowly. "Do you get along with your siblings?"

Aaron paused for a moment and thought about his brother. Scenes flashed though his mind.

"No...no we didn't. Madi, my brother

actually passed away...when we were both kids." Aaron didn't look at Madi.

"Oh, Aaron, I'm so sorry," Madalyne said mournfully. She put her arm around Aaron and pulled him close. "Aaron, I'm sorry. That was the same brother you talked about playing with as a kid." She rubbed his back. "I'm sorry, Aaron."

"Thanks... he uh... he drowned." Aaron peered at the circles of the old wood below him.

"We don't have to talk about it, Aaron, really."

He moved his hand along the wood. It was course and but felt easily breakable. He swirled his finger around a warp in the wood, watching it move all the way around the spiral until it reached the center.

Madi quickly wiped the tears from her eyes and changed the subject. "I wonder what this train was used for?" She looked around to see if she could find an explanation.

"It smells like horses. It was probably used to transport them."

"How do you know what horses smell like?" Madi responded, flirting a little as if to brighten the mood.

Aaron looked at Madi and instead of responding, he just smiled, as if to say 'thank you.'

Madi smiled back and got up and walked over to the train door. She stared out for a moment and then walked back over to Aaron. Taking him by the arms she said, "Come look at this."

Aaron got up and stood beside her, looking out. There was a large lake glistening from a mix of sunlight and moonlight. The lake was calm and blue. Darkness filled its edges, but the middle was lit with a reflection of various orange, purple, and pink sky and clouds. The moonlight created sparkles between the edge of the lake and the center.

It was absolutely beautiful. The train engine blew out a long whistle. Madi sat down along the edge of the doorway and held Aaron's arm, tugging at it gently. Aaron looked at her and saw the reflection of the sky in her eyes. She was beautiful.

He sat on the floor beside her. Crossing his arms, he rested his elbows on his knees with his hands hanging together between them. They sat along the edge of the car together, with their feet dangling over the edge.

The train passed the lake and a field of grass sprawled out before them. The wind blew and the greens waved below them. A herd of deer ran across the field in the darkness as fireflies lit up in the dusk.

The sun began to hide behind the mountains completely and the moon started to distinguish itself in the sky. It was the perfect summer night. Madi leaned her head against Aaron's shoulder and, in return, he wrapped his arm around her and held her close.

Madi let out a sleepy yawn, even though she was full of energy. Although it was getting dark, they both felt awake and the day still had plenty of time. They sat there and shared a few moments of watching the night close in together.

Madi lifted her head and looked into Aaron's eyes. His blue eyes peered back into her green eyes. Only moonlight reflected off both of them. She closed her eyes. Aaron closed his and moved his lips closer to hers. Without thinking twice, Aaron leaned in to kiss her.

Just before their lips touched, the train

bounced. They didn't kiss. They opened their eyes and scooted back from the ledge into the car. A loud screeching noise came from the back and the front of the train. Aaron looked out and saw nothing.

"We must be stopping soon." Madi stood up and looked around the train car as if to get a feel for her surroundings.

Aaron peered out toward the front of the train and saw thousands of lights up ahead.

So that's what a city looks like.

The city lit up in the night. Different colors glowed orange, yellow, and white. The patterns and designs of blue, red, and purple lights created words that were unreadable at this distance, but still looked breathtaking. It did look full of life, full of excitement, full of adventure. Earth was amazing. It was so different and advanced compared to his world.

"We have to get off the train before it stops, otherwise we could get in a lot of trouble for trespassing," Madi said, sounding worried. She paced back and forth, trying to think of a way to get them off the train without being caught or getting harmed.

Reality unfolded around them. Their moment of escaping from everything chasing them disappeared. They had to come back to their lives. They both had to come back to reality and realize the eventuality of facing everything they dreaded.

They looked out and realized there was really no safe place to jump off. It was all rocks and steep sides, and on top of that, although it was slowing down, the train was moving faster than when they first got on. It was sliding down the tracks at a frightening rate — too fast to jump off.

"Okay, just hold on. I'm sure we'll come to a place where we can jump when the train slows down a little more," Aaron said. "You look out that side and I'll look out here. It's no use pacing and blocking your thoughts with worry."

Madi rushed over to the other side and desperately looked for a spot. Summer air bashed against their faces. Their hair blew in the wind and the moon disappeared behind the clouds.

"Aaron! We might be able to jump coming up."

Aaron ran over to see what she was looking at. Madi pointed in the distance. "Right up there, it's — it's a…a…a road. Never mind."

The train continued to race and approached the edge of the city.

"There's nowhere to jump," Madi said slowly as she looked at the ground in disappointment.

"Then when we stop, we're just going to have to sneak off," Aaron said nonchalantly as he looked at the advancing city lights.

Chapter 12

The train rolled in through the train station walls and darkness encased the car as it went through a tunnel.

Madi and Aaron sat patiently in the back of the car as they waited for the train to stop. The wheels clanged on the steel tracks below. They sat close to each other in the darkness, listening to the sounds of the machine.

"I think I can see some light," said Aaron.

Madi leaned her head toward the door and squinted, her eyes peering out the front of the car. Madi instantly stood up and began to move for the door. Aaron grabbed her arm. "Just be patient. We have to stay hidden if we're going to get off without anyone knowing."

Madi paused and then sat down slowly next to Aaron.

The train exited the tunnel and light from factory lamps glowed across elevated walkways near the train tracks. The train's speed reduced to a crawl and Aaron and Madi backed into the far left corner of the car. The spaces between the boards of the old wooden car allowed them to peek outside.

They passed large factories and saw men standing along the outside of them. They had cigars in their mouths and appeared to be enjoying each other's company as they laughed and puffed out smoke.

Aaron looked directly into the eyes of one man but the blackness from the shadows inside of the car kept him secret.

"Aaron, there's men everywhere. How are we going to get off this thing?" whispered Madi.

"I'll figure it out, don't worry," Aaron whispered back as he continued to look through the crack.

Madi snuggled closer to him, as if seeking safety from the outside.

The train finally came to a stop. Madi began to move her shoulders and Aaron said, "Not yet."

She froze and a man crossed in front of the hole Aaron was looking through. He mumbled some words to a man on his left and then followed it up with a jolly laugh. The two men kept walking and passed the train car Madi and Aaron were in.

"Okay. Now, I need you to move over to the other side and see if you can see anyone coming," whispered Aaron.

Madi slowly slid over to the other side, not lifting her butt more than an inch off the dusty wooden boards. When she got to the right corner, she looked through the cracks in the wood.

"I—I don't see anyone. But I can't see that far," she whispered.

"It's okay. Now, you look across and out my door and I'll look across and out yours. See if you can see anyone coming from the front of the train."

Madi peered out the opposite door. "It looks good to me."

"So does mine." Aaron moved toward his door.

He scanned as far as he could without sticking his head out. In the distance, he saw light from a factory patio lamp, but no one outside. He quickly poked his head out the door and glanced around. Nobody was in sight.

"It looks safe," Aaron whispered. "Come on."

Madi moved over to Aaron. Aaron peeked

his head out to check again. Still no one. Hopping off the train car, he landed on the ground. It was a steep drop, about four feet. Madi put her feet over the edge and looked at Aaron.

"I'll catch you." Aaron smiled.

Madi moved her hands to the edge of the train car and lifted herself off. Aaron caught her and lowered her as she wrapped her arms around his neck. He carefully set her to the cold stony ground.

"Thanks," whispered Madi softly, with her hands still around his neck.

"Hey!" shouted a voice in the distance. "Hey! Come here! What are you doing?"

Aaron and Madi turned and saw a large man with a black beard wearing checkerboard red and black plaid coming at them.

"Madi, come on!" shouted Aaron as he grabbed her hand.

"Stop! Come here!" roared the man.

Aaron and Madi ran the other way and found a tunnel that led to another train stop. An orange light illuminated the brown stone archway as they ran through it. The worker came hurtling around the corner at them. Aaron tipped a pile of crates over that were stacked one on top another in the tunnel.

The wild man plowed through them, kicking one right past Aaron's head as he went around the corner of the tunnel. The crate smashed along the steel rails of the tracks in the docking bay they were entering.

No train rested on the tracks, but the light from one shined through the tunnel.

"Come on, come on!" shouted Aaron as he pulled Madi onto the tracks.

The whistle of the train blew loudly, reverberating off the brick-walled tunnel it was sleeking through. Madalyne turned her body sideways against the back wall and they crossed just before the train came to a halt. The man flew down the flight of stairs into the train docking area.

The train created a wall, cutting off the two of them from the man. The train lit up the docking bay with a beaming white light at the front of it.

"We're safe!" shouted Madi to Aaron as she hugged him.

Turning their heads, they saw the man stood on the other side of the train. They could see him clearly through a train car with two open doors.

"No we're not," Aaron said as he grabbed Madi's hand and continued to run.

The man bellowed out, "Security!" as he scrambled through the train car and chased them.

Aaron and Madi hustled through an underpass. It was triple the length of the first tunnel, but at the end were city streetlights.

"We're almost there!" said Aaron, running out of breath.

They made it halfway through the tunnel as the man shouted, "Stop! I'll have you both arrested! Stop them!"

Aaron and Madi exited the tunnel and sprinted across the street. The lights of cars, shops, and streets surrounded them and took them into their care. The man stopped chasing them once they were out of his sight, and they were safe. They still continued to run through the busy nighttime sidewalks full of people, though. Coming up on a small park with some trees, they slowed down. Madi and Aaron found a cold black bench and rested within the shadow of a young tree to catch their breath. Aaron started to laugh, and then Madi followed.

"That was…so…exciting!"

"I really didn't think a man his size could run that fast," Aaron said, still huffing.

"I didn't, either. He was really hustling." She took a deep breath. "Wow, I actually have so much energy right now."

"It's adrenaline."

"I know, but I have never had it like this. That was so much…fun!"

"Running is a little more fun when you're with someone." Aaron panted as he picked up a stick from the ground.

"What's that mean? Have you had to run before?"

"Once or twice." Aaron grinned.

"Oh, look at you. What were you running from, Mr. Bad Boy?"

"How about we go get some of that tea and discuss this another time?" suggested Aaron as he broke the stick in his hand and stood up from the bench.

"I'm going to hold you to that." Madi smiled as she also stood up. "I think there's a little teashop

over on Main Street, it's right over there, I think,"
she said, looking around and pointing her finger
down the road. "Let's go."

The road glistened from the lights of shops.
The colors of the city mixed and life glowed
everywhere, people were walking happily and
enjoying laughs, birds fluttered around food that
was dropped from late-night dinners, and cars
traveled up and down the street as people ran
across crosswalks.

"I think that's it, down there," she said,
pointing to a small little shop.

Madi and Aaron strolled up to the crosswalk
with a red hand. Aaron looked and didn't see any
cars, so he began to walk. Madi grabbed his arm
and said, "Aaron, what are you doing? You can't
cross yet." She pulled him back to the side of the
road.

Aaron paused. "Well, when can we?"

"When you see the little walking guy symbol.
We're in the city and I've heard they can be strict
about jaywalking here," Madi said. "Here, there's a
button, do you want to press it?" She gestured at the
crosswalk button.

Aaron ambled over, like a kid, to the small metal button with a worn yellow rim around it. He looked at it and then pointed his finger to press it. He pushed it slowly and then turned around to see if anything happened.

Madi giggled and said, "You're so silly."

Aaron pushed the button rapidly a few more times and then walked back over to Madi.

"Hmm, that was fun," Aaron said, not understanding the point of it.

The crosswalk changed to a glowing white walking man.

"See, now we can cross," she said.

Aaron looked at the cars as he walked by. Some of the people in them looked tired, some full of energy, and others melancholy. They reached the other side of the street and continued to stroll toward the teashop.

"My mom and I came here when I was a kid," Madi said.

"Do you still go here?"

Madi paused. She didn't look at Aaron.

"No...she passed away."

Aaron instantly turned to Madi just as she

did for him and said, "What? Madi, I'm — I'm so sorry."

"It's okay, I was only seven. But I miss her all the time still," Madi said, choking back tears. "I was going to tell you earlier, but I wanted to focus on you and I didn't want to ruin the fun we were having."

"Madi, I'm so sorry, and you wouldn't have ruined it. I promise you that."

There was a long pause as they slowed down.

"I guess there has to be a little bit of grieving in everyone's life, otherwise we would never be able to see or enjoy the beauties of living," Madi said, as if trying to explain it not only to Aaron, but herself also.

Nothing more was said for a while, but emotions were felt between them. Both of them had lost someone they loved dearly. And they actually did feel each other's pain. It was a real connection that they both understood.

"She was in a car accident," Madi allowed.

"You don't have to tell me about it."

"It's okay, it feels good to say how I feel to

someone I trust." Madi looked at Aaron. Continuing, she said, "I miss her. She loved me a lot and was always there, unlike my dad. She always supported me, and my dad only pushes me—me and my sister both, actually. But my sister is just a natural genius, so it was never hard for her. But for me, it is. My mom always wanted me to succeed in what I wanted to do, but my dad, he just seems to never approve."

They came up to the teashop door. The place had an old, wooden appearance. Inside it looked warm and friendly. The couches were a sharp, black leather, and the coffee tables looked hand crafted. A purple neon sign glowed above the doorway. It read: *Agape*

"I never knew what it meant." Madi looked up at the sign.

Aaron paused for a moment. He knew this word and what language it was in from studying he had to do as a child.

"It stands for a form of 'love' in Greek," he said delicately.

Madi paused and continued to gaze at the sign. Aaron looked over at her, but she didn't break her concentration away from the sign.

Aaron glanced at her eye and saw a tear form and then begin to roll down her cheek. Her other eye watered up and a tear, too, fell from it. Aaron put his arm around her waist and said gently, "Come on, let's go inside."

Aaron opened the door and led Madi in. She wiped her eyes and walked up to the countertop to order. A gentleman in front of them in line with a large white mustache and a scarf around his neck said a few words to a young lady behind the counter.

The counter was wooden with a black granite top. Glass cases ran all along it, except for an opening where the cashier stood. Inside the cases were cookies, cinnamon twists, gingerbread men, brownies, and many other little snacks.

Behind the lady was a chalkboard on the wall with different kinds of coffee and tea listed, and their prices. The teashop was lively, but not loud — active, but still peaceful.

There were Chinese letters decorated in picture frames around the room and also painted on the burgundy walls. The lights were quiet, not glaringly bright. The smell of baked goods scented the room, mixing with the aroma of the varieties of tea and coffee.

The girl behind the counter handed the old man a red cup with black letters reading 'Agape' along the side. Madi and Aaron stepped up to order.

"What do you want?" asked Madi.

"I don't know; I'll just have whatever you're getting."

"Could I get…" Madi paused and browsed the sign. "Oh, two Zip Xou Teas?"

"Of course you can," said the barista, not actually having a choice to say no. "It'll be $6.40."

"Oh." Madi felt around in her pockets. Her face looked worried until she pulled out a small piece of plastic from her front pocket.

"I almost completely forgot about money," Madi said to Aaron.

Aaron looked at the little piece of plastic. *What's that worth?*

He stared at the little piece of plastic in confusion as the barista swiped it through a computer. The lady handed Madi back her card and

Madi saw Aaron's puzzled face.

"My dad gave me a credit card since he's gone so much. I have to pay for myself a lot," Madi said, as though she had to explain why she had one.

Although that didn't answer Aaron's question, he figured it would make sense later.

"Have you ever had Zip Xou Tea before?" asked Madi.

Aaron thought for a brief second of all the teas he had. Nothing had ever been called Zip Xou before, they all had to do with leaves and plants that he and others collected.

He and the Captain of the Guard always drank tea together. While Aaron was out doing tasks for his father, he collected leaves from plants as he traveled between Upitar and Earth. The Captain, Ugine, did the same while he was out hunting or tracking threats to the kingdom. Aaron always liked having tea with Ugine. Even though the Captain was far older than Aaron, they were best friends. Having tea was calming and relaxing, and Ugine allowed Aaron to speak his mind, as long as he could do the same. It helped Aaron think, and the tea was always quenching. It was boiled over a small fire and Ugine always knew when it was ready to be taken off. He never failed to mix the right amount together to create a perfect blend. It put both their minds at ease and allowed Aaron to rest from the endless upcoming duties and rules of becoming the new king. It also allowed Ugine to peacefully get away from his violent life and, as he would say, reminisce over his younger years that he wished to return to.

Returning to the present, Aaron said to Madi, "I don't think so."

"My mom and I always got it. I think it's special to this store, though. I don't know…my tea knowledge isn't very broad. I know it's made with natural leaves and spices."

"It smells really good," Aaron said, sniffing a peppermint-like aroma.

The barista came back with two cardboard cups of tea.

"Careful, they're hot," she cautioned.

Madalyne took her cup and walked over to some seats. Aaron took his cup and pulled it close to him. Without thinking, he gripped it hard and the lid popped off. Tea spilled all over his stomach and leg.

"Oh my gosh! Are you okay?" shouted the barista to Aaron.

Aaron made a few noises and pulled his pant leg and shirt away from his skin the best he could. The barista grabbed some towels and asked one of her co-workers to come to the register.

"Here, go ahead and use the restroom back there to try to dry yourself," the barista said, pointing to the back of the shop.

Aaron waddled to the restroom. Madi looked worried and ready to come and help him at first, but then smiled at his clumsiness.

Aaron had never been in a restroom before and was confused about it. He saw sinks — something he knew about — and that was about it. There were three strange things, in front of one a man stood right up against, peeing into. Then there were little room-like things in the back. One of the rooms had an open door, so Aaron walked to it to see what was in it.

There was a toilet — something else he knew. *So, these are just like mini home bathrooms?*

He closed himself in one and locked the

door. Taking the towel, he dried his pants the best he could. Aaron took his right leg out because it was completely soaked and noticed that his dagger now had tea all over it. He dried it off and then wiped off his pants, attempting to dry them.

Aaron slid his pants back on after a worthy effort of cleaning and then exited the stall. The man who was peeing against the wall had left. Aaron examined the thing the man had been facing.

It had a little lever on it and Aaron gently touched it. Nothing happened. He looked around just to double check that nobody was in there with him. He saw only himself in the mirror. *One time.* He faced the thing and pushed the lever again. After pushing it hard, water flowed down from inside the thing.

Aaron took a step back and then watched the water stream down the walls of the thing. He gazed at it in wonder. The water stopped and Aaron let out a "Hmm."

He turned around and washed his hands in the sink. Afterward he saw a piece of paper towel hanging out of a box. He grabbed it and attempted to dry his hands. The small, single piece of paper wasn't enough. Aaron looked at the box and saw, through its black glass, some more paper towel inside. He looked for a lever, but didn't see anything. He put his hands on each side of the box and leaned in close to see the paper towel inside.

The box made a strange noise and more paper towel suddenly came out of it. Aaron took it and dried his hands some more. He kept putting his hands on the box and moving close to see the paper towel because that's how he thought it worked.

An old man with grey hair walked in and saw how Aaron was getting his paper towel. The man watched him for a second while Aaron just continued with his fascination of the machine.

The man mumbled, "We're doomed," and walked back out the door.

Aaron finished drying his hands completely and returned to the shop. The barista approached him, saying, "Are you sure you're okay?"

"Yeah, I'll be fine." Aaron handed back the towel she had given him.

"All right, here's another cup of tea. It's on the house; be careful this time." The barista handed him the cup of tea.

Aaron held it gently as the barista returned behind the counter to an older lady and conversed with her.

Aaron paid no attention to them but roamed to the center of the shop. He saw Madi sitting next to the window, facing the street.

Aaron sat down and Madi said, "You okay?"

Aaron laughed. "Yeah, I'll be fine." He smiled.

They sat in wooden chairs painted black with red cushions on them. Both looked out the window and saw city life before them. Madi lifted her cup to her mouth and slowly tilted it so that the tea flowed in. She closed her eyes. She smiled and then set the cup down.

"Try it," she said.

Aaron took a sip of the tea. He closed his eyes and a smile crawled across his face. With his eyes still closed, he said, "That's good. That's really good."

The flavor of the leaves tasted similar to something he drank before, just sweeter.

"Isn't it?" Madi agreed.

Aaron opened his eyes and looked out the

window. Madi began to talk, but Aaron didn't hear her. He was still looking out the window. He saw someone. Someone coming down the street. Someone that he knew. It was a water traveler. Dressed in human clothes, the traveler was moving quickly through the crowd of people in the direction of the coffee shop.

"Aaron?" Madi said, trying to get his attention.

"Yeah, yeah?" Aaron said, turning to Madi.

"Where do you live? I've never seen you before."

Aaron still didn't fully hear the question. He was focused on the man coming toward him.

"Uh, umm, just around." Aaron got up from his chair. "Will you excuse me for a moment? I see an old friend, I think, and I want to say hi really quick."

Madi looked out the window to see who Aaron was talking about.

"Umm, yeah, sure! Do you want me to stay here?"

Madi began to get up from her chair and Aaron, not even looking at her, said, "Yeah, just stay here."

"Okay," Madi said, sipping her tea as Aaron rushed out the door.

Aaron ran down the street to the man. He looked him in the eye and the man made a gesture for Aaron to follow him down an alley. This wasn't a coincidence.

Aaron came down the alley after the man and saw him standing beside a wall. When Aaron approached him, the man desperately said, "Sir. Master Aaron, it's so good to see you. My name is Imushial. I serve in the highest ranks of The Guard. I was told to find you and bring you home immediately. Something's happened. We've been attacked and your father needs you. He said it's urgent."

Chapter 13

Aaron took a beat, trying to comprehend what he just heard. The man continued to spew out words rapidly, but Aaron stopped him. "Wait, wait, slow down. What happened? Who attacked us?"

"We don't know, Sir. We believe it's the same people that have been sending the spies," Imushial said.

"Where did they attack us?"

"They hit the castle and the entire left wall has been destroyed," Imushial said frantically.

Aaron thought for a moment. He pondered the words the man just said. *What could have been that powerful?*

"We're not sure what it was, Sir, but you must come home this very moment. Your father has to speak with you. He did not tell me what it was about, but said that it was urgent and he must see you."

"I can't leave right now. I can come later, but I'm busy right now."

Imushial responded, saying, "With all due

respect, Sir, I have an order to bring you back home as soon as I found you — "

Aaron cut him off, asking, "How did you find me, anyway?"

"Your father told me the last place he knew you were. I've been tracking your dagger on this map. Once I saw it light up, I got here as soon as I could."

The tea. It must have activated the dagger when it spilled down my leg.

"Now please, Sir, we must go," Imushial urged.

Aaron thought quickly about how to explain that he had to stay. If he left Madi abruptly like this he would lose any chances of seeing her again and finding out more about her family. He had to buy some time and leave properly. He couldn't say he was with an Earth girl, because they would never understand. Besides, that might create even more chaos. He thought of something else.

"Imushial, you don't understand. Did my father tell you about my very important mission to find a certain girl? I was sent on this mission by him and I've found her. I'll be trying to take her captive in the next hour. Tell my father I will be there soon. I almost have her, and if I leave now, everything I have worked for will be lost. The mission may never be able to be completed again."

Imushial looked at Aaron and admitted, "Your father did tell me not to disturb you if you were in the middle of your mission—just tell you to come as soon as you can. Sorry, Master Aaron."

Aaron smiled; his clever lie worked. "I will be there as soon as I can."

"Thank you, Sir. Thank you. See you shortly," Imushial said as he ran off back into the city night.

Aaron walked around the corner of the alley, proud of himself. He quickly remembered Madi and that he really didn't have much time. He rushed back into the teashop, but recomposed himself as he walked through the door. He sat back down and Madi asked, "Was it who you thought it was?"

Aaron looked at his tea, still in wonder. He focused and said, "Yeah, yeah, just...a friend of my dad."

"Oh, that's cool," said Madi as she sipped her tea. "How does he know hi—"

"Madi, I hate to say this, but we have to get going. That man works with my father, and asked how he was doing. I guess my dad left work early because of some heart pain. I haven't heard from him but he usually keeps health issues quiet until he knows what they are for sure. I'd like to get home and make sure everything's all right."

"Oh my gosh. Of course! We probably should start heading back anyway," Madi said as she stood up.

Aaron stood also, with his tea still in his hand. Madi opened the shop door and exited as the barista behind the counter said, "Have a good night."

"You, too," Aaron said with the door closing behind him.

"Hold on." Madi walked into the street, waving her hand.

A yellow car pulled up and stopped beside her. Along the side of it read 'Taxi,' and on the top of it a glowing sign also read 'Taxi.'

Does she know this person?

"Come on," Madi said, waving Aaron over. "We'll just take a cab home."

Madi climbed into the backseat and Aaron followed. He closed the door behind him and Madi asked, "Do you take Visa?"

The man in the front of the car didn't even turn around. His voice was friendly, but strange sounding, an accent Aaron didn't recognize. "Yes, ma'am, where to?"

"8372 Silver Court West. Is that too far?"

"No, ma'am. It will be about fifteen dollars; is that okay, still?" the man asked as he eyed the street.

"That's fine, thank you," Madi said to the driver.

"I'll get you there as quickly as I can, then."

"Thank you," Madi said, turning to Aaron. "Would you rather we just go to your house?"

"No, it's fine, don't worry about it."

"Are you sure?"

"Yeah, I don't want to have to explain this to my parents later."

The man put the car into drive and joined the traffic. The inside of the cab had black leather seats and was dark in the back. The front had a machine that tracked the distance and the cost of the trip, along with other meters and gizmos along the dash. The steering wheel had a neon-red cover over it.

"What are your parents going to say when you get back?" Madi asked. "I haven't really thought about yours, but we've been out a lot and you've been away from home."

Should I say they're out of town, or they just don't care?

"My mom's out of town right not and my dad works all the time. Plus they don't really care; they're pretty lenient as long as I'm safe and home at a reasonable time," Aaron said, combining his two options.

The city lights glowed outside the cab as the cab driver moved in and out of traffic.

"Okay." Madi yawned while stretching. "I hope your dad is okay."

"I'm sure he will be," Aaron said, followed by a half smile.

Madi half smiled back and leaned her head against Aaron's shoulder.

"If you need anything let me know," she said.

"Thanks, Madi," he said, wrapping his arm

around her.

The lights of the city faded behind them. Aaron loved the city. The short moment he got to spend in it was better than he thought it would be. Everyone was so lively, and the places were so exciting. There was so much for him to take in that he had never seen before.

Aaron looked down at Madi; her eyes were shut. He didn't know if she was sleeping or not, but didn't want to disturb her if she was. She moved a little, only to place her head more on his chest and not his shoulder. Aaron looked out the window. He looked at Earth's one bright moon, at how it shined bright in the sky and lit the night.

It was beautiful. Its plain white and grey color looked so cool to Aaron, who grew up seeing yellow, green, and purple moons. The white looked peaceful and calming.

The taxi driver whispered to Aaron, "She's cute."

Aaron smiled and, trying not to wake Madi, whispered back, "Yeah, she is."

"When did you meet her?"

"About a day ago," Aaron said, not realizing

it until he said it; it felt like he had known Madi for a while now, but it had only been a day.

Aaron saw the taxi driver's eyes widen in the mirror. The driver said, "Wow. Only a day and you two look like you've been in love for years."

"Really?" Aaron said hopefully.

He didn't really know if Madi thought about him that way. He certainly liked her, but he wasn't sure if she felt the same about him. He had never really interacted with an Earthling other than occasional one-word conversations.

"Yeah, you two really must have…something…something special," the taxi driver said with a smile.

Aaron smiled and looked at Madi, still sleeping on his shoulder. Until now, Aaron never thought fully about himself and Madi. She was special. They could never be together, though. She was an Earthling, and he was a Upitarian.

Aaron loved every moment with her, but knew nothing could ever come out of it. He blocked these thoughts out of his head; he didn't want to think of leaving Madi.

The car pulled into a driveway and the driver

said, "We've reached your destination."

Aaron shook Madi a little and gently said, "Hey, we're here."

Madi rubbed her eyes and pulled her credit card out from her pocket. She handed it to the man, then fell back onto Aaron. The man swiped the card.

"Hey, come on now, sleepyhead," Aaron said.

The man handed the card to Aaron and said, "You guys are all set."

"Thanks so much, sir." Aaron unbuckled himself then Madi.

Madi, still half asleep, stumbled out the car door. The car backed down the driveway and drove off with its red lights fading in the distance. Madi leaned on Aaron, still trying to wake herself up.

"Come on now." Aaron picked her up, cradling her in his arms.

After taking her up the cement steps, he struggled to twist the doorknob, finally got it, and carried Madalyne inside. Using his elbow, he flicked the light switch that he saw earlier.

Aaron carefully hiked up the steps, Madi still in his arms. She had her arms crossed over herself and dozed happily. Aaron reached the top floor and walked into her room. The light from the moon lit the room well enough for him to see.

Aaron laid Madi in her bed and pulled blankets over her, tucking her in. Aaron smiled when he saw her sleeping peacefully in the moonlight. He backed out of the room until he reached the doorway where he stopped. Aaron smiled. She looked beautiful.

"Goodbye, Madalyne." He took a deep breath and hurried downstairs.

Aaron walked into the kitchen and looked for some paper and something to write with. He saw a stray piece on the counter and a collection of what he knew to be writing utensils near the fridge. He picked up a pen and wrote out a letter to her:

Dear Madalyne (Madi),

I had a lot of fun spending time with you and in all truthfulness I don't want to leave. I do hope to see you again, really, but right now I have to go. There are just some things that I can't explain. Maybe someday I will be able to. I hate that I have to leave you like this but it's for the better.

Goodbye,

Aaron

Aaron cried as he wrote the letter. He wanted to see Madalyne again, but he didn't know what was going to happen in his life. For the people of Upitar, he had to get back to his mission. And then what? Once he became King, who knew when he would have the opportunity to come and see her. As painful as it was for him to admit, there was no way an Earthling and a water traveler could ever be together.

Two tears fell on the letter by Aaron's name. He closed his eyes and breathed in slowly. He knew this had to be done.

Aaron hurried out the door and closed it behind him. He scurried to the pool of water that led him back to Upitar. He forced himself not to think of Madi. He ran faster and faster, away from her — the only thing he didn't want to run from.

Chapter 14

Aaron first grabbed his bag hidden along the outskirts of the pond. When he reached the shore of the pool, he stopped. He breathed slowly.

Aaron closed his eyes and let his tears fall across his cheeks and onto the ground. He wiped them away slowly with the sleeve of his shirt. He realized he was still wearing Madi's sweatshirt, but he knew he couldn't go back now. He would cave, and for her own sake, it was better that he just kept it. It would be hard enough reading the letter let alone finding the damp hoodie next to it.

Taking a look around, Aaron checked to see if anyone was near. No one. He didn't really care, though, if anyone saw him. He walked into the water and took a deep breath before plunging his head under the surface in bitterness. He held his eyes shut and then water traveled.

Rising from below the surface, he stood in the sunlight of Upitar. He got out of the water, not thinking as he set his feet on Upitar's soil. He changed back into his own clothes and made his way to the castle. Running through forest and plains, he traveled through pool after pool of water.

Aaron couldn't stop thinking about Madi. Every moment, she entered his thoughts. These feelings were different; they were special. He hadn't felt anything close to this before, even when his father presented possible princesses from the outer rim worlds for him to marry. Aaron tried to drown out his thoughts as he traveled home. Before he realized it, his home was in sight. Exiting the clear lake he was in, he trudged to the castle.

The tower guards noticed him off in the distance and sent word to his father. Men on horses surrounded Aaron within moments. The great animals trotted around the prince.

Their hooves and legs were massive; compared to Earth horses, they were practically double in size. One leg was almost the size of Aaron. They were all black and armor covered most of their skin. The men on horseback were all in guard attire.

"Climb on, Sir," one of the guards said to him as he reached out his hand.

Aaron took the guard's hand and was lifted

off the ground and onto the back of the horse effortlessly. The guard then let out a "heah" and the horse took off, galloping toward the castle.

Aaron held onto the cold armor of the guard while looking back at the hills in the distance. Memories of Madi endlessly flashed in his mind.

The horses stopped in the plaza in front of the throne room and Aaron went through the motions of swinging himself down. The Captain of the Guard met him as touched the ground again.

"It's good to have you back. Where's the girl?" greeted Ugine.

"It's good to see you, Ugine. Unfortunately, I still have work to do regarding that. Where's my father?" Aaron replied.

Ugine extended his hand toward the throne room doors. "Right this way."

Aaron approached but stopped when he saw the west wall. Bricks lay on the ground near where the damage had taken place. It was completely destroyed. Aaron could clearly see through it, straight up to the mountains behind the trees. Out of the ten thousand feet of wall, only one hundred feet was left. Aaron was speechless.

"We're not sure what it was," Ugine said.

The Captain put his hand on Aaron's shoulder and gently steered him to the throne room doors. "Come on, your father's waiting."

The entire castle was on alert. Men were stationed everywhere and everyone was paying attention to the smallest of details. Two guards opened the throne room doors, letting Aaron and the Captain enter. Aaron's father was leaning over a table with his side to the door. His finger pointed down at a piece of paper that looked like a map.

He was saying—almost shouting, "We don't know where they came from! We have scoured almost the entire globe of Upitar, and no city nor village has been built that we don't control or know of besides in the swamplands! They've gone unchecked for centuries, and it's the only place our enemies could be!"

Nine men surrounded the table with the King. There were two open chairs, one for Aaron and one for the Captain. An advisor of the king named Damarius responded to the proposal.

"But, Your Highness, the conditions of the swampland are too treacherous for life. No man, let alone an entire army, could live there! What would they eat? And how could they have blasted such a devastating hole in our castle walls? The walls are thirty feet thick by ten thousand feet long, and I don't care how big a stone is hurled at them, it's not going to do that much damage."

Aaron stood back with Ugine, listening in on the debate.

The King responded, "We don't know what we were hit with, and it certainly wasn't a stone. There are no remnants of one anywhere. We were hit with something we have never seen before and something, quite frankly, we may never see again. Our only choice right now is to search the swamp. It is the only place left!"

"Your Highness, more men will fall and die in that awful place than we have to spare! Our enemy probably wants that—"

The King cut him off, shouting aggressively while slamming his hands against the great wooden table. "Then what are you suggesting?"

There was a pause, and then Damarius responded, "I think it's Earthlings we're dealing with."

The King lifted his hands and turned away, chuckling. "The people of Earth?" He turned back around, speaking seriously. "The Earthlings can't water travel! It is a gift only our people know."

Damarius retaliated again. "They may have learned how! It is the only explanation. How else could they have gotten away so fast? Who else has that kind of power?"

The other men stood and began to shout, agreeing with the new idea.

Aaron became worried, about Madi. Out of the corner of his eye, he saw Ugine moving toward the table.

Calmly Ugine said, "It's not the Earthlings."

The roars ceased and they all looked at the Captain of the Guard. Ugine ambled up to the table and joined the men standing around it.

"We have all seen an Earthling, haven't we? They are not like the spies we've captured. The people of Earth do not have the same sort of camouflaged attire those spies had. When you look at that armor, you can tell it was made out of Konjoho leaves, and those don't exist on Earth. And Earthling technology is far more advanced than ours — "

Another advisor named Lar stood up from the table, pointing at Ugine. "You don't know that, Captain! You have not seen what Earthlings have buried inside their homes, or what forms of weapons they have." Turning to the rest of the men, Lar preached, "But we have all seen their moving machinery — those 'vehicles.' We have seen how fast those things are, haven't we, when on Earth? For all we know, they could have learned how to make things larger than ourselves travel and brought something powerful enough to do that to us." Turning back to Ugine, he continued. "And for all we know, you could be with them! You could be one of their inside spies trying to deceive us into going into the swamp!"

The men around the table, besides the King, grew in anger against Ugine and began to accuse him.

"Enough," the Captain shouted. "I have been loyal to my people and I am no traitor. If the Earthlings used one of their machines, there would be marks on the ground, or we would have heard it in the sky. We heard nothing! The wall exploded and we saw nothing! Now is not the time to take up arms against one another. Now is the time to trust one another, and to find our true enemy. The Earthlings have never wanted anything from us but to discover if we are real or not, and I don't believe that is important enough to them to take up arms against us."

Ugine took a breath and looked at all of the men around the table, including the King. "Now, what I am suggesting is that there is something else out there. Another race we have never seen before that has learned how to use our waterways." Ugine let his words sink in. Nobody else seemed to see it, but Aaron noticed Ugine shoot a glance to the King before resuming—a very unique glance that Aaron had never seen before. "Now this may seem absurd, but if we release a spy, we may be able to follow him back to his sender in order to find out where he came from."

The table grew quiet and they all pondered the idea. Aaron let the glance go, deciding to investigate it later.

"He will know something is planned," the kingdom elder, Gantrue, said.

"Not if he thinks he's escaping." Ugine paused briefly, then explained. "We bring a spy out in the night for what we say is a drill, to set him off guard. The spy will be brought out of the castle walls to a torch lit area. His hands are roped and we push him onto his knees in front of a log. An executioner will come out of the blackness. He will realize it is not a drill and we are going to execute him." The eyes of the men grew larger as they listened to Ugine. "I will give a speech stating his death sentence and the executioner will raise his sword. But before he strikes the man down, arrows — from our own men — pierce the armor of the executioner, me, and all of the guards. We will all fall and the spy, in a state of utter bewilderment, will act on it as an opportunity to run. When he takes off, we have more arrows fly back and forth between the woods and the castle so the spy believes it to be an actual battle. Then we will have someone secretly follow the spy until we find out where he came from."

All the men, including the King, leaned back in their chairs, taking the idea into consideration.

Lar said, "Yes, it sounds brilliant, but there is

a problem. How is everyone going to be struck without dying? Killing our own men isn't worth *possibly* discovering where these people are coming from."

Ugine said, "I know that. The arrows will be fake. We will pre-crack their tips so that they will stick in the armor, but not penetrate any farther. Also, the armor will be reinforced. We have armor in our catacombs that was designed to withhold many arrows. After it was forged, our ancestors discovered it was too heavy to travel in because one could not move fast enough. But we are not running anywhere, we are just standing and firing arrows, with maybe a little bit of covering. The spy will never notice. He will be too focused on his escape from death."

The men all breathed easily and began to smile, one by one.

"Yes, this could work!" shouted one of the members.

They all started to agree with the plan, except for one — the second in command to the Captain, Archival.

"With all due respect, sir, there's still one

more problem. Who is going to follow this man? None of us are fast or stealthy enough. He will be too crafty for us to keep up without him knowing."

The men all looked at each other and became downcast because they knew Archival was right. Not even the fastest guard—not even Ugine—could keep up with the spy.

"I will." Aaron came out of the shadows at the back of the throne room.

"Aaron, you cannot," the King said immediately.

"Father, I am the fastest and the best in the land, I—"

His father cut him off. "Aaron, if something happens to you, then who will become King? We cannot lose you."

"I'm aware of that, Father! But what good is a king if he has no one to rule over?" Aaron became pensive. "My people need me now, and as their future King, I will not sit back and watch. We are at war, and right now my services are needed—"

"Aaron, you have your own mission!" his father shouted.

"Father, if I don't do this now, then I may

never have a chance to be King, let alone would I want to be the king of a destroyed nation I could have saved. Sometimes you have to take a risk, because from risk comes progress. And you, and I, and everyone else in here knows I am the only water traveler that can do it!" Aaron took a breath after he finished.

There was a pause before the King spoke. Letting out a sigh, he said, "Very well. If it must be done...then, it must be done."

Archival spoke up saying, "Sir, we can not lose — "

"Aaron is right, Archival. He is the only one who can do this. It's time to discover who we are at war with before they wipe us out."

All the men around the table knew this to be true and agreed with letting Aaron go. Gantrue stood and raised his hands for silence. Once everyone quieted down, he spoke.

"There is one thing that has gone unaddressed, and it may be of importance."

"What is it?" asked Ugine.

Gantrue responded, "Do we know what happened on Earth as a result of the destruction of our wall?"

The men began to talk quietly amongst themselves. Aaron thought instantly, *the tree.*

"No, we do not know. The only one on Earth at the time was Aaron." Turning his head to Aaron, the Captain finished, "And unless you saw something, we know nothing."

Aaron paused. He ran every thought about the tree through his head and, most importantly, he ran Madi through his head. For her safety, he replied, "No, I didn't."

Ugine turned back to the rest of the men. "Very well. What we do know is that there was a Whispering Tree planted on the outside of the wall around the destroyed parts. Because it is no longer here, we know for sure that the corresponding tree was destroyed. The damage that occurred along with it, we will discover later, but right now we have a greater issue to deal with, and that's finding out who attacked us."

The men agreed, and Ugine stood and said to his second-in-command, "Archival, go and retrieve the armor from out of the catacombs."

"Yes, sir." Archival stood up from the table.

He nodded to the Captain and the King respectively and ran out of the throne room.

"Get the troops ready, this happens when the moons are high!" Ugine said to the rest of the men.

The men rose from the table and the King pulled Aaron aside. He looked him in the eye. Putting his hands on his shoulders, he said softly, "Aaron, be careful. And when you return, you must finish your mission."

Aaron looked back into the darkening eyes of his father and slowly nodded in agreement. The King lifted his hands from his son and shouted to the rest of the men, "When the purple and green moons are at their peaks, we bring out the bait."

The men cheered before exiting the throne room. Aaron knew most of them wanted revenge while few wanted peace.

Throughout the kingdom there was commotion. Two squadrons of archers had already been put together and were being instructed by Ugine about the plan. Pieces of black armor laid in rows behind the men, being cleaned by other guards.

Aaron walked over to a breastplate piece to feel it. It was cold and a little dusty. It looked thick, but only by a close-up inspection. Aaron tried to lift it, but struggled to get it above his waist. *No solider could ever run any distance in this.*

"Having some trouble?" Gantrue asked.

"No, it's—I'm just lifting it at an awkward angle." Aaron began to lower the piece back to the ground and practically dropped it.

There was no hiding the fact that Aaron wasn't very strong compared to most guards. Samuel always had the muscle while Aaron had the quick instinct. It didn't really bother him, though, except when others were around and he was reminded of it.

"It's heavy, but it will stop almost any arrow," Gantrue said to Aaron.

"It will serve us well, then," Aaron replied.

"Aaron! Come over here," the Captain shouted, waving at Aaron. "Now, listen. These men will be stationed in the trees on the left and the right. Try to stay out of their line of fire, because when it gets dark, they won't be able to see you in the shadows. Now, men." The captain redirected his attention. "We do not know where the spy is going to run, but whatever you do, don't shoot him or Aaron!"

Ugine looked sternly at them and then dismissed Aaron, saying, "Don't worry, Aaron, these are elite Forgotten Shadow archers, from the main archway of the castle. They don't miss."

Aaron nodded his head in understanding and walked away, a little uneasy. *Good. Don't hit Aaron. I think they got it. They won't miss. They shouldn't miss.* Ugine's voice faded out as he continued to give the men orders. "Breastplate and legs only, avoid the neck and head level..."

Aaron decided to go back to his home and rest because he didn't know when he would have another opportunity to sleep again. He needed all his strength for this task and was actually starting to feel worried about it. *What if I fail? What if I do get killed?*

Aaron walked up to his door and rubbed his hand along the smoothly crafted wood. *This is the mission I've always wanted. And now it's here, and now I'm starting to question it.* He twisted the cold copper handle and the door opened without a squeak.

His house was clean—bed made, floor swept, and not a dirty dish in sight. Aaron immediately moved to his bed and fell into it. Pulling his furs over himself, he buried his head and dozed. He forced out the worries of this mission and freely allowed himself to think of Madi as relief—what she looked like, how she acted, and everything they did together on Earth. Before long, he fell into sleep.

Chapter 15

Madi woke up the next morning refreshed. She rubbed her eyes in confusion, not remembering how she had gotten into bed. She remembered Aaron and leaned over to see if he was sleeping on her floor. He wasn't.

Madi got up slowly and looked around her room. He wasn't anywhere. She quickly ran downstairs, figuring he was asleep on the couch. She excitedly leaned over the back of the couch, expecting to see Aaron wrapped in blankets. He wasn't. When she didn't see him, her heart sank as the cushions absorbed her.

Was it all just a dream? No, it — it couldn't have been.

Madi had one last idea of where he might be.

She ran up her stairs but slowed down when she entered her room. Leisurely and pretending not to notice, she walked past her closet. Nothing happened. Madi peeked in and flicked the light on.

"Aaron?" she called. "Aaron..."

She sighed and flicked the lights off. *He must*

have gone home. She tried to cheer herself up. Madi walked down the stairs and into the kitchen to grab some food in order to take her mind off him. She opened the fridge and stared into it for a few seconds, not seeing anything she really wanted. Remembering it was time for breakfast, she pulled out the milk.

Madalyne noticed the note. She dropped the milk on the table as she read it and began to tear up. *I should have known he would disappear. Wow, that was stupid, Madi. How could I have been so immature and naïve?*

Madalyne let go of the tearstained note and went to her couch. She crawled up into a ball and leaned her head against the arm of the sofa and began to cry, not because someone had left her, but because the greatest connection she had ever felt with someone — the one she dreamed for — had come, and gone.

***

Aaron woke up thinking he was still on Earth somewhere inside Madi's house. He remembered when he looked around and realized he wasn't. His depressed thoughts were abruptly interrupted by the smell of food. A plate sat on his counter. *Father must have sent it.*

Aaron focused on the food, trying to push Madi out of his head. There was fresh fruit, cooked deer meat, and pure water.

Ugine entered his house and said, "Good, you're awake." He closed the door and picked up an apple. "You slept for over an hour; that's double the time you normally need. Out late on Earth?" he asked, sitting in one of Aaron's chairs.

"You could say that." Aaron stuffed deer meat down his throat, followed by water.

Ugine laughed and said, "Eat up, we're taking places in less than an hour."

Aaron looked out the window and saw the purple and green moons were almost high in the night sky.

"And here, put this on. It's one of our newest designs. It's made to blend in with the night, and it's incredibly light and warm." Ugine handed Aaron a suit.

It was black with a silk feel on the inside and

a rough outside texture.

"Thanks, Ugine," Aaron said, finishing the food on his plate.

"Be safe, Aaron." Ugine stood up. "I'll see you soon."

Ugine exited the house and Aaron pushed his plate aside. He changed his clothes and threw his bag over his shoulders. Leaving his house, Aaron looked around the kingdom.

Everything was in its usual order. Guards patrolled along the tops of the tower walls with torches; houses were shut, with most lights out. The kingdom was not asleep, but ready — everyone was in their positions. Aaron saw archers out of the corner of his eye. They passed him and halted at the entrance of the kingdom, waiting for further instructions.

The King came out of the throne room and approached Aaron.

"Listen closely, Aaron. You're going to be stationed in the woods with the archers. There will be an opening between the two archer squads where we hope he will run straight through, and then you can follow him." The King looked at his son. "We are hoping that."

Aaron nodded his head again in understanding. His father turned away and moved into the center of the guards. The King paused and looked around. After a brief moment of silence, he shouted, "For the Kingdom of Upitar!"

Everyone except Aaron shouted back, "For the Kingdom of Upitar!"

Aaron was focusing. He breathed in and out slowly. Archival waved his hands to the archers and they exited through the main gate. Aaron followed behind. The archway was lit with torches, and out in the blackness, a lone torch was planted in the ground next to a log. The archers split; half went into the woods and the other half stood alongside the castle walls. Then they divided again, with half on the right and half on the left of each side. There were ten archers in every square.

"Into the woods, Aaron," Archival said.

Aaron hurried through the small circle of light and into the woods. He knelt down by one of the archers stationed there. He had a clear view of the circle of light. Everyone was silent.

Aaron looked at the black armor worn by the

guards and noticed how it shined in the dark green and purple light of the night sky.

Looking through the archway, Aaron saw three figures coming forth. When they got closer, Aaron saw the prisoner, his hands roped. He was being pushed along by a guard and the Captain, who wore his full uniform. It was entirely black with a blue orb in the middle, with waves around it. His head was covered by a helm with a blue tassel on top.

The Captain and the guard continued to push the spy through the archway. They stepped into the light and the spy was shoved onto the ground in front of him. The Captain and the guard formed up with the other guards along the wall. The spy saw the log. He knew what it meant.

Looking back, the spy cried out, "What kind of drill is this? You can't do this!"

He trembled on the ground. His eyes raced along the edge of the castle walls, seeing the black archers lined up, ready to strike.

The Captain of the Guard came forth and spoke. "By order of the King, you are being convicted of 'spying against the kingdom, affiliating with destruction of the kingdom, and attempted murder of the King.'"

The spy looked around. His eyes grew wide as he realized what was happening. Now panicked, he shot looks back and forth.

The King stepped forth from the shadows and spoke aloud, "Your punishment is death."

The spy froze. From the panic in his face, all could see he was afraid of death. Then he smiled.

"You, too, will soon die, Your Majesty." The spy placed his head on the log and laughed mockingly.

The executioner stepped out of the shadows where even Aaron had not seen him hidden in the blackness. The dark mix of the purple and green night glistened along the executioner's sword as he pulled it out.

The executioner held it directly above the spy's neck. Everyone froze. The men in the woods drew their bows. Aaron held his breath.

The executioner lifted his sword. Arrows flew from their bows and struck the breastplates of the guards along the walls. The executioner fell to the ground, dropping his sword.

The spy lifted his head, seeing the waves of arrows fly past him. He looked behind him and saw the guards drawing their bows and taking cover. Aaron watched the spy as he pushed up off the ground.

The spy took one last glance at what was happening and darted off to the left of the castle. Not toward the middle of the archers, as planned. Dodging three arrows, the spy fled for the woods. It looked as though he was going to collide with an arrow Archival fired, but one Ugine fired intercepted it in mid air.

Aaron sprinted from his crouched position, sending up leaves and twigs.

The King shouted out, "Stop him!" as he was supposed to.

Aaron ran into the black woods. He dodged tree after tree, but still watched the spy run. They left the dim circle of light created by the torches on the castle and entered the blackness of the forest. The spy crossed Aaron's path by about fifty feet ahead of him. Aaron stalked him as an animal tracks prey. He observed every movement the spy made in the darkness, even matching his feet to the movement of the spy's in order to mask his own footsteps.

The spy glanced back constantly to see if he was being followed, but Aaron was always hiding in the shadows. He watched his target move through the hazy green and purple woods. The spy looked back once again and then, as if someone were directly behind him, made a dash to the right, moving deeper into the forest.

The spy was running somewhere specifically now. Aaron's heartbeat picked up. The spy was leading him.

The spy reached a small, murky swamp. He stopped, and Aaron, as if they were the same person, stopped as well. The spy looked around one last time.

This can't be it.

The spy rushed into the water and sank below the surface. Within a second, he water traveled. Aaron paused for a moment. He knew better than anyone he couldn't go too fast, otherwise the spy would see him in the water as well. But he couldn't wait too long or else the spy would get away.

Aaron breathed in and out once and then walked toward the pool, increasing his speed as he approached. When he reached it, his run turned into a jump and the jump to a dive into the pool.

Aaron water traveled. When he arrived, he remained under the water in order to take in his surroundings the best he could. The light of two moons — purple and green — glistened along the clear and clean surface of the water. They were still on Upitar.

Aaron saw a few ripples at the edge of the pool and knew the spy had already exited. Lifting his head slowly out into the night air, he looked for the spy and saw him running for more woods.

There was an open plain surrounding the pond of water they had come through. Aaron crawled out of the pool but remained flat against the ground until the spy reached the fifty-foot mark. The spy looked back again, but didn't see Aaron laying in the grass. As soon as the spy's head turned for the woods, Aaron dashed off the ground with full power.

The prisoner reached the woods and slowed to a jog. As soon as Aaron saw him reach the trees, he instinctively dropped to the ground.

The spy did look back again, just as Aaron predicted, but did not see him even though the light of the moons reflected in the grass.

This stuff works pretty well. Aaron felt the suit he wore.

When the woods began to consume the spy, Aaron again hurried after him. He entered the mouth of the forest just before the spy was completely swallowed.

The man jogged through the trees and came to an opening. There rested a small pond with the green and purple moonlight reflecting on it.

This will take us to the western mountains. Where is he going?

The spy, this time not checking behind him, water traveled. Aaron did the same as last time, not diving immediately into the water. When Aaron water traveled this time, he felt the sharp sting of ice water on his hands and face. He knew the spy would be out almost as soon as he appeared because of the freezing temperatures.

Aaron lifted his head out of the water slowly. It was lighter here than in the woods. The sun was slowly rising over the mountains and the steep slopes of the peaks were casting shade over the forests.

Aaron saw the spy swim out of the lake onto the frost-covered land. Swimming under the water, Aaron followed, not wanting to waste time in the lake. The spy ran into the woods, appearing to increase his speed to compensate for his decreased body temperature.

Aaron swam out of the lake and laid along the ground. He breathed slowly, trying not to slip into hyperventilation. To his surprise, the suit became warm immediately. It was remarkably dry and Aaron didn't feel at all cold.

You guys never cease to amaze me. Aaron was impressed by the craftsmen who made the suit. He rose from the cold ground and resumed following the spy who was running into a thin span of woods leading to the swampland.

Maybe they are in the swamp.

The trees in the woods began to disperse and the ground turned mucky, gripping the bottom of Aaron's feet with mud. They were far enough into the woods where the sunlight did not yet show.

The swampland had little moonlight shining on it as well. Aaron could see one more pond of water in the distance, though. Mud floated on the top of it to the point where it almost looked like land.

The spy stopped, and Aaron did the same. Walking over to one of the last remaining trees in the swamp, the spy brushed his fingers up and down its bark. Aaron hid behind some stunted brush. The spy pushed on a part of the tree and the section sank inward, but stayed together like a spider web. The spy's hand disappeared into the tree.

Aaron squinted to see if what he was seeing was really happening. The spy removed his hand with a device in the shape of a lantern from the tree. It was black metal on both ends and had a glass center. There were small lights. It looked complex — something not from Upitar.

Aaron couldn't make out what he was doing, but the spy fiddled with the device. Three lights lit up — a purple one on one end and red and green ones on the other. The spy worked with it some more and a thick red liquid poured into the glass center. Walking over to the water with the device, the spy entered the pool.

Aaron listened closely. He heard a twisting noise from the device. The brush was just big enough to hide him in the blackness, but the sun was beginning to rise over the mountains and cast its light into the edge of the forest. In a matter of seconds, light would shine on the swamp and Aaron would be revealed. For one of his precious seconds, Aaron crouched down in the mud and peeked his head around the tree. To his relief, the spy wasn't looking in his direction.

Aaron watched the spy twist the top of the device again. Aaron saw the shoulders of the spy turning toward him. Instinctively, he moved his head back behind the tree and held his breath as the spy looked behind himself. Aaron didn't hear anything—no movement in the water, nothing. The spy didn't see him, he was just checking.

Sunlight filled through the trees. A layer of light covered the swamp. Aaron was now easily visible if the spy looked, but he had to know what the spy was doing. Slowly he moved his head around the tree again, and to his relief, he saw the back of the spy.

The spy put a corner of the device into the water and twisted a part of it again. A black liquid poured out into the murky pond water, forming a small distorted black area surrounding himself. The prisoner then sank below the surface of the water and disappeared.

Aaron squatted behind the tree, waiting for him to come back. He waited, and after several moments passed, he had to assume it was safe. Aaron cautiously stood up from his crouched position and walked around the brush. The pond wasn't that big; it was more of a giant puddle.

The black area was still in the water. Aaron examined it; how it basically became one with the water. It was completely black and cast no reflection. Aaron walked into the water and stared at the circle. He touched it with his finger to see if anything would happen. Nothing did. Cautiously, he waded into the circle so that it encased him, too. It began to fade away as he waited for something to happen. He knew he had to do it.

Aaron sank under the water. Blackness surrounded him, and he water traveled. He felt a strange shock shoot through his body, but other than that, nothing was different. Opening his eyes, he saw that he appeared in clear water.

Aaron remained under the surface for safety. He was in something that was not natural as he saw a pool made of tiles and stones. He was in something made by someone. Aaron looked above the surface to see if he could see anyone.

He raised his head out of the pool and glanced around. The room was small, it was just the pool of water, three walls and an archway that were not more than two feet from the pool. There was some sort of a board with several markings on the right wall and a torch along the left. Other than that, nothing.

Regardless, Aaron had no idea where he was. He got out of the water but remained in the room. The tiles in the room were a burgundy color, but looked more red because of the torchlight.

The prince looked out the small archway. There was a large room with what looked like hundreds of other small archways. Aaron saw the spy at the end of the main room, entering through a larger archway.

Aaron quickly got out of the pool and peered around the giant room, trying to take it all in. The ceiling stretched over two hundred feet high and the walls were about four hundred feet by two hundred feet. He saw a few people, but figured they would never notice he wasn't from there.

Aaron moved at a brisk pace in the direction of the spy. The spy hurried through a tunnel illuminated by torchlight. Aaron followed him at a distance. The spy entered another large room with more archways.

What is this place?

The spy reached the end of the tunnel and rounded a right corner. Aaron followed closely, trying not to reveal himself. The spy entered another small archway and disappeared out of Aaron's sight.

Aaron hustled to the edge of the archway and peeked his head around. Again, there was just a pool of water. The spy must have water traveled. Aaron waited a moment to create some distance and then water traveled through the pool.

When Aaron surfaced, he saw other pools beside each other in what still looked like the same complex. There was a small platform area between a dozen pools and a giant staircase, which the spy was running up. There looked to be about one hundred steps on the stairs, which had the rigidness and agedness of ancient stone.

At the top of the stairs, light shined along the ceiling and the walls of what he thought to be an amphitheater. At the bottom of the stairs were two pathways that looked as though they went behind the staircase and led to the same place, only on a lower level.

Aaron took the right pathway, sneaking behind the stairs. He heard voices and people talking in the distance. Their voices echoed off the stone structure, but it was difficult to make out exact words.

Aaron saw a small tunnel and then, through that, what looked to be some form of a dome, with seats all around the inside. The seats were filled with people dressed in both black and red armor, and robes. The prince walked as far as he could in the tunnel.

It looked as though most of the people were at a higher level than the lower entrance. Aaron could only see a few people from his position, halfway through the small tunnel. They were shouting and looking around at others in the dome. Aaron took the torch that was illuminating the tunnel and removed it. He stepped on it and twisted his foot until the light went out.

Cautiously, he walked to the edge of the tunnel, but remained in the shadows for protection. Standing still along the wall of the tunnel, Aaron listened to the voices in the room that he could now hear distinctly.

Chapter 16

A man's voice said, "The humans ar—"

"The humans are not the problem at this time! The problem is the world of Upitar," said another voice, cutting the first one off.

The first voice responded, "Yes, but the world of Upitar and Earth are linked by the waterways, the same way we are linked with Earth."

The second voice said, "But the humans can't work the waterways like the people of Upitar—"

The man was cut off, by a new voice this time. It belonged to a male. It sounded insightful, yet secretive and powerful.

"Foolish ones who dawdle in the things that do not matter, have we forgotten the real purpose here? It's not the people we're after. It's the King, and more importantly, it's the orb. That is our first priority. We know that dark water is destructive now. An entire wall of their kingdom was destroyed by an arsenal we can recreate."

"Yes, my Lord. But the people will not tell us

where the orb is, let alone, allow us to take it," the first voice said.

The voice in command responded, "Do you think I'm unaware of that? The people of Upitar will not know. It is all planned out." He said with confidence, "Do not worry."

"When will we be striking, my Lord?" another voice asked.

"In five months."

A commotion arose in the chamber. Voices questioned, "Five months? Why not now?"

"Enough, enough," the superior voice said. "We need time to collect blood to make enough dark water for this attack, we need to exhaust them, and because of..."

Aaron was trying to process everything he heard. *Dark water? Blood?* He thought back to the device he saw the spy use. The black water must be called dark water.

The leader's sentence and Aaron's thoughts were interrupted by another voice. "My Lord! Emiliatek has returned!"

"Welcome home, Emiliatek. What have you discovered?" the leader's voice asked gently.

Aaron listened, and when Emiliatek spoke, he recognized the voice: it was the spy.

"My Lord, I have discovered the secret waterways in the chambers of the kingdom, just where they were said to be. They very well might lead to the orb's location. But before I go into details, I want to say thank you for sending men to save me."

Aaron froze. He knew no men were sent for the spy and they would soon discover it was a set-up. Aaron cautiously continued to listen to Emiliatek, hoping to gain more information on who these people were.

"Now, in the—"

Emiliatek was cut off by another voice that sounded curious. "What do you mean you were saved?"

The room went quiet.

Emiliatek spoke. "Just before I was to be executed, men from the woods fired arrows at my captors, and I assumed an army was sent to rescue me."

"No team was sent!"

"Humans?" another voice questioned.

The voice in command spoke, now dangerously angry. "No! You fool! It was a set-up!"

Aaron slowly began to back out of the tunnel.

"No, no, my Lord, I wasn't followed. I'm sure of it!" Emiliatek said, desperately trying to explain himself.

Aaron heard nothing but the string of a bow and the sound of an arrow piercing flesh. He saw Emiliatek's bleeding body fall past the tunnel. He never heard it hit the ground, though. The room must have had some kind of a bottomless pit in the middle, which Emiliatek was thrown into.

The voices in the chamber grew louder. Aaron saw shadows of men stand and move around the room.

"Search the entire castle! We have a spy in here!" the voice in command shouted.

Aaron turned and stumbled back toward the water pools. He tripped as he ran out of the archway and through the tunnel that wrapped around the stairs. Scrambling to his feet he crossed in front of the stairway and looked up at the ceiling.

Aaron caught a glimpse of men storming out of the top entrance of the dome. He looked into the eyes of one of them and froze. They made eye contact with each other. Peering into the dark eyes of the man, Aaron knew he had been noticed. He turned slowly and saw more shadows moving along the walls of the tunnel he was just in.

Breaking his silence, the man at the top of the stairs let out a cry. "He's here!"

Many men began to flood over the top of the stairs. Regaining his senses, he staggered into one of the pools of water.

Aaron submerged himself, looking through the clear water at the men running for the pool. He looked back at the top of the stairs and saw a man in an all-black robe at the top of the steps. His eyes were solid black, and larger than most. He looked heartless, chaotic, and deceptive.

Aaron didn't have time to see anything else because the men were up against the pool. Closing his eyes, he water traveled. Aaron opened them quickly to see if the men were still there. Not seeing anyone, he dashed out of the pool and found himself in another room like the first one. Outside of it was the giant room with hundreds of doorways.

He ran into the giant room, trying to

remember where to go next. Aaron heard the sound of men coming out from the pool he was just in.

"Stop him!" they shouted.

Aaron sprinted, not knowing where to go. He chose a doorway randomly and decided to try it. A siren sounded as Aaron fled. Massive stone walls came down, closing him off from all of the chambers around him.

Aaron didn't make it — he was trapped, the area closed off. Turning around, he saw five men in the giant room with him. Aaron examined his options.

Nothing! It's just a giant box! He panicked. Brick after brick. No door, no archway, no staircase, just a giant, bricked box.

He studied the men charging at him. Aaron noticed that each one had a vial wrapped around their waist with what looked like dark water inside. The men drew their swords and surrounded him. Aaron had only one option: he couldn't get off this world without one of those things, making his only option to fight.

The five men circled him and slowed down. They breathed heavily. They moved in a ring around him and one of them said, "So, you thought you could outsmart us, did ya? Sneaking into our kingdom."

Aaron drew his one weapon—the dagger attached to his leg—slowly and cautiously. The same man let out a laugh. "You think you're going to be able to fight us with that? This is a grown man's game, you know? You may want a grown man's sword."

Aaron breathed slowly.

"Come on, boy, let's fight!" the man said, antagonizing him.

Aaron looked around as the men approached him all at once from every angle.

"Oh, what? You thought you would get to fight us one at a time? Oh no, we don't play by those rules," the speaker of the group said, taunting Aaron.

Aaron breathed in and calmed himself. The man let out another mocking laugh. Aaron breathed out slowly and flung the dagger. The dagger flew through the air and pierced the man directly in the throat. Immediately after the dagger hit, Aaron was kicking him down and pulling it out.

The rest of the soldiers jumped into action. Before the first man's body hit the ground, Aaron kicked the sword from his hand into his own. He lifted the sword to block an attack. Aaron held the block with the man. With his dagger in his other hand, he stabbed the man in the stomach.

Withdrawing the blood-soaked dagger, he knocked over the body. The other three men attacked. Aaron swung the sword in his hand, parrying every attack perfectly. The man on his right took a jab at him. Aaron leaned behind the sword and swung his sword in front.

He rammed the blade into the handle of the soldier's. Instinctively, he twisted his sword and the soldier's flew out of his hands. Aaron kicked the soldier away. Using that momentum, he countered an attack from behind.

The man swung aggressively while Aaron deflected. The man took a step forward, swinging again. Aaron slid back to dodge the attack. While sliding away, he put his dagger back around his calf and used his sword to pick up the previously dropped sword. Aaron now had two swords in his hands, two men coming at him.

They both swung at Aaron from opposite sides. Aaron met them halfway. The man on his right broke the brief hold and came at him with a slash. Aaron parried it with the same sword by swinging it against the dirt.

The man's sword rammed against Aaron's sword in the ground. After the block, Aaron let go of the sword and took hold of the man's wrist, catching him by surprise. It was a quick and risky movement.

On his left, Aaron still held the first hold, not allowing him to break through or release. He forcefully swung the man on his left into the man on his right. The two fell to the ground on top of each other. Aaron threw the sword in his hand. It sliced through both of them, pinning them to the ground.

He hustled over to the men, kicking up the other sword from the ground. He plunged this one through them, piercing their hearts. A pool of blood seeped into the dry ground below.

Aaron heard a shout behind him. He turned and saw the man whom he had only kicked running at him with his fists. The man swung at Aaron, but Aaron moved and grabbed his wrist, twisting it and pulling the man toward him fiercely. Lifting his knee while pulling the man, Aaron rammed his knee into his chest. The man choked and sank to the ground. Aaron kicked him across the face while on his way down. The man fell, remaining silent.

Aaron looked at the two men he had pierced together. He knelt down next to them, one still gasping for air.

"You know, the funny thing is, I'm not even from around here." Aaron took hold of the vials around the men's waists and yanked them off.

He quickly removed the vials from all of the others as well and rushed over to one of the sealed walls that led to many pools of water. He felt the wall — it was solid.

Any moment a doors going to open and there's going to be someone or something I can't defeat. He paused and looked at the vials in his hand. They were smaller than the ones the spy used, about the size of his fist. He looked inside them. The water was indeed dark.

"Dark water," he said to himself.

Aaron looked at the wall and then at the vials. He put all but one in his pocket. Aaron stepped back and hurled it at the brick wall that blocked his escape.

The wall exploded in a mix of a black and purple smoke. Dust and bricks flew everywhere. A giant hole had been blown through the wall, and into the next chamber. Hundreds of pools were on the other side.

There's more?

He had no time think. Aaron clearly saw the pool of water he planned to use for his escape.

Behind him, he heard the walls opening and saw men rushing at him with weapons. Aaron smiled. He knew they couldn't catch him now. Hurrying toward the hole, he pulled out another vial.

Aaron twisted the top off and entered one of the several rooms with a pool he now had access to. Arrows flew near him, mostly hitting the outsides of the room, with a few zipping past his body. He tilted the dark water vial, dumping the liquid into the pool. The vial was completely emptied and the pool turned entirely black. Without wasting any more time, Aaron jumped in and submerged himself. Not knowing if it would really work, but not having another option, his heart raced. He held his breath. Feeling the pull in his gut, Aaron water traveled.

Chapter 17

Aaron appeared in a lake. He surfaced above the water and quickly swam for the shore. When he reached it, he didn't look back. Hearing the voices of men behind him, he realized he was not safe yet.

Aaron ran into the woods alongside the lake and arrows zinged through the woods beside him. They stuck into trees and the ground below his feet, leaving the forest wounded. Aaron spied a small pool of water ahead. He looked back and saw dozens of men rapidly closing in behind him.

Suddenly he felt an arrow hit his pant leg. The arrow ripped through the suit's legging, yanked him to the ground, and pinned him to the root of a tree just at the edge of the water he was aiming for. Aaron couldn't move; the arrow was firmly interlaced with the metal in his attire.

He looked back frantically. The soldiers were dashing through the woods toward him. Aaron squirmed to try to get free or break the arrow, but the tip was made with a metal core and wouldn't budge, as it was firmly driven into the tree. Aaron pulled out his dagger in one last desperate attempt. He leaned over the pool he wanted to use to escape and struck the dagger into the water. It glowed green and Aaron began to write.

"Please, Father, please!" Aaron said to himself under his breath while he wrote.
He spelled out: Help

Aaron watched the green words float in the water. He scanned behind him and saw the men drawing close. He checked back at the pool of water desperately, waiting for a response, and then again back at the men.

He began to sweat. His heart raced. Death was closing in all around him. Aaron looked at the pool in desperation, hoping to receive any form of relief.

"Please, Father."

Aaron stared at the men, who now completely encircled him. About three dozen men were in the woods. A soldier in black stepped forward. Aaron observed him closely and knew it wasn't the leader he had seen in the meeting room.

"You are a brave one, aren't you? I am

General Radosha. Now, tell me, where are you from? Actually, no, I already know that. Who sent you, is my real question?"

"What do you want?"

"That doesn't answer my question," Radosha said. "My question was, who sent you?"

"My name is Aaron Archien, heir to the throne of Upitar," Aaron said boldly.

Radosha shouted proudly, "Still not an answer to my question, but regardless, would you look at what we have here? You really are a magnificent capture! Let me guess, Daddy sent you because he's too afraid to set foot outside the kingdom walls?"

"I chose to go on this mission, actually."

"So, it is the King of Upitar who is behind this!" Radosha looked at him. "Hmm." Turning his head in the direction of the rest of his men, he shouted, "Did Father tell you you may die?"

He turned back toward Aaron and drew his sword. It had a black satin handle with a red ruby in the center. The blade was black, like the handle. It looked intricate and expertly crafted.

Aaron thought of something to save his life—

a reason they would want him to live. He spoke, revealing his mission. "If you kill me, you will all suffer."

"Right, of course," Radosha said, not even looking at Aaron.

"Listen to me! It has been prophesied that someone on Earth is about to destroy the waterways, and I have to stop them. If they destroy the waterways, you, too, will be affected."

The general paused and then looked at Aaron. "We are well aware of the prophecy that you speak of." He smiled and leaned close to Aaron. He knelt down and came directly up to his face. "And it's already taken care of." Radosha smiled and then he stood back up.

Madalyne. No.

"Aaron, son of King Archien, you fought well, and it will be my pleasure to kill you."

Displaying an evil smile, Radosha wrapped his hand around the hilt of his sword with a lusty desire to use it. He pointed the tip of sword at Aaron's neck and then lifted it toward the sky before swinging. Just before the sword struck, an arrow punctured his upraised hand. The sword dropped and Radosha turned in rage.

All around the forest were guards in black. Some were on horses and some were on foot, some had bows and arrows, and others, swords. They flooded the woods and the lakefront. Hundreds of men—Upitarians.

In the distance, Aaron saw a guard with blue symbols and a blue tassel on his helmet—Ugine. Radosha opened a dark water capsule with his good hand and tossed it into the pool of water next to Aaron and himself. He shouted, "Hide my trails!" to his men as he dove into the dark water and disappeared.

As soon as he jumped, a man appeared by Aaron's side, freeing him. The man used both his hands and tugged at the arrow.

"It's stuck," Aaron said, trying to explain.

The man pulled harder on the arrow and whispered something under his breath. The arrow suddenly broke loose from the tree and the man landed on the ground. Aaron quickly turned and saw an enemy soldier in the pool, splashing around. The dark water was gone and so was Radosha.

An arrow ripped through the enemy's head

immediately after he cleared the pool of the dark water. Blood now filled the pool.

"Here, sir," said the man who had freed him. He handed Aaron a sword.

Aaron took it and said, "Thank you." Before running off to join the battle, he took a second look at the man.

"Imushial? Is that you?"

"Yes, sir," Imushial said with a smile.

"Thank you, Imushial." Aaron clapped his hand on Imushial's shoulder and then hurried off.

He met up with the Captain on his horse and shouted to him, "Ugine!"

"Aaron, grab hold!" Ugine extended his hand to Aaron.

They clasped arms and Ugine pulled him up. All around them were Upitarian men, but few enemies. Most of them lay dead on the bloody ground, but some escaped. Ugine let out a loud whistle that echoed through the woods, touching the ears of all of his men. They began to rendezvous around him. Ugine let out a "heah" and his great black horse took off.

"Thank you, Ugine," Aaron said.

"You had us scared there for a minute," Ugine responded. "Your father got the message and we were on our way immediately. Your glowing dot showed that you weren't far from the kingdom, actually."

"So what took you so long, then?"

"Oh hush," Ugine said, giving the reins a whip to make the horse go faster.

Chapter 18

The guards followed behind Ugine in a pointed formation across the meadows, back to the kingdom. The sun was still high in the sky. The regions behind the castle were the ones he explored the least. Most were woods that became swamp and were of no use for exploration, because the water was too shallow to travel through. Nevertheless, Aaron at least knew where he was now.

The army came over a hill and the kingdom walls were in sight. They rounded the back and side walls around to the front, where the main gate was already open for them.

The great horses galloped through the main archway and inside the kingdom walls. Ugine's horse came to a stop before the throne room, where the King stood, waiting. Aaron leaped off the horse and was met by the arms of his father.

"My son!" his father cried as he grasped Aaron.

Aaron returned the hug and then pushed away from his father, saying, "Father, I am safe, but we must act quickly now."

"You're right. Into the throne room," his father said, leading the way.

They entered and the same officials who were there last time were in attendance. Ugine and Archival entered shortly after Aaron and his father.

Aaron explained everything to them at the table. After he had done so, they questioned him.

Archival was the first to comment. "Now, are you sure, Aaron, that you were not on the planet Upitar?"

"I'm sure of it."

"Not just on one of the outer rims?" Archival added.

"Yes, I'm sure of it. It was some other planet; one we have never seen before."

Aaron pulled out the three dark water vials he had left. "Look, these contain the dark water that they used to travel through. And this is the same stuff they used to destroy our wall. When it touches something other than liquid, it just…explodes."

The men gawked at the vials. Ugine lifted one up to the torchlight to examine it more closely.

"So, you're telling me if I were to throw this

at that wall over there, it would explode?" Archival said, lifting one up and gesturing it at the wall.

"Yes! Our kingdom is already damaged enough—don't throw it!" Aaron shouted.

"I just want to see if it's true!" Archival said.

"Put it down, Archival; that's an order!" the King barked.

Archival set the vial down. "My apologies, Sir."

The King now spoke. "Aaron, you said they were after me, but more importantly, the orb. Did they say what for?"

"No, Father."

"We're going to have to strengthen defenses then. We do not go out of a state of high alert until I say." The King turned to Orik, the official messenger of the Kingdom of Upitar when it came to its involvement with the outer rim worlds. "Orik, I need you to notify and request support from the outer rim world of Horexa. Tell King Vanihar that King Diadosia and the Kingdom of Upitar is in need. See to it that only he receives the message." He directed his attention to Asmore, Bith, and Kninto, official messengers within the world of

Upitar. "Bring together the entire army. Now that we have access to our enemy, I want us ready to strike."

All across Upitar were extra guards. Not all were stationed around the kingdom; many were in reserve throughout the land. In total the army numbered around forty thousand.

"We'll send our own spies to discover what they can, using the three vials we have left over. In the course of their mission I want more vials to be retrieved so a counter attack can be organized." The King stood from the table. "Captain, put together a team."

"Yes, sir," Ugine said, standing as well.

"Should I go with them, Father?"

"No, Aaron, it's best for you to finish your mission. Let us not forget that the waterways are still in danger. That is our first priority. We have found out where these people are coming from, and now Upitar needs you to focus your skills on stopping this prophecy. Even if we win the war, we will soon perish if it is fulfilled.

Aaron didn't respond, but accepted what his father said this time without arguing. Gantrue rose from his seat and the room became silent.

He looked at Aaron. "What is to become of Earth? Did you learn this?"

"No," Aaron responded.

Gantrue said, "The people of Earth are in danger themselves, then. If it is the orbs they're after, is not there one on Earth, as well as the five outer rim worlds?"

"Yes—" the King replied, but was cut off by Gantrue.

"Then in danger they are, too."

"The people of Earth can defend themselves," Bith said.

The elder shook his head in disagreement. "You think that?"

"The people of Earth are more advanced than us. Their weapons are far more destructive than our own—than anything this unknown race has," the member replied.

"So young you are," Gantrue said. "It does not matter what weapons the people of Earth have, they cannot beat the waterways. All water travelers have the ability to appear and disappear. And this unknown race has the ability to appear, cause destruction rapidly, and disappear. With the vast number of waterways, destruction on Earth is entirely possible with the weapons this unknown race has. Who is to say they won't learn how to use the weapons of the Earthlings? Water travelers are fast learners and can adapt quickly, you do know this."

The elder sat down and the room remained silent. Aaron thought of one person: Madi.

Gantrue continued, "This unknown race will either enslave the people of Earth, or kill them, if they stand in the way of their plans."

Aaron's emotions for her pulsated through his body.

Archival broke the silence. "The people of Earth are not our concern! If we fight our own battles, we won't have to worry about them. If it comes to the people of Earth having to fight, then so be it."

"Enough, Archival!" The King extended his hand, ordering Archival to sit.

Madi is in danger and she didn't even know it.

"Aaron," his father said, "I need you to come

with me. The rest of you get moving."

The King went to the back of the throne room and Aaron followed. The rest of the men exited the main entrance, while Aaron and his father left through the back entrance into the rest of the castle.

Father and son went up the great spiraling staircase that led to the living quarters. They reached the top. To the right stood the door of Aaron's and Samuel's old room, and to the left was the great oak door of his father's room.

"Come with me," his father said, opening the door to his own room.

Aaron had only been in his father's room twice—when his mother disappeared and when Samuel disappeared. The room was huge. Bookshelves ran along the right wall, with hundreds of books. On the left was a great fireplace with a crackling fire.

Shelves rested above the fireplace and two red, comfortable-looking chairs were stationed in front of it. Halfway between the entrance and the chairs was a large circular table. There were few chairs around it and it looked as though it was more for decor then dining.

At the back of the room was the King's bed. It could easily and comfortably hold five people, and was crafted out of a rare wood called Ollardi-Whis. It was practically flame resistant and few knew where to find it. Swirling designs were carved into both the headboard and footboard. Four large wooden pillars stretched toward the ceiling but formed a canopy above the bed before touching the ceiling.

Hanging from the top of the bed were nylon sheets that wrapped around it, giving it an enclosed feel. Beside the bed was a stone nightstand with a glass of water, a candle, and a few books that his father would probably never read on top.

There was a giant rug in the middle of the floor that once belonged to a wild beast. It stretched almost the length of the room and had a tail that wrapped around itself. Its head wasn't at the end, but was instead mounted onto the wall above the fireplace. It had three great horns sticking out and then curling upwards. Aaron had always been told stories about these creatures. They were called rothans, and his great-grandfather killed this one.

Aaron stood in the doorway, scanning

around. His father stepped over to the fireplace and stood in front of the rothan head.

"Come here, Aaron."

Aaron hesitantly walked up to his father. His shadow flickered from the fire's light. The room was not well lit because the curtains were completely closed.

"What I'm about to show you is for kings only. Since you will be replacing me as king one day and we don't know how much time I have left, I think it's time you know. Granted, I may have a lot of life left, but if our enemy strikes me down, then you must take over."

Aaron remained silent.

"Do you understand, Aaron?"

"Yes, Father."

His father nodded. The King lifted his hand up to the great Rothan horns and grabbed hold of the far right one. He gave the horn a pull and, as if it was a lever, it dropped. The fire roared greatly and then went out; the fire that had been blazing was no longer there — not one glowing ash. The room was barely lit by the candle on the nightstand.

"Come," the King said.

They crossed the threshold of what was once the fireplace, now covered by stone. The back wall of the fireplace was gone. There was a short tunnel instead, that led to a staircase.

Aaron continued to follow his father into the darkness, not sure where he was stepping anymore. His father struck some things together and a torch shined. Aaron saw him put rocks back into his robe pocket and an empty sconce on the wall.

They went down the staircase and the King began to talk.

"Long ago, when the kingdom of Upitar was first established, there was more than one of our kind. There was another race, from a world called Senapin. They were also water travelers and they could do everything we could. They could go to Earth, and back to their world. They, too, had their own orb. But there was only one waterway that linked our two worlds. Regardless of our efforts, we could never make it to their world, nor they to ours, through any other waterway. We tried taking the same waterways from Earth, but they always went back to their world and we to ours. A theory proposed that even though the orbs are the source of the waterways, it is our blood that determines what orbs we are linked with, controlling where we go. You see, when you water travel to Earth, you link with the Earth orb, and when you come back to Upitar, you're linking with our orb. The people of Senapin were not linked with the Upitarian orb. Their blood was linked with the Senapin orb and the Earth orb, just as we are linked to the Earth and Upitarian orb; therefore, they could only travel between those two worlds."

Aaron and his father reached the bottom of the staircase and came to a wooden door in a great stone wall. The massive wall stretched in both directions, as far as Aaron could see in the small circle of light. The wooden door looked old, like that of the door he and his brother had gone through as kids.

"Is this all making sense to you so far, Aaron?" his father asked.

"Yes."

"Good. There was no way between our two worlds, except for this." The King pushed the latch down on the door to open it.

The door squeaked as it opened into a huge

chamber. It was rectangular, with walls stretching about one hundred feet by two hundred feet. The two hundred-foot sides were on the same side as the door.

In the middle of the room was what looked like a trench that stretched from one side to the other. The trench was about fifty feet wide. Aaron's father tapped the wall with his torch and a ball of fire formed. It flowed toward the middle of the ceiling and branched off left and right, forming a giant ring of light.

"Magic!" Aaron exclaimed.

"Yes, son. In the ancient days the Keeper of Upitar was said to be more... involved."

Aaron now saw what looked like dozens of archways with their own tunnels along the walls. At both ends of the trench were two archways, stretching thirty feet high, with gates in front of them. The room was mostly stone; the trench contained some dirt, and around the room were the remains of old wooden barrels and crates.

Aaron's father began to explain. "When the kingdom was being built, our ancestors were allies with the Senapins. The river that used to flow here was what connected our two worlds. But when something happened between the keepers, the river was cut off and its source covered so it no longer flowed. Every Senapin who remained on Upitar was killed afterward by magic, so the stories claim."

"What happened?"

"No one knows, the stories only say that the keepers blocked this waterway because evil was spreading, and even that is an old tale."

"But they could still go to Earth?" Aaron asked, trying to gain information on Madi's safety.

"That's right. But they can never come here, and we can never go there. It's been so long now that their world has been forgotten, and I thought they would have forgotten about us. Apparently something is happening on Senapin, and they desire to go to war with us."

"What do they want from our orb?"

The King paused. He said in full honesty, "I do not know, Son."

The two of them remained silent for a moment and then the King spoke.

"You need to get going, Son. Your mission is still of dire importance and I fear it may be related to the Senapins, as well. Some supplies have been packed and are waiting for you outside the throne room doors. Go." The King pointed at the staircase.

Aaron paused and looked at his father. He was thinking more about Madi than his mission. She was in danger.

Aaron responded to his father out of instinct, saying, "Yes, Sir."

He turned and ran up the staircase to the main throne room. He exited and breathed in the fresh, outside air. There, on the steps, stood Imushial.

"Here you are, sir. The King had me prepare some stuff for you." Imushial handed Aaron a bag of supplies. "Food, clothes, and a few other things."

"Thank you, Imushial." Taking the bag, he emptied it into his own.

Aaron headed to the main archway and stopped. He looked back at the throne room. At his house. At the hole in the kingdom wall. He took it all in, because he knew what he was about to do might prevent him from ever seeing any of it the same way again. The prince turned and hurried out through the main archway.

Chapter 19

Aaron dashed out of the kingdom and straight for a lake not far off. He had to find Madi.

After water traveling through the lake, he rushed across the grass toward the pool of water that led to her. He took the usual trail and quickly found himself in the pond near her house. Stumbling up the path, he scurried through the small woods.

He slowed down and caught his breath when he saw her house. The sun was setting in the distance and all the lights in the house were off except her room. Aaron sat there for a moment on the twig and grass covered ground. He breathed in the fresh air and pondered what he was planning on doing and the consequences that could come from it.

No matter what came to his mind, he still wanted to do it. He decided no matter what the outcome, it was worth it. The prince got up and snuck around to her porch. The light didn't turn on this time.

It must be on a timer.

Aaron snuck up to the top of the porch, trying to cause the fewest amount of squeaks in the wood. He reached the top and then lifted himself slowly over the rail onto her roof.

Quietly, he tiptoed across the shingles of the roof. He came to her window and paused one more time. The sky was purple with a mix of orange and pink. The clouds exploded with life through the entire sky.

Aaron turned his body and looked through the window. He saw Madi seated on her bed, holding the glowing stone he had given her from the cave, the flowers he had given her laying next to her. She held the stone between her fingers and then moved it around in her hand until it landed on her palm, where she grasped it firmly.

She looked heartbroken, and it was because of him. Aaron lifted his hand to the window. He knocked on it gently with a smile.

Madalyne turned and saw Aaron. Her face flooded with color as she became overjoyed and rushed over to the window. Without hesitating, Madi slid the window open and hugged Aaron immediately.

"Aaron! You came back," she cried with her arms still around him.

Suddenly she let go of him and backed away, her face giving no expression.

"Why?" she asked.

"Madi, I have to tell you something."

"Tell me why you left. And who even are you?"

Aaron breathed. "You want to know?" He looked around. "Can I come in?"

Madi nodded but stepped away.

Aaron calmly climbed through the window. "Okay. Madalyne, I need you to listen to me."

"Okay. Tell me what's going on," Madi said in complete willingness to listen as she sat on the edge of her bed.

"You mind if I sit, too?"

Her eyes looked at the spot next to her and then at Aaron. She didn't say anything but Aaron still sat. He looked into her attentive eyes.

"Madi...it's actually something I have to show you." He stood up from the bed.

Aaron extended his hand out to Madi and,

although hesitant, she took it, saying, "Okay…"

Aaron led her out the window and down to the pond.

"Here, sit down," he said, crouching by the edge of the water.

Madi sat next to Aaron and briefly smiled.

"Now, what I'm about to tell you, you must never tell anyone. Do you understand?"

"Umm, yeah, okay…"

"Not any of your friends, not your father, not even your grandmother."

"Yeah, I understand."

"Not anyone, Madi."

"Aaron, I get it! I won't tell anyone!"

"Okay," Aaron said, standing up. "Take my hand."

Aaron extended his hand and Madi took it. He began to wade into the pond and Madi stopped him.

"What are you doing?" She chuckled.

"Madi, just trust me. There's something I have to show you." Aaron pulled her hand.

Madi smiled at Aaron and followed him into the water.

"Now, on the count of three, I want you to go completely underwater and close your eyes."

"Aaron, that's gross! What do you want to show me?" She asked with laugh.

"Madalyne, just trust me."

"Fine, I'll play along with your game...because I think it's cute. Pretending to be a water traveler for my entertainment."

"Yeah," Aaron said, with a hint of irony in his voice.

Madi squinted a little and smiled, seeming to pick up on a hint of the irony.

"Now, on the count of three." Aaron took Madi's other hand. "One...two...three."

Both Madi and Aaron ducked under the water. Aaron opened his eyes to ensure she was completely submerged. She was, and had a smile on her face while under the water. Aaron closed his own eyes and squeezed Madi's hands.

They water traveled.

Aaron opened his eyes and saw the cleanness of the water. He lifted himself while pulling Madi's hands above the surface, causing her to quickly stand up as well.

Aaron watched Madi as she wiped the water out of her eyes. She cleared both and opened them. She looked at Aaron, still with a smile on her face, and then quickly looked around. She was silent. She looked back at Aaron in utter wonder as she took in the world of Upitar. They were no longer on Earth. There was daylight instead of moonlight. Trees and fields surrounded her instead of homes and streets.

Aaron said gently, "Madalyne, I am a water traveler."

Madi stared deep into Aaron's eyes.

"I'm what your grandmother spoke of, what your grandfather searched for, and what your father is looking for. I am one of them. Yes, we do exist."

She spoke no words, but only stared. Her face was blank. She continued to look into his eyes. Aaron looked back into her eyes, not knowing what to do. Madi slowly shook her head, upset. Her eyes became watery.

"Take me back."

Aaron's mouth opened slightly as his eyes grew wide with a mix of shock and confusion.

"Take me back, Aaron," Madi demanded.

"Madi—"

"Aaron, take me back!" Madi cried.

"Okay. Okay. I'll take you back." Aaron took Madi's hand and went underwater.

Madi held his hand loosely and dropped below the surface. Aaron didn't know what else to do—how he was supposed to respond or react.

Aaron opened his eyes under the water to make sure she was completely under. She was. He looked at her face. It wasn't happy and playful like before, but grave and upset—her eyes held shut, and her face sorrowful.

Aaron water traveled. When they appeared in Earth's water, he stood up in the small pond. Not even having to lift her hands, Madi stood up in the water. She waded right past Aaron onto the shore. Aaron tried to stop her, saying, "Madi, please listen."

Madi already reached the damp land. She turned to him. Tears were in her eyes as she said, "Goodbye, Aaron. We can't be together, we can't see each other, we can't talk anymore—nothing. This has to be goodbye this time."

Madi turned and ran up to her house, wiping her eyes. Aaron stood in the pool of water, not knowing what to do. He watched her leave him as she went up the path and through the trees until she was gone.

Aaron stood in the pond. He looked down at his reflection rippling in the murky water. He slammed his fists against the surface.

I don't get it!

"Giving up that easy, aye, sport?" said the voice of an old man.

Aaron looked toward the top of the small hill where the voice came from. There stood the same creepy old man Aaron saw on his first night. He was leaning against a cane, looking down at Aaron.

"I heard some splashing in the water and decided to do some investigating," the man explained.

Aaron looked at him, wondering if he saw them water travel.

I didn't see anyone. He didn't…he couldn't have… I'm sure of it.

"Now I'm no guru, but she wants you to see her again," the old man said with a chuckle.

Aaron climbed out of the pond and approached the old man. He shook his Earthling clothes, trying to dry them the best he could.

"I'm sorry, sir, but you don't understand." Aaron didn't want to be enlightened by some old Earth pervert.

"It's not a matter of understanding the situation or not. It's a matter of understanding people — humans. And it's not hard to see that she's in love with you, and love's more powerful than whatever your little trouble is," the old man said, leaning more heavily on his cane.

Aaron pondered what the man said. He was shocked that something wise actually came out of his filthy mouth. But maybe, just maybe, he was right. Aaron eyed the old man, studying his face.

"Thank you..." Aaron said, still thinking about what he said.

Before the man could reopen his mouth, Aaron knew he was right. He knew there was something different, something truly special between him and Madi.

"I've studied the human race for a long time. I know a lot about us," the man said, with a smirk that had a more deep and perverse meaning.

"Yeah." Aaron ignored what the man

actually meant and sighed. He then turned so he was not looking at the man but at Madi's window, and just before taking off toward her house, he mumbled, "Well, I'm not human."

Aaron ran up Madi's yard to her window. He moved quickly, not too concerned about being quiet. Within moments, he was stepping across her roof over to her window.

She was inside on her bed again. Her head was buried in her arms as if crying. The window was cracked, either because the man really was right or in her sadness she didn't notice that she hadn't shut it all the way.

Aaron slowly slid the window open. He watched Madi the whole time to see if she would hear him, not knowing what he would say if she looked up at him. He managed to open the window without startling her.

Aaron didn't know what else to do but to climb inside her window as softly and quietly as he could. He climbed in carefully, setting his foot down on the padded bench below the window for stealth. He moved his entire body inside the room without making much noise. Aaron then lowered his feet onto the floor and crept over to her bed.

Maybe she already knows I'm here?

Aaron stood at the post of her bed. Madi stopped crying, but didn't look up. Aaron was about to open his mouth, but Madi spoke first.

"Go away, Aaron."

"Madi, listen. Don't you think I knew the risk of telling you this? Madalyne, I—"

Madi cut Aaron off. She lifted her head, showing her blushed face with tears flooding down.

"Aaron, you don't understand. It's too dangerous for you here. My father has sworn to destroy your race. He believes you exist and will stop at nothing to put an end to you all. Nothing can ever become of us because of that, Aaron. I won't put your life at risk. If my father found out, he would trap you, or even kill you!" Madi put her hands on her forehead. "Everything makes so much sense now. How so many basic things seemed new to you. Aaron, Earth is different from your world. You know that! If—if anything were to become of us, how would our cultures mix?" Madi exhaled heavily. "Oh my gosh. I can't believe this."

"Madi, I know. I've thought about all of this.

Just hear me out. You can't let someone else's decisions establish yours. I know your father hates my people, but if you're going to let a grudge rule your life, then you will be so wrapped up in a world revolved around it that you're going to miss some of the greatest experiences in life. And this may sound crazy to you, but I don't know — I just think there's some kind of fun in being secret and having our own life that nobody knows about."

Madalyne wiped her tears and Aaron sat on the end of her bed opposite from her and crossed his legs.

"Really, your father would never have to know."

Madalyne smiled and coughed out a little laugh. She looked at him and said, "But, Aaron —"

Aaron cut Madi off this time. "But what, Madalyne? I feel like my father is a bigger issue than your father."

The two laughed and shared the moment of thinking about the difficulty of their fathers.

"Your father?" Madalyne joked.

"Yeah," Aaron replied, with the same amount of energy. "My father is going to be a little more difficult."

Aaron scooted closer to Madi with his legs still crossed. He clasped his hands together and said, "Now, just...let me say everything."

"Okay."

Aaron breathed out and then looked at Madi. Her eyes glistened from the tears that still lingered around her face.

"My father is the king of my world, and I am the prince."

"What?" Madi shouted. She put her hands over her smiling face because she couldn't keep it composed. "What do you mean 'prince' and 'king?'" Madi asked, bursting with curiosity.

Aaron replied, "It's exactly as I said."

"King of what?"

"All of Upitar; that's the name of my world."

"How big is it?"

"About half the size of Earth, but there's also five outer rims. They are separate worlds that connect to Upitar through water traveling. They have their own kingdoms, too. My father is the king over the entire world of Upitar, though."

"What? That's...that's just crazy! And does,

like, whatever he says go?"

"Yeah, but he has officials and a council that advise him and he often speaks with the outer rim leaders before major decisions are made. He basically makes all the decisions for Upitar, though. It's complicated and I can explain it later," Aaron said, not wanting to discuss the politics of his world.

Madi looked up at Aaron and a little smile moved along her face. "And you're...you're a prince?"

"Yes." Aaron said, returning the smile. "Now, the difficulty is that people of Earth are forbidden to come to Upitar unless they're taken captive," Aaron said, not sounding worried. "But my father has been pressuring me to find a princess to marry, because he is afraid he is going to be killed or die from some random disease soon. So we can just say you're a princess from one of the five outer rims. And eventually we could tell him the truth, but by that time he would understand."

"Jumping a little ahead, here, aren't we?" Madalyne said sarcastically.

"Oh, okay. Never mind. I just thought you

would have fun being a princess for a little bit."
Aaron dangled the opportunity in front of her.

Madi looked at Aaron, clearly wanting to,
but in her mind she was allowing her worries to
debate her opportunities.

"The chance to be a princess doesn't come
around that often," Aaron said, adding more weight
to her decision. "Don't be afraid, I will be with you
through whatever comes."

Madi gazed at Aaron for a moment. "Sir
Aaron, I would love to."

They laughed and Madi wiped her eyes
again. Neither of them could believe they were
actually going to try to make this work. Against all
odds, and though he was forbidden to even
communicate with Earthlings, and her father had
sworn to destroy water travelers, they were going to
try to make this work.

"I can't believe that...all this time...you were
real. Water travelers are real." Madi tried to wrap
her head around it as she leaned against the
headboard.

She suddenly bolted forward toward Aaron
and shouted, "Do you know what happened to my

grandfather?"

"No, I really don't. I'm sorry," Aaron said, expressing his sorrow for her grandfather.

"It's okay," she said, looking away.

Getting up, Madi walked over to her window and ran her fingers along the wooden handle.

"So my grandfather was always right. And he knew it."

Madi continued to feel the wooden handle on her window. Aaron came over to her and looked at the handle she was touching.

"This was a gift from my grandfather. I never met him, but this was left to me in his will. One was given to all of his grandchildren. It says 'They're Real', I think. But when you look at it in the moonlight, it almost looks like there's a different word in front of real."

Aaron quickly looked at the handle, finally knowing what it said. The letters were engraved differently than Aaron was used to. He felt the wood again. It felt the same as the fallen tree in Granny's backyard. Aaron gazed at the handle. It meant something—it had a deeper meaning—but he just couldn't figure it out.

"Hey, so, this might be a weird question, but if you're a water traveler, then why are you on Earth in the first place?" Madi said, turning away from the window and looking at Aaron.

Aaron paused for a moment. He didn't look at Madi. "Umm, I—I am on a mission for my father."

Madi, trying to get a look at Aaron's face, asked, "What's your mission?"

Aaron paused again. He couldn't tell her the truth. They had gotten this far and he didn't want to blow it all by telling her he had to kidnap and kill a girl.

"I—I just have to find someone on Earth; it's critical to my people. I still do, but I can do it later," Aaron said, finally looking at Madi at the end of his sentence.

"Who is it? Maybe I can help, you know?" Madi said cheerfully.

"I don't know. I was just given her general location, and when I am close to her, a red dot on my map will begin to glow," Aaron explained.

"That's so fascinating. How does it do that?"

"Our maps are intertwined with the orbs that

allow water traveling to happen, and it's said that the orbs are linked with our blood and… Never mind, it's really complicated." Aaron didn't want to explain how he would find the girl, because it might lead to what he had to do.

"Well, let me see your map," she said. "I know a lot of people around here, and maybe I can help."

"Okay fine," Aaron said, not knowing what harm showing her his map could do.

He took his bag off his shoulders and opened it up.

"That's why your clothes are always wet," Madi said.

Aaron looked up at her. She was smiling with her hand almost covering her mouth. He smirked and admitted, "Yeah."

He pulled out the rolled-up map from its snug position. It was a tattered piece of paper that looked quite old. Madi stood by his shoulder, looking at the map as he unrolled it.

The paper crackled a little as he did so. On the inside was a layout that showed all of Earth. It was three dimensional, showing elaborate peaks of mountains. The map immediately began to shift and zoom in on his location after opening it.

"What's happening?" Madi said, shocked that a paper map was transforming as if it were a digital screen.

"Just watch," Aaron said as he waited for the map to stop moving.

The map quickly arrived at Aaron's location and a blue ring appeared around the area Aaron was to search. This was the first time Aaron had looked at the map in days. Aaron's green dot soon appeared inside the blue ring.

"That's me, there," Aaron said.

The map zoomed into just being a flat surface with a few undistinguishable features. They watched the map closely. A small red dot appeared. It shined brightly, right beside Aaron's dot.

Aaron froze. His heart skipped beats. He stopped breathing.

"Go over there!" he shouted as he pointed to the doorway.

"What? Wh—"

"Just go over there!"

Madalyne hustled over to the other side of

the room. The red dot moved with her. Aaron looked at Madi and then at the map again. He began to sweat.

"Go over there!" Aaron shouted again, pointing to the other side of the bed.

The dot moved again, as Madi did.

Madi was the dot. Madi was her. She was the girl he was supposed to find. Madi was the girl who was prophesied about.

Madalyne is the girl I have to kill.

Chapter 20

Aaron stopped. Panic raced through his mind. He didn't know what to do. He couldn't kill an innocent person, let alone Madi.

No no no no no no no! This isn't... This...no, this can't really be happening!

"Aaron, what's wrong?" Madi asked, starting to sound worried. "What does this mean?"

Aaron didn't respond. He began to sweat more. His fingers shook as he held the map.

How can it be Madi? After all this, how can it be her? No, no. It can't be! It can't be.

Aaron knew it was. There was no denying it. It was either kill Madi or let his people perish. And he couldn't tell her. How could he? There was no way out of the fact that it was her.

"Aaron, what's wrong?" She asked again, sounding more worried.

Aaron thought fast and he thought deep.

How can she destroy the waterways? If she's the one prophesied to destroy them, then how is she going to do it? He shouted in his mind, "*How can I save her, but also save my people? If she lives, then she will destroy the waterways and my people will die! If she dies, then..."*

Aaron turned toward the window. His open hands turned to fists and he slammed them against Madi's bench.

"Aaron! Tell me what is going on!" Madi became defensive and afraid.

Aaron gazed out the window. His eyes traveled into the sky. The light rippled along the clouds and then a vigorous gush of wind blew through the trees.

Then, something came to him — one possible way out. One extremely risky idea. A way to save both his people and Madi. The chances of it working were slim, but it was the only thing he could think of. The only dubious thing that might have a chance of working.

Aaron turned back toward Madi. He took her hand.

"Madi, here, sit down," he said sitting on the bench.

Madi tried to figure Aaron out as he tried to wipe the panic off his face.

"Madi...I — I was sent on a mission to find you," Aaron said, facing Madi.

"Okay..." Madi said, lowering her eyebrows and squinting slightly.

"My people are in danger because of your future. It's been prophesied that you are going to find a way to destroy the waterways," Aaron explained.

"That's absurd!" Madi defended.

"Madi, it was prophesied."

He looked at her and then calmly said words he hated. "My mission was to find you and...kill you."

Madi dropped Aaron's hands and stood up. She stepped away from him in fear.

"Madi, listen. I'm not going to," Aaron said extending his arms, trying to keep her calm. "My race is in danger because of you, because destroying the waterways will cause Upitar to be unstable and well, perish. But I've never been a fan of killing and I'm not going to start with you. I think I know another way. A way that will keep you alive, and keep the waterways and my people safe."

"I would never want to destroy them

anyway!" she shouted.

"Yes, you would. Think about it. If it meant for your father to give up his ridiculous revenge hunt, you would. If you knew a way, which apparently in your future you're supposed to, you would destroy the waterways in order to save your father from becoming consumed by revenge," Aaron said, explaining it to himself as he spoke.

Madalyne responded immediately and passionately. "No! Aaron, I love my father, but never would I kill an entire race because of his delusions!"

They took a moment and breathed. Madi was telling the truth, and Aaron knew it.

"It doesn't make sense, then! If it was prophesied, it has to come true," Aaron said, burying his hands in his hair.

"No, Aaron. Your mission was to stop me, right? Granted, killing me seemed like the way to do it, but you have already stopped me, haven't you? If I had never met you, then maybe I would have. But because of you, now I never will."

The words made Aaron feel euphoric. His eyes widened as a smile came across his face with a breath of relief. Then, he remembered something. "That makes sense to us, but my father will never buy it. He wants you dead." Aaron was coming to the harsh realization of his father's immutable hatred for Earthlings.

Madi sighed. Aaron knew she understood because she faced the same amount of stubbornness from her own father.

"Now, I have a plan that might—just might—work. It's never been done before, but it's the only thing I can think of."

Aaron moved close to Madi. "But you have to be okay with it."

Madi slowly nodded her head in agreement. Aaron then said carefully, "Okay...You have to become a water traveler."

"What?"

"Madi, it's the only way. Think about it. As a water traveler, I would not have to kill you because you would be one of us. Then, in my father's eyes, as a water traveler you would not want to destroy the waterways. You would be one of us and he would see you that way."

***

Madalyne looked down at the carpet. She got lost in the brown texture it presented in the yellow room. It was all real. This wasn't some kind of a dream. She wasn't able to stop time and think, she had to quickly make decisions that would affect her for the rest of her life.

Her father loathed water travelers — her life would be jeopardized in her own home. She looked around and then closed her eyes. The main question that ran through her head was: *Is Aaron worth it? Is this...person...I met only a matter of days ago worth risking everything?*

She felt something, though. Something she had never felt before, even with the other guys she had known. It was like an entirely new emotion. When she was with him, it was as though music played all the time, even though no music was around. Even with the fact that it had only been a few days, she didn't want to regret never finding out.

Several minutes passed before she came back to reality, the gridlock in her head resolved. She opened her eyes and looked up at Aaron.

"Then I will become a water traveler," she said, almost excitedly.

"Are you sure?" Aaron asked, his large, caring eyes gazing at her.

"Yes. It's the only way to keep peace. And I think it could be—I don't know, fun. A little adventure. Aaron…" she said, looking up into his eyes. "You and I met for a reason. I knew it from the moment I saw you. And I can't deny that, or any of this."

They both smiled, not broadly or grinning, but simple smiles. She didn't know why, but she felt warm with joy. Everything seemed more magical: the sky, the grass, her room, Aaron.

"We have to go now, then," Aaron said. "How long before your father comes back?"

Madi pulled out her phone and looked at the date. "Still…five days." She was shocked they had that much time left.

"We'll have to move quickly, then." Aaron looked around the room. "Change into something you're okay water traveling in, and pack something warm into my bag," Aaron said, taking his bag off his shoulders. "Even though we can water travel, the Keeper is far away," Aaron explained.

"The Keeper?"

"The Keeper of the waterways. He is the keeper of the orb and has the power to give anyone the gift of water traveling."

"Does he exist?"

Aaron sat down by the window. "Yeah, I think so. As the future King, my father has shared most of the oldest secrets of the kingdom with me. When I was a boy, my father told me this one."

"How far away is he?"

"The top of Mount Romeatir. It's the highest mountain in our land." Aaron packed some of Madi's things into his bag.

"We can't just water travel to it? Isn't there some kind of pool somewhere?"

Aaron's mind seemed to go blank, thinking about this.

"Umm, yeah. There is one. But it's in the bottom of the castle, and there's no way of getting to it without someone knowing." Aaron looked out the window as his mind seemed to go elsewhere.

Madi noticed something was wrong. He

appeared to be thinking about something, and it wasn't the trip they were about to make, or the pool.

"What's wrong?" she said softly.

Aaron looked out the window. "That's where I lost my brother."

She immediately sat beside him and put her hand on his leg. "Oh, Aaron, I'm sorry."

"He didn't drown, Madi. He did something called miss-traveling," Aaron said. She could tell he was trying to explain and warn her. "When that happens, it's said that water travelers are sent to the Reverse, which basically means they've died. Nobody's ever come back from there, so it's concluded that they're dead. The idea of the Reverse just gives us a little hope that they could be alive; my father said he doesn't know if he believes it exists."

Aaron looked out the window. Madi could tell memories of his brother were running through his mind.

"Don't stop believing in hope," she said.

Aaron smiled. "I won't."

He stood up and lifted up his bag. Madi followed by his side and grinned at him. She gave him a moment before speaking.

"I'm happy to be doing this...especially with you."

"Me too." Aaron smiled back at her. "Come on, I would like to get as far as we can while it's still night." He put a leg out the window.

Madi shut the lights off in her room and rushed back over to the window. She took Aaron's hand as he sat on the ledge, waiting for her. She gazed at the wooden handle.

Yes, they are.

Aaron climbed out into the fresh night air and Madi followed, holding his hand.

The two ran off into the night toward the pond behind her house. They stopped at the edge of the pool and peered into it. Aaron quickly looked around to see if anyone was nearby.

"Are you ready?" He asked.

"Mhm." She followed Aaron into the water and he turned so he was facing her. The beautiful night sky clashed in harmony with the darkness of the water.

"On the count of three," Aaron said.

I am actually going to water travel. Madi

watched his eyes as the world faded around them.

"One…two…three."

They dropped under the water. Madi squeezed Aaron's hands, and he squeezed hers back. Madi kept her eyes open, even under the water. She saw Aaron open his eyes to make sure she was safely under the surface. Aaron shut his eyes, and she shut hers. They water traveled.

Chapter 21

Aaron and Madi lifted their heads above the surface of the water and breathed the fresh air of Upitar. Aaron glanced around, quickly checking if anyone was near. After seeing that it was safe, he let go of one of Madi's hands.

"Come on," Aaron said, pulling her to the edge of the water.

They climbed out and jogged briskly through the grass. The sun had also set in the part of Upitar they were on and the purple moon was out. Madalyne gazed at it in fascination.

"It's purple?" She pointed at it.

"Welcome to Upitar," Aaron joked. "Now everything feels new to you, doesn't it?"

"Is this what it's like for you on Earth?" Madi asked, beginning to realize why Aaron seemed to understand so little.

"Yeah, but Earth has so much technology that it's overwhelming."

"Oh my gosh! That's why you were so amazed and confused about everything! Like driving and opening a car door and the city and lights and the thermostat! You'd never seen any of that before!" Madalyne giggled.

"What? Don't make fun of me!"

"I'm not! I think it's kind of cute, actually."

They ran up a giant bluff toward the next pool, hands still locked. The moonlight was behind them, glowing on their backs. Madi gazed at her free hand, how it was a shade of purple. It obviously baffled her even though it was so simple. They reached the top and lights illuminated the kingdom, not far away in the distance.

"What is that place?" Madi said, desperately curious.

Aaron outstretched his free arm, saying, "That is the Kingdom of Upitar. Where I live, and my father, the king, rules."

Madi let go of Aaron's hand and took a step forward.

"It's so…big," she said, trying to take it all in. "It's beautiful."

The kingdom was massive, especially to an outsider. From one end to the other it had thousands of lights and homes with a giant stone wall wrapping around all of them.

Aaron pointed out the main building of the kingdom, his father's home with the throne room on the first floor. It was in the middle and had two main pillars in front and what looked like three levels, each getting smaller as they rose. The craftsmanship of the building was elegant and the architecture looked advanced compared to the rest of the city.

"Another time, I'll show you around," Aaron said, coming up alongside Madi.

"It's unbelievable," Madi said as she gawked at it.

"My father wants to expand it, actually. From wall to wall the kingdom is pretty small compared to others. My father wants people from all over Upitar to be able to reside close to the worlds capital."

"That makes sense. I mean, compared to the capitals on Earth, its not that big. Although, it's absolutely beautiful."

Aaron took a moment to try and look at it like she was. "Having lived there my whole life, I never really noticed its beauty. It's always seemed so ordinary to me. But, I see a little more now — the stone that was hand crafted into lions, the patterns and art carved along the walls, the magnitude of the castle. It is nice to just sit and look at it like someone who has never seen it before."

Madi was still gazing at it.

Drawing her away from the view, Aaron said, "Come on, we have to get going, though."

"It's so beautiful here. Everything's so ancient and fantasy-like," Madi said happily.

"Yeah…it is," Aaron said, taking her hand.

She smiled at him and he at her before they barreled down the other side of the hill.

They ran at almost a 45-degree angle from the castle's front gates. At the bottom of the hill were woods again. Not far was the pool of water the spy used in escaping. They ran through the dark woods, trying to distance themselves from the castle as best they could.

"We're going to have to be quiet through here," Aaron said, in almost a whisper. "There may be a few guards roaming the woods and the side of the castle and we don't want them to find us."

Madi whispered back, "okay," and remained

silent.

They ran through the thick woods, trying to avoid fallen branches and any other debris that might make noise. They came to an open clearing that led to the castle gates and main archway. It was a vast amount of open space and would take more than a few seconds to run across.

Aaron and Madi stood at the edge of the woods as Aaron viewed the castle. There seemed to be little commotion going on, but nothing appeared to be disordered because guards still walked along the top of the castle walls.

Aaron looked the other way to see if anyone was coming toward the castle. The clearing led to a hill — once they descended, they would be out of sight of the castle and the guards on patrol.

Aaron looked once more in both directions to make sure they would be safe.

"Okay, we're going to run across. As soon as we reach the bottom of that hill, we'll be out of the sight of anyone in the castle. The guards on top of the walls might not be able to make us out in the blackness, but it is possible. They've noticed things like elk and some have claimed Amtu trotted across before. And the kingdom is in a state of high alert, so we have to be careful."

"What do you mean?"

"We're kind of in the middle of a war," Aaron said, not looking at Madi but at the top of the castle where the castle guards were.

"What? Wha—"

Before Madi could finish, Aaron squeezed her hand and said, "Come on."

Aaron pulled Madi out of the woods and the two sprinted as fast as they could. The darkness embraced them. Aaron checked the castle and saw only four guards looking out. They continued to run, but Aaron looked back again to see if he could figure out what was going on. *Why did most of the guards leave?* Aaron turned his head back to focus on their destination and, upon doing so, a loud roar sounded from the castle.

Aaron and Madi reached the edge of the hill and slid down the other side, fearful because of the roaring cheer they heard. Aaron turned around and snuck back up the edge of the hill. He lay with only his head peeking over the crest of the hill.

Madi crawled up next to him and asked,

short of breath, "What was that?"

"I'm not sure," Aaron replied in wonder.

The guards on the top of the tower were lifting their fists and shouting. The echo from the castle reached Aaron and Madi with a crisp blare. Then torches rapidly approached the exit of the main gate of the castle.

Guards on horseback flooded out into the clearing. They stayed in formation, riding directly toward Aaron and Madi.

"Madi, we have to go! Come on!"

He sprang up and Madi followed in fright. The two dashed again as fast as they could. Fear filled them and adrenaline rushed through their veins.

The torchlights quickly approached. Aaron looked around for a place to hide. There was nothing—no trees, no water, not even a few stones, just open field. The closest hiding spot was almost a mile away.

Aaron tried to decide if they had time to run back to the woods. They didn't. Guards were already running alongside the trees.

Aaron took his best guess at the path the

guards were going to take and made almost a complete right turn. Madi did the same without question. Aaron gave up his last bit of energy and slid on the ground. Madi rolled onto the grass next to him.

"Lie among the grass!"

Aaron saw the army rise over the hill in their armored attire, torches in hand. Black figures galloped down the hill Aaron and Madi lay on.

Aaron opened his bag. His hands shook dramatically. He yanked out the piece of armor he had acquired from the spy and unrolled it over Madi.

"Don't move," he ordered.

He pulled out a dark blanket packed from Madi's house and threw it over himself. They laid in the grass in complete stillness.

Shouts from the men grew louder and louder. Neither could see anything. The ground shook as the mighty feet of the horses hit. The landscape vibrated more. Aaron tensed, trying to avoid any kind of movement.

Suddenly, torchlight was visible through his camouflage. The shadows of horses flashed by as the ground trembled violently. Aaron saw the hoofs of a horse land directly in front of his face. He shook from fear.

Aaron looked to his side and saw the shadow of a horse coming right over him. It didn't jump, it didn't change its path at all; it stomped through the small space between him and Madi.

There was a loud crack. Aaron waited for pain, but didn't feel anything. If it cleared him, it must have struck Madi. Aaron thought the worst. She might be dead.

The prince stood up, revealing himself. He spread his arms out to defend Madi and force the horses to go another route. He heard nothing, though: no horses, no shouts, no breathing of anything. Nothing but the trotting of horses behind him.

When he opened his eyes, he was stunned not to see any horses charging at him. He turned his head sharply and saw that they had all passed. He immediately dropped down to Madi and threw the armor off her.

"Madi!" he whispered

Aaron didn't see any damage to her body.

She's safe, right? "Madi!" he said, louder.

Madi lifted her head and turned her face toward Aaron.

"Madi," Aaron said, taking a deep breath.

She gave him a smile showing she was okay. The smile didn't last long, though, before her features turned to agony.

Alarmed, Aaron asked, "What's wrong?"

Madi lifted her right hand toward Aaron. Her middle finger, ring finger, and pinky all dangled at strange angles. She couldn't move them. One was beginning to bleed.

"Okay, hold on. Just lay there, okay?"

Aaron reached hastily into his bag. He rummaged around and pulled out a small vial, which contained a brown liquid. He turned back to Madi and popped the vial open. A small pool of blood had already formed under Madi's hand.

"Okay, this may hurt a little, but let me see your hand."

Madi tried to lift her hand, but the excruciating pain on her face showed she couldn't.

"Okay, that's fine. I'm going to lift it for you. This is going to hurt, but it will help." He was trying his best to keep her calm.

Aaron lifted Madi's arm. Blood fell off the bottom of her hand.

"Can you roll over?" Aaron asked.

She rolled over, revealing the palm of her hand. It was covered in blood and Aaron saw why. The middle finger's bone stuck out in the direction of the center of her palm. Aaron blocked his panic and quickly poured the liquid on her hand. He dumped it along the open wound and her broken fingers. He even poured out some on her arm.

Madi's face turned red in agony. She bit her bottom lip, but held in her scream. The wound bubbled. The liquid began to form a skin-like texture around the bone and all of her arm. Within moments, the area was cocooned in a new layer of rigid, skin-like material, and the bleeding stopped. Madi breathed in and out slowly and heavily. Her face relaxed and her muscles became less tense, indicating that her pain had reduced to a tolerable level.

"What is that?"

"Medicine. It creates that material, cerol, to cover open wounds. It's also good for sore spots and helps block out pain," Aaron explained.

"Thank you," Madi said gratefully, partially in shock.

"That's the first time I've ever had to use it. I'm glad it worked," Aaron said, touching her arm. "Do you feel able to keep moving?" he asked, knowing they had to.

Madi stood up. Her arm remained bent at the elbow and frozen.

"I...can't move my arm."

"Yeah, it also locks all of the muscles and nerves it's poured on. Everything still functions, but you just can't move it. It helps the area heal faster," Aaron said. "I poured some along your arm as well because I didn't know what might also be broken in there. You will be able to move it again in about two days."

"Oh, so it's kind of like a cast," Madi said, inspecting her arm.

"Yeah, whatever that is."

Madi looked at Aaron and shook her head with a laugh.

"Come on, we're coming up on our next pool of water."

They continued, trying to keep a brisk jog. Madi looked off in the distance at the fading torchlights.

"Do you know where they are going?"

Aaron took a moment to watch the torches before responding. "War."

Chapter 22

The words felt weird rolling off Aaron's tongue. Upitar had never been at war, and the fact that they were going and he wasn't with them was even more strange.

Aaron was one of the best fighters in all the land. As much as his father protected him, everyone knew it was true. He only lost one scrimmage — to Ugine, and that was a year ago.

"Oh, what's an Amtu?" Madalyne asked curiously, obviously wondering from when Aaron mentioned the guards claiming to spot some from atop the kingdom wall.

"It's...umm." Aaron thought about it for a minute, trying to figure out how to describe it. "It's like an elk, but much bigger. A baby's antlers stretch about eight feet from tip to tip, and when full grown, they can grow between eighteen and twenty feet. And they have massive tails. They're big and bushy and tend to be about a foot or two thick, stretching to whatever the length of the antlers are. They're really fascinating, and they taste amazing, I guess."

"Are they dangerous?"

"Most of the time, from what I've been told. Many years before I was born, during my grandfather's reign, I've been told that his Captain of the Guard used to ride on one. Ugine's tried to, but he's only come across one once."

"Who's Ugine?" Madi asked, sounding confused about half the sentence.

"He's...well, he's just a close friend of mine, and the current Captain of the Guard — technically third in command after my father and I."

"Wow, you're second in command?" Madi asked in realization.

"Technically. Ugine usually has more say on most matters, but that's because I'm not around for most decisions," Aaron said, looking away. "I really don't enjoy kingly duties and stuff like that."

"Why not?"

"I'm not ready to be king, and I don't know if I ever will be. I don't want that life. I want to be free and not tied down to my kingdom."

"I get that. Like a routine job, but with also being responsible for thousands of people," Madi said sarcastically.

"Yeah. Both just seem kind of repetitive — which to me is a synonym for decaying," Aaron said.

They reached a pool of water with a river running into it. On the far side, connecting to the pool, was a mesa, no more than a five-minute climb.

"That's Leading Tip," Aaron said. "It used to be the marker that my ancestors used during the Building of the Kingdom Era. This pool here will take us to a plain near the base of Mount Romeatir."

"How far is it from there?"

Aaron hesitated, but said, "Not too far."

Aaron jumped into the water, creating an ample splash that crashed onto Madi, causing her clothes to soak. She laughed, knowing that staying dry wasn't a possibility, and then jumped in as close to Aaron as she could, causing water to splash against his face in return.

The water was chilly, but not too cold. Madi rose and wiped the water out of her eyes with the arm that was able to move. Aaron was barely visible in the purple moonlight that reflected on the surface of the water.

"On three," he said.

Aaron took Madi's free hand and counted to three. When he reached the number, they both sank under the water and Aaron water traveled. Rising above the surface of the new pool, they heard the noise of roaring water in the background.

Madi opened her eyes and had to tread water with her legs and one good arm as she turned her body around. Like the water they were just in, there was a mesa connecting to it, this one with a graceful waterfall. Water gushed over the top and into the small lake they swam in. The waterfall was not huge, but enough water came over it to force someone under the surface. At the top were two rocks shaped like pillars.

The moon had just moved directly in between the two pillars from their view. Its purple beams shot across the water, creating a majestic sparkle on the surface. The water wasn't uncomfortably cold and it wasn't a nasty warm—it was the perfect cool and refreshing temperature. Madi's eyes gazed at the moon, taking in the celestial sight she had never seen before.

Aaron swam over and looked as he treaded

water alongside her. They were there when it was just right.

The waterfall's calming roar drowned out the noise of their worries. Nobody was repeatedly telling them they had to do things, the fear of the future wasn't daunting to them. Everything just felt right. Nothing felt out of place. They were exactly where they should be. The moment was full of not worrying and peacefully enjoying the world around them.

The moon moved out of the small window and went behind the right rock. The peaceful moment ended, but the joy from it remained.

Aaron spoke as he treaded water. "We should get going again." And he began to swim to shore.

He made sure Madi reached the shore first. Once on land, she awkwardly shook her wet clothes out the best she could. Aaron dropped his bag off his shoulders and opened it. He pulled out both his new and old armor. Tossing the new set to Madi, he said, "Change into this. The mountain will get cold, but you won't feel it if you're wearing that. That will also stay dry."

Aaron rummaged through the bag and pulled out a spare change of dry clothes as well. One for himself, and one that Madi had packed for herself. Aaron awkwardly looked around for a place to change. Scanning the area, he noticed Madi doing the same thing.

There was really nothing there but open plains. The mesa where the water flowed from yielded no trees, no caves, not even an abstract formation in its rocks where someone could change privately. It was just a wall with water flowing down that ran for what looked to be a few hundred feet. The two looked at each other and laughed.

"Here," Aaron said, pointing behind Madi. "There's a rock over there, and we'll both be in darkness anyway. You go over there behind the rock and face that way and I'll go over to the other side of the lake and face the other way."

"Okay." Madi laughed.

Aaron headed over to the other side of the lake while Madi walked behind the hardly adequate stone. Aaron wanted to look back to make sure she wasn't visible, but couldn't because of the possibility she might be. Aaron had to assume she wasn't and began to change.

***

Madi quickly changed her top, even with only one working arm. She took off her wet pants and was sliding on her dry ones when she saw a glow from a pair of eyes not far from her.

Her heart stopped for a second before she breathed again. The eyes glowed in the moonlight and looked right at her. They moved near her, coming faster and faster. Madi choked for words. A growling noise came from the direction of the eyes. Madalyne came to her senses and shouted out a cry for Aaron as she dropped to the ground, getting as close to the rock as she could.

The eyes were now no more than ten feet from Madi, drenched in purple moonlight. They belonged to a creature that looked smaller than her, but the demented growls still struck her with fear.

The creature reached the leg of Madi's dry pants and bit them violently with its teeth, but threw the pants aside when it tasted no flesh. Madi looked for something to defend herself with, but saw nothing in the short time she had to react.

The thing viciously turned back for her. It crouched on its hind legs and sprang at her head. Its wide-open jaws revealed piercing teeth. Aaron hurdled over the rock, thrusting his dagger into the creature's head and driving it to the ground. Pulling the dagger back, he kicked the dead creature to the side. Its body flopped along the ground and remained lying in the withered grass.

Aaron slid his dagger back into its sheath along his leg and scooped up her pants. His eyes were closed when he turned around.

Aaron extended the pants to Madi.

Madi took the pants out of Aaron's hands, thankful that he kept his eyes closed even after she had taken them. She kissed Aaron's cheek.

"Thank you."

Aaron didn't reply, as if he didn't know what to say, but walked back to the other side of the rock.

Madi finished changing and then came around the rock to Aaron.

"You can open your eyes now." She giggled.

"Okay." Aaron opened his eyes and said, "You okay?"

"Yeah," Madi replied. "What was that?"

"It was a night finder. They're like Earth possums, but with rabies."

"Hmm. Sounds about right."

They continued walking, and before their eyes, Mount Romeatir revealed itself in the darkness. The closer they got, the more visible it became. The mountain was enormous. It stretched up and beyond the clouds that concealed parts of the sky. As far as the two could see, it reached up and continued.

"Wow," Madi gasped. "How big is it?"

"It's said to be about eight thousand meters," Aaron said nonchalantly.

"Eight thousand?" Madalyne shouted. "Aaron, I don't know about you, but I can't climb that high!"

"It's okay. I can water travel most of the way. But when we reach the higher altitudes is when it gets a little tough, because the water's frozen. Then we can't water travel. But there's a path, I think."

"Aaron, has anyone ever made it to the top?"

Aaron didn't answer her at first.

"Aaron?"

"No. But no one's tried in over six hundred years, and the equipment I have with me—"

"Aaron—"

"Madi, we can do it. Once we make it to the frozen zone, we'll be fine. My father has told me stories about it that were passed down to him."

"How many miles is it once we reach the frozen zone?"

"I'm not sure," Aaron said. "The thing is, the mountain really isn't hard to climb. There's a path that's said to be pretty easy to walk up."

"Then why has no one ever made it to the top before?"

"I don't know. The last people who tried were from another kingdom that was at war with ours. They knew of the legend of the Keeper being at the top, and the orb also being there. They wanted the orb because of its power, but could never make it to the top. After we defeated them and a treaty was signed, they said that they had tried, but always found themselves back at the base of the mountain. They never got very far before finding themselves starting all over. And I think the reason why they couldn't make it to the top is because they wanted the orb to use it for war. Since the mountain is where the orb rests, it has some connection with it, therefore not allowing them to make it to the top."

"And since we're not using it for war but for peace, we will be able to make it through?"

"Yeah!"

"I guess it makes sense. I really hope you're right," Madi said, trusting Aaron. "Because a lot is riding on this."

The two reached the base of the steep mountain. A rocky trail led up to the mountain and ascended around an edge and out of sight. Aaron set foot onto the mountain's rocky base and Madi followed, standing by his shoulder. Aaron took a breath in and then breathed out. "Let's hope this works."

They walked up the path without experiencing trouble. The terrain was easy to navigate, with a few steep inclines here and there. The purple moonlight shined brightly, allowing them to see most of where they were going.

As they progressed, the ground grew colder. Small patches of snow had accumulated along some of the rocks and a few icy puddles caused them both to lose their footing a couple of times. Aaron had to watch himself and Madi, because she only had one available arm to catch herself when she stumbled.

"Aaron, I don't think there's any water on this mountain."

Aaron looked around. "You might be right. How far would you say we have gone?"

"I'm not sure. Maybe a mile?"

"The trail may get worse, but I think we're still making really good progress."

Madi agreed and they continued to hike. It continued to be steep, but it seemed easier. It also began to get warmer. The snow was melting and the icy puddles were thawing away.

"Either this suits doing a wonderful job at keeping things warm, or something else is going on," Madi said, poking her finger in a small puddle of water.

They continued to hike until the temperature was just like a summer night. The ground and rocks were dry. Aaron and Madi stopped and looked around. Everything seemed the same — familiar. They had already walked through this part.

"Aaron," Madi said, "we're back at the beginning."

Aaron looked around. "Then it is true. I don't get it! We never left the trail, and we continued to hike upward. This doesn't make any sense."

"Aaron, we're just missing something," Madi said, trying to keep their hopes alive.

"I know, but I don't get it. There were no pools to water travel in, there were no forks in the road or secret paths. It was just a plain path that went up the mountain."

Madi suddenly had an idea.

"Wait!" she said. "I think I figured it out! You said this mountain was the holder of the orb, so it's linked with it, right?"

"Yeah, I think so."

"So it's not that someone must have the right motives to get up the mountain. The reason we can't get up it is because the mountain is protecting the orb. It's like a defense; it plays with our heads," Madi said.

"So how do we get up?"

"We don't. We go down."

Aaron squinted a little in confusion.

"What?"

"Maybe it's because I'm new to all this, but the mountain holds the orb, and the orb is what makes water traveling possible, right?" Madalyne asked.

"Yeah."

"So maybe that's just it. The mountain is like water. When you water travel, you don't go above the water, you go down, under it," Madi said, looking at the mountain. "Maybe in order to get to the top, we must go to the bottom."

Aaron looked at the mountain and said, "It doesn't really make sense, but, at the same time, it does. Maybe that is the secret. It's worth a try, I guess."

Aaron and Madi walked back to the beginning of the mountain and looked for a place to start. Then they journeyed around the edge of the mountain as if it were a giant circle.

They were on no visible path. They had to make their own way by scaling stones and jumping off high points. The air became more dense. The thickness of the clouds consumed them. Their visibility became impaired due to the fog and the darkness of the night.

Madi held onto Aaron's bag so she didn't lose him.

"Aaron, we can't go any farther," she said. "I can't even see my feet."

"Yeah, you're right."

Aaron turned around and took Madi's hand that had been on his bag.

"I have to search through my bag." He gently released Madi's hand so she would stay calm.

Aaron crouched down and opened his bag. He dove his arms into it and moved things around, doing the best he could to see with his hands.

Aaron pulled out a piece of wood and laid it on the ground, and kept two rocks in his hand. Striking the two rocks close together, he made sparks fly, causing a brief second of light in the abyss. Aaron struck them a few more times near the small wooden torch he had pulled out until it lit.

The torch grew bright and allowed them to at least see each other. Aaron scanned what he could with the torch, looking for a spot to rest. He took Madi's hand and carefully walked over to the wall of the mountain.

The ground was firm and the wall seemed well structured. There was a small, open area of ground along the side of the mountain.

"We'll rest here for the night," Aaron said, crouching down and looking through his bag again.

Madi looked around the place, a little concerned. It was cold, barely lit, and the ground looked hard. She crouched down and leaned against the wall of the mountain, wrapping her arm around her knees. Resting her chin on top of her arm, she watched Aaron.

Aaron pulled out a huge blanket brought from Madi's room. Then he pulled out another, and another, until there were five comforter-like blankets on the ground. Madi lifted her head. She smiled at the sight of a comfortable sleeping spot.

Madi got up from the wall and walked over to the blankets. There was a pink, a green, a yellow, and two black ones. Madi picked up the yellow blanket and rubbed it across her face. The softness brought a warm smile. Aaron continued to rummage through the bag until he turned it over and dumped everything out in front of him.

Madalyne walked over to him with the

yellow blanket around her shoulders. She crouched down and asked, "How does everything fit in that small bag?"

Aaron sat on the ground shaking the bag to make sure it was emptied completely.

"It's magic," he said. "It's a magic bag that can hold — well, I don't know how much. I've never filled it up all the way. And it keeps everything safe from the moisture when I water travel."

Madi picked up the bag, looking at it with curiosity. Tossing the bag up, she stuck her free hand in it in order to feel the bottom. It appeared to be no bigger than what she felt.

"Life forms can't go in the bag." He laughed.

"I don't get it, though. Where does it all go?"

"I don't know. When you put things in, it just all fits. The more stuff you put in it, the more vast the space inside the bag appears when you look in," Aaron said, trying to explain.

"Hmm." Madi decided not to try and figure it out anymore.

Aaron looked at everything he had dumped out. He appeared to only know what half of it was.

"Is this your stuff?" he said, pointing at

some of the objects he seemed unsure about.

"Only those four things are," Madi said, identifying what was hers.

Aaron picked up the remaining items. There were eight things. Four vials, a folded cloth, a white rope, a paper wrapped up with a string — keeping it bound — and a small circular object with a hollowed-out center and two holes on each side.

Aaron looked at the small circular thing. The top of it had a small indent. Peering into one of the holes, he tried looking at Madi through it, but couldn't see straight through.

Aaron picked up the paper and untied the string. The paper unfolded showing black ink. Aaron read it aloud:

> Aaron:
> I put together a few items for you. I hope they help you on your journey. I wish you the best of luck and the best of courage.
> Purple Vials — you should have two. They are a very rare medicine for if you get sick.

Red Vials — Drink one of these if you need warmth immediately. They're only for emergencies, Aaron.

White Rope — Light one end of this on fire and it will keep the area warm, and burn for three days.

Folded Blanket — The folded thing is a blanket. It's waterproof and can be used for warmth or coolness. Just think of what you need and it will do the rest.

Whistle — Aaron, no one knows you have this. It is the Whistle of Elrob. I trust you with this, Aaron. Do not lose it. It is not safe in the kingdom. I will explain more when the time is right. It will create noise if you need it, though.

Imushial

Aaron smiled when he finished the note.

"Imushial," he whispered. "You never stop helping, do you?"

"Who's that?"

"He's...well, he really is a friend of mine. It's a gift from the same person who met me at the coffee shop," Aaron said.

He looked at all the items again and then placed everything but the rope and the folded blanket back in the bag.

"Let's see this blanket," he said, unfolding the small square.

"Wait. He was a water traveler too?"

"Mhm." Aaron nodded. "I bet you've been around us and never even known it before."

"Wow." Madi sat; slowly realizing the stories from her childhood were not just made up. "So if he was from Upitar, was your father really ill?"

"No." Aaron stopped unfolding the blanket. "The kingdom was attacked, and my father requested me as soon as possible."

"Attacked? By the same people the kingdom is at war with?"

"Yeah. We believe we were attacked by another world called Senapin — one we didn't know still existed until recently."

Aaron explained all he could to Madi about Senapin as the two resumed opening the blanket. Fold after fold the blanket grew in size and thickness until it took both him and Madi to continue unfolding it. Madi used her body with her free hand in order to get it open and frequently dropped it, but Aaron only laughed with her. When it was completely opened, the blanket could easily cover the ground with room for both of them, with it also being poufy.

"Magic?" Madi giggled.

"I guess so."

Aaron laid the magic blanket on the ground along the wall of the mountain, using it to provide padding from the cold, rocky ground. He then spread out Madi's pink, green, and yellow blankets on one side and the other two on the other side. He rolled the edges of the magic blanket in a little, too, creating a soft barrier to prevent he and Madi from rolling onto unpadded stone. The two black blankets were then placed on one side and the colored ones on the other.

"Do you think we'll even need this?" asked Aaron, wiggling the white rope.

"Not for warmth, but it would be a nice light."

Aaron agreed and lit the tip of the rope. It illuminated the area better than the torch and let off a gentle warmth. Aaron put out the torch, in order to save its light, and put it back in his bag.

He climbed into the giant bed, moving over to the side with the two black blankets. He sat on his knees and said to Madi while she was still standing, "I claim this side."

"Oh do you? You better not set foot on my land then," she said, crawling into her side. She climbed under her blankets and poked her head out. "Or else I'm going to cast a spell on you."

"A spell? Are you a wizard now?"

"I might be." Madi raised her eyebrows.

"I guess I'll keep my distance then."

Aaron threw his blankets over himself. Lying there, he bumped Madi's foot with his toe. She simpered, looking over to him without moving her head. Looking away, she lay her foot against his.

The purple haze mixed with the rope's fire created a small ring of light that was more of a cozy tint than anything. Both their heads rested against the magic blanket. Aaron turned toward Madi and she toward him.

"It's a lot warmer than I thought it would be. I'm actually starting to sweat a little."

"Just think of it cooling you off," Aaron said with a reminding smile.

Madi thought of cooling off and the blanket obliged her.

"It's working!" she shouted as she sat up.

Aaron laughed. "Of course it is."

Madi fell back onto the magic blanket and closed her eyes.

"I'm glad I climbed out my window with you that night."

Aaron paused for a moment then said, "I am too."

He closed his eyes. The two of them both fell fast asleep in the cozy bed with the fog wrapping around them, the purple moon shining, and the white rope glowing.

Chapter 23

"What is it?" the King asked upon being awoken from a brief sleep.

"It's Ugine. He's found the tree and made contact," a guard said.

The King sprang up, throwing off his blankets. He put on his burgundy robe while walking out the door of his room.

"Stay on guard," he ordered.

The King rushed out of his room and down the stairs into the main throne room. He came in through the back entrance, facing the secret door that rested behind the throne. Guards stood on both sides of the door, safeguarding it, wearing their black armor with the hilt of their swords against the palm of their hands and the blades touching the ground.

They remained motionless and expressionless. When they saw him, both simultaneously twisted their swords so that the blades ran perpendicular to their bodies, but not a word was spoken.

The King took no notice, as it was a custom he had grown up around. He opened the door and closed it behind him. Hustling down the stairs with a torch in one hand and the other gripping his robe, he reached the bottom of the stairs and dashed into the main room, which had five tunnels on each side. He quickly took the third tunnel on the right. The light glowed with him as he ran down the tunnel. At the end of the long hall was a door.

The door was not smooth; it was ridged and soft in some parts, and bore indents and rivets. It was made out of a tree's wood that retained its original state. The door had no handle and no lock.

The King released his robe and rested his palm against the door. Its ancient texture embraced his aged hand. Pushing gently on the door, it opened — not with squeaks, but with the sound of crackling. Upon opening the door, a blue light flooded through the cracks and shined on his face.

The King pushed harder on the door, allowing himself to squeeze in. When he fully entered the room, he saw that in the center of the circular room stood a giant, ancient tree. It stretched to the ceiling of the room, which was only about twenty feet high, and canopied over all the room. The flowing branches stretched out and held blue leaves that glowed. The roots of the tree sprawled out across the rocky floor, along the walls, and into the ground below.

The King looked in awe at the great tree. He had never actually seen it before, because there was never a need to. Even though enclosed, its blue leaves still flourished with life. Three butterflies circled around the tree, living in its open arms. They were a mix of yellow and red and blue. Their wings fluttered gracefully and peacefully as they flew around the tree.

After gazing at the tree in amazement, the King closed the door behind him. He walked up to the trunk of tree and observed it, not sure what to do. The King glanced up and down at the tree and then finally said, "Ugine, are you there?"

Out of nowhere, Ugine's voice was heard. "Yes, my Lord. I can hear you."

The King was shocked that it actually worked. He put both hands on the tree as if to examine it and said, "This is astounding! How can I hear you?"

"They're called Whispering Trees. They used to be for planning attacks, but since our land has been at peace for so many years, they seem to have been forgotten about. The one you're speaking into is the main one of them all. If you speak into any Whispering Tree from anywhere, it can be heard from that one."

***

Ugine was actually at the base of a small mountain with a lake, in the east. It was dark where he was, but the torchlight from the army encamped around him provided visibility. Archival and a few other guards were with him. The army was not far from a forestland that also lay below the mountain. With the camp behind them and the lake to the east, the mountain rested to the northeast, where guards were stationed to keep watch.

The kingdom was short on guards but still maintained enough to keep the people inside the walls and the King safe. Most of the army had been summoned to go with Ugine and fight. The army was filled with the ranks of the best fighters, and some mediocre ones, as well.

The tree Ugine stood in front of was significantly larger compared to the ones around it. The trunk was almost three entire arm's length around and a little blue leaf glowed at the top of it.

Sound came from the direction of Ugine's tree as the King spoke, and from the King's tree as Ugine spoke. There was no hole, no cracks in the bark—the words just came from the tree.

"This is fascinating. We can use this for so much! How many of these are there, Ugine?"

"I'm not sure anymore, sir. I've only stumbled across a few in my time. In some of our old books, though, it's said the seeds used to be saved so they could be planted all across the land. Maybe if you actually visited the library built for your grandfather and read a few books instead of only discovering things by word of mouth, you would know these kinds of things," joked Ugine.

"Now is not the time, Ugine," the King rebutted. "What information do you have on our enemy?"

The tone of the conversation quickly changed from warm and friendly to serious.

"We are resting in the valley of Simul. We have men on watch on a cliff of Mount Haspure. We're planning on opening the first vial and pouring it into the lake so the first team can be sent."

"Proceed as planned," the King ordered.

"Yes, sir," Ugine paused. "Sir, I know this may sound rash, but I think it would be wise if we seek the Earthlings' help this time. We are encountering another world, one that wants to go to war with us, and the power they may possess might require us to join with the worlds we know now."

The King responded sharply, "We will not affiliate with the Earthlings, Captain. We never have, and we are not going to start now."

"I understand this, sir, but our enemy has weapons that are greater than ours. If we cannot overpower them they—"

"Ugine, the Earthlings are not reasonable with us, nor us with them. Our two kinds are not—"

"King Diadosia, you have seen their weapons! This enemy has blown a hole in the wall of our kingdom. A wall that, if it were our men, every one of them would have been killed! We cannot win this fight alone!" Ugine shouted angrily, in defense of his men.

The King rebutted with the same amount of frustration. "I will not work with the Earthlings! They are a people that cannot be trusted. Have you forgotten they are the ones who will destroy the waterways? Have you forgotten they are said to be the ones who will destroy Upitar? Have you forgotten what Earthlings do? Ugine, if we bring them here, they will do nothing but overpower us and enslave us at the first opportunity! We are on our own."

There was a brief pause before he spoke again.

"Ugine. We are a people who have persevered through greater turmoil than this. We are a strong race. Even when fighting our own kind — water travelers — we will be an equal match. Whatever weapons they do have can be used against them, and I do not doubt that you will have any trouble in doing that. Do you understand?"

"Yes, sir," replied Ugine in obedience.

"Carry out the attack, then. Report back to me when you have word."

"Very well, sir."

***

The King sighed after finishing. He looked around the room and at the tree. The butterflies were no longer in the air, but on the ground, with their wings sprawled out as if they were resting along the roots of the tree.

The King looked at the butterflies, but didn't allow their calmness to influence his thinking to be rational. Instead, he stormed out forcefully. Unknowingly, he stomped on some of the tree's roots. The King slammed the door behind him and proceeded to tramp back to the top of the castle.

Chapter 24

Aaron woke up from the sun shining in his eyes. He wiped them and stretched his hands up to the sky. His entire body straightened out and he felt wide awake. He looked over to Madi, who was still sleeping, and smiled. Then he paused, realizing something. It was daytime. The sun was up in the sky.

Aaron stood up in the homemade bed and looked around and up to the sky. The sun was above the mountains. Aaron walked out of the bed, away from the wall of the mountain. He moved to the edge and before him was a massive canyon.

The canyon stretched far, at least a mile. And it was overwhelmingly deep. The drop gave Aaron chills as he stood along the edge, looking over. It was beautiful, though. The stones changed color from dark grey, to blue, to a calm red. The sun reflected off the stones, adding to the beauty of the canyon. Its massiveness became more peaceful the longer Aaron stared at it.

From where Aaron and Madi first set foot on

the mountain, this canyon wasn't even visible. The fact that they had wandered around the mountain in the night, barley avoiding this, gave Aaron shivers. He glanced back at where they came from. If they had taken a few more steps, they would have both fallen over the edge. Aaron looked back at the campsite, realizing how near it was to the edge of the cliff. He laughed nervously because of how close they had come to dying.

Aaron looked at the canyon one more time. Taking it in and enjoying its beauty. Madi sauntered up behind him with the yellow blanket over her shoulders.

"Wow!" she exclaimed. "It's so beautiful! And it's huge. We were really close to it, too."

Aaron laughed and agreed.

"What time is it?" asked Madi.

Remembering what caused him to spring up in the first place, Aaron looked up at the sun. It shined bright as it climbed above the mountains.

"Almost seven-thirty!" he shouted.

Aaron hurried back to the campsite and began to pack things up quickly.

"I feel like I got so much sleep, though,"

Madi said.

Aaron stopped packing for a minute. He turned back to Madi and asked, "How much sleep do Earthlings normally need?"

"Between six and nine hours."

"That's crazy! Upitarians only need around half an hour, maybe an hour if they're really tired. And that's what I don't understand; I slept for about three hours as well. When we fell asleep it was about four in the morning."

"Half an hour?" Madi shouted. "I could get so much done if I had that kind of time!" Madi began to help pack and said, "Aaron, not to be mean, but—your people seem kind of behind, don't you think?"

Aaron finished folding the last of Madi's blankets and stuffed it in his bag. "Yeah," he laughed. "We are. But, unfortunately, that's how they like it. Well, most of them. I don't, really."

"What do you mean?"

"Well, my people enjoy keeping things simple. They like the world they live in and are still discovering new things about it to this day. The creatures of this world are also different from the creatures of Earth, and our people tend to take pleasure in discovering them at a slower rate. Things are just much more simplified here. And I guess there's nothing wrong with that, but I would just like to see some new stuff—some lights, technology, some advancements, you know?"

"Yeah, I understand. I mean, it does seem basic and peaceful here; it's only about survival and keeping everyone safe and then enjoying each other's company, right?"

"Yeah, that is true. I think since we all see the Earthling world, we notice the consequences that come with the advancements. I guess none of my people are ready to take the risks of progress. Well, and the fact that my father doesn't want to, plays a big role in it. He doesn't like the Earthlings," Aaron said sorrowfully as he looked down at the ground below him. "But I, personally, would be all for some progress."

"Why doesn't your father like us?"

"It was rumored—but never been confirmed true—that the people of Earth and the people of Upitar tried to become allies long ago. But when we came to Earth, we were captured and the Earthlings tried to harness our gift of water traveling. One man apparently escaped and ran to the nearest pool of water. He made it back to Upitar and told the King everything that had happened to him and his companions. The King sent in a rescue team, but when they came to where they were being held captive, they found all of the others had been killed.

"The team burned down the place and brought back the bodies of the men. They were cast off in coffins into a lake not far from the kingdom, called Lake Blairora. The coffins sank shortly after they were cast off due to their design, and it's said that they have rested at the bottom of the lake ever since. Nobody has ever been able to swim all the way to the bottom, though, to see if the legend is true. I don't know if it is or not, but my father has believed it his entire life. Also, when he was a boy first learning to water travel, he got lost on Earth for a night. He was taunted and beaten in a city by thugs. He believes all Earthlings are similar to the people who hurt him and the people who captured our ancestors, so he holds a grudge—and fear, too, I think—against the people of Earth ever since. He doesn't want war, though; he just wants nothing to do with them."

"That's awful. Not everyone is like that. Those were thugs, reckless criminals who did that, and even if what happened to your ancestors did happen, people are different now."

"I know, I know. But my father is consumed by it. When you let your life be controlled by a grudge, you go nowhere except in the circle it decides, causing you to miss out on everything else life has to offer," Aaron said. "I've tried to tell my father that, but he won't listen. When I become King, I will again seek to make peace with Earth and not keep them excluded from us."

"Some people are just stubborn. But maybe I can change his mind before someone who doesn't even want to be king, has this stress to deal with as king, " Madi said with a smile.

"Maybe." Aaron laughed.

They resumed packing until all that was left was the magic blanket. Aaron picked up one side and Madi happily picked up the other, without Aaron even saying anything. She did the best she could to hold the edges of the blanket with her one movable hand.

They danced, folding the blanket together. The tips of their fingers ran across each other with their palms holding the blanket in place.

Aaron moved to one end of the blanket and Madi the other, with both of them still holding the first fold. They walked the second fold in, and then the third. The blanket shrank as they folded it until Aaron could finish folding it by himself.

They watched the blanket in amazement as Aaron folded it. It shrank and compressed until it reached the original size—no bigger than the palm of his hand. He picked up the bag and tossed it in, ending the job.

"That's remarkable!"

"Yeah, it really is." Aaron still didn't understand it himself. He shrugged. "Magic, I guess."

Aaron threw his bag over his shoulders and walked to the edge of the mountain. He peered off the cliff and looked around.

"You ready?" he asked, looking back at Madi.

Madi confirmed and they continued to scale down the mountain.

The farther down they went, the more available foot space disappeared, until they came to the point of being cautious with every step. They were not completely leaning against the wall yet, but it was coming close to it.

"Aaron."

Aaron didn't hear her, but continued to walk with extreme caution.

"Aaron," she said again, breaking his focus.

Aaron turned his head sharply to hear her.

"We're going to run out of room," Madi said.

Aaron glanced ahead, trying to see if the walking space increased. Not seeing anything better, but not wanting to give up, he said, "Just a little bit more. We'll go as far as we can."

"Okay," Madi said softly, beginning to sound worried.

They eventually had to lean against the mountain for support. Aaron held his head high, not wanting to look at the intimidating view below them as they continued to place their feet carefully. Madi followed until Aaron lost his footing and breathed heavily against the wall. No stones had fallen, and nothing had flown past him.

"We're out of room." Aaron looked at his feet again.

The next step was a drop-off that looked as though it plummeted to the bottom of the canyon. Aaron was about to give up when he noticed the path continued a little less than a jump away. On the other side of the jump, there was more land with a tunnel that looked like it ran into the mountain.

"We made it!" Aaron proclaimed.

"What do mean?"

"Shimmy over to me!"

Madi did so, and when she reached him, she saw the jump and the entrance. With fear in her voice, she said, "I don't think I can jump that far, Aaron."

"Yes you can. I know you can. I'll go first, and when I make it, I can grab you if you come up short," Aaron said, trying to reassure Madi.

"Aaron—"

"I'll go first." Aaron backed up the best he could and prepared to jump.

"Aaron, no, plea—"

"I'll be fine. You'll be fine. Trust me."

"Aaron, I only have one arm to grab on

with!"

"And I promise I won't let that one arm go. Trust me."

Aaron gave Madi a wink, as if it might help her worry less. Stepping close to the edge, Aaron tensed his muscles and leaped. His body glided through midair. He came down, only clipping the edge of the cliff with his two hands.

"Aaron!" Madi gasped in fear.

Aaron pulled himself up and stood on what little ledge was available before the entrance to the mountain.

"See, no problem at all." Aaron smirked.

"No problem? No problem, Aaron, you almost died!" Madi yelled, sounding worried and afraid.

"Madi." Aaron looked directly into her eyes. "I will catch you. I will jump down this mountain with you if I don't."

Madi closed her mouth and swallowed in the dry air. She breathed in and tensed her muscles as she stood along the edge. Giving it all she had, Madi launched herself across the gap. Aaron eyed her the entire time — where she was, where her hands were — it looked like she was going to make it.

Suddenly, Aaron noticed she was going to come up short. He extended his arms over the edge for her to take hold of. His heart paused. He knew he had to grab her hand. Her fingers stretched out and spread apart toward him. Like the clap of hands, he caught hers.

Madi didn't scream, but only breathed heavily as she hung over the edge.

"See?" Aaron said with a smile.

"Just bring me up, Aaron," Madi cried, looking down at her death.

"I'm sorry I made you jump."

Aaron began to lift her up onto the edge of the cliff. Halfway up, he heard and felt a large crack behind him. The piece Aaron was kneeling on broke.

The stone ledge tilted and dropped Aaron, along with Madi. Aaron thought frantically, remembering every detail he saw as he fell over. He looked for something to grab — anything to hold on to. There was nothing.

Aaron and Madi fell over the edge. Their backs slid along the ridged mountainside. The armor Madi wore held up against the clawing rocks, but Aaron's began to rip into shreds as they increased speed. The two barreled down the mountain.

Rocks and dust flew into their faces. Aaron felt his armor disintegrating and sharp pains of stones piercing his body. His flesh was cut open and stung as they slid along the mountainside.

They both quickly scanned for a way out, but saw nothing. He leaned back on his bag the best he could in order to keep his flesh off the stones, for the bag had not been broken yet. Aaron thought of the magic blanket. *Maybe it can protect us!*

Struggling to roll onto his side, he tried to open the bag. Before he could, he felt himself falling and then splashing into water. Holding his breath, he felt the rush of the current and stinging pain in his back. Aaron instinctively swam to the surface and thrust his head above the water.

He was in a cave with a gushing stream. Light shined down on him from a hole in the ceiling. He fought the water as he looked for Madi and land.

"Madi!"

Aaron saw a dry stone shore ahead of him that rose above the surface of the water and swam desperately to it.

Before he reached the shore, he saw Madi's arm flailing in the water. Turning away from his harbor, he swam against the current for Madi. The pain in his back diminished with his fear of Madi being swept away. Water splashed in his face, decreasing his visibility in the already dim cave.

Keeping his eyes open even with the water in them, he saw the current hurling Madi toward him. Aaron stretched out his hand instinctively, grabbing Madi's arm. He pulled her close and used his last burst of energy to swim to the shore. Reaching refuge, he slammed his free palm along the dry stone ground.

A few ridges in the rock allowed him to grip it securely. He lifted Madi onto the surface first and then dragged himself up. Lying on his stomach, he coughed water up from his lungs.

Madi lay on her back and began to cough as well. Aaron choked up more of the water and then tended to Madi. She rolled onto her side and continued to gasp for air. Aaron crouched down, trying to help in any way he could.

"Madi, I'm so sorry. I'm so sorry."

Madi finished her coughing, to his relief, and opened her eyes again.

"I should have never asked you to jump."

"You told me you'd catch me," she said, choking up some more water. "And you did."

Madi's positive humor gave Aaron a quick chuckle.

"I'm okay," she said, sitting up.

They regained their breath and began to look around.

"Where are we?" asked Madi.

Aaron looked around the empty cave. It was larger than he initially thought. The light shined on the violent river behind them, with some of its luminosity spilling onto the dry land where they stood.

"I...I don't know," Aaron replied.

The piece of land was connected to a wall that ran into the darkness of the mountain. Aaron opened his bag and pulled out his torch and lighting stones. The torch lit almost immediately.

"I guess we'll have to find out." Aaron

stepped along the dry ground. "Are you okay to keep going?"

"Has Mr. Adventure become afraid of taking risks now?" Madi said, taking a few steps ahead of him.

Aaron gave a wry smile and joined Madi.

She stood close to him as they continued into the darkness together. Madi took hold of his sleeve as they journeyed. The cave became narrow, and the noise of the water faded behind them.

"It's almost as though something carved this."

"You're right. It's rare that water makes these kinds of bumps on the walls." Aaron ran his hand along the tunnel.

The walls were like a series of endless hills connected to each other.

"Speaking of water, where do you think that river would have taken us?" Madi asked.

"That's a question I ask a lot, and I'm sure others do, too. The fact that every source of water leads to another place is on my mind a lot. But sometimes you have to know when to put your curiosity aside and remember what you're supposed to be doing."

"Well, I think when we're not trying to create peace and save our two worlds and all that stuff, we should find that out some time." Madi stopped, pointing at the ground. "Hey look! We're still going down!"

"We...are," Aaron said as he scanned the ground.

"Maybe we are do—" Madi was cut off by a howling noise. "What was that?"

He knelt down and drew his dagger. "I'm not sure," he said, gripping the hilt.

They continued, caution in every step. The howling noise came again, causing them both to freeze. Aaron held his torch out in front to see if he could make out anything in the distance.

"I...I'm not sure what it is," Aaron said as he continued to walk. "Stay behind me, Madi. Ice men are rumored to roam Mount Romeatir."

Madi clenched the back of Aaron's shoulder with her hand. Aaron still held the light out in front of him. There was another howl, quickly followed by another.

The closer they got, the louder and longer the

cries became. One last piercing howl echoed through the cave and didn't stop. Aaron gripped his dagger forcefully; ready to defend Madi from whatever came into their ring of light.

Chapter 25

The howl stopped. Aaron waved the torch in front of him one last time. He peered at what he could see from the small amount of light his torch provided. A gust blew down the tunnel. Aaron's hand shook because of the unexpected wind. He didn't see any figures, only a fuzzy blue that consumed the exit of the cave.

"That isn't a creature!" Aaron said, moving faster to the end of the tunnel.

Aaron began to jog. Madi looked past Aaron and saw the same thing he did.

"It's—it's a blizzard?" Aaron asked as he closed in on the exit.

They continued slowly now, knowing what awaited them at the end of the tunnel. Immediately outside was a hurricane of wind and snow. The blizzard made direct contact with the end of the tunnel—nothing else could be seen outside the exit. A howl came again and echoed down the cave.

"It's the wind," Aaron said, almost confused. "The wind runs along the rocks and creates the howling noise." He touched the frozen tunnel walls.

Aaron handed the torch to Madi. "Here, hold this for a minute."

Madi took the torch and watched Aaron. He slowly stuck his hand into the blizzard. The tips of his fingers gently entered the storm in front of them. He didn't feel anything harsh, only a peaceful breeze.

Aaron put his entire arm into the blizzard to see if anything felt different. Pulling it back out, he said in astonishment, "It's calm!"

"What do you mean?"

"Here, you try." Aaron took the torch from Madi and lifted her hand up to the storm.

He took her hand and stuck it into the blizzard and he could tell from her wide eyes that she too felt its gentleness.

"That's amazing!" Madi said, pulling her hand out of the wind.

"Madi, we have to be close. Come on!" Aaron proclaimed as he took her hand.

Aaron gently and cautiously took his first step into the storm. His foot touched icy ground, but he felt no overpowering wind or additional coldness. He took another step, putting his entire body into the blizzard.

He didn't tense or yank her quickly; he only tugged her hand gently, pulling her in as well. Madi fully entered the storm with Aaron and both still felt only a peaceful breeze running by.

"Aaron, can you hear me?"

"Yeah, perfectly fine!"

"How? How does this...?"

"Magic, I would guess."

Aaron and Madi continued to walk along the icy path with their hands intertwined. Aaron stopped abruptly but continued to pull Madi so she would come up along his side. When she did, Aaron knew she realized why he had stopped. They remained still, looking up.

They were in the center of the storm. The blizzard was swirling all around them—far in front, behind, above and below.

The path they were on continued to an ice structure in the shape of a dome. The most wondrous thing they saw, though, was what was in the center, swirling around the middle of the path.

A giant ring of water that was thicker looking

than blood flowed around the trail. The water was a deep blue color. Inside its spinning flow were white clots. The ring circled inside the center of the storm.

The size of the open space in the eye of the storm and the ring of water swirling around the long path were intimidating. They were massive and Aaron and Madi were but minnows in a pond with a giant fish.

"What is it?" Madi said, with a hint of fear in her voice.

"I'm not entirely sure, but I think I might know. I've only heard stories of this place, but no one's ever found it. Its existence has only been a rumor, a scientific guess. It's called the Reverse, the place where water travelers go when they miss-travel," Aaron said.

"You think those clots of white flowing around in the ring could be their souls?"

"They might be. I didn't even believe this place existed."

Aaron started moving again along the path. Madi followed. Looking at the bridge below them, they noticed it was only floating in the midst of the storm, with no support beams to hold it up. The ring of blood-like water circled overhead, around and below their feet, and then back up again. The magnitude of it was greater than anything Aaron had ever seen.

Stepping under the ring, Aaron got a chance to look directly up at it. It flowed with a mix of grace and violence, with the spots of white moving at different rates, sometimes surfacing. Aaron watched the water and the spots for a moment.

Are you in there?

Madi gawked at the ring as they stood in the center of its orbit. Breaking her connection with its beauty, she looked at Aaron, still lost in its cycle.

"You're thinking of your brother, aren't you?"

"He could be in there, Madi. Lost forever," Aaron said, not breaking focus with the ring.

Madi put her hand on Aaron's shoulder.

"Aaron, he might be, but you don't know that. If he is, we will find a way to get him out and bring him back. What happened is not your fault."

Aaron closed his eyes.

"There's something I have to tell you, Madi." Aaron turned, opening his eyes. He looked back and forth, but not at Madi.

"My brother didn't miss-travel by accident. I am the reason he's gone."

"Aaron, don't blame it on yourself," Madi pleaded.

"No, it is because of me. It was because of my pride, my jealousy, and my anger. My damn anger that I let blind and take control of me."

There was a pause before Aaron resumed. Tears formed in his eyes.

"My brother didn't miss-travel by accident, Madalyne. When we were young, we were in a pool of water we shouldn't have been in. My brother and I got into a fight in the pool and things turned violent. I knew my brother would water travel soon in an attempt to outsmart me. But when I saw him begin to, I — I grabbed his hand and pulled it above the water."

Tears fell down Aaron's face as he told the story.

"I killed him, Madi," he said, turning back to her. "I caused him to miss-travel! I deliberately held a part of his body out of the water! I killed him, Madi! Because of me, he's either dead or lost in something like that forever!" Aaron shouted as he gestured at the ring of water. "It wasn't his fault that he miss-traveled, it was mine!" Aaron screamed, confessing the truth — the story that no one had ever heard before. He fell to his knees and buried his head in his hands.

***

Madi backed away. She didn't take her eyes off Aaron as she slowly shook her head. Not lifting his head, he shouted, "My own blood, Madi! My jealousy of him becoming King and my loathing for him caused me to commit murder!"

Emotions Madi didn't want to feel hit her. She felt betrayed. The one thing — the one thing she thought was perfect, wasn't. She watched Aaron's head turn back and forth in his hands as tears fell onto the snowy ground below them.

He killed him.

She looked at Aaron.

He was so young.

His arms and knees were against the cold ground.

Still, it was a life.

He violently ran his hands through his hair.

But, as a child, did he really know?

His forehead was now pressing against the ice.

Children are different. But they still know. Would I have controlled myself? He couldn't have known — he couldn't have controlled his emotions at that age.

Aaron looked up at the swirling water around them. Madi backed up, still alarmed and in a state of uncertainty. Aaron didn't look at her, only at the water.

He has to live with this, daily, for the rest of his life.

Aaron was breathing heavily. "I'm sorry!" he shouted.

He did know. Even as a child, he knew.

"Samuel, I'm sorry!"

And he hates himself for it.

His head fell back to the ground, where it crashed onto his arms.

And he's...he's...

He continued to mourn, the world shut out.

He's different now, but still controlled by regret.

"Aaron." Madi spoke to him directly.

He didn't move.

"Aaron!" she shouted.

Aaron slowly lifted his head, his eyes still closed.

"If you wallow in your past and allow it to haunt your future, then how will you ever change anything? Your past is your past. If you don't forgive yourself, then the problem will never find the solution. Your brother might still be out there, and I will help you find him!" Madi said with every fiber of compassion in her being.

"Madi, you don't—"

"Aaron! The more you hold onto your past, the less you will be able to move on! I know this haunts you, but it doesn't have to, it shouldn't have to. You have done amazing things. You want to do what's right now, and your brother is out there somewhere." Madi knelt down next to him and put her arm around his back. "He has to be, and we will find him. Now, come on. Whether you want to or not, we're going to keep moving. I did not risk my life to stop this adventure here."

Madi lifted Aaron up. She wrapped her arms

around him and held him tightly. She didn't let go. Aaron, after several moments, put his arms around her. She squeezed him, not letting him move. Letting go, she turned away, ending the conversation.

Aaron didn't argue or become angry. He just remained silent, soaking in what Madi said. They continued, moving out from underneath the ring of water toward the small dome at the end of the path.

The dome was made completely of thick ice and nothing could be seen through it. Aaron and Madi walked up to it and entered through the archway that connected to the path. The space inside the dome had a blue light to it from the light reflecting through the ice.

The inside was large and empty. In the center was a stone statue of a grey lion. It looked frightening, with its mouth open as though it was roaring, with its cold, stone teeth clearly visible. It had a mane of stone that wrapped around its head and its tail, which extended in the form of an "S" with a small ball of hair facing upward at the end.

The lion stood on its hind legs, and its front paws faced out as if about to devour its prey. It was taller than the two of them, but not by a lot. Regardless, it caused an intimidating fear in both of them.

Chapter 26

Aaron studied the lion closely. It had one feature that stuck out more than others — its eyes. They weren't stone like everything else, but instead some kind of a blue jewel. When Aaron made eye contact with them, his connection with the eyes was hard to break.

Aaron didn't have to point the eyes out to Madi because she had already seen them. He finally broke contact and began to look around the lion, searching for something — something next, the next piece. They were in a giant dome, with only one way in. There was nothing else in the room.

"I don't get it," Aaron said, looking down, disheartened.

"What do you mean?" Madi said, breaking her own connection with the statue.

"Where do we go next? There's nothing else — no trail, no door, no pool of water, nothing. This can't be the end."

Madi looked around the room and seemed to realize what Aaron was saying. The dome was completely sealed except for the entrance.

"There's nothing here but this stone lion, and it's not even big enough to have a secret passage under its paws or anything. It's just sitting there, causing fear, because this is the end. There is nothing else," Aaron said softly in discouragement.

"There has to be something, Aaron; get hold of yourself. This isn't the you I climbed out the window with," Madi said, walking close to Aaron. "That you is funny, adventurous, smart, caring, and joyful, and he's always thinking of something, even when I think we aren't going to make it. And if you still want to try to save your brother and make me a water traveler and bring peace to our worlds, then you'll help me."

Aaron smiled, as if to say, "I'm not going to admit it, but you're right, and thank you."

Madi took one of Aaron's hands and pulled him back by the lion. "Now, come on, let's figure this out."

Aaron stepped to the front of the lion.

"Maybe its tail's a lever or something." Madi pushed on the tail. Nothing happened; it didn't even budge.

Aaron stared back into the eyes of the creature and watched the blue jewels. He felt something from them. He analyzed the lion: its features, its paws, its stance, its mane, its mouth. He knew he had seen it before. Aaron compounded everything he had taken in and searched the catacombs of his memory.

That's it! The kingdom! It's the statues along the wall!

This lion was identical to the one apart of the castle wall.

Aaron lifted both hands up to the palms of the lion, stretching up to be level with the lion's. He waited. Nothing happened. He waited some more, peering into the blue eyes of the lion. He stared deep into them.

Aaron removed his hands from the lion's paws. *Something's still not right.*

"Madi, come over here!"

When Madi came over to Aaron, he said, "Put your hands against the lion's palms."

"I can't," Madi said looking down at her casted arm.

"Madi, we're going to have to break the

cast."

"Is my arm going to be okay?"

"It might hurt a little bit, but Madi, this is the only thing I can think of. Along the kingdom wall is a statue of this same lion, and also the lion representing Earth. If this is the lion of Upitar, then someone from Earth has to connect with it."

"If you think it will work, then let's do it. I'll be okay."

Aaron took his bag off his shoulders and rummaged through it. He pulled out the magic rope and the rocks used for making fire.

Lighting the rope, he said, "You have to burn the cast off if you do it prematurely."

Madi didn't say anything, but only watched the fire and then looked at her arm.

"Taking it off won't hurt, but moving it will, okay?"

Madi nodded her head and held her breath.

Aaron started to burn off the cast. As it smoldered he calmly peeled and unraveled the skin-like material from her arm. Madi's lips pressed against each other as her arm became free.

"Easy. Breathe in and out, okay?" Aaron

said, quickly glancing at her eyes.

Madi groaned as Aaron reached her wrist.

"Just a little bit more," he said.

Madi cried out in pain as Aaron burned the cast off around her hand, except where her bone had come out.

"Okay, we're done. You okay? Can you move your arm?"

Aaron helped Madi as she slowly extended her arm.

"My arm's not bad, it's my hand that I don't know if I'll be able to open," Madi said, looking at her half-clenched fist.

"You only have to open it when you touch the palm of the lion."

"I know." She faced the lion.

She stretched her arms up to reach the paws. Aaron helped as she lifted her wounded arm.

"Now, just slowly open it," he said.

Madi let out a second cry of pain as she opened her hand. Her fingers only skimmed the bottom. She wasn't tall enough to line her hands up with the lion's paws.

"Don't push yourself."

"I'm okay, I almost have it."

Madi stretched her good hand up as far as she could and opened her wounded one wider. Then she felt something pulse through her veins. Something very strange—something she had never felt before—but it allowed her to stretch the way she needed.

Madi's hands fully reached the lion's paws. She leaned against them for balance, trying to relax her wounded hand. Her green eyes looked into the lion's blue eyes. All of a sudden, the ice dome around them began to melt rapidly. Turning into water, it spun around them and the lion.

"What's happening?" Madi shouted.

Aaron explained quickly. "It's just like the tale. On the wall of the kingdom there are two lion statues with water flowing around them. The lion of Upitar has blue eyes, and the lion of Earth has green eyes, like yours! I don't know what's happening now, though!"

The lion dissipated in the water. The mass of water flowing around them turned into misty green air and slowly transformed to fog.

"Very good, Aaron," said a voice from

outside the greenish fog.

The fog began to fade away as old vegetation became visible around them. They now stood on a circular platform made of dark, yellow stone with carvings etched into it. It was separated from the rest of the faded yellow stone ground by a small stream, only as thick as Aaron's fist, which wrapped around what they stood on. The platform was connected to a mountain by a walkway that appeared to be floating. A portion of the brown mountain's rock face was visible, with the rest covered in ancient forest. On all sides was nothing but open space and clouds.

The fog faded almost completely.

"But that doesn't mean she is the lion of Earth," chuckled the voice. "You do need an Earthling with green eyes in order for the magic to work, though, so, again, very good, Aaron."

Aaron and Madi looked around. Memories flashed through Aaron's head. He tried to block them out and focus on the voice.

"Who are you? And where are you?" Aaron demanded.

"Hmm. Someone's had a long journey,

haven't they?" the voice said.

Aaron stepped in front of Madi. He reached down and drew his dagger.

"Bahh haha! Put down your little sewing needle, Aaron, I'm not going to hurt you or Madalyne," the voice said humorously. "I mean, without me, you wouldn't even be here! You two were really… I mean, you were smart, but there were a few things you almost missed."

"Who are you?" Aaron boldly asked.

"Okay, okay, put the little thingy away. I don't want you to throw it in my eye or something."

"I won't throw it, but I'm not putting it away until I see you," Aaron compromised.

"You really are a wise one, aren't you? Very well. If that thing comes flying at me, though, I'm not going to be very happy."

Aaron held his dagger at the ready. A few feet in front of them appeared a man dressed in long yellow robes. He had a long bushy white beard with five beaded tassels running down each side of it. He held a wooden staff in his hand with a small blue sphere on top; white streaks ran through the sphere and down the staff.

Aaron backed into Madi, acting as a wall between her and the man.

"Who are you?"

"No need to be afraid, Aaron. You were looking for me, weren't you?"

Chapter 27

There was a brief pause. Aaron relaxed his muscles and eased his firm clutch on his dagger.

"You're the Keeper?" he said with a hint of joy.

"Call me Yerowslii. 'Keeper' makes me sound like some old legend — not that I'm not old, or a legend..." Yerowslii said. "But yes, I am the Keeper of the Orb of Upitar. Welcome, Aaron Archien, prince of the Kingdom of Upitar."

Aaron stepped away from Madi and to the man, feeling it was safe to approach him.

"And hello, Madalyne Harper, daughter of Michael Harper," Yerowslii said, lifting his chin and tilting his head so he could see her better.

"H — h — hel — lo," Madalyne stuttered, still seeming to recover from her fear.

"How do you know our names?" Aaron asked.

"Ohh, I have watched you two for quite some time now." He paused. "Why don't we go inside?" Yerowslii turned and waved for them to join him.

Aaron looked at Madi, who still seemed worried. She came up next to him for safety and they started to follow.

"Don't worry, I'll be on my guard," Aaron whispered into Madi's ear.

Yerowslii rolled his eyes as he heard them whispering.

They all stepped away from the platform, Yerowslii leading the way, with Aaron and Madi following at a safe distance behind. To their left was what seemed to be a stone barrier, which kept them from falling off the long, floating walkway they were on. On their right was the same thing, but with vegetation intertwined and tangled around the aged barrier.

The platform they set foot on had trees wrapping around its back like a crescent moon. The front connected to the pathway that led to the mountain. Behind the trees was a drop-off that led to sky. They walked to the mountain in the center, which had a large tunnel running through it. On the other side of the tunnel, it looked like a mirror image of the side they just came from.

They all moved through the tunnel, but

instead of coming out the other side, they came to two old wooden doors with horizontal metal handles. The doors were large and folded with the walls of the tunnel — they were bent, with a curve in their middles, not straight lines like most doors.

Yerowslii opened the left door for Aaron and Madi.

"Right this way," he said cheerfully.

Aaron and Madi entered the mountainside, Aaron leading. They walked up four wooden steps and found themselves in a home, a giant home inside the mountain.

A wooden post rested in the middle of it, seeming to hold the structure together. At the back of the room were five great windows, forming a bay that overlooked the entire land below the mountain, that is, what could be seen through the thick cloud cover. The windows formed 170-degree angles with each other, and the ones that connected to the walls formed 130-degree angles. On the other side of the post, to the left, was a staircase ascending into another part of the home.

The room was filled with dozens of tables with miscellaneous trinkets on them. Things swung up and down, some things with orbs, things attached to ropes, complex-looking schematics, numerous telescopes, vials, deciphering devices, mystical-looking disks with carvings and numbers on them, locks, wooden objects, sculptures that changed shape, and many more things that Aaron couldn't even begin to imagine their purposes.

The door closed behind them with Yerowslii saying, "Sorry for the mess. I haven't had guests in a few…Well, I guess you could say eleven years, technically, but that was completely unexpected."

Yerowslii came up the steps, passing Aaron and Madi, who were still trying to take in everything they saw.

"Something to drink? I have some very nice tea, made fresh from eruingia plants." Yerowslii crossed behind them and strolled into the kitchen.

"Uh, yeah, yes, please," Aaron stuttered.

"Alrighty. I'll grab some snacks, too; you both look a little hungry," Yerowslii said from the other side of the staircase.

Yerowslii pulled a lever with two orange painted rings around it. The part of the home where he stood—a square about fifteen square feet—

started to move. The entire structure — the floors, the walls, and everything that sat in that square — began to interchange. The house transformed, moving the square outside of the mountain.

The floorboards and walls were floating. Magically, the floorboards expanded in the direction of the rest of the home until they became one. The walls extended and reconnected, and the roof ascended at an angle to enclose the part of the house that moved, completing the reconnection process.

During all of it this, objects in the square also changed. An old ironing board poofed into a rack of pans, a furnace turned into a stove with a lit fire, and a hand water pump transformed into a sink.

The wood on the walls expanded inward and a china cabinet filled with plates inside appeared. Small gold strands ran along the glass door of the cabinet. The plates inside shook slightly during the transformation process, but became calm once it was done.

Yerowslii didn't react at all to the change of the home, but merely opened one of the cabinets in his newly-formed kitchen and pulled out a few tea bags. He looked back at the stove. It had one fire burning, but nothing over it.

"Hmm," he said, and pointed his finger at it.

A teakettle formed out of nowhere, with water inside. Yerowslii smiled and resumed rummaging through his cupboards.

"If you two want to go over there by the middle window, I'll meet you in a minute," Yerowslii yelled.

Aaron and Madi looked at each other and then wandered over to the middle window. The view was spectacular. Clouds rippled across the sky, and sometimes a small pocket allowed them to see the land below. All they could really make out was green, but they could still see it.

"Okay!" said Yerowslii, gliding over to them holding three cups of tea, two in one hand and one in the other.

He joined them by the window and whispered to himself, "Didn't think this one through, did I?" Yerowslii looked around. "Aaron, would you snap the fingers on your right hand for me? Mine are a little occupied."

"Um, yeah, sure," Aaron said, raising his

hand. Aaron snapped his fingers. Nothing happened.

"Oh come on, now, don't be rude," Yerowslii said to the house. "Try one more time, Aaron."

Aaron looked at Yerowslii and then at the house. He raised his hand and snapped his fingers. The square they were in began to move. The windows on the right and left of the middle window broke their connection easily. They opened up like two doors, allowing the square the three were standing on to travel away from the rest of the house. That section of the home now extended far out above the clouds, but still remained connected to the house through the floorboards, which stretched out into the sky with them.

Black metal railings with intricate patterns built themselves all the way around them. Beautiful flowers wrapped around the black rails as they formed. Chests on the platform turned to seats, and an old wooden table turned to a white stone outdoor dining table. The clutter on it vanished. The floorboards became grass and the two windows became one, forming a giant, square window.

Yerowslii set the cups of tea on the table and

extended his hand out at the rest of the home. Plates appeared out of thin air in his hand and, with his other hand, he set the table.

"Ah, I forgot the snacks!" Yerowslii said. "Please excuse me, I'll be right back. Have a seat, take in the view! I'll only be a moment!"

Yerowslii dashed back into the kitchen while Aaron and Madi took their seats around the table. Madi still held her arm in the bent position it was in when the cast was on it. Although the cast was off, it was still damaged and seemed to hurt her to move it.

The view was really stunning. They were not looking through a window now, but instead seeing everything around them clearly with nothing in between. Madi got up from her seat and went over to the rail. Leaning over it, she dipped her free hand in the soft clouds. Cupping her hand, she scooped pieces of the cloud as it moved along the sky. It was thick and remained misty even when taken from the rest of the flow.

"Don't fall," Yerowslii said, returning with the food.

The food looked like bread, but it was in the

shape of a spiral. Its crust was a complete layer of golden brown, flaking at the cracks. Aaron and Madi both peeled off a piece and took a bite.

"Better than what you thought, isn't it?" said Yerowslii when he saw their eyes widen. Aaron and Madi didn't expect bread to taste so good.

"Now, enjoy your food and I'll explain a few things." Yerowslii sat down and crossed his legs. He leaned his staff against the table and interlocked his fingers.

"Yes, I am the Keeper of the Orb of Upitar. As you know, my name is Yerowslii, and, as you have probably figured out already, I am a wizard. From my observatory, I am able to see millions of miles and across universes with my telescopes. That is how I have kept my eye on you two."

Aaron swallowed his second bite and took a sip of the soothing tea.

"I see you both are a little more at ease now, food always tends to do the trick," Yerowslii said. "So, you want to become a water traveler, now, do you, Madalyne?"

Madi looked at Yerowslii with raised eyebrows.

"The telescopes, remember?" Yerowslii said, answering her question.

Madi swallowed the unfinished piece of bread in her mouth and let out a "yes, sir" immediately after.

"Madalyne, you do not have to call me 'Sir,' or 'Mr. Wizard,' or 'O Great Water Ball Keeper.' Call me Yerowslii, or Yeros, or even Yellow. Whatever suits you best, really," Yerowslii said, trying to calm her more. She showed a small smile, trusting him a little more.

"Now, I haven't taught someone in over two thousand years, but we'll see."

"Two thousand years?" Aaron asked, perplexed. "How have you even been around for two thousand years?"

"Actually, I've been around for three thousand, two hundred, and eighty-seven years. Or maybe three thousand, two hundred and eighty-eight? Or nine? When you get to be my age, it doesn't really matter." Yerowslii chuckled.

"To answer your question, though, it's the orb. As long as the orb is here, I am here. I was linked with it at a young age, when I became the

Keeper, and it is what keeps me alive. That is, I am safe from death by natural causes, such as sickness and old age. I am still vulnerable to things such as swords, or being squished by a boulder. Luckily, I have been able to hold my own against the tangible things of this world," Yerowslii explained.

"You don't look that age," Madi said.

"Well, what is one who is over three thousand years old supposed to look like? We all stop growing after a while, you know." Yerowslii took a sip of his tea and then shook his head. "I forgot I brewed eruingia plants; not the taste I was expecting." He blinked his eyes a couple of times. "Now, back to the matter at hand. Tomorrow we will go to the Orb of Upitar, and I will do everything in my power to give you the gift. Nightfall is dawning on us, though. I have prepared two guest bedrooms for you to stay the night." Yerowslii stood up from the table and collected the teacups.

Looking around, they found the wizard was right. The sky had turned to an orange-pink as the sun began to set off in the distance. Aaron and Madi stood from their seats as well and followed

Yerowslii back into the house. The platform they were on retracted and the house turned back to its original state — windows intact, tables as normal, and the objects throughout the house how they were when Aaron and Madi first saw them.

"Right this way," Yerowslii said, leading them to and up the staircase.

The second floor had a hallway made of wood like the rest of the home, which extended to the right and the left. The left side was shorter, but they could see that the hallway made a right turn around a corner.

At the top of the stairs and just to the right, on the left side of the hall, was the first door. The door was normal this time, not like the two main doors at the entrance in the tunnel.

Yerowslii turned the clear crystal knob of the door and opened it. The room was clean and organized, with not a speck of dust. Yerowslii held the door open for them to walk in. The lighting in the room was fading due to the decreasing sunlight.

Yerowslii tilted his staff toward a candle that rested on a wooden dresser on the right side of the room. The candle lit instantly and the room filled with a dim light.

A decent sized bed with a blue and white patterned quilt rested on the left side of the room. A casement window was opposite from the door. The room looked well-kept, but also old. The blanket's patterns and shades were ones Aaron didn't recognize at all. Aaron ambled over to the wooden desk and ran his figure across its smooth wood surface. He had never felt this particular wood before, either. The room was like a forgotten world to him. It was so old, and had many things he had never seen before; so many things that may have not even come from Upitar.

"Now come along, Madalyne, your room's down here," Yerowslii said, waving Madi out of Aaron's room.

Aaron followed behind Madi and Yerowslii. Not far down the hall, to the right, was another door. Yerowslii opened the door and it was like that of the first, except for its state of cleanliness.

Mounds of dust fluttered into the air from the whoosh of the opening door. Madi sneezed.

"I guess the room hasn't been dusted in a while." Yerowslii stroked his white beard. "Hmm.

No problem."

The wizard lifted his staff out and away from his body. The dust rose into the air from the bed, the dresser, the window, even the walls and ceilings. It then flew into the sphere on the staff Yerowslii held.

"All clean." He smiled.

"Now, if you need anything, my room is down the hall and to the right. Don't be afraid to wake me," Yerowslii said, exiting the room.

Aaron waved to Madi and said, "I'll drop your stuff off in a couple minutes once I get it all unpacked."

Closing the door, Yerowslii said, "Good night."

Yerowslii and Aaron walked back down the hall, where Aaron's door was still open. Yerowslii stopped at the threshold and turned to Aaron.

"Aaron, would you care to join me for a walk?"

Chapter 28

Aaron didn't know what the wizard meant by going for a walk, but the option to say no didn't seem available. Not that Aaron wanted to say no. He wanted to talk to the Keeper; he wanted to learn some of the oldest secrets and the answers to his questions.

"Sure," Aaron said.

"Come with me." Yerowslii tilted his head, indicating that Aaron should follow.

They walked down the stairs and out the front door, with Yerowslii closing the main doors behind them quietly as if he thought someone was already sleeping.

"Do you remember this place?" he asked Aaron.

"I...don't know. It seems familiar."

"Maybe a little stroll will jog your memory, then," Yerowslii said, grinning and gesturing for Aaron to walk beside him.

Aaron and the wizard walked side by side down the tunnel, this time in the opposite direction of the platform.

"You have indeed been here before. Quite some time ago that was," Yerowslii said.

"Things do look familiar, but it's more of the atmosphere that I remember, I think."

They reached the end of the mountain tunnel and stepped into the open air again. This side was exactly the same as the previous side, with a railing-like stone wall, a few worn trees, and aged vegetation. The only thing different was the platform. Instead of a large yellow stone tablet, there was a pool of water. Just a small, circular pool of water.

The two reached the pool and Yerowslii said, "Now, turn around."

Aaron spun and everything made sense. This pool of water connected to the one in the catacombs of the castle. The one he encountered when he was a boy and Samuel and he snuck into the chamber and found the sacred pool. The long tunnel was the same dark and horrifying tunnel he had seen a creature coming through.

"Do you remember this place now?"

"Yes! Are you the monster I was afraid of?

The one that came and looked at me in the water?"

"Yes, that was me," Yerowslii said. "I was coming to greet you, and then you water traveled."

Yerowslii turned back to the pool of water and sat on its edge, dipping his feet in the coolness. Aaron did the same, realizing he was sitting across from one of his childhood fears. Aaron relaxed in the cool water, finally knowing what he saw.

"That's when everything turned sour, and I talked to my first visitors in a long time. Your father and Ugine." Yerowslii began to tell the story. "They rushed out of this very same pool of water. Your father was speaking gibberish because of his fear. Ugine had to explain what had happed to your brother. I said I saw nothing besides you, and the only real explanation was that he miss-traveled."

Aaron looked down at his reflection in the rippling water. The moonlight glowed a clean blue color, which meant all of the moons were up. He didn't want to think of his past.

"So, was Madi right about finding this place?" Aaron said, looking for complete clarification and a chance to change the subject.

"Yes, she was. Partially. The magic to the

mountain is, yes, that one must travel down the mountain in order to go up it, and one must travel up it in order to go down it." Yerowslii moved his feet slowly in the water. "But you would have not made it here if it wasn't for me." He lifted his chin and looked up into the sky.

"And what is that supposed to mean?" Aaron leaned forward.

"Oh, what? You thought that the cliff you were on just happened to break, causing you to go sliding down the mountainside and into a secret cave? In all honesty, it was a sturdy cliff. Travelers like yourself think the jump is their last challenge before making it to the end. But, you see, no one has ever found out that you're supposed to fail the jump. They all have successfully made it and took the cave. The cave leads nowhere, in case you were wondering," Yerowslii said. "It just goes back to the start of the mountain path."

"Wait. So you mean you had a part in that?"

"Would blasting the side of the mountain with a little magic count as having a part in it?" Yerowslii chuckled. "And the same with Madalyne. She wasn't tall enough to reach the paws of the lion, even stretching as much as she could! I had to work a little magic there, too, to give her a little extra boost."

Aaron was baffled at hearing this. "What else have you done?" he asked, thinking through his life.

"Oh, just those two things, I think. I don't really leave the mountain anymore. I've just become content with enjoying the beauties of the world around me. There's so many of them, you know. If you just take a moment to stop and look around, the world will open itself up to you."

Aaron took a moment to look around him. He looked in the pool of water, thinking of home, and then Samuel, and then Madi. A thought came to him.

"Did you play a part in pushing me to go back to Madi when I first met her, or after I told her I was a water traveler?"

"No, I did not. But I can tell you the orb probably did."

"The orb?"

"You see, Aaron, the orbs are alive. They're not just magic spheres with water, they're beings. They have minds of their own, and often times they speak to us, giving their input on things without us even knowing."

"So the orb is what I felt telling me to go back."

"I would not be surprised. It must have known you would be the only way to stop Madalyne from fulfilling the prophesy. You trusting her must have been the key to changing the fate of our worlds."

"Do you think the waterways are safe now because of us?"

"I believe they are."

"How do you know? Can you hear the orb?"

"Sometimes. When it speaks to me. But there's another reason I believe them to be safe."

"What's that?"

"I was the one who made the prophecy long ago. The orb revealed it to me and I traced the bloodline all the way ahead to Madalyne. That is how the map to her existed."

"So, we're safe?"

"Yes, but Madalyne still must become a water traveler if you want to prove it to your father."

"Will he listen if she is one?"

"I do not know. I cannot read minds, nor can the orbs. Aaron, you should know something." He paused. "Your father has grown different. He has a dark side. I took notice of it long ago."

"Because of Samuel?"

"Because of Samuel, but also because of your mother."

Aaron hadn't thought of his mother in years. She disappeared when he was only two, so his memory of her was scattered. Yerowslii looked at Aaron and tilted his head. He seemed to notice the lack of understanding in Aaron's face.

"Do you know what happened to your mother, Aaron?"

"She miss-traveled, didn't she?"

Yerowslii looked at Aaron with soft eyes and then closed them. He took a breath and answered, "No, Aaron. Your father only told you that to keep you from being afraid, or from looking for her."

"What happened to her, then?" Aaron asked in shock.

"She was taken captive by a creature called the Rashikaa. A pet to a deadly hunter on Senapin."

Samuel was right. "My brother used to tell me stories like that. I thought he was just trying to scare me," Aaron said, completely baffled.

"He spoke the truth."

"Is she alive?" Aaron desperately asked.

"I do not know, Aaron."

"Do you know why she was taken?"

"No. I only saw the creature strike and take her. It appeared on Upitar and returned to Senapin in a matter of moments."

"What did my father do?"

"Your father sought my wisdom. That's when his I first took notice of his corruptive traits."

"What did you tell him?"

"He wanted to hunt the beast, but didn't know how to track it or how it came to Upitar. He wanted me to use my power to create secret pools to Senapin. I said even if I could do that, I would not. It would put him and the entire world of Upitar in danger."

"There's a river in the catacombs of the kingdom!"

"I know of it, Aaron." Yerowslii extended his hand for Aaron to relax. "I helped create it. But I

could not destroy it. I only could block the water so
the river would no longer exist."

"How did you block it?" Aaron asked.

"With a powerful spell."

"Can it be broken?"

"Only by another Keeper."

"One like you?" Aaron said, looking at
Yerowslii.

"Yes."

"Are all of the Keepers wizards?"

"Wizards or Sorceresses. It's very rare that
one is not one. It's only happened once."

"How many Keepers are there?"

"Fourteen—one for every orb. Well, thirteen,
now, actually," Yerowslii said looking at his
reflection in the water.

"What happened to the fourteenth?"

"The fourteenth Keeper was the Keeper of
Earth. He was killed."

"By who?"

"Earthlings," Yerowslii said, beginning to tell
the story. "Torath was the Keeper of Earth. He was
a wise and peaceful man—a good friend of mine,
too. The orb rested far above the Himalayan

Mountains on a floating peak, like this one. It was a small peak, though, with just a pool and an ancient pavilion where the orb stood. The mountain's magic was very clever. A layer of clouds circulated around the floating peak, hiding the orb. If anything flew through it, it merely came out the other side, not seeing anything. But near the base of the Himalayas where his home was, Torath decided to meet a group of villagers he had never seen before. Torath didn't desire to harm them, he actually wanted to befriend them. While he was traveling to greet them, he came past a dying Himalayan marten—cute little creatures. It broke his heart to see the animal dying, so he used some of his magic to heal its wounds. While his back was turned five armed villagers approached him. They called him a sorcerer but he didn't notice them. Before he stood up, three spears pierced his body. One of the men took his staff and broke it. The men continued to spear him to death before he could escape. I know he could have killed those men before they killed him, but Torath chose not to. I would not have been so merciful."

"Did you see all of this through your

telescope?"

"Yes. After the first spear was thrown, it was too late for me to rescue him. By time I got there, they had taken his body and burned it."

"That's...awful," Aaron said, not knowing how to respond.

"It hurt deeply to lose my friend."

"I'm sorry, Yerowslii... What happened to the orb?"

"The orb still remains resting in its home, waiting for a new Keeper. But it no longer stays above the Himalayas. It travels all over the Earth in order to remain safe."

"When will the new Keeper come?"

"Soon, I would say. Some of the other Keepers and myself have been watching whom we believe it to be for some time now. We're just waiting for a few more things to happen before we know it's him for sure. Every orb needs a Keeper, though, otherwise it will die over time."

"Even the Orb of Senapin?"

"Yes. Even the Orb of Senapin, Aaron."

"Yerowslii, what do you know of Senapin?"

"Little, anymore. I wish I could tell you more

about Senapin, but I can no longer see it. I haven't been able to for many years. The world of Senapin disappeared from sight. Where it used to be it is no longer. I cannot see it with any of my telescopes, no matter how powerful their magic. I know it still exists…but, Aaron, it is dangerous. The dark magic within Senapin is powerful and the Keeper is not to be trifled with."

"Who is he?"

"Herrathos, a ruthless magic user. He is evil, Aaron, immensely evil. I fear he will show himself again one day, but when that time comes, I will not be able to stop him. I feel his presence constantly growing stronger."

"Can you stop him now?"

"Not on Senapin. He is far too powerful there. And it would be unwise for me to leave the Orb of Upitar during this time."

"So how do we stop him?"

"By keeping the orbs safe. They are what he's after, and without them, he will not be able to do what he desires."

"What is that?"

"I do not know, Aaron. But the other Keepers

and I will handle that, you must focus your attention on the matter at hand. Your father is expecting you to return with Madalyne any day now. And it is more important at this time to create peace within our world, and maybe even between Upitar and Earth."

Aaron did the best he could to put Senapin out of his mind, but it still haunted him. Facing his father worried him more, though. Aaron looked in the small pool at the clear water that splashed around his feet. Flashbacks of the kingdom and his father and his brother all traveled through his head.

Aaron quickly backed away from the water, splashing Yerowslii with his feet as he exited.

"What's the matter?" asked Yerowslii.

"You said this was the same pool that I came through as boy, which means my father could come through it any moment and find Madalyne!"

"Oh, calm down, Aaron. That's an irrational thought, why would he come here? And besides, this may be the same pool, but I destroyed the connection between the two pools... It was too dangerous."

"What do you mean? How did you destroy

it?" Aaron asked, scooting back over to the pool.

"It just wasn't safe for your father to have such easy access to the orb. Your father has many secrets, Aaron; many I don't even know. He has a great amount of evil somewhere in him. The orb wasn't safe." Yerowslii stroked his long beard.

"What do mean?"

"I've only noticed it in him, Aaron. I know little about it, not even where it came from. Just be on your guard."

Aaron didn't respond. He had noticed things changing in his father but he thought it was just because of stress from being king.

"And the orb in my staff is linked with the Orb of Upitar. I have the ability to destroy or create waterways how I choose, most waterways. The one in the catacombs was created by more than one Keeper, five of us, actually. And it will take at least five to destroy. Every body of water that is eligible for water traveling must be linked somewhere. As for this one, it is linked elsewhere now. I've only had to adjust the waterways a few times, like when the kingdom was built. It's difficult to design specific links between Earth and Upitar — or any world without the help of two or more Keepers, that is — but it can be done. On the other hand, adding waterways that stay in Upitar — the ones where you water travel and just appear somewhere else on Upitar — are simple. All I need is a drop of untouched water."

Aaron took his feet out of the pool of water and walked over to the edge of the platform. He looked over at the clouds and said, "There's so much I don't know about."

Yerowslii laughed. "Me too, Aaron, me too...And you're never going to know everything while you're alive."

The wind blew, tossing Aaron's hair around.

"Careful now, you don't want to fall over the edge. I can't fly."

Aaron turned around with a small smirk on his face.

"Do you know what's at the bottom of this mountain?" the wizard asked.

"Umm...the ground?" Aaron responded, confused by the question.

"Well, yes." Yerowslii laughed while rolling his eyes. "But it's certainly not as close as it appears.

The ground you're seeing through the clouds is really a greater distance than you can see with your eye. This mountain is actually floating."

Aaron was shocked. He looked over the edge, trying to see if he could see the end of the mountain as it floated over the ground. He turned back to Yerowslii, saying, "What do you mean it's floating?"

"This mountain is a floating mountain. It floats above Mount Romeatir. It's still called Mount Romeatir, but its official name is The Floating Top of Mount Romeatir. That's why no one can find it. Even if one flew on a harom to the visible top, the real top floats far above the clouds. The portal is the only way to reach it, unless one flew far past the clouds or used some kind of magic."

"Then what am I seeing as the ground?"

"The clouds perform a mirage. They amplify the land below so we can see it all the way up here. The clouds act as another form of defense in hiding the orb. In amplifying the ground, they also cast the mountain far out of physical sight, and that of most telescopes. In fact, the clouds work like a telescope. Looking through our end, an object is maximized.

But looking through the other end, an object is minimized and looks farther away than it really is. It's quite amazing, and I haven't entirely figured out how it works myself yet."

"Wow," Aaron said, gawking over the edge of the platform.

Yerowslii laughed and continued to soak his feet in the water. Aaron returned back to the pool. Off in the distance, a howling noise in the wind was heard.

Yerowslii lifted his right eyebrow when he heard the noise. Aaron began to talk as he sat.

"Quiet," Yerowslii ordered.

Aaron stopped as Yerowslii turned his ear to the sound. The noise came again over the mountain.

Chapter 29

Yerowslii arose out of the pool quickly. Gripping his staff, he peered at the end of the tunnel, the side of the mountain, and then over the edge of the platform. Seeing nothing, he looked to the top of the mountain and down its back. Scanning the back of the mountain, the Keeper saw movement in the trees.

"What's wrong?" Aaron asked, sounding afraid.

The noise came again and Yerowslii snapped immediately to its direction. It was a howl, like that of the wind, but it had more tone to it — a voice.

"Come quickly!" Yerowslii said grabbing Aaron's wrist and dashing to the door of his home.

The howl was heard again, with different pitches and levels. Yerowslii turned his head back and forth quickly and then said, "Inside."

They entered the home and Yerowslii bolted the door behind them.

"What's going on?"

"Snow shadows." Yerowslii rushed over to

his windows.

The wizard swung his staff across all the glass. Fog covered them completely. "This doesn't make sense," he muttered.

Yerowslii came close to Aaron and said, "Now—"

Before he could finish, a cry came from upstairs. It was Madi.

Both Yerowslii and Aaron's eyes stopped moving. They turned immediately and bolted up the stairs. Crashing open the door, Yerowslii rushed into the room with his staff in hand. As soon as the door opened, the frozen tail of a creature swung down at him. The Keeper wrapped the tail around his staff almost immediately and pulled it close to him. The tail was long and stretched to the other end of the room, where Madi lay on her bed. Standing over her was a creature that didn't seem to have an entirely defined shape. It was frosty looking, like ice, and its body fluctuated. It had two large horns on its head and an open mouth with sharp icicles for teeth.

Its stormy body was standing on what appeared to be four legs. The window was broken open and cold air rushed through it. Yerowslii and Aaron were in the room on the opposite side of Madi. The wizard clenched his staff aggressively, the tail of the creature still wrapped around it.

The snow shadow was about to sink its frozen fangs into Madi when Yerowslii whispered a spell under his breath. He yanked his staff, pulling the creature by the tail. The snow shadow's hind legs were dragged from the bed. It clawed viciously for Madi as she scrambled against the wall of the bed. The sound of wind blew violently from its mouth as it hungered for her.

Yerowslii let out a loud yell. He yanked the creature again, this time completely away from the bed. It turned at the wizard and let out a stormy howl.

"You're in the wrong parts, snow shadow!" Yerowslii yelled.

The creature lunged for Yerowslii with its frosty mouth open. The wizard swung at the side of its head. He knocked it up against the wall and spontaneously pointed his staff at the creature. A fireball unleashed from the staff's tip.

The flaming ball hit the creature and turned

its frozen form into a puddle of water. Yerowslii delivered another fireball. The creature evaporated. It was dead.

"Check on Madalyne!" Yerowslii ordered as he rushed over to the broken window.

"Are you okay?"

"Yeah, I'm fine." Madi tried to catch her breath.

"There are more coming," Yerowslii said, turning to them.

"What are they?" Aaron asked.

"Snow shadows! They're trained killers that live deep in the Humaris Mountains," Yerowslii said as he checked on Madalyne.

"Listen. Downstairs behind the staircase is a chest. Push it aside and you'll see a hatch. Lift the hatch — it's where I keep my swords. I have a sword in there that's enchanted from the outer rim world of Yarif. The handle is red — you can't miss it. It's the only sword I have that can strike and kill these creatures. What I need you to do is go to the furnace and put as much heat into it as you can. It's powered by magic, so you'll be fine. You've been in my house long enough for it to like you," Yerowslii said, standing up.

"But wha—" Aaron was cut off by Yerowslii.

"The house needs to be heated up to ward off the snow shadows. They won't be able to enter if it's over one hundred degrees. I'll fight them off as long as I can, but you must get the house heated."

"Why don't I fight them and you heat it? We don't know how!" Aaron yelled.

"Because I'm the only one who can draw them all away from the house. Now listen! The furnace will know what you want! Just—"

Before Yerowslii could finish, another snow shadow jumped through the window.

Yerowslii spun and blocked its jaws with his staff. He twisted it sharply, spinning the creature onto its icy back. Yerowslii yanked his staff out of its teeth, breaking some of the icicles. He drove the bottom of the rod into its icy head. The bottom of his staff ruptured, causing the snow shadow to incinerate.

"Go!" The Keeper shouted as he ran and jumped out the window.

The window shut and locked behind him, then filled with fog. Yerowslii rolled onto his roof and checked his surroundings. He turned and jumped up the side of the mountain until he reached the top. There was a large slanted ridge down the back of the mountain, with only a few trees scattered about until it reached the bottom, then it thickened with brush. The farther down the back of the mountain, the more trees there were. Yerowslii looked off in the distance and saw shaking within them.

Bursting through came a pack of about twenty snow shadows. Yerowslii lifted his staff into the sky and a large flash of light came from its tip. The staff glowed vibrantly for a moment. He saw that from the edges of the mountain near the house, some of the snow shadows rerouted and started to run to him.

"It's been a while, hasn't it?" the Keeper said to himself.

Five leaders of the pack pulled ahead of the rest. Yerowslii aimed his staff and released blasts of fire. He knocked down and finished off three of the shadows. The other two evaded and rapidly reached him.

One dove overhead, while the other went for

his ankles. Yerowslii allowed the one jumping to bite his staff. Swinging it downward, he swooped it into the other shadow. That sent the two creatures tumbling along the mountain only to be finished by a consuming inferno.

The rest of the pack surrounded him and, instead of striking, immediately rendezvoused. Yerowslii watched the pack circle him savagely. The wizard struck his staff against the ground and a ring of fire came to his defense.

"Come and join me," he whispered.

Three of the snow shadows pounced at him. Yerowslii twirled his staff—first in front of himself, bashing one. Around his back, striking another. Ducking, one flew above him, but was followed by a fireball. The first two were knocked into the ring of fire and evaporated.

Five more dashed toward him. The first was nailed on the top of the head. Yerowslii then rammed the butt of his staff behind him directly into the mouth of another. Two more leapt for his back, and a rupture came from the bottom of his staff, destroying all three.

The fifth shadow leapt from the flames at his

side. Yerowslii parried the fangs of the creature with his staff. The snow shadow held onto the middle of the staff as Yerowslii held it horizontal. With great effort, the Keeper spun while twisting the staff, sending the snow shadow into the blazing fire on its back.

***

Aaron and Madi made it to the bottom of the stairs. Stumbling over to the chest, they tossed it aside, opened the hatch, and scanned the eight swords that rested on a rack in the compartment. Aaron frantically wrapped his hands around the hilts of the swords to see if he could tell which was correct. He knew he had the right one when the hilt glowed red and then returned to normal when he grabbed it.

"Come on!" he said, pulling the sword out of the compartment and running over to the furnace.

Madi stayed close to Aaron. She tried to stay behind him in order to protect herself.

"Okay, he said it would just work, didn't he?" asked Aaron in a hurry as he looked at the furnace.

"I don't know! He said we would figure it out!" Madi said, confused.

A pounding came against the door. They looked at the entrance.

"Okay, you're going to have to try to figure it out," Aaron said as nicely as he could as he got ready to defend them both.

The pounding came again. Then again. The door snapped against the side of the wall. The locks flew across the room and bloodthirsty howls followed.

A snow shadow bolted up the stairs with its paws sliding across the wooden floor. It saw and directed itself toward Aaron. He charged at the creature as it pounced at him. Taking it head on, Aaron swung the sword at its jaw.

He brutally struck the creature and it fell against the floor. Aaron drove the sword through the shadow as it laid wounded along the floorboards. The blade of the sword flared, causing the snow shadow to evaporate from the brief moment of intense heat. Aaron looked at the sword in awe. He had never used, or even seen, an enchanted sword before.

Aaron looked back at Madi. She was frantically looking for something to burn, a switch to pull, or even a sign that would explain how to start the furnace. There was nothing: no wood, no lever, no sign.

Another shadow leapt up the stairs. Aaron moved so he was hiding around the side of the steps and when the creature came flying up, he swung the sword into its thirsty mouth. The bottom half of the frozen jaw fell off and evaporated. Aaron twirled his sword as the snow shadow backed up in pain. Before it could turn and rendezvous with its pack, he drove the weapon through its head.

Aaron saw Madi standing in front of the fire. Suddenly it appeared to get bigger. The fire roared and flames shot up. Heat flooded through the pipes and into the house.

"I figured it out! It's just like the blanket!"

Aaron turned to her and saw a snow shadow next to her, slowly stalking her on its paws. A windy cry blew from its mouth and it pounced. Aaron jolted from where he stood at the entrance of the house.

The creature lifted its head high and dove with its icy jaws open for Madi's head. The cold tip of a tooth touched her nose, but the head moved no farther. In between its eyes was the burning sword. Aaron had thrown it from across the room and pierced the creature. The snow shadow fell over and was consumed by the elevated temperature of both the sword and the blazing furnace.

Aaron rushed over to Madi and picked up the sword before it fell to the ground. Madi thanked him with a glance of gratefulness, but refocused on the fire. They both needed it to survive. Aaron turned back to the entrance, seeing two more shadows come up the stairs.

They were slower than the first couple. Another came down the stairs. They crept in as a group, closing in on Aaron and Madi. They howled from the heat of the home, but continued their hunt.

They came closer and closer. Aaron stood in front of Madi in an effort to protect her. They were backed into a corner. Aaron extended his sword, ready to strike the first one that attacked.

They saw a bright flash from the outside. The night sky lit up and even shined through the fog on the windows. The creatures lifted their heads and dashed out the front door.

Aaron and Madi looked around for a moment and realized it must have been Yerowslii. They quickly focused their attention on increasing the heat in the house. With the two of them feeding it, the fire grew larger, and pumped more heat into the home.

***

Yerowslii continued to fight the shadows as they attacked him. Striking one, then twirling to strike another. He clubbed and ignited snow shadow after snow shadow. With a moment to breathe, he looked onto the horizon. The sun was still far from rising, but the light of his home was bright, the furnace was burning fiercely.

The fog from his windows had begun to turn to steam. It was time — the house was above one hundred degrees. The Keeper turned back for the bottom of the mountain but, before going down, created a wall of fire, cutting off the rest of the snow shadows. He then turned and jumped off the edge of the mountain.

Descending it rapidly, the wizard swung back onto his roof. The lock on the inside of the window was lifted by a nod of his head and Yerowslii dove inside. He rushed down the stairs. The window locked behind him.

The wizard flew toward the furnace. He was met by the tip of a sword poking his neck.

"Put that thing down before I turn you into a donkey."

Aaron lowered the sword and shouted, "You're okay!"

"Of course I am," Yerowslii said. "The house is hot enough, now, Madalyne, you can stop."

Yerowslii waved his staff across the windows again, this time evaporating the remaining dew on them. Running over to one of his telescopes, he looked and saw the snow shadows retreating in the distance.

"Ravaged mutts," he muttered.

Aaron began to sweat, as did Madi. Yerowslii noticed them both becoming fatigued from the heat. He walked over to his well and pumped water.

"Just a moment, now." Water spilled over his

floor.

Yerowslii continued to pump, but began to circulate the water into a small floating ball. When the ball grew to about the size of his head, he stopped pumping. All of the pumped water was off the floor. Some evaporated from being so close to the furnace.

Walking over to the center of his house, he lifted his staff slightly. The ball split into three canopies that connected with the floor.

"Step inside one," Yerowslii said.

Aaron and Madi each stepped into their own shield of water. The temperature was cool inside. The bubble was hollowed out like a dome, only the walls were water.

"We'll sleep in these for the night," Yerowslii said. "I'll go get some blankets. The floor's kind of rough."

Yerowslii was back in a mater of seconds with six magic blankets like the one Aaron and Madi had used the previous night. Aaron and Madalyne examined their bubbles. She poked her hand in the watery wall in amazement. It stayed completely composed, floating around her fingers as she moved them through it.

Aaron did the same. Yerowslii enjoyed watching the moment. He knew so much was new to them and what it was like to realize how little one really knew, because he too once thought that he knew so much about his world.

Yerowslii tossed two magic blankets to each of them. "You know how to use these."

"Are you the one who made these?" Aaron asked.

"With the help of a friend, yes," Yerowslii responded, opening up his own.

They opened up their blankets and created areas to sleep.

"Are we going to be safe to sleep?" Madi asked.

"Do not worry, Madalyne. We are safe. I know a lot has just happened, but try to get some rest. Tomorrow is going to be a busy day," Yerowslii warned.

The wizard noticed Madi was struggling to make a place to sleep because of her broken hand; she still wasn't able to move it without feeling pain. He chuckled to himself and waved his hand a few times. Madi's blankets lifted into the air and began to unfold. Within seconds, her entire bed was made for her.

"Thank you, Yerowslii," Madi said, followed by a smile.

"We'll take care of your hand in the morning. I'm no healer, but I know of something that is."

"Really?" she asked, excited to get her hand and arm back.

"Without a doubt in all the hairs of my beard," Yerowslii said.

Aaron and Madi laughed at the joke as a way of calming their fears.

"What were those things again, Yerowslii?" Aaron said, climbing into his bed.

"Snow shadows. They're trained killers. Which means someone wants me, or you guys, dead, because they don't attack for sport. We will discuss this in the morning, though. Now what's important is rest," Yerowslii said.

Aaron and Madalyne concurred, but he knew they didn't really agree. Yerowslii knew they were stirred up from recent events. Their minds raced. Danger was real to them now.

The wizard hummed a spell to calm their nerves. Aaron and Madalyne heard the melody and quickly began to doze and drift off to sleep because of the magic it entailed. The melody even put the Keeper himself in a fog, until the room was silent with them all breathing steady as they slept.

Chapter 30

Aaron and Madi woke up the next morning before the sun came up; Aaron first, but not far ahead of Madi. Yerowslii was already awake and sipping a cup of tea in front of the window. Aaron rubbed his eyes and stretched. He stumbled over and sat down in a chair next to Yerowslii.

"Good morning," Aaron said.

"Why, good morning, Aaron. You're just in time."

"Just in time for what?"

"Shhh. Just watch." Yerowslii nodded at the view outside the window.

Off on the horizon, over the water, the sun began to rise. It glistened and swept through the land, brightening the world. It glowed beautifully along the trees, the mountains, the water, and the clouds.

"Even after some three thousand years of watching the sun rise, it never gets old."

"It's like life itself is waking up," Aaron added.

"A good observation, Aaron." Yerowslii continued to watch the sun climb into the sky.

"Maybe you can explain this, Yerowslii," Aaron said. "Why am I sleeping so much? I slept for three hours the night before, and, if I'm thinking correctly, I slept for about four hours last night. I'm a water traveler, so I only need half an hour."

"It's because of Madi, Aaron. You've been around an Earthling for a while, and, if I do say so myself, I believe you have grown quite close to her," Yerowslii said. "Some of her earthly traits are starting to rub off on you, and yours on her. She too will be waking any second now."

Just as Yerowslii said, Madi woke moments later. She remained laying down in her bed, but stretched.

"Good morning, Madalyne. You just missed the sunrise. Would you care for a cup of tea, though?" Yerowslii shouted as he leaned his head back in his chair.

"Good morning, Yerowslii." Madi climbed out of bed. "I would love a cup of tea."

Yerowslii made two cups appear in his hand and then lifted the teakettle that was already resting on the table. The tea's aroma filled the air as he poured. One he gave to Aaron, and the other to Madi when she reached the table.

Madi sat down and Yerowslii said, "I was just explaining to Aaron the reason for your sleeping habits. If you haven't noticed, you've been needing less sleep. Basically that's because you've been with Aaron so much."

Madi looked upward with her eyes, showing she was thinking about it. "You're right. I've never been able to wake up when the sun was rising and feel so fresh."

Aaron and Madi both sipped their tea, Madi with her good hand. The wizard said, "That's a very strong tea. It will give you two the maximum amount of energy needed for today."

Aaron and Madi finished their tea and set their cups on the table. The wizard gave them a moment to breathe and enjoy the morning before he asked, "Are you ready, Madalyne?"

She picked up her teacup and looked at it. It had a glossy white inside with a blue patterned outside. Yerowslii knew she was pondering this choice.

"I am."

"Splendid!" The wizard made the cups on the table disappear with the flick of his wrist and a clap of his hands.

They rose from the table. The teakettle and unused tea bags all flew into the kitchen, into the sink and cupboards accordingly.

"Come over here, you two," Yerowslii said, standing in the middle of his home.

They joined him and stood close. The wizard lifted his staff and closed his eyes. He hit the ground with the butt of his staff. Wind blew up at them, sending their hair and his beard skyward.

The whole house began to shift, things moved and changed shapes and forms. The staircase that led to the upper level moved in front of the small steps at the entrance of the home. The staircase then dropped in reverse through the floor. The top step became the bottom and the bottom step became the top. A new staircase was formed, one that led into a basement.

The new staircase ran directly under the small steps at the entrance to the house.

After the transformation process finished,

Yerowslii said, "This way, now."

He led them down the steps. The deeper they descended, the darker it became, until no light was visible. The staff Yerowslii held began to glow, lighting the way. The staircase was long. It was made of an old wood — sturdy, but ancient.

They finally reached the cold surface of the bottom. In front of them was a giant stone door. It had glowing lines running all over it. Parts of the lines glowed blue briefly, then faded away. They had no distinct pattern.

Aaron and Madi stood back as the wizard approached the stone. He touched the center of the door with the tip of his staff. Holding the staff with both hands, he closed his eyes. The Keeper slowly breathed in and out.

Something unlocked. The lines on the stone all glowed blue, and then the light rushed to the edges of the door. The door slowly opened by itself. Nothing could be seen inside — it was just black.

"On the other side of this portal is an ancient place only a few have ever been to. It's the domain of the Orb of Upitar. Do you still want to do this, Madalyne?"

Madi nodded her head, confirming her decision.

"Very well." The wizard entered the blackness and disappeared.

Aaron and Madi looked at each other. Neither moved toward the black stillness. Aaron took Madi's hand. She held his in return. They stepped through the portal and into the blackness.

They came through the other side of the portal into the mystical domain of the orb. The space was like that of a cave, but with trees flourishing around the edges. The room had a mystical green and blue glow to it.

Three rabbits roamed the room, mostly around the center. There was a ring of water that circled a small island. On the little island was a stone mound with three small pillars sticking out of it. On top of the pillars rested the Orb of Upitar.

The orb was large — bigger than the distance between Aaron's shoulders. Its blue and green aura flowed around inside of it. Yerowslii stood by it, facing the doorway when they entered. Aaron remained still when he saw the orb. After the moment of astonishment, the prince walked over to it slowly.

"It's…it's actually real."

"Of course it's real!" Yerowslii shouted with roaring laughter.

Madi came up to the orb as well. Her eyes glowed. It was so captivating, so beautiful.

"Madalyne, would you touch the orb?" Yerowslii said.

Madi looked at Yerowslii in hesitation as to why he wanted her to touch it. After all, it held the waterways of Upitar together.

"It is all right, Madalyne. You're not going to break it," the Keeper said calmly.

Madi reached out with her available hand. She looked at Aaron.

"Oh, this isn't how you become a water traveler yet," Yerowslii said. "I just thought it was time your hand became completely healed from that nasty wound."

Madi's face grew excited. She looked back at Yerowslii and he nodded for her to touch the orb. Madi placed her palm and fingers against it, feeling its smooth surface. Her hand instantly became healed — bone back in place, pain completely gone, cast faded away.

She moved her arm, hand, and fingers around freely without feeling any sort of stiffness.

"You, too, Aaron. Your back looked a little cut up from that slide down the mountain," Yerowslii said.

Aaron touched the orb.

"My wounds healed, I don't feel the pain or cuts on it anymore."

"I already fixed your armor, if you hadn't noticed," Yerowslii said.

Aaron did the best he could to look behind him.

"Thank you, Yerowslii!" Madi said, giving the wizard a hug.

"Yes, thank you, Yerowslii," Aaron also said to the wizard.

"You're welcome. Now, the time has come for you to become a water traveler and learn the ways of water traveling, Madalyne. Aaron, could I have you wait on the other side?" Yerowslii said.

"Umm, yeah," Aaron said, looking at Madi.

"It's okay, go," Madi said without a touch of fear.

"Okay." Aaron looked at her to make sure she truly wanted to.

She did.

Aaron backed up and disappeared back through the portal.

***

Madi watched him leave and then turned her head to the wizard.

"Are you ready?"

"I am," Madi said with a nod.

"Okay. Stay standing inside the ring of water," Yerowslii said, moving himself in it completely.

The ring of water rose higher and higher, turning into a curtain of water, until the top closed, sealing them inside with the orb.

"Put both your hands on the orb."

Madi put both hands on it. It was smooth and refreshing, just like the first time. Yerowslii raised his staff and put the tip of it against the orb. His staff glowed.

The Keeper lifted his rod off the orb and then

touched the tip to Madi's head. He lifted the staff off her, but a small sphere continued to glow on the top of her head. The sphere slowly sank into her head until it was no longer visible and was completely inside of her. Glowing lines pulsated through her veins. Madi felt her blood moving all throughout her body. Her heart pounded. She felt her gut being pulled in two directions — toward the orb and somewhere else. She couldn't breathe. She closed her eyes. She felt as though all her blood rushed to her heart.

Madi inhaled and her lungs filled with air like never before. Her gut relaxed. Her blood returned to normal and she couldn't feel it moving through every vein anymore. She breathed steadily, feeling normal again.

"You have been given the gift. Madalyne Harper, you are now a water traveler," the Keeper said.

Madi took her hands off the orb and looked at Yerowslii. The capsule they stood in turned completely to water; no air was inside. Both of them held their breath, but no motions were made. The Keeper's hair and beard floated gracefully in the water along with Madi's hair.

Yerowslii nodded to Madi. It was time. She had to do it alone, not with anyone. By herself. *I don't know how. I was given no instructions.*

No direction of thought. Nothing. Madalyne could feel her lungs compressing. A bubble of used air froze in her lungs. She felt pain in her chest. She closed her eyes as if to squeeze some air from them. *I need air! I need to breathe!* She couldn't leave the capsule because it seemed wrong in her heart.

She focused. She did the one thing she knew how to do — think of it. Then Madi felt something — a pulling in her gut, like she had before, but it felt new — like a new sense this time. She felt a rush in her veins, as though all of her blood stopped and then flowed another way.

Madalyne opened her eyes and lifted her head up for air. Looking around, she found she was back on the mountain on the other side of the tunnel.

I did it! I water traveled! Breathing in the world around her, her heart beat rapidly. "I water traveled!" she said aloud.

Excitement and awe coursed through her.

She took a moment to let everything set in. *I did it. I really did it.* Madi stuck her head back under the water and did it again, returning to the capsule of water in the ancient room.

Yerowslii opened his eyes. He knew she had water traveled. Starting from the top, the capsule of water quickly drained into a small ring after she appeared.

"You have done it, Madalyne. You are a water traveler," Yerowslii said with wide eyes.

"I did it! I did it! I water traveled!" Madi shouted as she hugged the Keeper.

Yerowslii laughed, happy for her.

Madi wanted to do it again. This newfound ability fascinated her.

"Shall we go back to Aaron?" Yerowslii said.

Madi touched the orb again, enjoying the magical moment.

"Yeah," she said turning away from it.

They returned to Aaron. The room was dark again. Yerowslii's staff beamed light around them in the blackness.

"She is a water traveler now, Aaron." Yerowslii informed him.

Aaron looked at Madi. He seemed speechless. He took Madi and squeezed her close to him.

"I can't believe it," he said, still hugging her.

Yerowslii laughed favorably with them. There was no going back; their lives were forever changed.

Chapter 31

Aaron, Madi, and Yerowslii returned to the top of the house. Aaron's bag was already sitting on the floor, packed and ready to go.

"Who packed my bag?" Aaron asked, picking it up.

"It looks like my house changed how it feels about you," Yerowslii said as he looked around his house and smiled.

The wizard stood in front of them after Aaron picked up his bag and swung it around his shoulder.

"Are you ready to return?"

"It's been wonderful staying with you, Yerowslii," Aaron said.

"And it has been wonderful having you. Come anytime you like!" Yerowslii said happily. "Now, I have one more thing to show you. Come with me."

Yerowslii led them up the stairs and down the hall this time. A door was on the right, and another on the left. Yerowslii opened the door on the left while pointing to the door on the right, saying, "That room there is mine. It's a mess and I would probably lose you inside."

Inside the other room was a spiraling staircase. It wasn't very tall and appeared to lead nowhere. They stepped up it, Yerowslii leading the way.

The staircase was cut off by a hatch in the ceiling. Yerowslii opened the hatch and climbed through to the roof. He lifted Madi up first, and then Aaron. They were on a small cliff in the mountainside, overlooking the water below the clouds. The cliff was grassy, and a pool was near the back wall.

"This pool takes you to a place not far from most of the main waterways on Earth. You can come and visit me anytime. Just ring that buzzer over there so I know you're here." The wizard pointed to an abnormal rock in the side of the mountain.

"Once you reach Earth, you will never forget where the pool is. It's impossible to find if you've never traveled through it, though. Trust me, I made sure of that."

"With magic?" Aaron asked.

"Magic....and a good hiding spot." Yerowslii jokingly complimented himself.

"Thank you, Yerowslii," Aaron said.

"Be safe," Yerowslii said back.

Madi gave the wizard one more hug and so did Aaron. Then they entered the pool of water.

"Shall I go first?" Madi asked.

"I'll be right behind you."

She smiled, knowing he wanted to watch. Madi took a deep breath and sank below the surface. Closing her eyes, she vanished.

Immediately after she water traveled, Yerowslii said, "Aaron, finish what you must first. Be on your guard, though. For the unknown is beginning to darken our world."

He knew the Keeper was talking about Herrathos. Aaron nodded, and then water traveled.

***

Aaron and Madi appeared on Earth, Aaron surfacing after her.

"You really are one now!"

Madi laughed, not knowing what to say.

"Come on. It's time to go to my father and end this hatred," Aaron said, climbing out of the muddy pool.

They both looked up and saw upside-down trees growing on the ceiling above them. Some of the branches of the trees were long enough for him to reach. Aaron and Madi seemed to be in an indent on the side of a cliff. There was a mouth-like opening that overlooked a massive body of water.

A vine dangled into the mouth of the cave. Aaron leaned out, and looked up at the edge of the cliff.

"We can climb this vine to the top. It looks thick and sturdy enough." Aaron said, feeling the vine.

He grabbed it and said, "Follow me," as he began to climb it.

Madi shook the mud off her body like a dog. She wasn't used to water traveling into a muddy puddle. Not letting it slow her down, she followed and climbed the vine as well. They arrived at a cliff side on Earth overlooking an ocean.

"The whole time, this has been here." Aaron

looked around. "I know exactly where we are. I must have passed this place dozens of times."

The landscape was field-like, with a few lush trees and a river. The air was chilly from the ocean, but nothing close to freezing.

"If we take this river, it puts us right back in the main channels," Aaron said, leading Madi over to it.

Aaron tiptoed around. "Now that you can travel by yourself, I can do things like this!"

He took off running and dove into the river. Madi laughed as she chased him. He disappeared in the river before she reached him. Water traveling through it, Madi was caught in Aaron's arms on the other side.

They took a series of waterways, playing around the entire time, laughing at and with each other. Madi experienced her new ability and Aaron remembered what it was like to have someone to play with while traveling.

They reached the final waterway that would lead them to a pool right outside the east side of the kingdom. While they had a chance to, they took a moment to recompose themselves, sitting by the edge of the pond they were about to travel through.

"Now, let me do most of the talking. I'll explain everything to my father. Don't be afraid, but he's probably going to assume I've brought you back to kill you."

"I know," Madi said in understanding. "Aaron, what if he still says no?"

"No matter what, Madi, I will keep you safe."

She smiled and leaned against his shoulder. He smiled back, wrapping his arm around her and pulling her close. Their fears grew together. They knew the possibility of death was becoming very real.

From behind them, the sound of horses was heard. Aaron turned around sharply. Madi saw in the distance men in black armor and giant horses galloping at them. Aaron stood up as though watching over Madi.

There were eight men on horses.

"Archival," Aaron muttered.

The horses surrounded Aaron and Madi in a trot.

"Play along," Aaron whispered.

"Aaron! I see you have returned! And not alone, you have brought the girl," Archival said from atop his horse.

"Good day, Archival. Indeed, I have. I was just on my way to the kingdom with her. Where are you moving to?" Aaron asked.

"We are returning from the war. A scout team has brought back precious information for the King, and we are making sure it gets back," Archival said, waiving a rolled up scroll.

Resuming his trot around them, Archival said, "What do you say we give you a lift? We wouldn't want this rodent escaping."

Actually hearing the hurtful words from another Upitarian scared Madi. She kept quiet, but still began to shake a little from fear.

"That won't be necessary, Archival," Aaron said.

"Nonsense! It would be a disgrace to the kingdom not to help you."

"Archival, this is my mission."

"Aaron, I won't let you return to the kingdom alone. Your father and Ugine would look at me in shame if I did such a thing. My men and I will transport you." Archival extended his hand to Aaron.

Aaron's face expressed his consent.

"Put the girl on the back of the horse I'm on," Aaron said.

"Nonsense!" Archival said, gripping Aaron's arm and swinging him up onto the horse. "You've had a long journey, now relax." With a snap of Archival's fingers, another guard grabbed Madi by the arm and laid her onto the front of his horse.

Madi tried to remain calm. *Keep it together. Just breathe.*

The guard held her down firmly with his arm and she let out a small yelp.

"Quiet, mutt!" Archival barked at her. He snickered at the sound of Madi crying, and she knew it took every fiber in Aaron's being to restrain himself from turning and ordering the guard to release her.

"Heah!" Archival shouted, whipping the reins on his horse.

The small team of horses took off galloping across the open field. Aaron held onto Archival's armor as he bounced up and down.

Madi's body flailed around on the other horse. She hit the arms of the guard and then the neck of the horse with every bounce. Madi glanced at Aaron, showing the anguish she felt.

"Slow it down!" ordered Aaron.

The horses shifted to a slower pace.

"What's wrong, sir?" Archival asked.

"I — I feel sick...I think I caught something while on Earth. All of this galloping is making me feel very nauseous."

"Very well," Archival said, seeming slightly annoyed. "Keep it to a soft trot!"

The horses continued, this time at a slower speed. Madi was able to lay across the neck of the horse this time without bouncing up and down.

Thank you. Madi gasped for air.

The horses traveled a few miles before the kingdom was in sight. They came around from the side and up the main valley. Madi recognized the hill she and Aaron had hidden behind and the woods they traveled through. The squad came through a giant archway that stretched immensely high and the trumpets blew loudly.

They entered the kingdom. Archival

dismounted his horse and shouted, "Aaron has returned! And he has brought back our perpetrator!"

Aaron dismounted as well and briskly moved over to the horse Madi was on. The guard carelessly threw her off the horse and onto the ground. Her body hit the hard dirt.

Aaron help. I don't know how much more I can take. Tears formed in her eyes. She tried to hold them back.

"Careful!" Aaron shouted. "I want to kill her at full health."

Wai — no. He's — he's still pretending. Or was I set up? Is, is this a sacrifice? No, keep it together. Think rationally.

"Come into the throne room, Aaron. Your father and Ugine are both in there, in a meeting with the council. They will be happy to see you, and…that," Archival said.

Aaron took Madi by the wrist. He grasped it gently, but acted as though he was squeezing it viciously.

Archival threw open the doors of the throne room and led the prince and his catch in. "Your son has returned! And look who is with him!" Archival bellowed as he gestured at them.

The King's eyes, and those of the men around the table, widened when they saw Aaron and Madi.

"Well done, my son!" the King said, rising from his chair.

Chapter 32

Aaron felt the room was different than usual. The atmosphere and most of the people — even Ugine — had a look of lifelessness. The table and the men were the same, but something felt strange. Aaron noticed all along the edges of the throne room were archers and swordsman, alternating in a pattern one after another.

"Bring her forward, my son, and strike her right here. Give me her head and you, my son, will be ready to succeed me as King." His father stood in the middle of the throne room, waiting for Aaron.

Aaron brought Madi forth and the great doors closed behind him. He met his father in the middle of the room. Madi was on her knees, quaking next to Aaron. The candles glowed bright, the room was silent — everyone still. Aaron looked into the stone eyes of his father.

"Father, and officials of Upitar, I have brought forth the girl of Earth, the one prophesied about by the Keeper of the Orb of Upitar."

There was a pause. The prince looked at

Madi and then back at his father. "But we were wrong about her. This girl does not have a desire to put an end to us. We were wrong about having to kill her to stop the prophecy. We were wrong about her, and we've been wrong for far too long about the people of Earth. They are not how we have thought them to be!"

Aaron's father looked lost and he stood in confusion.

"Father. I have found who I want to court to be my queen. It's her." Aaron pointed to Madi as she lifted her head. "She has a pure heart and wants nothing but peace!"

The King backed up. His mouth twitched, but no words came out. All of the officials stood to get a better view.

"Father, I understand. You are confused—"

"She's from Earth! An Earthling, Aaron! Our enemy!" the King roared.

"Yes, Father, she is an Earthling! But I know she is not out to destroy us."

His father looked filled with rage. He turned away from his son in dishonor.

"And...she has the gift now. She is a water

traveler," Aaron said, delivering what he thought was the winning point of the argument. "She's one of us, Father. One who uses the waterways like us. A water traveler."

The room was silent. Madi was now on her feet. She said softly, "Sir, your son —"

She was cut off by a loud roar from the King. His face was irate. Blood rushed to the surface of his skin.

"Silence! You have betrayed the Kingdom of Upitar!" The room shook. "Teaching an Earthling to water travel? That is treason. It's anarchy!" the King bellowed.

Aaron shook his head desperately in disagreement. "No, Father! I was with Yerowslii, the Keeper of the Orb! You can ask him!"

"Deceptions and deceits flow from your lips! You are no longer my son! Instead," the King said, "your fate will be the same as hers."

Aaron's eyes pleaded. He didn't understand what he just heard. He thought this would work. He thought they were safe. He thought his Father would listen.

"Kill them both!" the King ordered.

Aaron's eyes raced, looking for Ugine, the one man he could trust. He saw him standing, not moving, not looking away. Ugine was expressionless and statue-like. But before Aaron could plead with him, his father shouted again, "Kill them both!"

Aaron instinctively grabbed Madi by the hand and turned for the door. The bows of the archers were raised and arrows from their quivers drawn. Aaron's mind focused only on the door. The swordsman drew their swords. Guards moved at them, closing in on them, flooding the throne room floor.

Archival blocked the door. Aaron ran, facing Archival, who now had his sword drawn. The guard swung his sword fiercely down on Aaron. Still focusing on the door, Aaron dodged to the side, pulling Madi out of the way as well. Aaron shifted his weight and rammed into Archival, knocking him aside. They desperately pushed open the doors.

Arrows whizzed by, barely missing their heads. Aaron pulled Madi outside and made a run for the main archway. Madi squeezed his hand tightly. Running with more energy than they knew they had, the two made it halfway through the archway before the King shouted, "Stop them! Bring them down!"

The archers on top of the archway turned to the King's voice in what seemed like confusion. There were only half the amount of archers in place.

"Kill them!" the enraged King shouted.

Aaron and Madi reached the end of the archway. The archers turned and ran to their posts. The first one to reach the end drew his bow. Aaron and Madi were out the gate and into the outside world. The archer tightened the arrow against the string of his bow.

Aaron and Madi continued to flee. The arrow was fired. It rippled through the air. Aaron and Madi darted. The wind howled. Aaron turned his head to look back and saw the arrow strike the ground just behind his ankle.

They made it out of the archer's range, but they weren't safe. Horsemen were behind them, riding with their swords drawn.

"Aaron!" Madi cried out in confusion.

Aaron squeezed her hand and continued to escape. The ground was firm under their feet. "Into the woods!" Aaron shouted, leading the way. "They will have to follow us on foot!"

They hurried into the woods. They dashed desperately past hundreds of trees. Aaron pushed through branches forcefully, with their feet plowing through the murky ground.

The guards behind them dismounted quickly and continued to pursue them. A pool of water was visible, and Aaron knew exactly where it led. He pulled Madi and made a dash for the pool. They plunged into the water and then disappeared, but he knew the guards were close behind.

Rising out of the water, Aaron pulled Madi up before he even opened his eyes. Aaron was fast—the fastest—but he was anchored down by Madi. Stepping onto the shore, he wiped his eyes and continued to run for his and Madi's life. They sprinted across an open field.

The field turned into a field of rolling hills. Aaron and Madi went up and down until they were looking down on a river. Glancing behind them from the top of the hill, Aaron saw the army. He turned, gripping Madi's hand, and ran down the hill. Their feet scrambled for ground below them as they descended.

The guards gained on them. Aaron and Madi leaped from the hill into the river, in an effort to save time. The water splashed around them and the current pulled them both under. Water traveling, they came to a foggy marshland.

Aaron yanked Madi through the swampy water onto dry land. They fled into the fog. Guards emerged from the water and, back in the distance, Aaron saw flames from their torches in the foggy air.

The lights pursued them. Aaron and Madi frantically hurried, constantly sinking in thick mud. The black armor that Aaron once hunted beside now pursued him. The prince had become a fugitive. The torchlight that once guided him now sought to destroy him.

Aaron and Madi reached firm ground. Aaron looked for where to go next. In the distance was a lake that led to Earth.

"We need to make it to the city somehow." Aaron caught his breath for a moment, then picked up the pace again.

"Aaron, we can't do this! We can't outrun

them! I'm running out of energy and who knows how long it will be before you see an arrow through my eye. We have to outsmart and lose them somehow!"

Aaron knew she was right. He couldn't outrun the guards with Madi, and she couldn't escape on her own if they split up. The city was still several miles away, even with water traveling, and by that time they would be within an archer's range.

Aaron looked back, and something caught his eye. It struck him hard and deep, like he had been betrayed and abandoned. As much as he understood, he didn't. Seeing this hurt more than hearing his father order their deaths. Coming through the fog was the one he trusted — Ugine, sword in one hand and torch in the other.

To see Ugine's face as his pursuer shattered all he had come to know. He knew Ugine had to follow the orders of the King, and the King felt the girl was the greatest threat to the people of Upitar. Because it was evident that Aaron would rather die than give her up, Ugine had to follow the order. Yet actually seeing Ugine — his best friend — obey the King and come at Aaron, with a sword and torch in hand, left him distraught.

Aaron turned his head away from Ugine, trying to block him out. Aaron and Madi reached the edge of the lake. Jumping in, they dove under and water traveled, appearing on Earth. It was dark, but lights from houses glowed in the blackness. The houses were recognizable.

"We're in my subdivision! My house is right over there!" Madi pointed in the direction of her home.

"We can't go there, Madi. They will find us or they will watch the house until we come out. If they see we're the only ones there, they will suspect something. It's your one safe place—we can't compromise it!"

Madi understood. The house would be under watch if the guards knew they were the only ones in it, and her dad still wasn't home—not that him being there would help anything.

Aaron and Madi scanned around for where to go next or what they could do to throw the guards off. Her eyes locked on a house. Her mind seemed to be working on something.

"Aaron! I have an idea!" Madi took off, now

leading Aaron.

They ran up to a house with a few lights on. Madi put her palms against the window, trying to push it to the side. Nothing happened.

"What are you doing?" Aaron looked around in a panic.

"Just follow me!" Madi said as she ran to another house and did the same thing. "Sometimes people's windows are unlocked. If we can sneak into a house, we can fill up a bathtub with water and water travel through it. Because any pool of water large enough to submerge yourself in must be linked to another pool of water, right?"

"Yeah, I guess."

"The trick is, though, before we travel, we will pull the drain plug, causing all of the water to disappear. By time the guards get there, the water will be gone, or even the owner of the house might be awake!"

Not seeing another option, and thinking it was a pretty good idea, Aaron agreed. He remembered something then — one house that might unlocked.

"Follow me!" Running off into the blackness

and looking back, he saw the guards emerging from the pond and splitting into groups.

Aaron raced through the woods with Madi behind him. They came down over a hill with a pond at the bottom.

The pond was the same pool of water Aaron traveled through to get to Madi's house. They ran around the pond, with the echoes of the guards' voices coming through the woods.

"I thought we weren't going to my house," Madi said.

"We're not!"

They ran up the hill that led to Madi's backyard, but instead of going to her house, they went in the opposite direction, through a few sparse trees and down a small hill. They came to a home with a basement porch light on and a glass door. The top of the house had one room inside lit. It was the home of the old perverted man that Aaron met when he first began his journey.

Aaron put his hand on the handle of the door. "Please," he whispered under his breath.

He pulled the handle, and the glass door slid open.

"Yes!" Aaron sighed. "Hurry, inside!" Aaron said, bringing Madi in and closing the door behind him. He locked it and saw guards cautiously scanning the area in the distance.

"How did you know?"

Aaron looked around the room with the little light available. "Umm...he's an old friend," he said, not looking at Madi.

Aaron found another room and flicked a light on. It was a bathroom, and along the back wall was a tub. Madalyne sighed with relief.

She ran over to it, pushed the drain in, and turned the water on. The running bath was loud, but began to fill with water. Aaron shut the light off so the guards wouldn't see them.

"Now we have to be patient," he whispered.

The silent blackness didn't stop their hearts from pounding, only amplified them. The bath had reached almost halfway when they heard footsteps upstairs. Creaks came across the ceiling as someone walked across the floor and then stopped. The feet walked again, and then stopped.

"How much water do we have?" Aaron whispered.

"A little over halfway," Madi whispered back.

The tub wasn't safe to travel through yet and the footsteps continued again, this time walking away from directly over them on the second floor. It was worse, they were coming down a flight of stairs. Each step was a pounding quake that echoed in the house. In the distance, Aaron could see the figures of the guards beginning to close in on the home.

The footsteps hit the main floor.

"Aaron, you go first. If anything happens, it will be easier for me to explain myself to the owner of the house than you. I can at least hide here and call the police to scare away the guards; you can't."

Aaron didn't like the idea of leaving Madi behind, but he knew she was right.

"Fine."

The footsteps moved at a brisk walk, then changed from a walk to a hustle. Aaron and Madi breathed deeply. Light flooded as someone opened the basement door and started down the stairs. Guards surrounded the house outside in the blackness.

"Aaron, go!" Madi whispered frantically.

Aaron moved and sank into the tub. He was completely engulfed by the water, and then disappeared. Madi rolled in immediately after him. Under the water, she pulled out the plug and closed her eyes. A firm hand grabbed her shoulder and pulled it above the surface of the water right as she water traveled.

She was gone.

***

Aaron appeared in a giant raindrop falling through the sky. It crashed against a stony surface, setting him free. More raindrops continued to fall from the sky and break against the surface.

Aaron looked around. He was on a giant circular disk in the sky. The disk had ancient carvings along it that he didn't know how to decipher. Scanning out and around him, Aaron saw plains below him and mountains miles away in the distance.

The disk was very large and had a spiraling staircase connected at one point on its edge. The structure was the color of coal and felt remarkably solid. The staircase circled down to a pond a vast distance below. The pond and ground were visible, but too far down for Aaron to jump and survive.

Looking up, he saw the storm releasing the life-sized raindrops. Aaron had heard of this place before in an old book. It said that this was where all unstable waterways exited. He had never been here, but he had never taken an unstable channel like the bathtub.

Aaron looked around for Madi. He didn't see her anywhere. Not on the platform, nor in another raindrop. He looked up and began to panic.

What if she doesn't make it?

Aaron waited. He breathed, trying to calm himself down. Still no Madi.

Aaron ran everything through his head. The water was the right level. It was deep enough. She knew she had to be under it completely in order to travel safely. The guards were still outside. The person…the person was in the basement.

Then it hit him. He knew what happened. Because of fear, Madi must have traveled too soon.

She miss-traveled. She was gone.

Madi miss-traveled.

Aaron choked for air. He gripped his chest and looked toward the storm. No Madi. A giant raindrop crashed on him. Still no Madi. He wailed loudly and fell to his knees, burying his head into his hands. Tears flooded from his eyes.

"She's gone! She's gone!" Aaron shouted in devastation and anger. Because of him, both his brother and Madi were dead. He knew it. Madi miss-traveled.

Chapter 33

Madi awoke. She rubbed her eyes and found herself laying in a bed. She was tucked in and cozy.

"You took a nasty gulp of water there," said a voice.

Looking up, she saw a man sitting in a chair in the corner. The house was different than the one she had been in. It was more of a wood hut, and the room looked like it belonged in a beach house on a deserted island. Outside the window in the wall near the foot of her bed were giant, lush trees. Sunlight shined inside and illuminated the room.

The man in the chair had short dark hair and looked slightly familiar. He was sitting back, relaxed, and looking at Madi with blue eyes.

"Are you all right?"

Madi finally came to words. "Yes, yes. Thank you." She still felt confused.

"You washed up on the shore, unconscious. You're lucky the water came out of your lungs," the man said, standing from the small wooden chair.

Madi sat up and leaned against the

headboard. Her legs were still tucked under the blankets. She wore different clothes, too. They were slightly big, but still fit comfortably.

The man walked over to the nightstand by her bed and lifted a cup of tea. Handing it to her, he said, "Here. It will help keep you from getting sick. That water you were in was cold."

"Thank you," she said, gently taking the cup of tea and sipping it.

The man smiled warmly in return.

"Is she awake? Oh, she's okay! Sweetie, she's alive. Come here!" said another man, looking through the doorway.

This man was larger. He was wearing what appeared to be overalls. His grey hair was gone on the top and thinning on the sides. He was smiling, showing most of his teeth, a few were missing.

"Oh, sweetie, you're awake," said a lady as she pushed the two men out of the way and came into the room.

The lady was large as well — not round, like the man, but still heavy. Her brown fuzzy hair was tied back into a giant bun. Sitting on the bed, she asked, "How are you feeling?"

Madi responded shyly, "Good."

"Oh, sweetie, let me introduce myself. You're probably so confused right now," the lady said warmly. "My name is Elinore, and that's my husband, Jimuian, and that's...Now, where'd he go?"

"Hmm?" The round man said, looking around and then down the hall. "I don't know."

"I'll introduce you to him later," Elinore said, turning back to Madi. "Now, I know you're probably scared and lost right now, but we will explain. What is your name, sweetie?"

"Madalyne..." she responded, still feeling shy.

"Oh, what a beautiful name," Elinore said. "Now this may be hard for you to hear, but Madalyne...you have miss-traveled. You're on the Island of the Reverse now." Elinore didn't make eye contact with Madi until a few moments after telling her.

Madi looked around. It had already crossed her mind that this was what had happened, but she hadn't accepted it yet.

"I'm sorry to have to tell you this…but things

aren't all that bad! The rumors you've probably heard about this place really degrade it."

The Reverse? The shock was still hitting Madi.

"I'll give you some time to be alone," Elinore said, standing up from the bed.

The round man nodded to Madi with a smile and they left the room. Down the hall, Madi heard Elinore say, "Poor girl, she's so young."

Everything began to hit Madi. She was trapped. Trapped in this place. Her life was now chained to this island.

I have to be dreaming. This can't be real.

Madi threw the blankets off. In denial, she ran out the door, wanting to see it for herself. She stepped into a hall with steps leading directly into sand. The hall was long and looked to have more rooms attached to it. The roof was made out of bundled weeds, and the building itself was made out of dried wood.

Madi barreled onto the sand. The tiny grains of sand shuffled through her toes. She moved the best she could along the mini sand mountains, to the shore. She stopped. Past the shore was some water, but past that was — nothing, just endless sky.

The water dropped off, falling over an edge, but nothing was after it. Just open sky, endless, open sky.

Madi turned around. Three mountains stood there, one on the right, one in the back on the left, and one in front of the left one. They had lush green trees on them and what appeared to be more shacks.

The land was an island. Along each side, land eventually ended. The shore only ran around the front quarter of the island. The rest was sandy beach and forests.

Madi turned back to the shore and sank into the sand. She was trapped. Away from everything—away from Aaron, the one she risked all this for. Madi began to cry and buried her head in her arms.

"I'm sorry," said the voice of the first man, coming from behind her.

Madi didn't answer.

The man continued. "When I first came here, I was sad. But my sadness quickly turned to anger, and my anger to rage. I tried to rule the people who were already here. I tried to take power. I loathed this island," the man said.

Madi lifted her had and watched him as he slowly looked around the island and then down at the sand.

"The raging fire already inside of me grew and consumed me even more. Night after night, day after day. I didn't know if it was my hate for the island or the pain that no one came to get me. After a while — a long while — it changed me. This island broke me. It showed me life differently. It forced me to take a step back, to examine myself and my life. I know it sounds absurd, but I really began to enjoy the place. It's peaceful. You have nothing to do but eat, sleep, and be happy."

"I had so much to live up to, though," Madi said in her self-pity.

"You think you had a lot to live up to?" the man said, and then chuckled. "I had a lot to live up to," he said. "Do you know who I am...Who I was?"

Madi looked at him. She studied his face, trying to figure out why it looked familiar. "I don't, I'm sorry. But I'm not from Upitar," She admitted, and then regretted saying it as she looked at the sand.

"You're not? Then...then, are you a Senapin? Or Outer-rim?"

"No, I'm... Promise you won't kill me?"

The man laughed. "You could be the Keeper of this world and I wouldn't hate you."

"Okay," Madi said, letting out a small giggle. "I'm from Earth."

"An Earthling! Really? That's amazing! How did you learn to water travel?" the man asked, sounding fascinated.

"I was trained by the Keeper of the Orb of Upitar, Yerowslii."

"Yerowslii trained you? You must be one very special girl!" The man still sounded baffled. "But how did you even find him? How did you come to Upitar?"

Madi looked off across the water.

"A boy named Aaron and I... Well, I guess you could say we fell in love. And he brought me here, to Upitar that is." She smiled when Aaron's name rolled across her tongue.

"Aaron?"

"Yes," Madi said, still thinking of him, "and now that I think of it, he'll find me. I know he will!"

"Aaron?"

"Yes, Aaron. Aaron Archien."

The man looked off into the distance. "Wow, my brother fell in love with a pretty one, and an Earthling."

There was a pause. Madi turned her head back around to him slowly. "Your brother?"

"Yes, allow me to introduce myself. My name is Samuel Archien. Pleased to meet you," Samuel said, bowing in greeting before Madi. "And you are, my Lady?"

"Madalyne Harper." She stood up to join him.

"My pleasure. An Earthling — that is extraordinary," Samuel said. "The people here would love to meet you. Would you like to go to the village?"

Madi looked at the hut she walked out of, slightly confused.

"Oh, that? That's not the village. That's just a small clinic where we take care of the new people that come," Samuel said, pointing at the shelter she had walked out of. "Come with me. There's a lot to this island that's never talked about." Samuel turned and walked away from the shore.

The clinic was on the left when the shore was at their backs. Behind the hut were the mountains and lush trees. Madi hiked beside Samuel through the thick sand.

"This might be a silly question, but has anyone ever tried to water travel back?" Madi asked.

"By no means is it a silly question. The truth is, it doesn't work. Nothing happens. One just sits under the water and doesn't go anywhere. Water traveling doesn't exist here."

"Oh." Madi sighed, wishing the answer was different.

They reached the edge of the trees. A well-used trail traveled into the dense forestland. The tree trunks ranged from about half of Madalyne's arm span to four entire arm spans. Dark green vines swung from them, stringing the forest together.

Great trees stretched out their leaves along the land, providing shelter for the creatures below. Birds flew overhead — some much larger than the birds of Earth, and some much smaller. The trail wrapped around a mountain and the climate was calm and warm. It looked like some construction was being done on the path to make it a sturdy wooden path from the village rather than a stomped-weeded path.

Madi and Samuel came to an open clearing with more elaborate huts, which formed a village. People walked around in joyful spirits. A fire burned in the middle of the village with a cauldron over it. A lady sat on a porch in a chair, and a small child ran around the front of the house. Some of the people looked different than most. Something about them seemed unusual.

Madi also saw someone with a tail, and someone with fins that blended into their skin. Everyone conversed, though. The men looked busy working on things, and everything was lively. When Samuel and Madi entered the village, the people slowly stopped what they were doing and smiled.

"This is Madalyne, a girl of Earth," Samuel said.

The people approached them, saying hello and kindly greeting Madi. One lady brought a bowl of soup to Madi and, without taking no for an answer, gave it to her. Madi sipped the soup, not knowing what else to do. When the flavors touched her tongue, she smiled. It was delicious.

The person with fins shook her hand.

"Trobu, from the outer-rim of Vasipor," Samuel whispered in her ear.

Madi smiled back at the person. A few of the younger men smiled and nonchalantly showed off their muscles.

"Now, now, boys," Samuel said. "I believe she's taken. I'll show you my house, Madalyne. You're welcome to stay as long as you like." Samuel opened his arm to the back of the village.

Madi followed him to his home. It was made out of the same material as the others, but looked to have two rooms and an upstairs.

"Built it myself," he said. "I built most of these, actually. It was the least I could do."

Madi and Samuel walked up onto the front porch, where he opened the door for her. The inside was beautiful. The wood was smoothly crafted and all of the furnishings looked delicately fabricated.

It did have two rooms and an upstairs, as she suspected. The first room they walked into had a chest against the left wall and a few other things, like chairs. In the back right corner was a rising staircase. The other room was connected to the right wall. It was a dining room with a great, dark wooden table in the middle. Along the back wall was a kitchen set-up with a water pump, furnace, and culinary station. On the other wall was a window overlooking the village.

"Can I make you something?"

"I'm fine, thank you," Madi replied.

Samuel walked into the kitchen and Madi followed.

"Go ahead, have a seat."

She pulled out a chair and sat down, saying, "Thank you."

Samuel sat down with two cups he had grabbed off the counter, and gave one to Madi.

"It's tea," he said. "I know you must be thirsty. I wouldn't know what to ask for in a foreign place, either. Take it; I'm sure you'll like it." Samuel pushed the teacup to her. "So, tell me about Aaron. What's he like now? How tall is he? Does he have hair on his face? What's he sound like?" Samuel's wide eyes burst with curiosity.

Madi giggled a little. "Well, he's a little bit taller than me, and his face is smooth. And he's wise, funny, quick on his feet, kind…" Madi thought more about Aaron than the conversation. "Trustworthy, and loving."

"He sounds so grown-up. I wish we had gotten along when we were young. I wish I had been different." Samuel looked down into his cup. "What did he say about me? If he said anything about me."

Madi smiled caringly. She waited until he made eye contact before saying, "Samuel, he misses you so much. It eats away at him that you're gone, and that it was because of him."

Samuel looked up with watery eyes. "I was so harsh to him, Madalyne."

"Samuel, it hurts Aaron as much as it does you. Your brother truly misses you."

"Really? Madalyne, I would give anything to have another day with my brother. I long to fix the things between us. I was such a fool, the way I lusted for the throne. I taunted him with it. I tortured him, Madalyne. I want to fix that. I don't care about that all-consuming power anymore. It doesn't matter. All the desires I had — they mean nothing. Loving people, Madalyne, that's what really matters. It just took me so long to realize that."

"You two are a lot alike. You both hold things against yourself," Madi said. "Aaron will come, and you two can reunite and dismiss this. But letting it torture you as punishment doesn't have to be the outcome. You both regret everything that happened, but letting these things take root in your mind — plaguing you both for the rest of your lives — is not just. Let this go. You have admitted your faults, now accept peace and be free from it." Madi tried to cheer him up.

Samuel lifted his head. He looked at Madi with teary, blue eyes. He smiled and said, "I can see why he likes you."

They laughed and then there was a knock at the door.

"Come in!" shouted Samuel.

"We're going to have a festive dinner tonight to celebrate Amishikia's birthday. Will you two be joining us?" Elinore's voice said.

"Why, of course," Samuel said, standing up.

"Thank you, Elinore, we'll be there in a minute."

Madi got up from the table and they went out to join the rest of the village. The light source, which looked like a small sun, was rapidly setting over the mountains. All of the people of the village, young and old, were enjoying each other's company around the fire. There were no more than one hundred of them living on the island.

***

Aaron sobbed on the platform for a full day. He remained motionless, with his arms and knees against the stone. He wept for the loss of Madi, and for the regret of his wrong against Samuel. The giant raindrops splashed against his back, but he still didn't move.

"What are you doing?" said a stern voice. "Get up!"

Aaron turned his head and saw Yerowslii standing there. Fog surrounded the pillar.

"She's gone, Yerowslii. She miss-traveled." Aaron wept.

"I know that! Stop your whimpering and get

up!" the Keeper bellowed.

Aaron got to his feet. His back cracked and his knees shook from being against the stone for so long.

"Are you going to give up that easily? Sitting here, moping in your misery?" Yerowslii yelled. "Find her!"

Aaron only looked at Yerowslii in confusion. *Find her?*

"You heard me!" the Keeper shouted.

"Yerowslii, she miss-traveled! She's gone!"

"Gone where?" the wizard said, challenging his statement.

"The Reverse!"

"So you know the place, and yet you sit here in mourning!"

Yerowslii's words struck Aaron. His face slowly changed from a tense rage to suspicion.

"Does the Reverse exist, Yerowslii? Is she alive?"

"Aaron," the wizard said, "I do not know. But what I do know is this: back in the beginning when all of the Keepers were chosen, we were given our orbs, the worlds they belonged to, and the power that came with them. Now one Keeper, Ashipir, was given the smallest world. Over hundreds of years, he slipped into rage and anger and cut his world off from the rest of ours. He, his orb, and his world has never been seen since. I searched for it, looking through my telescopes, but found no signs. His world is missing. I have come to believe it is hiding now, like that of Senapin. With some form of magic, I think he linked every waterway to his world, but only if the traveler has a part of their body above the water, thereby creating miss-traveling. Before his world disappeared I would not have proposed this because when one miss-traveled something felt lost. As though that person truly was gone forever. But since the absence of his world, something feels very different. I no longer feel that loss through the orbs and yet I still feel the presence of his orb ever so often. And with him being a Keeper, it would make sense why no one can escape. He must have enchanted the waterways in that world with a spell. I say and believe this because in a frenzy of seeking the truth, I pillaged Ashipir's chamber in the Council of the Keepers. I searched everything, read every book and scroll, examined every picture, searched every atom of the room. In this, I came across two things. One was Ashipir's desire for and thrill of taking risks. And the second was a phrase. All along his walls, in his books, and behind his paintings it said this: *A place to go and a reason to leave.*

"I believe this means that in order to leave the world of the Reverse, one must have a reason, and they also must have a token of some sort. An item from another world — something for them to travel to, a place to go."

"Yerowslii, even if what you say is true, what would be my reason to leave?"

"Peace," the Keeper said. "Aaron, you have a unique position. You are the heir to the throne of Upitar, and you have made peace with an Earthling. No one has ever been in your position. You, Aaron, possess the capability to bring peace between Earth and Upitar, and maybe even all of the worlds."

"How can I bring peace when my father wants to kill Madalyne and me?"

"Senapin is growing powerful; I can feel that threat in the Orb of Upitar. Your father is going to need your help soon, Aaron. And when that happens, it will open many doors for you."

Aaron took in what was said. It hit him. Even if he wanted to deny it, Yerowslii was right.

"But that's if the Reverse exists," Aaron said. "What about Madi? What's her reason to leave?"

"Love," Yerowslii replied. "Aaron, Madalyne risked everything for you. She left her world to become a water traveler for you. And the fact that neither of us really knows if this world exists — that you might die if you try to get there — is a risk in itself. And it's a risk you're willing to take because of true love. You're risking your life for Madalyne, like she did for you."

Aaron felt a pounding in his chest. It was possible and it was time. He wanted to risk it. It was worth it — the smallest chance that she could still be alive was worth it.

"Now, Aaron, you need to listen. If the world exists and I am right about how to get off it, it's not going to be easy. Ashipir was obsessed with risk and danger. And he was quite clever, too. If what I predict about the world is true, then I also fear great risk is going to have something to do with getting off it."

"I understand," Aaron said with a nod, ready to go.

"Are you sure?"

Aaron nodded.

"Very well. Now listen to me. You will be on Earth for some time, Aaron. You and Madalyne must stay there until the time is right. I will send for you for you when the time comes."

This hit Aaron differently. He didn't understand.

The Keeper noticed the confusion in Aaron's face and said, "Aaron, your father is going to need your help soon. When that time comes, I will send for you. When you return, your father will need you. Saving him is how you can sway him. Hide on Earth and do not water travel. Do you understand?"

Aaron agreed to comply with the Keeper and nodded. "I'll wait."

"Good. You will know when it is time to return to Upitar. I will send for you," Yerowslii repeated.

Aaron slowly nodded his head, but still didn't completely understand.

"Now go," the Keeper said.

Yerowslii faded away with the wind, and the fog disappeared from around the platform. Aaron ran to the edge and looked at the spiraling staircase that circled down. He rushed down to the bottom, where a circular pool of water rested.

Aaron stood in the mystic pool of water. He took a deep breath and held it in. Closing his eyes, he plunged under the water and stuck his hand above the surface. Aaron deliberately miss-traveled.

He felt a strange pulling in his gut. He knew he had traveled, though. Lifting his head above the water, he found himself near the shore of an island.

So you do go somewhere.

Aaron felt a small current. It was pulling him to the edge of the water and onto the shore like a string leading him. Aaron obeyed and swam to the shore. Stepping on the sand, he looked around, taking everything in.

It exists.

It was night on the island. Off in the distance, Aaron saw a light glowing on the mountainside. Seeking to find Madi, he started to hike in its direction.

Chapter 34

Children danced around the great roaring fire as they tried to sing songs in harmony. Elders laughed and drank island alcohol out of large wooden mugs. Madi was with Samuel, Elinore, and Jimuian.

"I love parties!" Jimuian shouted drunkenly.

"Oh dear, give me that. You've had quite enough," Elinore said, taking the mug out of Jimuian's hand.

Jimuian squinted, as if trying to see Elinore better.

"I've only haaaadddd..." He breathed in and then finished. "Thre-fou-eleveny drinks, dearie. I being fine."

"Yes. Clearly," Elinore said, holding the mug with one hand and the other hand on her hip.

Samuel laughed and patted Jimuian on the back. Elinore leaned over to Samuel and whispered in his ear, "She's looking a little tired, sweetie. Why don't you get her a bed?"

Samuel looked over at Madi. Her eyes were

flickering, and her head lowered and then snapped back up in an endless cycle of drowsiness.

"I think you're right," Samuel said to Elinore.

"You want her to stay with us? We have an extra bed."

"That's probably best," Samuel said.

Elinore nodded and walked over to Madi, who was on the other side of Samuel.

"You ready for some rest, sweetie? Jimuian and I made a bed for you."

Madi nodded, apparently too tired to speak any words.

"Alrighty. Let's go, then."

Madi stood up and stumbled behind Elinore.

"We're heading in for the night. I'm not coming back out to get you later, understand, Eleven-di-six?"

They continued walking into Elinore's home. Samuel followed, making sure Madi got there safely. Elinore left the door open after they walked in. She unlatched something on the back right wall of the downstairs room. A folded, pre-made bed with a pillow fell out and bounced against the floor.

"Here you go, sweetie. Sleep well." Elinore

gently tapped the bed.

Madi smiled and crawled into the bed. Samuel knew she was asleep instantly.

"Goodnight," Samuel whispered to Elinore and returned outside.

The party lingered. Almost all of the children and women were in bed, and most men were becoming less sober. The fire crackled and its warmth spread. A cold gush of wind blew over the sands. Samuel felt something tapping his body. He got up and looked around. Nothing was there. Something felt distinctly strange. He heard whispers in his head saying, "The shore, the shore."

Getting up, Samuel began to walk to it curiously.

"Where you going, Sammy?" Jimuian said.

"I...uh, I just want to go for a walk and some air."

Jimuian laughed and then fell off the log he was sitting on.

Samuel ran. Something felt off. His heart raced. He burst out of the forest onto the sand. He saw a figure in the distance. It was running toward him.

Samuel drew his dagger from around his ankle. It was like Aaron's, crafted with a golden handle and a gem in the middle. But instead of a green gem it had a yellow one, and a golden blade instead of a green one.

Samuel held the dagger, ready to defend himself. The figure moved closer and closer. Samuel squinted, trying to make out who it was. They weren't slowing down. Samuel crept into the shadows and prepared to attack.

"Stop! Who's there?"

The person didn't stop. They seemed focused on something.

"Stop!" Samuel shouted.

***

Aaron continued. He was close to the trees. A figure sprang from the edge of the forest, dagger in hand. Aaron saw the person lunging at him with the weapon. He quickly turned, taking the wrist of the person. Twisting the wrist, Aaron threw the person to the ground and then pounced on him with his dagger now in hand.

The person lifted himself violently, throwing Aaron off him. Aaron flew onto his feet, backing away.

"Who are you?" a man's voice shouted.

The two stood at a safe distance from each other; the man against the trees and Aaron with his back to the shore.

"I'm not looking to disrupt your peace or your culture!" Aaron said.

"You're moving awful quickly to be new around here!"

"I'm just in a hurry," Aaron responded, still gripping his dagger. He could see it was someone close to his age. The voice sounded familiar.

"Who are you?"

Aaron sighed, buying time to think. He had came this far; he had nothing to lose in giving away his identity. "My name is Aaron Archien."

"Aaron? Aaron?" the man said in a hoarse voice, dropping his dagger. "Aaron, it's me! I'm your brother, Samuel!"

"Samuel?" Aaron said as the hairs on his head rose slightly. Dropping his dagger in the grainy sand, Aaron cried out, "Samuel!"

They embraced each other with tears and open arms.

"I'm so sorry, Brother. I'm so sorry I sent you here!" Aaron cried.

"Brother, I forgive you. I have longed to apologize for myself acting so wretchedly to you."

Aaron hugged his brother firmly.

"It's in the past, Samuel." Aaron cried.

The brothers held their embracing hug. Forgiveness brought healing to both of them. Tears fell from their faces because neither had lost the other forever.

Madi burst out of the forest onto the sandy beach.

"Aaron!" she cried out, running to him.

"Madi?" Aaron turned. "Madi!" He ran to her.

They embraced and Aaron lifted her off the ground, spinning her with his arms wrapped around her back.

"How did you know I was here?" Aaron asked with his hands still wrapped around her back.

"I felt something! Something woke me from

my sleep and I felt it pulling me down to the shore. It was you."

"It was the orb. They're alive, and we can feel them sometimes," Aaron said, releasing Madi and looking around the Reverse.

They were all in wonder.

"I'm going to get us out of here," Aaron said, refocusing.

Samuel laughed, coming to them. "Out of here? You've only been here ten minutes. How are you going to get out of here?"

"I spoke with the Keeper of the Orb," Aaron said, letting go of Madalyne and excitedly turning to his brother.

"Yerowslii?" Samuel asked.

"Yes, how did you know?"

"High in the mountains is a cave." Samuel looked up to the back right mountain and then back to them. "On the walls there are ancient hieroglyphics. One of them shows fourteen circles with fourteen names above them. We believe they symbolize all fourteen worlds and Keepers. Yerowslii is the Keeper's name written above the circle that appears to be Upitar," Samuel said.

"Fourteen? What else is in that cave?"

"Just ancient hieroglyphics, and yes, fourteen."

"Does Senapin has outer rim worlds?"

"You know of Senapin?" Samuel asked.

"Never mind that," Aaron said, remembering what was important at the time. "Does it say anywhere, 'A place to go and a reason to leave'?" Aaron asked.

"It might. Most of it's written in a language no one on the island can read. We've only been able to decipher what we could from the shapes."

"Samuel, you need to take me to this cave. It may hold the way out of here."

Madi suddenly fell over into the sand. Aaron turned to her quickly and knelt down to check on her. She was sleeping.

"She's exhausted." Samuel laughed. "Why don't you both get some rest, and we'll go to the cave in the morning? Come on, you can stay at my place. Madalyne was sleeping at one of the villagers' homes."

Aaron was confused, but agreed. Samuel led the way while Aaron carried Madi in his arms. They reached the village and Samuel directed Aaron to Elinore's place.

As they passed, Jimuian lifted his head from the ground and said, "Another one? Why hellooo there! We're not normally like this." He waved his arms at everything around them. "We're very people actually a civilized! Glad to meet you're, sir. I am most certainly sure that I'll swim with you later!"

"Don't mind him, he's had one too many drinks," Samuel said, opening the door to Elinore's house.

The door hit Samuel after Aaron laid Madi on the bed and tucked her in.

"Will she be safe her?" Aaron asked, looking up.

"Yeah, the people here are friendly," Samuel reassured.

It was weird for the brothers to see each other again. They walked out of the house and closed the door behind them.

"Good night, Jimuian," Samuel said, leading Aaron to his house.

"Good night, Sammy! I will see you!

Tomorrow!" Jimuian said, raising his head and then collapsing onto the ground.

Samuel led Aaron into his house and then shut the door behind them. He showed his brother around the home and then took a seat at the table.

"Honestly, Aaron, I can't believe you're here. My brother, Aaron." Samuel extended his hands to his brother, still in amazement.

"I can't believe you're alive. I…I didn't think this place existed," Aaron said, returning the same amazement.

"What's new? Tell me about your life, Aaron! Tell me about my brother!" Samuel said with overwhelming joy.

The brothers began to talk with each other, sharing their lives, what had happened, how they were doing, and what life was like for the both of them. Aaron spoke about Madalyne and everything that had happened. He brought Samuel up to speed on their adventures, the water tower, Granny, the city, the wall, Senapin, taking Madi to Upitar, the mountain, Yerowslii, the orb, Ugine, and especially what happened with their father. It was nice for Aaron to open up to someone he could trust.

Samuel loved hearing his brother's stories as much as Aaron loved hearing Samuel's.

"He actually wants you dead?" Samuel asked.

"Both of us," Aaron replied. "Yerowslii said I need to stay away from Upitar until Father needs me. Then I guess when I come back and save him, he will push this aside."

Samuel sipped a cup of tea. "No," he said. "You can't save him. Madalyne has to. Think about it — if she saves him, it will show him that he's wrong about the people of Earth."

Aaron sat back in his chair. "That does make sense," he said. "Do you think Madi will want to go back to Upitar?"

"I think she will go wherever you are. I don't say this often because most of the time it's not true, but there really is something special about you two. She is the one who was supposed to destroy the waterways, and you are an heir to the throne, and that makes you both unique."

They laughed together.

"So, 'a reason to leave, and a place to go.'" Samuel thought. "Hmm."

"Yeah, and Yerowslii said it would most likely be a risk, whatever it was. Got any ideas?"

Samuel swirled what was left in his teacup. He looked out his window. "I have one," he said.

Aaron raised his eyebrows and looked at his brother.

"It's risky, Aaron, that's for sure," Samuel warned.

"It's supposed to be."

"If I'm wrong, you'll die." Samuel looked his brother in the eye. "Is that the kind of risky you're prepared for?"

"What is it?"

Samuel leaned forward across the table. "At the end of the shore are stones that overlook the drop-off. The drop-off is basically a waterfall. Along the waterfall are these cloud-like things, but they're all water, no fluffy stuff. Just clumps of floating water. If you could hit one and water travel through it, with your place to go, it might—just might— work. That's if your reason is adequate, too, I suppose."

"And if we don't make it?"

"The last person who jumped kept falling

until he disappeared. The next day we found his body splattered along the forest path. This is a small world, Aaron; it repeats itself. If you stand on one end of the island and look through a telescope, you'll only see the other end."

Aaron breathed in, pondering the devastating thought.

"Anything else you can think of?"

"Not like that. Nothing that risky," Samuel said.

Aaron sipped his tea. "Tomorrow when we go to the cave, maybe we'll find more definite answers."

"'A place to go and a reason to leave,'" Samuel said, sitting back in his chair again. "That makes sense, because what is a good reason to leave? What would be my reason to leave this place? I don't have one, and the people trapped here don't, either. At least, not something adequate enough. None of us have a reason like yours. For the most part, we live in peace here. People get married and start families, we have fun, we enjoy each other's company. But…The thing is, we want nothing more than to leave. We can never amount to anything here, Aaron. We're isolated from everything and everyone. Worlds move and advance around us, but we will never get to experience or be a part of any of them. It's like being locked in a room for your entire life. You can have fun every now and then, but you want nothing more than to leave, to live life again. Well, all of us besides Elinore and Jimuian; they're living happily together here. Story goes she miss-traveled and Jimuian couldn't live without her, so he did the same in order to be with her. And now they don't want to be anywhere else."

Aaron looked out the window and saw Jimuian on the ground, sleeping.

"He does like to drink." Samuel laughed.

Aaron chuckled a little.

"If Yerowslii says he needs you on Earth, though, we better get you and Madi off this place as soon as we can. Father could need you any time if Senapin attacks. We should get some rest. Tomorrow's going to be the longest day of both of our lives," Samuel said.

Aaron agreed. He followed Samuel who unlatched something on the opposite wall in front of the chest, close to the door. A bed folded down.

"What's that?" Aaron asked, referring to the chest Samuel pushed aside.

Samuel looked at it. It was something he had forgotten about over the years.

"It's some of my old stuff," he said, not opening it. "Clothes, boots — some of the stuff I was wearing when I came here. Would that count as a place to go?"

"I don't think so. Yerowslii said it had to be a token like thing." Aaron pulled out the rock from the cave he and Madi had been in. "Something like this, I think."

Aaron dangled the glowing rock while it remained chained around his neck. Samuel reached into the collar of his neck and pulled out a similar stone.

"Like this?" he said, showing the stone he saved when he and Aaron were in the same cave.

"You held onto yours!"

"Of course I did! It was a piece of home I could never grow out of, and I couldn't get rid of it, even when I tried. I tossed it from the top of the mountain once in anger, and the next day while I was walking it fell from the sky and around my neck. I think a bird dropped it from its mouth. After I broke down on that mountain, I decided to keep it, and I've treasured it ever since."

"I'm glad I came here, Samuel. I would have never seen you again if I hadn't."

"I'm grateful to see you again, Aaron, but I wish it wasn't here," Samuel said with a laugh.

They both laughed a little and after laughing they stood silently for a moment. Samuel hugged his brother and Aaron hugged back. Stepping away, Samuel had tears in his eyes.

"It's good to see you again."

Aaron also had tears. "Yeah, it is."

"See you in the morning?"

"Yeah."

On his way up the stairs and into his room, Samuel said, "Get some rest, Brother."

Chapter 35

Aaron woke up to the smell of food cooking. Samuel had the table completely set with fruits, drinks, meats, and vegetables. The sun shined brightly through the windows, having already woken up the land around them. Samuel was cooking and Madi sat at the table, drinking a cup of tea.

"Good morning, sleepyhead." Madi smiled. "Or should I say good afternoon?"

"Good morning," Aaron replied with a smile. "How long was I out for?"

"Just over eight hours," Samuel said, turning around with a pan in his hand and dumping the food onto three plates. "We didn't get to sleep until...early this morning, actually."

"Eight hours?" Aaron asked loudly.

"Yes. Our sleep patterns are more like Earth here. I don't know why, but everyone just sleeps more." Samuel sat at the table. "Eat up, we need to get going. The days aren't as long here, either, and the mountain at night can be dangerous."

Aaron ate the food before him and even took seconds to make sure he wouldn't go hungry. Samuel explained the plan he and Aaron came up with last night to Madi. Aaron then told her about the water clouds below the island.

"Madi, do you still have that stone I gave you when we first met and traveled to the underwater cave?"

She pulled out the stone from around her neck.

"Would you look at that? We all have one!" Samuel said.

"That is your place to go," Aaron said.

Madi nodded. "So, if the cave doesn't have the answer we're looking for, we're going to jump?"

Aaron nodded, confirming it.

"What if we don't make it? We splatter and die?"

"I know it sounds awful, but if the cave doesn't hold the answer, then this will have to work," Samuel said.

Madi was silent as she tried to comprehend what was ahead of them.

"What's my reason to leave?" she asked.

They all looked at each other awkwardly. Aaron had shared with Samuel what Yerowslii told him, but not Madi.

Breaking the silence, Samuel said, "Well, you do love each other, don't you?"

Aaron and Madi looked at each other, the moment being rather humorous. They had never even kissed. But then the moment became real, it became true. Aaron and Madi realized they had never said anything about it, yet they both knew it. Whether it was love or not, they felt something very powerful for each other.

Samuel severed the awkwardness of the moment by saying, "Well, you may have never expressed it, but it's noticeable to anyone's eyeball."

They all laughed, mostly because of the stillness of the previous moment. Samuel stood up, ending the moment. Afterward, Madi still didn't look okay with the idea, but she didn't say anything. They finished breakfast and then prepared for what they were about to do. Samuel and Aaron packed their bags. They were similar, both magic bags.

They all left the shelter of the house and

embraced the fresh air. The island was lively as wind blew through the trees. Jimuian was chopping logs near his home so there would be firewood for the next party.

"We're going up to the cave, Jimuian. If we don't come back before tomorrow's daybreak, come for us."

"Will do, Sam. Be safe up there," Jimuian said, nodding to Samuel and then Aaron and Madi before returning to chopping.

Samuel led Aaron and Madi to a trail not far from his home. It was a grassy and wide trail that appeared frequently cleared.

The lush trees of the island were bent over, mostly shading the edges of the path, but with a line of sunlight streaking down the middle. As they progressed, the trail became less tilled and there were more overgrown weeds and fallen branches. Sounds in the woods came from creatures Aaron and Madi had never heard before. The mountain had a mysterious and secret feel to it, like things hid in its shadows.

"How far up is the cave?" Aaron asked.

"A little over halfway," Samuel answered.

"What are those creatures we hear?" Madi asked.

"It's a variety of different species. Most of them are peaceful, so don't be afraid."

"What kind of creatures have you seen here, Samuel?" Aaron asked.

"Many are similar to those of Upitar. There are a few distinct ones. I have seen two haroms flying around the tops of the mountains, and a herd of amtu roaming the forests. Those were sights to see," Samuel said, turning around for a moment so he could see Aaron and Madi's faces

Remembering something, Samuel let out a laugh while he asked, "Is Ugine still trying to tame an amtu?"

"He's certainly trying, but they're hard to come by on Upitar anymore."

Samuel chuckled. "They're hard to come by anywhere. I remember one time Ugine sat up all night with a massive rope, waiting to catch one he thought he saw prancing around in the woods."

They all laughed.

Samuel continued to lead Aaron and Madi up the mountainside until, in the distance, they saw the entrance to the cave. It looked like a massive stone with a hole in it, surrounded by an area of short grass. A few moss-coated rocks stood near the entrance. Light shined on the grass in front of the cave where dozens of butterflies roamed in the warmth.

Green, blue, yellow, red, orange, purple, and multi-colored butterflies floated in the presence of the cave. They walked up to the butterflies and looked at the mouth of the cave.

"This is it," Samuel said. "Kind of a tranquil place, but I can't help feeling a hint of secrecy."

"Yeah, I feel it, too." Aaron stepped forward into the mouth of the cave.

Light from the outside spilled over into the entrance. The cave's dark brown walls led down into blackness. Aaron fully entered with Madi and Samuel at his side.

They were swallowed up in the darkness of the cave for a moment before seeing light near the back. The cave had a hole in the ceiling, providing the luminosity.

"Wow," Aaron said in wonder as the secrets of the cave became visible.

On the inside, there was a small pond in the back with remarkably clear blue water. Fish of all colors, like those of the butterflies, swam in harmony. Along the walls of the cave were glowing sapphire texts and hieroglyphics. They were scattered and in no order.

"Can you read them?" Samuel said, asking Aaron.

Aaron looked around the cave, moving his head in all different directions.

"No," he said, still baffled.

Aaron spotted something he could read on a drawing of the fourteen worlds, with the names of their Keepers above them. The names were in his native language, but that was all.

"That's where I learned of Yerowslii," Samuel said, coming alongside his brother to examine the glowing sapphire pictures.

"Aaron," Madi said from the other side of the cave.

He turned and saw Madi facing the pool of water and appearing to examine the text on the wall of the cave across from it.

"Aaron, I think I found something," she said.

Aaron and Samuel moved over to Madi and looked at the same text. Neither of them could read it, but she seemed to be intrigued by it.

"Do you know what it says?" Aaron asked.

"No. But you might," Madi said, pointing to the pool of water and crouching down.

Aaron and Samuel watched Madi and did the same. They looked where she was pointing in the water. A reflection of the letters on the wall could be seen, but through the reflection they were in another language.

"'A place to go, and a reason to leave,'" Aaron said, reading the text out loud.

"Then it's true," Samuel said, reading the text to himself multiple times.

"Is anything else visible from the reflection?" Aaron scanned the surface of the water for an answer. "No."

Nothing else could be seen in the reflection.

"Maybe this is it, then?" Aaron said standing up. "Maybe this is the waterway to get us out of here."

Aaron waded into the pool. The water came up to his waist and the fish circled him. He turned back when he reached the center of the pool and looked at Madi and Samuel with wide eyes. Taking the stone from around his neck, he clenched it tight.

Madi and Samuel watched Aaron anxiously. He held his breath and dropped under the water. His body became completely submerged in the pool. The fish stopped moving. Aaron's body sat in the stillness of the water, but he didn't disappear, he didn't water travel.

Opening his eyes, he rose from the water in anger. Striking his hands against the pool, he sent splashes up around. He knew what this meant. He was going to have to risk it. He was going to have to risk Madi and jump.

Madi's top lip barely covered her bottom lip. Aaron could tell she knew it, too. Samuel looked down at the floor of the cave. Aaron knew what he was thinking: the island was inescapable for him. As Aaron began to wade out of the water, he noticed something.

The fish in the pool faced him, blocking his exit. They all seemed to look him in the eye. *They want something.* Aaron looked into their small fish eyes, seeking an answer. The first fish in the line broke from it, followed by the second, the third, and the rest, in order, and began to circle him.

Aaron watched as they swam gracefully around him and then meandered to the back of the cave and reformed their line. Aaron turned around as they glided. They looked him in the eye again.

Aaron walked toward the fish, back to the far side of the pool. He came up to the middle fish, an orange one. Facing it, he looked in its orange eyes. The fish peered into his, and then looked past him. It looked up at the ceiling of the cave.

Aaron turned and looked toward the ceiling. He saw something that could only be seen from the back of the pool. It was an indent, as if part of the ceiling had broken off and a small wall along the ceiling could now be seen. On the ceiling wall was something written in giant letters — letters that Aaron still couldn't read.

Aaron tried to look at the message in the reflection of the water, but he couldn't. It was too high up for the angle to work. The message still stuck with him, even though he couldn't read it, it imprinted on his mind. It was something for him to know, not for now, but for a later time.

"What is it?" Samuel asked.

"More writing I can't read. But I don't think I'm supposed to right now, I'm just supposed to know it's here."

Aaron turned back to the fish, looking for something more — an answer, or where to look next. But the fish didn't show him anything. They all swam back into their small caves within the pool. He looked at them in wonder as they entered their homes and turned so they faced him. There was nothing more for him to know, nothing else they had for him at the time.

Aaron turned back to his brother and Madi and exited the pool. He walked past them to the entrance of the cave. Samuel and Madi turned and followed him in confusion.

"So, what now?" Samuel asked.

"We have to jump," Aaron replied. He put his hand on Madi's shoulder. "And we're going to make it."

They didn't ask another question, they only followed Aaron, traveling back through the woods. Within half the time it took to arrive at the cave, they were back in the village.

"Sammy! Good to see you made it back safely. How was your trip?" Jimuian asked when he saw them.

"Good," Samuel said, as Madi entered his home and Aaron stopped half way. "Sort of. Maybe not what we were looking for, but still good."

"Well, at least you got some exercise, right? I should go up the cave. I need some exercise," Jimuian said, putting his hands on his belly.

Samuel laughed at the man's joke and patted him on the back before leaving and walking with Aaron to his home.

Aaron sat with Madi at the table and started talking. Samuel followed into the kitchen and started a fire with a pot of water over it.

"Will it work?" Madi asked, staring at Aaron.

"Madi, it's our only choice."

"What if we're not supposed to have a choice?"

"It wouldn't work like that. All of these signs, all of these writings — Madi, it will work."

"And if it doesn't, we splatter." Madi's hands made a splattering against the ground gesture.

"Madalyne." Aaron put his hands over

Madi's. "It will work."

Madi looked back at Aaron, her starry eyes showing she wanted to trust him.

"Okay," she said, still sounding unsure.

Looking away, she stood up from the table and went to the upstairs portion of the house.

"Just give her some time," Samuel said, turning to Aaron.

"What do you think?"

"I think it's risky." Samuel looked at his brother. "But I think it will work."

Aaron remained silent, in agreement with his brother.

"Make sure you're packed. Nightfall sets in even quicker this time of year," Samuel said.

"I'm set," Aaron said, standing up from the table.

"Here, have a quick cup of tea," Samuel said standing and pouring a cup for Aaron. "Sit down and drink it, then you can go talk to her," Samuel insisted.

Aaron took the tea because he knew it was for the better. Samuel enjoyed a cup of tea with his brother as they sat in silence. They took in the moment, after so many years of waiting, they were in each other's presence again. Aaron finished his tea and set it on the table.

"Thank you, Samuel."

"You're welcome, Aaron."

In that short period of time, the sun was already beginning to set over the island. Aaron went upstairs. There was a large bed along the right wall, overlooking a closet. Along the back wall was a wooden patio, showing the setting sun. Madi sat on the side of the bed, looking out the patio doors as the sky turned orange and purple.

Aaron came around the bed and sat next to Madi. He wrapped his arm around her and pulled her close. Her head fell onto his shoulder instantly.

"I'm scared, Aaron," she said with tears forming in her eyes.

"I am too," he said. "Madi I never wanted to put your life at risk again. Not after what happened on the mountain and while we were running from my dad. That pain, knowing I was the reason you almost died twice...I know it would never be more than actually losing you. But, Madalyne, I promise you, we will make it out of here. I feel it in my gut, this will work. I wouldn't even be remotely up for it if I wasn't absolute confident about it."

She turned, burying herself in Aaron's chest. Tears fell from her eyes as she cried.

"So much has happened in the past few days, Aaron." She looked up. "And, it's a lot."

"Yeah, it is." He lay back on the bed and she against his chest. "I would have it no other way, though."

Madi rubbed his chest. "Nor would I." She looked up at him. "What I really fear…is losing you. Not for a moment have I wanted to go back to the life I lived before this."

"Nor have I."

They lay on the bed until the sun had completely set, but in the end, both seemed ready.

Together they exited the home and entered the warm night air of the Reverse. With the consent of Aaron and Madi, Samuel had notified the village so they could watch. They figured there were only two outcomes and the village watching them would only confirm one. Torches met them as they stepped out of the house. Elinore approached, giving Madi a hug.

"I'm going to miss you, dearie, even though its only been a little while. Come back and say hello, or maybe I'll come to you!" she said, trying to reassure Madi.

"It's been a pleasure having you, the day or two you were here," Jimuian said, nodding to Aaron and then giving Madi a hug.

After their goodbyes, Aaron, Samuel, and Madi led the way, with the rest of the village following. They came to the sandy beach and soaked their feet in the shoreline. The rest of the village waited while Aaron, Samuel, and Madi walked into the water. Torchlight shined behind them as they waded out to where the current started to gently pull them toward the edge.

A great stone stood in the water along with other stones, creating one last spot of land before falling into the abyss. The night sky above them was composed of billions of stars, guiding their steps with the light of the night. A thick line of stars streaked across the sky, forming a faded blue and purple river.

They climbed onto the rock.

"It's only been one day and you're taking

off," Samuel said jokingly, but with tears in his eyes.

"I know where you are now. And I will get you off here, soon," Aaron said.

The brothers hugged and Samuel waited at the base of the stones. Aaron took Madi's hand and they walked up the stone, the space below them began to narrow.

Aaron turned back to Samuel, tears accumulating in his eye. "See you soon, Brother."

Samuel smiled and nodded his head, not actually able to say goodbye."

"Goodbye, Samuel," Madi said.

Samuel also nodded to Madi. He knew they had to go.

Aaron and Madi climbed up to the tip of the rock that overlooked the endlessness. The mysterious water clouds glistened in the starlight as they hovered in midair far down the falls. The water fell down an intimidating plummet until they could no longer see it.

"I can't do this, Aaron," Madi said, backing away.

"Madi, listen. We're going to make it. We're going to be safe."

"Aaron, I can't! What if it doesn't work?"

"Madalyne, I wouldn't put you through this if I didn't think it was going to work."

"Aaron, it's never been done!"

"Trust me, Madalyne."

Madi's green eyes looked into Aaron's blue ones. The mist floated around them. There was no roar of water, just a gentle stream as it fell over the edge. The torchlights of the villagers flickered behind them, and the stars of the night shined peacefully above them.

"Aaron, I—"

Aaron gently put both of his hands on Madalyne's cheeks. Without thinking twice, he leaned in and kissed Madi's lips. She relaxed.

He pulled away and opened his eyes, seeing her open hers.

"Trust me."

Aaron took her hand and walked to the edge. They looked down into the abyss.

"One…two…three," Aaron said.

Aaron and Madi jumped. Falling alongside each other, they dropped down the waterfall toward the water clouds.

Chapter 36

Aaron and Madi fell through the air. They picked up speed and the wind rushed against their cheeks as air bashed their faces. All their hair stood up because of the force at which they were descending as they rapidly approached the water clouds.

Aaron planned to water travel first because his reason to leave was to bring peace, and Madalyne's reason was love. She knew if he wasn't gone, then she wouldn't be able to leave. They continued to pick up speed as they approached a cloud of water. Unlocking their hands, they spread themselves out, preparing to hit the cloud.

Aaron looked into Madalyne's eyes and smiled. She smiled back and the moment slowed just before she hit the cloud of water.

Closing her eyes, she waited to water travel. She held them shut. Feeling the water engulf her, she tried water traveling. Her gut pulled and then remained still. Suddenly, she wasn't falling anymore, but she still felt water around her. Her hands interlocked with Aaron's. Opening her eyes, she saw Aaron floating across from her. He slowly opened his under the water and looked back at her.

Looking below them they saw land, and above them they saw the ceiling to a cave. Both of their faces exploded with happiness and relief as they stood out of the pool.

"We made it!" Aaron shouted as he stood, lifting Madi out of the pool. "We made it!"

Madi cried out with joyous laughter. Aaron took Madi and squeezed her close. He kissed her again on the lips. Their foreheads remained touching and they laughed with overwhelming happiness.

Madi looked up and said, "Where are we?"

She looked around. They were in a cave, but it wasn't the same cave where they received the rocks, though it had the same glowing rocks on the ceiling. It was small and dome-like. The water was warm and there was an entrance with light shining through it.

"Let's go see," Aaron said, climbing out of the water.

Madi swam to the edge and Aaron took her

hand as she too climbed out of the pool. Outside was a narrow path that led to a small floating pavilion. It was warm and the path had grass growing on it. On both sides of the path were drop-offs that led down to the purple and pink sky below it. The pavilion was white and looked ancient.

Madi couldn't believe what she perceived at the center of the pavilion — an orb. It was like that of Upitar, but had more blue than green. They walked across the bridge and into the pavilion. Looking around the ancient structure, they saw writing all across the ceiling. In every translation Madi could read, three in total, they all said, 'Earth.'

***

"This is the Orb of Earth!" Aaron said. Astounded he continued to glance at everything.

"Where's the Keeper?"

"Yerowslii said he died long ago," Aaron said, touching the orb.

"So there's no Keeper?"

"Yeah. The mountain's magic is protecting it until a new Keeper is chosen."

Aaron looked at the orb. Evening clouds glowed below them. Plants had wrapped around some of the pillars of the white circular stone pavilion. Aaron had both his hands against the orb.

"Madi, come here," he said. "Put your hands on the orb."

She complied.

"We have to throw it over the edge," Aaron said, looking into the orb.

"What?" Madalyne asked, backing away.

"Madi, I know it sounds crazy, but think about it. It will destroy the waterways to Earth. That will keep any water travelers from coming to Earth—keeping Earth safe, and keeping us safe."

"It just seems like a last-resort idea."

"Yerowslii told me I would have to live on Earth for a while, Madi. I didn't understand at the time, but he told me I soon would, I think I understand what he meant now. He wants me to destroy the waterways. Destroying the waterways to Earth will force me to stay here, away from my father. Madi, Yerowslii won't let the waterways be completely destroyed, he'll use magic to keep things in balance. It will be just for a moment in time, just until it's time to go back."

"When will that be?"

"He didn't say. He just said he would send for me."

Madi seemed to process Aaron's words. "Cutting the waterways will also slow the war between Earth and Senapin. And Upitar and Senapin would not be able to attack Earth."

"See, I think this is the right thing. It's the only thing that actually makes some sense."

"But how will we get back? We have to water travel to get out of here. We will have to go back to Upitar, and then work our way back to Earth by finding waterways near where I live," Madi said.

"We'll have time. The orb has to hit the ground first. And it's not the shell that holds the waterways, it's the sacred water within the shell. After it breaks, the water has to evaporate for the waterways to be destroyed."

"Do you really think this is what we're supposed to do?"

"I don't feel anything else. I only want to make sure you're safe. Do you feel anything?"

"No...I feel the same way."

There was a moment of silence between them and the orb. Aaron put his hands on the orb and said, "Will you help me lift it?"

"I can't believe we're doing this," Madi said.

She joined Aaron and the two lifted it up off its stand. They held it high above their heads and, with a great heave, Aaron and Madi hurled the Orb of Earth over the edge. The sphere plummeted down and disappeared with a *poof* through the clouds.

Without wasting any time, they turned and ran back to the waterway they came through. Jumping in the pool, they water traveled and appeared on Upitar. Not knowing where they were, they took a series of waterways and within a matter of minutes, Aaron finally started to recognize some of the terrain. He didn't know how they had gotten there, but he remembered it.

Once Aaron fully knew where they were, he realized where they had to go. They traveled swiftly to a waterway Aaron knew of, keeping watch for anyone. They reached it without a problem. Traveling through it it led them to another pool on Upitar, where the pool that led to Madi's was just across a short field.

Dashing across the field, they jumped into the pool and sank below its surface. Both disappeared in an instant and reappeared in a pond. Aaron and Madi lifted their heads above the surface of the water and knew they were safe. They made it to Earth.

Their hearts raced as they splashed the water in relief. Leaving the pond so as to not cause a disruption in the neighborhood, they ran up to Madi's house. No guards were there. Entering in the house, they locked the door behind them and fell on the floor, out of breath.

"We did it...We did it!" Aaron said.

Madi smiled. She seemed too exhausted to formulate words. The two fell asleep on the floor in front of Madi's door.

Aaron woke up after a short thirty minutes. He looked around, feeling full of energy again after a brief nap. Soon after him Madi woke up too.

"Only needing thirty minutes is nice isn't it?" Aaron asked, still sitting on the floor with Madi pushing him against the door as she stretched.

"I could go for another nap in a few hours."

She yawned and leaned against Aaron.

While they sat against the door they discussed what they were going to do.

"How long do you think Yerowslii will take?" Madi asked.

"I don't know. I don't think it will be too long."

"Well, you could hide out, and when my dad's away on business trips, you could just stay here," Madi suggested.

"I was actually thinking of your grandmother's. She knows I'm a water traveler."

"How?" Madalyne's eyes were wide.

"I don't know. But that's what she whispered in my ear when we left her house — that she knew my secret. I think if we explain things to her, she will let me stay."

"I guess it's worth a try," Madi agreed, astounded.

After taking a moment to plan out what they were going to say, they drove over to Granny's. Aaron felt weird. So much had happened.

They pulled up in the driveway of Madi's grandmother's. Madi knocked on the door and they waited anxiously. Granny opened the door, smiling widely when she saw them.

"Hello, you two."

"Hello, Grandma!" Madi said, hugging her grandmother.

"Hello, Granny." Aaron smiled.

"Come in, come in. Tell me what's new," Granny said, waving them in.

Aaron and Madi entered the home and took off their shoes.

"Sit on the couch, I'll be there in a second," Granny said on her way to the kitchen.

Just like last time, Granny came out with three cups of hot chocolate. She set them on the coffee table and took a seat in her chair. "So, what adventures do you have to share with me?"

Aaron lifted his hot chocolate off the coffee table. His hand shook from nervousness, as he was about to ask Granny to let him stay.

"Well—" Madi said, but was interrupted by the phone ringing.

"Oh, hold on one second." Granny got up from her chair. She walked over to the kitchen and picked up the phone, "Hello? Oh, hi, sweetie. How are you? Today? Really? Well, Madalyne's here right now. Shall I tell her? Okay. Will do. Okay, see you soon, honey."

Granny hung up the phone and returned to the room.

"That was your father, Madalyne. He said he's coming home early. He misses you and wants to see you. You might want to get home quickly."

Madi looked at Aaron and then at Granny.

"Oh, go on, sweetie. Aaron and I will chat. I'm sure your father just wants to say hi. You can come back," Granny said.

"I'll be fine," Aaron said, reassuring her.

"Okay," Madi said, wanting to see her dad again.

"See you soon, sweetie," Granny said.

"Bye, Aaron," Madi said with a smile. She kissed him on the cheek and then said, "Bye, Grandma."

"What, I don't get even a hug?" Granny said.

Madi laughed and hugged her grandmother and then walked out the door. They heard the car start and pull away.

Chapter 37

"So, tell me about yourself now that she's gone, Aaron. And you can be truthful with me. I know you're a water traveler." Granny chuckled.

"Madi does, too," Aaron said. "Granny, a lot has happened. I need your help."

Aaron told her everything, about Madi, all they had been through, and that he no longer had a home.

"So, you need a place to stay?" Granny asked, concerned for him. "By all means, stay as long as you need. No one but myself and Madi will know."

"Thank you, Granny," Aaron said with a wave of relief.

"It will be nice having a traveler in the house again," she muttered.

"Granny, I wanted to ask you. How did you know I was a water traveler?"

"It was from the way you acted and moved. Most of all, I saw something in you. Something I have not seen in someone in a very long time,"

Granny said.

Aaron looked puzzled.

"There's something I think I should tell you, Aaron. I am married to a water traveler."

Aaron's eyes widened. He couldn't believe what he was hearing.

"My husband was not taken; he had to leave. Partially because you and your brother were born. After your birth, he could only visit me occasionally. After your brother miss-traveled, we knew he would not be able to come back for a long time, out of safety for our children," Granny said, revealing her secret. "When we first met and fell in love, he showed me the world of Upitar. While he was away, we used to talk through the Whispering Tree in our backyard. The one that was struck by lightning. He used to sneak to the outside of the Kingdom wall and talk with me."

"What was his name?" Aaron asked in shock.

"His name is Ugine."

END OF BOOK ONE

Made in the USA
Lexington, KY
15 September 2014